SO-AGA-908

not
for
trade
6 50

EINSTEIN'S
BRIDGE

Other Avon Books by
John Cramer

Twistor

Avon Books are available at special quantity discounts for bulk purchases for sales promotions, premiums, fund raising or educational use. Special books, or book excerpts, can also be created to fit specific needs.

For details write or telephone the office of the Director of Special Markets, Avon Books, Dept. FP, 1350 Avenue of the Americas, New York, New York 10019, 1-800-238-0658.

EINSTEIN'S
BRIDGE

JOHN CRAMER

AVON BOOKS NEW YORK

This is a work of fiction. Names, characters, places, and incidents either are the product of the author's imagination or are used fictitiously. Any resemblance to actual events, locales, organizations, or persons, living or dead, is entirely coincidental and beyond the intent of either the author or the publisher.

AVON BOOKS
A division of
The Hearst Corporation
1350 Avenue of the Americas
New York, New York 10019

Copyright © 1997 by John Cramer
Published by arrangement with the author
Library of Congress Catalog Card Number: 96-30722
Visit our website at **http://AvonBooks.com**
ISBN: 0-380-79279-6

All rights reserved, which includes the right to reproduce this book or portions thereof in any form whatsoever except as provided by the U.S. Copyright Law. For information address Avon Books.

First Avon Books Trade Printing: June 1997
First Avon Books Hardcover Printing: June 1997

AVON TRADEMARK REG. U.S. PAT. OFF. AND IN OTHER COUNTRIES, MARCA REGISTRADA, HECHO EN U.S.A.

Printed in the U.S.A.

QPM   10   9   8   7   6   5   4   3   2   1

If you purchased this book without a cover, you should be aware that this book is stolen property. It was reported as "unsold and destroyed" to the publisher, and neither the author nor the publisher has received any payment for this "stripped book."

To Albert Einstein and Nathan Rosen,
who discovered the Bridge
within the mathematics of general relativity,
and to Charles Lutwidge Dodgson,
who organized the first Snark hunt

• Acknowledgments

This novel was a long time in the making. It was originally intended to be a hard science fiction novel, set in Waxahachie, Texas, and about people doing high-energy physics, that would take advantage of the publicity and interest surrounding the construction of the world's largest particle accelerator, the Superconducting Super Collider. It was about 80 percent complete when the U.S. Congress canceled the project in 1993. I was unable to even look at the unfinished manuscript for about a year after that event. Ultimately, it was rewritten from scratch. Needless to say, the present form of this novel was shaped as much by the cancellation as by the original project.

I am deeply indebted to many people for their help and advice during the approximately five-year period that this work was in progress. I particularly want to thank my wife Pauline for all her help and encouragement.

I'd like to thank the following people (listed alphabetically) for valuable scientific and technical discussions contributing to this novel: Gordon Baker, Greg Bear, Gregory Benford, David Clements, Robert Forward, Anthony Garrett, Geoff Landis, Henry Lubatti, Vonda McIntyre, Mike Morris, Grazyna Odyniec, Ken Young, and Matt Visser.

I'd like to thank the following people (listed alphabetically) for taking the time to talk with Pauline and me during our visit to Waxahachie: Wendell Bigham, Wendell Chen, Helen Edwards, Les Faciane, Gil Gilchrise, Ronnie and Sylvia Hastings, Richard Holleyfield, Buck Jordan, Jim Owens, Stephen and Claire Ann Pierce, Ken Reed, Wil Reuter, and Barnie Taylor.

I would like to thank the following people (listed alphabetically) for reading various versions of the manuscript and making valuable suggestions: Amanda Baker, Jennifer Brehl, Ethan Bradford, David Clements, Karen Cramer, Kathryn Cramer, Pauline Cramer, John Douglas, Geoff Harries, Mark Howe, Mark Hurst, Henry Lubatti, Bede Pittenger, Susan Protter, Karen Savage, Janet Seyboth, and Richard Seymour.

• PART I
May 23, 2004

January 29, 1987

Throw deep!
> —President Ronald Reagan, when asked his thoughts on initiating
> the Superconducting Super Collider project

You're going to make a lot of physicists ecstatic, Mr. President.
> —Director William Miller, Office of Management and Budget

*That's probably fair, because I made two physics teachers in
high school very miserable.*
> —President Ronald Reagan

May 11, 1987

*It would be wrong to say I'm against the SSC. It's great
scientifically. In fact, it's mind-blowing. The problem is that
over the past five years there has been a slow starvation of
what I call "small science." I say first get small science in good
shape and then by all means proceed with the SSC.*
> —President-elect James Krumhansl, American Physical Society

PART I
May 13, 2002

• 1

THE SKY-FILLING DISK OF THE DIM YELLOW-ORANGE SUN WAS JUST
rising on the east coast of the northern continent when the new universe was discovered. The Hive Mind's latest breed of extradimensional Lookers signaled the find, triggering rapid transmissions that
rose to a screaming pitch on all frequency bands as communications
from separated components stitched across the planet. The Hive Mind
gave orders. Resources must be refined, machines must be constructed,
energy banks must be recharged, a new strategy of conquest must be
put into place. Workers all over the planet scurried to fulfill their tasks,
refining materials, producing parts, assembling machines, simulating
alternate courses of action, making ready for the next great attempt at
Hive colonization.

The Hive Mind was immortal, and it was very old. A million years
ago it had slowly come to awareness of its own existence as an ordered structure overlaying the disorder of its Hive. It had made the
leap of self-insight, viewing the instinctual behavior and the stilted,
almost random, actions of its components: Workers, Soldiers, Flyers,
Queens, and Drones. The Hive Mind smoothed their neural programming, turning their narrow rote behaviors toward a more holistic purpose.

The other Hives were the principal threat to the Hive Mind. Most
were much older, larger, and better established. The Old Hive dominated the ecology of the entire southern continent. The Sea Hive had
developed Swimmers that extended its hegemony into the ocean,
somehow communicating through water with sound instead of normal
electromagnetic waves. The North Hive had developed Ice Workers
that could work even below the freezing point of water and could
make Nests and tunnels under the polar ice cap. But none of these
proved to be a match for the Hive Mind's new intelligence-directed
assaults.

In a few brief millennia the Hive dominated the planet. It had killed
off all of the other Hives, along with most of the planet's other life-
forms. By exercising choice and vision in its multiplicity of decisions,

the Hive Mind found by chance the process of selective breeding. Soon the few surviving non-Hive species of the planet had been modified into domesticated resource gatherers and food processors. Applying selective breeding to its own Queens and Drones, it soon developed fast long-range communication between its components.

The resulting increase in the speed and number of the Hive Mind's constituent parts greatly increased its awareness and volume of sensory inputs. This endowed it with a new attribute: curiosity. Systematically it began to explore its world. It encountered fire and found uses for it. It began to savor the subtle differences in the native materials of the planet and investigated how they behaved when heated with fire. It discovered refining and smelting, and it learned to use metals and ceramics as structural materials and tools.

Then it discovered the stars. By selective breeding it developed special units, Lookers, with eyes that had greatly increased optical resolution and broadened frequency sensitivity. The Hive Mind discovered that by combining simultaneous inputs of many Lookers, it could gain more information about the mysterious bright objects in the sky.

It began to notice certain regularities in the motions of some of the sky objects. From these regularities the Hive Mind's first theories and mathematics emerged, as it deduced the existence of a solar system with planets and a force of gravity that held them in regular orbits.

Its emerging science of astronomy served as a model for other discoveries that followed. Slowly, as the millennia passed, the secrets of chemistry and biology and physics were revealed, as the Hive channeled Workers to perform measurements and experiments that would verify or falsify the theories that the Hive Mind had devised. It developed Workers so small that they were only complex molecules and used these to experiment and explore. It began to understand the universe in which it lived.

The chain of discoveries ultimately led the Hive Mind to begin a new program, high-energy physics. Its tireless Workers constructed a large electromechanical structure that stretched in a long straight line spanning a considerable stretch of flat plains on the southern continent. The machine accelerated electrons from the north and from the south and brought them into head-on collisions at the center of the machine, while millions of specially designed Lookers observed and communicated the results of the collisions before succumbing to radiation exposure and dying, to be replaced by fresh units.

As these investigations were progressing, a remarkable thing happened. A particularly violent collision event opened a communication channel to another universe. The Hive Mind began to exchange signals with another species through the channel. It was a strange and stressful experience, communicating with an Otherness, a non-Self, a non-Hive. It had endured this stress for a time, gaining valuable information and concepts. Then, when the Otherness had seemed to lose some interest in communication, it had used its technology to kill the Otherness.

It found a way to manipulate atoms through the communication channel, producing and controlling molecule-size Worker machines in the other universe. These first made many more of themselves, then began to produce full-size Workers, Soldiers, Flyers, Queens, and Drones in the other universe. Soon a new Hive Mind formed there, eradicated the Otherness, and assumed control of that world. The Hive Mind had a sister, a sibling in another universe with which to communicate. It was an Otherness that was also Self. This was very satisfying.

After this initial success, the Hive Mind sought to reproduce again in this way, using the new technology it had learned from the non-Self Otherness. It succeeded in the first three attempts, so that Hives in five universes were in communication.

But then something had gone wrong. Seven successive attempts to reproduce had failed. A wrongness had developed in its basic strategy of contact and assimilation. The Hive Mind carefully analyzed the accumulated data of the failed contacts, applying models and simulations in an effort to understand. The simulations suggested that some opposition had developed in the other universes and that this had frustrated the recent efforts.

Now the Hive Mind had a new strategy, and its extradimensional Lookers had just detected another universe on which the technique could be tried. It marshaled its planetwide resources, anticipating the new apotheosis of Self that it would soon bring to another pristine world.

• 2

GEORGE GRIFFIN INHALED THE SCENTS OF PINE AND SUNSHINE-
heated rock, feeling the tensions and stresses of the week drain from
his shoulders as he stepped forward to the precipice. Below his vantage point on the peak of Montoisey was a kilometer of steep drop-
off. At its base the green and brown Plain of Geneva spread out like
an intricately detailed map. He had reached this high platform of bare
rock by taking the cable car above the French village of Crozet, riding
the chair lift to Montoiseau, then hiking the last three hundred meters
lugging his fifteen-kilo backpack, the British Airways baggage tag still
attached, that contained his parasail.

He turned to savor the sweeping panorama from this high point of
the Jura Massif: the Alps before him dominated by the white spectacle
of Mont Blanc, the blue sweep of Lac Léman, and the green richness
of the Rhône Valley. This was a beautiful and very special place, a
place of power. The bankers, the diplomats, the high-energy physicists
of the world all came here to do their important work.

The parasail wing, a bright pink horseshoe of polyester and Kevlar,
lay on the rocky slope behind him. George knew from the feel of the
wind teasing at his beard that its velocity was all right. Nevertheless,
he checked it with his small wind gauge. The LCD readout hovered
around twenty-one kilometers per hour, comfortably below the
twenty-six danger level that would prevent control.

He was about to do a solo from a cliff, which was reputedly a bad
combination. His parasail group in Seattle wouldn't approve. They
considered flights without a partner risky and launches from a cliff
edge downright dangerous. But he didn't much care what they
thought. He was always careful, and he trusted his own skills. If something did happen one day, well, *c'est la vie*. Nobody lives forever,
and the danger gave shape and bite to the experience.

He turned from the cliff edge to face the parasail, grasped its front
risers and brake lines, and pulled hard. The wing responded, rising
like a great pink kite until it was almost overhead, arching above him
like a bright pink air mattress designed for a giant. The polyester cells
fluttered and sang as the wind off the Plain of Geneva gave them life

and form, tugging at the leg loops and chest straps of his harness, urging him upward. George scanned the thin Kevlar lines and the long parallel cells, searching for subtle irregularities or snarls that might kill him. Finding none, he turned and walked to the edge of the precipice. As he reached the edge, the wind rose to meet him and lifted him off. He was flying free, and a rush of exhilaration hit like a great wave.

George reminded himself that flying and falling have identical feelings, at least for a while. He quickly checked the variometer of his GPS monitor. It was okay, although his rate of descent was a bit too high. He adjusted the speed tabs until the indicated descent rate was where he wanted it. Finally he had time to consider comfort. He moved the molded seat into position, releasing the painful cutting tension of the leg loops, and then deployed the speed bar and moved his feet to it. Now he was relaxed and comfortable and in full control. This was what he had come a third of the way around the world for.

He grasped the thin Kevlar steering lines, made a few experimental swings, then angled out over the Plain in search of the thermal, marked by a spiraling hawk, that he had spotted from the chair lift. He soon found it and began to spiral upward, too. His variometer indicated that his rate of descent was now a negative thirty meters per minute. The updraft had overcome the pull of gravity, and he was truly flying.

George now had time to look around at the familiar landscape near the CERN laboratory where twelve years ago he had lived and worked. He loved this place, the spot where he had spent most of the best years of his life. He was glad to be back, glad to have a free Sunday here.

He studied the French Alps, seeking peaks he had climbed and climbing routes he had used with CERN coworkers years ago. Looking far to the southeast, he could see the city of Geneva at the edge of long Lac Léman, the city's famous jet fountain making a white exclamation point in the distance. He remembered pleasant walks with Grace through the twisty streets of the old part of Geneva, exploring the little shops and looking for good but inexpensive restaurants. Closer he could see the Geneva airport, where he'd arrived yesterday, and the V-shaped CERN main campus, sprawling across the Swiss-French border and pointing in his direction. To his right he could see the CERN north area, with its hangarlike experiment buildings and cross-shaped office complexes. Farther north he could see the town of Gex spilling down the slope of the Jura, and near it he thought he could make out the buildings above the tunnel that contained the old LEP accelerator and the detector, where he had worked for four years before moving to Fermilab. That tunnel, which burrowed under the Jura Mountains, the French countryside, and the airport, now housed the new LHC accelerator and the ATLAS detector, his group's principal competition.

George pulled on the right control line and stepped on the speed bar, terminating his lazy spiral and angling out toward the CERN campus, searching for another thermal. The view, the solitude, the control, the element of adrenaline-laced danger, it was all wonderful. It made him feel young again.

He recalled that once long ago when he was a student looking for a summer job, a personnel clerk at an employment agency had pointed out that George's job application form listed his recreational activities as reading, writing, skiing, glider flying, and wind surfing. These, the man advised him, were all solitary activities that branded him as a loner. The major corporations were looking for team players. The man had suggested that George perhaps might want to change his entries to amateur acting, softball, volleyball, and touch football. George had declined.

Dammit, he *was* a loner. Since adolescence he'd detested team sports. Even paragliding he preferred to do alone, without the bother of arranging to go with a partner or group. He was at his best when he was working on a problem alone, with nobody asking questions or offering distractions, when he could hone his concentration to a white-hot pinpoint focus that cut through the crap and got to the roots of the puzzle.

Yet, somewhere along the twisted path of his professional and academic career, he had stumbled into experimental particle physics, perhaps the most overorganized and team-oriented form of experimental science. He did not really mind working with a thousand other people, harnessed together to build and milk data from the largest, most expensive, and most complex experimental hardware in the history of the human race. But every day he endured the frustrations of having to work with a group, unable to make decisions and take actions without consulting others, touching the proper bases.

Loners, no matter how good, did not make much of a splash in experimental particle physics. Loners were not the stars of the field, the guys who went to Stockholm to collect the Nobel prize when their group discovered something spectacular. It was the operators, the hyperactive organizers who could put together a team of eight hundred physicists and fifteen hundred technicians and could badger everyone into working at maximum output for three or four years who rose to the top and got the glory and acclaim.

People like Jake Wang, the spokesman and leader of George's group at the SSC, the Chinese wild man who offended everyone and was the butt of more jokes than George could count, people like Jake got the acclaim. Somehow he always managed to understand the physics a few microseconds before anyone else in the room and to push hard in the right direction before anyone else had decided what the right direction was. George and Jake had been graduate students working together at the SLAC laboratory in California long ago.

Jake had been a very green graduate student then, his English not very good, his physics ideas off-target, his behavior in confrontations tending toward overt hostility. While George had followed his own planned course with reasonable success, he had watched and noticed as Jake had transformed himself, asking subtle questions in private and remembering the answers, working hard until he became an articulate speaker, demonstrating a consummate mastery of the physics literature, learning to argue and convince without offending, learning how to tell other people what to do and have them do it. A year after George had gone to CERN, Jake had left SLAC with a reputation as the most promising new Ph.D. in experimental particle physics. He had gone on to a good postdoc, a better faculty appointment, and to Jake-initiated research that by a stroke of luck had made quite a splash and had led to his becoming spokesman for the LEM collaboration at the SSC. Jake was probably headed for a Nobel prize. The LEM group would earn it, and Jake would collect it.

George, as a group leader in LEM, was probably as high as he would ever go in the hierarchy of high-energy physics. LEM would be his last experiment. For the next twenty years he could look forward to grinding out data, solving technical problems, doing good physics in harness with a thousand others.

But, dammit, he wasn't here to think about Jake. He had a free Sunday to enjoy the Swiss and French Alps, and he was going to take advantage of it. He would paraglide until the thermals died and then land beside his rental car in the Crozet parking lot.

Soon enough he would have to return to the dead-flat plains of Central Texas, where the Superconducting Super Collider threaded through its circular fifty-three–mile tunnel carved into the limestone stratum of Austin Chalk, where the LEM detector lay deep in an underground cavern, there presided over by Jake Wang like a great dragon guarding his hoard.

• **3**

WHEN THE SIGNAL FROM THE SUMMONING APPLIANCE ARRIVED, TUNnel Maker was feeling homesick for his clan-herd. Through the transparent station wall he saw the Makers' Sun, appearing as no more than a very bright star at this distance. An optical enhancer would be required to make his home planet visible.

It was a great honor to be Creator of Bridges, but that honor carried with it the necessity of living in this lonely cometary cloud outpost at the outermost fringes of the great gravity well of the Makers' Sun. In three more orbits he would be able to return to his home planet.

Responding to the signal, he budded a wall aperture, waited while it dilated, and floated through the opening and into the passage. The signal had interrupted his transtemporal meditation linkage with home and produced a dull ache in his occipital orbs. He flowed along the curving passageway. The summoning appliance, he thought, had probably been activated by a false initiator. It had happened before. For the three orbits he had held his present position every such initiation had been a false one.

When he reached the equipment enclosure, he addressed the data station, interrogating its status indicators and accessing the neural nodes. The stored data began to flow into his sensorium. He turned the emerging patterns to orthogonalize them and paused to contemplate their meaning. Then he flowed backward in delight and wonder.

His long period of waiting was over. Here, at last, was a true find! The extradimensional scanners had actually detected a sequence of enormous nucleus-scale concentrations of energy in one of the neighboring Bubbles. The concentrations were very close in time, and any one of them would have been large enough to establish a Bridge.

Tunnel Maker's feeling of depression lifted. He would at last be able to do the work he had been trained to do. If all went well, he would be able to construct a Bridge, contact a new civilization, and exchange information and culture with them. New intellectual riches would flow from the contact, to be enjoyed by every Individual of the race of Makers. It would be a great contribution, and it might allow his return to the home world very soon.

This was important news. It was a true find, the first discovery of intelligence in another universe in two dozen orbits. Tunnel Maker paused. Should he call for the assembly of the Concantation of Individuals immediately, communicate the discovery, and secure the needed resources for attempting contact? No, he decided, he must be more cautious. He would lose considerable status if he called together the Concantation, only to have it revealed subsequently that some natural event or malfunction had produced the signal. First he must be very sure, must perform a careful review of the evidence. Then he must eliminate absolutely the possibility of a detector malfunction. He linked through one of the neural nodes to his sensorium.

The sensory representation displayed the time stream of data from the candidate Bubble. There was an irregular succession of marginally significant clusters of ultra-high-energy concentration. These came systematically from the same coordinates within the candidate Bubble. The time pattern seemed random, sometimes off, sometimes on, but taken as a whole it was clear that the peaks of intensity and their frequency of occurrence had both been increasing with time. The single ultra-high-energy event that had triggered the summoning appliance had been large indeed and represented an energy density many orders of magnitude larger than a thermonuclear explosion or supernova. But after that triggering event, the subsequent signals had tapered off and now had stopped altogether.

Tunnel Maker paused to consider the evidence. Was there any possibility that this observation could be the result of some natural phenomenon in the neighboring Bubble? An active galactic nucleus, perhaps, or a pair of neutron stars or black holes orbiting toward merger? The neural circuits of the initiator had been trained to eliminate such irrelevant phenomena, but there was the possibility that they had been confused.

He reviewed the data. First, the transdimensional wavelengths indicated that the concentration of energy was tightly localized, of approximately the size of a proton. That argued against a phenomenon of stellar, neutron star, or black hole dimensions. Second, the energy was definitely positive rather than negative, eliminating the possibility that the Bubble of interest was an inaccessible antimatter time-reversed universe. Third, the phenomenon repeated again and again at essentially the same general coordinates, but primarily at two specific points within those coordinates. That argued against some phenomenon involving ultra-energetic cosmic rays. And fourth, the intensity pattern showed a tendency to increase irregularly and then halt, as if some tuning and improvement process were in progress. It was difficult to imagine any astrophysical catastrophe that could simultaneously be so energetic, so localized, and so repetitive.

Tunnel Maker, with a rising sense of excitement, decided that the case for a signal from a high civilization was convincing, that no plausible argument could be made for a natural phenomenon. This had to be the work of intelligence! Somewhere a great machine had been fabricated by intelligent beings and was accelerating protons or electrons and bringing them into collision. As the beings gained experience with its use, the machine was being steadily improved and the rate and magnitude of energy densities achieved were rising. In the neighboring Bubble Universe some alien race was doing high-energy physics experiments.

His sense of elation shifted to concern. As well as opportunity, there was a serious responsibility here. There was a high probability that the high civilization in that Bubble was now in grave danger from the Hive. The civilization must be contacted and given aid. The magnitude of the energy density concentrations had been more than sufficient to initiate his summoning appliance, and they were undoubtedly sending transdimensional signals that were attracting attention elsewhere in the Cosmos. The Hive might soon attempt to destroy their world. The race for the survival of a civilization was on.

Tunnel Maker, feeling some urgency now, accessed the neural node that would assemble the Concantation of Individuals. Huge resources would have to be marshaled in a short timescale. A Bridge must be opened. An emerging high civilization was in great danger and must be contacted and helped by the Makers. Time was short, and this opportunity must not be missed.

• 4

IT WAS A PLEASANTLY WARM SPRING DAY IN MEYRIN. ROGER COULton had decided to sit outside under the pale green of the trees outside the CERN cafeteria as he ate his lunch. He glanced at the croquet lawn in front of him. The grass had been transformed from an ugly brown to an emerald green in the past few weeks, and later this afternoon the serious CERN devotees would be there playing their quaint game, like Alice and the Queen of Hearts.

Through the trees he could see the upthrust rock slab of the Salève and behind it other mountains surrounding Geneva. The sun was shining, and there was no wind to disturb his papers.

He frowned at the symbols on the pages of the laser-printed Mathematica notebook before him on the round white table. Neatly typeset in a subdialect of the language of mathematics, they laid out the anatomy of a failed idea. For the past two months Roger had felt like a drowning man trying desperately to stay afloat. He had been grasping for some variation of his basic approach that might save his new procedure for calculating particle masses from first principles. He was becoming very sure that his efforts were futile. His new procedure was beautiful, elegant, brilliant, and wrong.

In theoretical physics it was not unusual to spend time exploring a few blind alleys. That was part of the game. But this particular idea had looked so promising. In his recent seminars he had been able to use it to impress his colleagues. He was about to move to a new job, a big upward step, and his newly elevated position was due in no small part to the impression made in his interview seminar discussing his new approach. He still could not quite bring himself to believe that his beautiful idea was wrong.

A shadow fell across the papers and remnants of his meal. Roger squinted up at a tall broad-shouldered figure outlined in the yellow alpine sunlight and the green of translucent leaves.

"Hello," the man said. "I believe you're Roger Coulton. I was at the talk you gave at Les Houches last March. Very nice work." The face was vaguely familiar. He had sandy blond hair, a gray-streaked blond beard, and the rugged tan characteristic of the high-altitude UVladen sunlight of mountain climbs. His accent marked him as American, probably from the Midwest. He was holding a marbled-white CERN cafeteria tray and smiling. "I'm George Griffin. I'm an experimentalist with the LEM collaboration at the Superconducting Super Collider. You're obviously working, and I don't want to bother you, but I didn't want to pass up the opportunity to say hello."

Roger waved his hand in a gesture of welcome and moved his backpack from the other chair. "Please sit down, George," he said, feeling somewhat relieved to be distracted from his troubles. "I was not, I regret to say, doing anything useful." He gathered his papers and put them back into the pack. He glanced around the outdoor seating area of the cafeteria. It was becoming crowded, and he was alone at this table. Roger liked to talk to experimentalists. It was a good way of hearing the news about experimental results early, and they usually didn't want to discuss the details of his recent theoretical work.

George sat down across from him, poured beer from a brown Kronenberg bottle into a glass, and took an appreciative sip. "It's a great cafeteria that serves beer at lunchtime," he said. "The good folk of Ellis County, Texas, would never permit such civilized customs, even if they were allowed by the uptight image-conscious Department of Energy bureaucrats. Imagine the reports their safety task forces would write about the hazards of alcohol in the workplace."

Roger shook his head. "The U.K. science bureaucracy stands second to none in the tediousness of their safety," he said. "I moved here from England as soon as the opportunity was offered, and I've lived here for three years. The physics is excellent, the pay is twice what I'd get in the U.K., the food is wonderful, and the scenery is beautiful."

"But you'll soon be leaving CERN to learn about the Waxahachie way of life at first hand," George said. "You've accepted the senior fellow position with the SSC's Particle Theory Group? I'm surprised that you were willing to move." He waved his hand toward the south, where the Alps, punctuated by Mont Blanc, ringed Geneva.

I was a bit surprised myself, Roger thought. "It wasn't an easy decision. But ultimately physics decided it. I realized that the CERN LHC simply does not have enough energy to address the most interesting physics questions. Now that the SSC is at last coming into operation, it's where the action is for theorists as well as experimentalists, so I'm going there.'' And hoping the change will blast me out of my present morass, he thought.

"Are you leaving soon?'' George asked.

"I move to Texas in a few days,'' said Roger. "My boxes of books and papers are already on their way. It's going to be an adventure for me, living in the States. Especially in Texas. I misspent my early youth watching old cowboy videos.''

"It's going to require a certain change in lifestyle,'' George said. "Are you married? Where do you live here at CERN?''

"I'm single,'' said Roger. "In the U.K. I had rooms at Cambridge before coming to CERN.'' Roger felt a twinge that might have been guilt. He never mentioned King's Lynn, where he'd spent the first ten years of his life in near poverty. "Now I have a nice flat in a housing complex in St. Genis, across in France. It's near a wooded area with a path beside a stream where I like to walk, and my flat has a pleasant view of the Jura Mountains. As a theorist it would have appealed to me to live in a town named Thoiry, which is just down the road, but I couldn't afford the rents there. How's the housing situation at the SSC? Where do people live?''

"Hmm,'' George mused. "How can I explain Texas? Let's consider it as a problem in conformal mapping. Instead of Geneva you have Dallas—very tall buildings, like Geneva a banking and insurance center, a few small lakes but no big ones, no mountains at all or even significant hills. It's very flat, with rich black topsoil over limestone. Good farmland, especially for growing cotton. Can't say much for the wine.

"Instead of the Genevois Calvinists and the French Catholics you will encounter hard-shell Southern Baptists and other subspecies of Texas fundamentalists. You'll love them. Narrow-minded, gossipy, very strict about the appearance of rectitude, uprightness, and Christian living, but somewhat more relaxed in private, behind closed doors. They also have a strong work ethic, which is good for the SSC lab.

"Lots of evangelists around, moving from town to town and making a big show of hellfire religion. You'll drive past their big circus tent revivals, hear them on the radio, and find it difficult to avoid them on the local TV stations. There are lots of small churches in the countryside and some very big ones in Dallas and Fort Worth. Dallas is known is some quarters as the very Buckle of the Bible Belt.''

"Delightful," Roger said and laughed, then frowned as he considered the prospect of experiencing American-style fundamentalist Christianity at close range. Griffin seemed to be going through a familiar spiel, one he'd probably delivered many times before, but that was good. Roger was interested.

"Instead of Meyrin," George continued, "you will have Waxahachie, the town nearest the SSC campus and approximately at the center of the ring. Waxahachie might be best described as Texas-Victorian. It was a cotton boomtown around 1900. It has a wonderful Victorian courthouse, and many lovely old gingerbread houses of that boom period still decorate the town. After World War I, the cotton boom faded and Waxahachie went into hibernation until about 1988 when the SSC came along. Now it's a boomtown again, but this time it's a physics boomtown."

"That's a bit difficult to imagine," said Roger, draining the last sip of apple juice from his glass, and turning it upside-down on the tray. The small yellow wasps were beginning to take an interest in it.

"And I suppose St. Genis maps into Maypearl to the west of the SSC campus," George continued. "Maypearl is certainly the low-rent district, but I wouldn't recommend living there. It's a depressed cotton gin town, not very pleasant unless you like beer joints populated by migrant workers, sharecroppers, and mean unemployed drunks."

"So where do people live who work at the SSC?" Roger asked.

"Be prepared to buy a car and drive it," said George. "There's essentially no public transportation, and the places you will need to go are far apart. As for housing, as usual, it's a matter of taste. Some have apartments in De Soto or South Dallas, where there's something of a singles scene. A few are buying and remodeling the classic gingerbread houses in Waxahachie. Others live in newer houses on one of the lakes to the south, with maybe a dock and a boat for water skiing. Then there are those who have bought into the Texas mystique and have set themselves up as mini-cattle-barons on a hundred-acre spread, with a couple of horses, a dozen head of prime livestock, a few ranch hands to do the actual work, and an air-conditioned ranch house. The land around Waxahachie isn't too expensive, so you could buy into that kind of setup for the equivalent of a few years' salary. For example, your new boss Bert Barnes, the head of the SSC Particle Theory Group, has become a gentleman rancher in that style. Stetson, high-heel boots, and all. You're going to love his barbecues." George combed his fingers through his beard, as if appreciating the thought.

"I don't think I'm quite ready for gentrification," said Roger, who had already met Bert and had already formed an opinion. "What's the culture like in Dallas proper? Can one find films and theater, bookshops and coffeehouses and intelligent conversation?"

George smiled. "You must understand that I'm a faculty member at the University of Washington, so I live in Seattle, which is about twenty-seven hundred kilometers northwest of Dallas. But over the past few years, while the SSC was getting started, I've come to know the Dallas area fairly well. I think you may have a problem, Roger. Dallas is a big city, but its culture, like its religion, tends to be concentrated at the surface.

"The Dallas big rich support the showy cultural forms, the symphony, the opera, the ballet, the usual repertory theater company, and a well-appointed art museum with some minor works of first-rank painters and major works of third-rank ones. They like culture they can point to and be seen at. They like big names, but they're not all that picky about the quality of the end product.

"The center of Dallas is a complex of sterile office buildings staffed by a mobile population that vanishes at 5 P.M. You'll find the film scene at the suburban shopping malls, with movie theaters that have a dozen screens and can occasionally spare one of them for the odd foreign film. The bookshops are mainly chain franchises, and they're also at the malls. Come to think of it, that's probably where the coffeehouses are, too, so that the housewives can pause on shopping expeditions to grab a quick espresso or latte. Perhaps you'll need to locate near a shopping mall, Roger."

Roger winced. He wondered if George might be having a joke at his expense and looked closely at him.

"Seriously," said George, apparently getting the message, "there's intelligent conversation to be had, but you'll have to go looking for it. There are some big universities in Dallas, Fort Worth, and Arlington, and there are supposed to be good bookstores, coffeehouses, and student pubs near them." George paused and stroked his beard again. "Look, Roger, I'm making it sound worse than it is. There are good and interesting people living around the SSC, and you just have to find them yourself. Culturally, Dallas isn't London, or even Seattle, but it's a city with an enormous vitality and frontier exuberance that's quite fascinating in its own way."

Roger swatted at the yellow wasps. "I can see," he said, "that I'm in for a period of adjustment." He looked upward at the sunshine filtering through the trees. Griffin seemed to have come to the end of his Texas observations. "Permit me to change the subject," he said. "Why don't you tell me a bit about the experimental program at the SSC and the big detectors? During my visit there two months ago, I only talked to the theorists. I'd rather not be so uninformed about the SSC's experimental program when I show up there and begin telling the experimentalists what physics they should do."

George smiled. "The most important thing I can say about the SSC," he said, "is that the damned thing, after years of political battles, DOE bureaucratic interference, budget fights, technical glitches, and magnet tinkering, is finally up and running. I consider that a miracle. The whole project was almost killed by the U.S. Congress several times in the mid-1990s. It was very close. Only a major effort spanning the whole eight years of the Bush-Dole Administration, particularly by Allan Bromley, Bush's Science Advisor, and John Deutsch, his Energy Secretary, saved the SSC from an ugly premature death. Bromley and Deutsch engineered the one-billion-dollar Japanese contribution to the SSC, and at their instigation many of us in particle physics made frequent pilgrimages to D.C. to talk to congressional staff about the value of the project. I was at Fermilab working on CDF at the time, and for a while we were spending more time lobbying for the SSC than discovering the top quark. Have you ever tried explaining particle physics to a lawyer?"

Roger laughed. "I have trouble enough explaining it to my colleagues," he said. He sensed that Griffin was giving him another familiar spiel. "But how well is the machine running? I've heard the luminosity is low."

"The beam luminosity did start out very low four months ago, when they first reached full energy. The machine team is still working on some beam instabilities that occur while ramping up to full energy, but the luminosity is building up to the design values on a nice curve. The two major detector systems, SDC and LEM, are both working well, and both are now taking data."

"Ah yes, you should remind me of what the acronyms stand for," said Roger. "To be properly admitted to the high priesthood, one must first memorize all of the holy acronyms."

George grinned. "SDC stands for *Solenoidal Detector Collabora-*

tion. It's a big barrel-shaped superconducting solenoid coil with elaborate wire chambers on the inside and layers of calorimeters and muon detectors on the outside. It collects data mainly for the hadronic sector, the heavy charged particles from the collision. LEM stands for *L*epton and *E*lectro-*M*agnetic Processes, the processes it's designed to detect.

"I should add, for your cultural edification, that some of our rivals have had the temerity to suggest that LEM stands for Jake's *L*arge *E*mpire of *M*inions or the *L*oony *E*xcursion *M*odule. It's a large open-geometry superconducting toroid for detecting leptons and photons.

"LEM is working fine at the moment, but some of the electronic components are already failing. We're worried. Some of the radiation-hardened detector circuits are turning out to be not as radiation-hard as we'd expected, and we badly need to replace them with better ones. I'm here at CERN to compare notes on radiation damage problems with people in the LHC detector groups. One of their experts, Wolfgang Spiegelmann, is going to spend next month working with us at Waxahachie."

"Anything, ah . . . interesting in the data you've collected so far?" Roger asked.

"Well, we haven't yet discovered any Higgs bosons with LEM, if that's what you mean. Neither has the SDC, but we're all looking hard. The students claim that Jake Wang has already written the paper announcing the discovery of the Higgs. He only has to fill in a few numbers and paste in some graphs when we actually find it. He expects his Nobel prize any month now." He smiled and combed his beard again.

Roger looked across at George. "Of course!" he said. "I'd overlooked that minor detail. You must work with Jake." He smiled sympathetically, realizing that he had probably hit upon yet another of Griffin's favorite topics of conversation.

George shook his head. "I don't think you understand, Roger. Nobody works *with* Jake. I work *for* Jake, just as everyone else in the LEM collaboration does. All of Jake's detector projects have started with the letter *l*, all have produced excellent physics, and all of them have left a trail of broken minds and bodies in their wake.

"The story goes that a prominent particle physicist suffered an unexpected heart attack, dropped dead, and immediately found himself standing before St. Peter at the Gates of Heaven. St. Peter carefully examined his earthly record, asked some pointed questions about several referee reports the physicist had written, and finally decided to admit him to Heaven. As he was passing through the Pearly Gates, the man noticed to his right an enormous particle detector that looked like LEM, and standing before it was a solemn oriental man in a tailored gray business suit, checking papers on a clipboard against some details of the detector.

" 'Why, that's Jake Wang over there,' said the physicist. 'Is he dead, too? I saw him at the SSC just last week.'

" 'Oh no,' said St. Peter. 'That's God. Sometimes he likes to play at being Jake Wang.' ''

Roger laughed. "I heard the same story at Cambridge about Disraeli, but I think it probably fits your friend Jake better. Even in England I'd heard stories about his rages and personality quirks."

"Yes," said George. "Unfortunately, all of those stories are true. Of course, it is possible to adjust to him. In fact, there are many time-tested ways of adjusting to Jake . . ." He smiled. "A nervous breakdown, alcoholism, heavy tranquilization, a quick drink of strychnine, a change of profession . . ." He smiled.

Roger raised an eyebrow. "That bad . . . ?" he said.

George shrugged. "It's the price that fate has extracted from me in exchange for my involvement in the best experiment on the best accelerator in the world. Usually I think it's worth it."

• 5

ALICE GLANCED UP AT THE RUNDOWN BUILDING AS SHE PAID THE cab driver. She frowned. Could this really be the New York headquarters of the famous Wagner Publishing Company, the publisher of all her novels? She stepped around the derelicts near the entrance, walked past a sleazy-looking guard by the doorway, and entered the building's lobby. There was no mistake. The building directory listed WAGNER PUBLISHING COMPANY, SUITE 401.

When she pressed the call button for the elevator, feeling a bit uneasy, the guard laughed unpleasantly. "No elevator this week, lady," he said. "The stairs are over there." He laughed again.

She felt growing concern as she walked to the stairway, remembering that her financial and literary future depended on this publisher. Weren't the big New York publishing houses supposed to have fancy offices on Fifth Avenue?

Alice was breathing hard when she reached the fourth-floor landing and pushed through the fire door. She looked around, feeling somewhat reassured. Apparently Wagner occupied the entire fourth floor of the building. The elevator lobby was nicely decorated and furnished. It was adorned with a large gilded Wagner Books logo and a long glass-covered display exhibiting the covers of some of their recent publications. She noted that although her most recent novel, *E as in Earthworms*, had just come out and was selling very well, it was not among the paperback books in the display case. Prominently featured was George Bush's recent *Saddam, Boris, and I*, along with *Fabulous Washington Sex Scandals, Madonna's Secret for Thinner Thighs, The Financial Secrets of Football All-Stars*, and *How to Psychoanalyze Your Cat*. Nonbooks, she thought. I hope at least that stuff pays the bills here.

Alice smoothed a wrinkle at the sleeve of her loose white jacket and brushed a fleck of lint from the side of her elegant light blue dress as she approached the reception desk. "Miss," she said, "I have an appointment with Janet Renfrew. Please tell her that Alice Lancaster is here." Alice liked the sound of Lancaster, which was her pen name. It looked better on a book than Lang, the name she was born with, or Brown, the name of her late husband.

The receptionist picked up the handset of her telephone, dialed a number, chewed her gum for a while, and then replaced it in its cradle. "I can't reach Janet because the phone system is acting up again. Guess you can go on back to her office. It's in the back of Room 447. Go straight back to the first partition and turn right, then left to the wall and another two rights and a left. Ya can't miss it."

Alice wondered briefly if this was a joke but decided that the receptionist didn't seem sufficiently amused. She ventured through the door and was immediately confronted by a barricade of cardboard boxes filled with books. She took a long detour around the obstacle, took several turns along the lines the receptionist had suggested, and was soon completely lost in a warren of narrow passages, small offices, partitions, piles of printed matter, and desks. No room numbers were visible anywhere.

A young man wearing faded jeans, a T-shirt advertising a defunct 1960s acid rock group, worn running shoes, and a new-looking camel-hair sport coat approached her. ''Can I help you?'' he asked.

She asked him how to find Janet Renfrew, and he guided her along several more hallways to a room filled with people, all talking rather aggressively into telephones. ''That's our collections group,'' he said.

''Book collections?'' Alice asked.

''No,'' he replied. ''Bill collections. Go to the far end of the room. Janet's in the little glassed-in nook back there by the windows.'' He smiled and waved, then turned away.

Relieved at finding Janet, Alice threaded her way to the door of the indicated cubicle. Through the glass door panel she could see a young woman with curly black hair, presumably Janet Renfrew, whom she had not yet met in person. The woman seemed to be screaming into a telephone.

Alice wondered if she was intruding on a private matter, maybe a lovers' quarrel. She thought perhaps she should sneak away and wait outside for a time. But before she could put this plan into action, the woman inside saw her, smiled and waved, mouthed the words ''your agent,'' and rapidly terminated the telephone conversation.

The woman strode to the door and opened it wide. ''Alice! My dear!'' she said, embracing her. ''I'm Janet. So we meet at last. Come on in. Can I get you some coffee? Sit down! Did you have any trouble finding your way here? How's the writing going? You must tell me about the new book you're working on.''

Alice sat in the chair by the cluttered desk. On the desk was an open manuscript that had the obvious stain of a recent coffee spill on its center. Alice was feeling uncomfortable and confused. She wondered if she had made a mistake coming here. Last month Alice had not been present when her agent had negotiated the new contract and advance for her yet-to-be-written novel. Then, to her surprise, Janet had invited her here and sent a plane ticket. Alice would have brought her agent along, but he was away on a West Coast business trip.

Janet had taken over her books at Wagner from her previous editor, Damien Howell, who had been fired last year in the aftermath of the most recent of a continuing series of leveraged buyouts, corporate takeovers, and consolidations of publishing lines and imprints. Damien had been a wonderful editor. He had been largely responsible for successfully launching her writing career and had helped her to put her life back together after Steve died.

Alice was still uncertain about Janet as a replacement for Damien. Janet had been involved mainly in the production phases of her last book. She had, to her credit, arranged for the *Earthworms* paperback to have a cover that had beautiful artwork and was embossed with large gold letters and a peekaboo cutout. That was a first, and Alice had liked it very much. Janet and Alice had so far communicated only by fax, the Internet, and telephone. There had been several pleasant and encouraging telephone conversations, but this was their first meeting.

"Getting here from LaGuardia was no problem," Alice said. "I just jumped in a cab, and three traffic jams later I arrived. Finding your office once I was on the right floor of the building was far more challenging. There was a nice young man in jeans and a camel-hair coat who was very helpful."

"Oh sure," said Janet. "That was Albert Jukes. He's my boss's boss, the executive publisher of the corporation. Isn't he nice?"

Alice blinked. "I must be getting old," she said. "I thought he was an office boy. Isn't he rather young for a position like executive publisher?"

"He's older than he looks," Janet said. "Albert likes to walk while he's thinking, so he frequently runs into our visitors. He calls it 'management by walking around.' Would you like some coffee?"

Alice nodded. "Yes, please. Black."

Janet picked up the telephone and dialed a number, hung up and dialed a second number, then a third. Finally she slammed down the receiver. "Shit!" she said. "This telephone system is utterly worthless. Who needs 'voice messaging' when you want to ask the damned receptionist to bring in some fucking coffee?" She stalked out of the cubicle, returning after a while with two steaming mugs. She handed Alice a mug bearing the Wagner Books corporate logo emblazoned in gold.

"Well," Janet said, putting both elbows on her desk, placing one hand under her chin, and looking across at Alice, "we're going to be working together, and we need to get better acquainted. So tell me how a nice girl like you wandered into the business of writing disaster thrillers that are crawling with bugs."

Alice laughed. "Sometimes I wonder about that myself," she said.

"I was a couple of years out of college and working as a newspaper reporter for the *Tallahassee Democrat*. My byline at the Democrat was Alice Lang. My late husband was a sharp lawyer with political ambitions. We had a nice house and a very active social life aimed at furthering his career. But after a while I found that I needed some creative outlet as a pressure relief valve. I'm a naturally inquisitive person, and I thought about doing some freelance investigative reporting. There were plenty of things going on in Florida that were potential subjects for investigation. But my husband, Steve, was concerned that if I looked under the wrong rock I might antagonize one of his rich clients. So I decided to do something else.

"I found that I was always buying a certain kind of paperback at the supermarket, the ones with the pictures of crawly creatures and metallic letters on the cover. Whenever I was feeling depressed or overstressed, I'd read one of those and I'd feel better. Then one day it suddenly hit me that I'm actually a much better writer than the people who were writing those books. I had plenty of source material from my job at the *Democrat*, so I decided to try writing one myself. The result was *A as in Arachnids*, my first novel published by Wagner. I adopted the Alice Lancaster pseudonym to avoid embarrassing Steve, but he still wasn't too happy about my second career."

"You implied your husband is dead," said Janet.

"Yes," said Alice. "Steve was killed in a mountain-climbing accident in Switzerland at just about the time when my second novel was coming out."

"I'm very sorry to hear that," said Janet, looking directly at Alice.

"It was a long time ago," said Alice and sniffed.

Janet nodded. "So tell me about your plans for your latest project."

Alice took a cautious sip of the coffee and placed the mug on the desk. She reached into her briefcase, extracted the summaries of her earlier books and the outline of the one presently in progress. She handed the packet to Janet. Then she took a deep breath and started her carefully prepared opening. "You must have read this outline of my new book already, when the new contract was being negotiated last month. You'll recall that all of my books are techno-disaster thrillers with similar themes involving plagues of dangerous insects and vermin. *Arachnids* was about spiders from a failed genetics experiment attacking a small isolated university town. My most recent published novel, *E as in Earthworms*, is along the same lines. Earthworms from a worm farm in a small Mississippi town are mutated by a hazardous chemical spill and develop an enzyme that dissolves human and animal flesh. My agent says that *Earthworms* is my breakthrough book. It's only been out for a month, but he projects that by the end of the year it could sell over one hundred thousand copies, provided Wagner is willing to go into a second print run.'' She paused, hoping to hear a confirmation from Janet.

"Just a minute," Janet said. She rummaged through several drawers of her desk, then stood, cursed, and walked to a file cabinet against the wall. After looking unsuccessfully in two of its drawers, she extracted a folder from the third drawer. She returned to her desk and scanned its contents for a moment. "Yes, it *is* doing very well," she said. "So far at least," she added cautiously.

Good, Alice thought, she's noncommittal but positive. Her agent had plans to negotiate next time for a multibook contract and a much bigger advance.

"In fact," said Janet, "it's doing well enough that for your new one we're considering a major promotion, with advertising and a big push to the bookstore chains. How would you feel about going on a promotional tour?''

"I'd love to," said Alice. "I enjoy talking about my writing, and I think I do it well.''

"Good," said Janet, "so let's talk about what you have in mind for your next book.''

"Of course," said Alice. She pointed to the outline she had placed on the desk. "As you will recall, the new novel is called *F as in Fire Ants*," she said cheerfully. "It's set in Waxahachie, Texas.''

"Wax-a-hachie . . ." Janet repeated slowly. "An unusual name for a town, sounds Native American. Why does it sound so familiar?''

"Perhaps you remember it because it's been in the news lately," Alice answered. "It's a small town south of Dallas, the county seat of Ellis County, Texas, where the Department of Energy has recently spent over eight billion dollars to build the Superconducting Super Collider, the world's biggest particle accelerator. They had some start-up problems, but now the accelerator is completed and running. There have been several recent news reports and magazine features about it.''

Janet frowned and looked suspiciously down at the outline. "Wait a minute, Alice. Your new book isn't *science fiction*, is it?'' There was a rising note of alarm in her voice.

"No, of course not," Alice assured her. "As I told you, it's a techno-disaster thriller involving dangerous insects, strictly within the genre. Scientists from the SSC laboratory will be characters in the book, but I had scientists in *C as in Cockroaches*, too. Nasty ones. The most important characters are the Waxahachie townspeople and the local cotton farmers. The disaster element comes from colonies of fire ants, mutated by the radiation from the accelerator, that grow to enormous size and attack the community."

"Fire ants?" Janet looked puzzled. "Is that something you invented?"

"Oh no," said Alice, "they're quite real. They're a very nasty pest, an aggressive variety of ant that has been moving north into Texas from Mexico for the last few decades. They're difficult to kill, they have a poisonous, debilitating bite, and they have a way of coordinating attacks so that a group of fire ants will crawl onto the victim and all bite at the same time. It's believed that they use some kind of pheromone chemical to signal when it's time to sting."

Just then Albert Jukes, a newspaper in his hand, opened the door. "Excuse me for interrupting, but you've got to see this, Janet. Remember how Promotions decided to go for a full-page ad in the *Times* for the new Bush book? Well, it looks as if they had a minor typo in the copy!" He held up the page of advertising, which featured SODOM, BORIS, AND I BY GEORGE BUSH in very large letters.

"Oh God!" said Janet, striking her forehead.

"But think positive," Alice said brightly. "Perhaps it will boost sales to gays!"

After Albert left to spread the news further and they had stopped laughing, Janet said, "It sounds like the fire ants of yours would be great at picnics."

"Oh, they'll definitely put in an appearance at a picnic," said Alice, "but for the purposes of my novel an item of great interest is their tendency to attack electrical devices, particularly those that hum, and to eat the electrical insulation. Apparently they're the main cause of electrical fires and the failure of large electrical appliances, particularly air conditioners, in the Waxahachie area. Think of that in relation to all the electrical equipment at the Superconducting Super Collider."

Janet wrinkled her nose. "Are these big ants? They sound awful."

"Actually not," said Alice. "As ants go, they're very small but very aggressive. They've already killed off most of the larger ant varieties in Texas, along with much of the small animal population like rabbits, moles, and field mice. Perhaps fire ants are so aggressive and poisonous as a way of compensating for their small size."

"Uh-huh." Janet nodded. "I know men like that."

Alice reviewed the project, going over the outline of the novel and her recent progress in writing and research and emphasizing her track record of always meeting her book deadlines. She could tell that Janet was growing progressively more enthusiastic. Now is the time, she decided, to bring up her request. She reminded herself that she must not let Janet know how important this was to her. She flashed her most charming smile. "I should mention that there's a favor I'd like to ask of Wagner in connection with this book, Janet," she said.

Janet suddenly looked suspicious. "What's that?" she asked sharply.

"As with my other books, I'll need to go to Waxahachie and do some on-location research and interviews for a few weeks. For that to be effective, I'll need the cooperation of the people who run the Superconducting Super Collider laboratory. But if I tell them I'm there to do a disaster novel in which the laboratory is attacked by giant mutant fire ants, you can imagine what their reaction will be. I'd be about as welcome as an astrologer at an astrophysics convention."

Janet frowned. "Astrologer?" she said. "I don't understand."

"I'll need valid press credentials," said Alice. "The Randolph Corporation, which owns Wagner, also publishes a big line of magazines. One of them is *Search*, the weekly science magazine. I need you to obtain press credentials for me from *Search* under my real name of Alice Lang that will get me into the SSC laboratory as a science reporter."

Janet blinked, then rolled her eyes heavenward. "My God, I can't do that, Alice," she said. "Professional ethics are involved. If any news organization were caught giving out phony press credentials, they'd lose credibility, and nobody would trust their reporters."

Nobody trusts their reporters now, Alice thought. "Look, Janet," she said, "the credentials don't have to be phony. As I told you, I was a full-time newspaper reporter when I wrote *A as in Arachnids* and *B as in Blowflies*. It was only after my husband was killed that I used the insurance money as a stake to quit my job and support myself with freelance writing. But I always *liked* writing science stories, and I found that I could do them better than the other reporters. Even though I don't have much science training, I think I have a real knack for science reporting.'' She didn't mention that one of the reasons she quit the *Democrat* was because she wasn't allowed to do more. They had nailed her to the Lifestyle section.

"In fact," Alice continued, "*Arachnids* was based on a news story I did for the *Democrat* about a research project at Florida State University in which a lot of spiders escaped from their cages. I could perhaps arrange to do the SSC story for the *Democrat*—I still have friends there—but I'd get far more cooperation if I had press credentials from a national magazine. *Search* could commission Alice Lang to write a real story about the SSC laboratory. Perhaps about the women technicians and scientists there, or the effect of the laboratory on the lives of the townspeople. If afterward somebody named Alice Lancaster writes a successful disaster novel about the SSC, even if they discover the connection, it would be, shall we say, just a spin-off of the research for the magazine story.'' She felt instinctively that she'd convinced Janet, and she smiled.

"Hmmm . . .'' said Janet, brightening. "That's not bad, Alice. If they commissioned you to do such a story, they would certainly provide you with press credentials and maybe even arrange some contacts for you. Slipping you into the laboratory would also make a good angle to reveal later when we promote the book. Come to think of it, I used to see a guy who now works for *Search* in editorial. I haven't heard from him for a while, but he's very nice. Perhaps it's time for me to renew the acquaintance . . .'' She reached for the telephone.

• 6

GEORGE GRIFFIN GLANCED UP FROM READING *THE TIMES* OF LONDON and looked out the window of the 777. The fjords of Iceland were passing by below. Brown and green fingers of land seemed to grasp at the incredibly blue water. He recalled a charter flight from Luxembourg to Washington, D.C., that had landed at Reykjavík to refuel.

He had bought a fluffy gray Icelandic sweater for Grace at the airport shop, but he had not gone into the city. Too bad. He might never have the chance again. He wondered if Grace still wore that sweater.

He looked at his watch. They were an hour into the ten-hour over-the-pole flight from Heathrow to Seattle. It was 1:30 P.M., London time, and 5:30 A.M., Seattle time. It was his practice to try to sleep as much as possible on transatlantic flights, but he certainly wasn't sleepy. Perhaps he could get some work done on his report before British Airways started shoving food and drink at him. He didn't enjoy writing inconclusive reports, but it was necessary, and he might as well get it over with.

He opened his briefcase and removed the magic glasses and the data cuffs. He switched on the small computer inside and made that sure that its sensor flap was extended outside when he latched the briefcase lid, then slipped it back under the seat in front of him. He pressed a switch recessed in a thick earpiece of the magic glasses, then put them on. He draped the flesh-colored data cuff around his left wrist, just in front of his wristwatch, and secured it with the Velcro joint underneath. He repeated the process on his right wrist and activated the calibration process, flexing finger, twisting wrists, and bending elbows.

The glasses produced a display screen presented vertically in front of him and a horizontal keyboard etched in bright lines in midair. He reached out, grasped the screen, and moved and stretched it until it filled the full area of the seat back in front of him, then positioned the virtual keyboard to a more comfortable position at the surface of the tray table. He called up the report he'd been working on earlier and began to type and revise.

The smell of food at last attracted his attention. He realized that he had missed lunch waiting at Heathrow and was very hungry. The flight attendants were rolling the food cart down the aisle, dispensing dinner to the passengers. George saved his file and exited. He was slipping the data cuffs and magic glasses into his pocket just as the male flight attendant placed the food tray before him, exactly where the keyboard had been.

"What were you doing just now?"

George turned. The question had come from the older woman seated next to him. Earlier she had asked him to put her carry-on in the overhead rack and thanked him, but otherwise she hadn't spoken nor had he. George noticed a thick paperback historical novel stuffed into the seat pocket in front of her. She reminded him of his grandmother, although he supposed she was only about fifteen years older than he was.

He smiled, surveying the food on the tray. "I was using my computer to write a report," he said. He opened the zip of a small plastic bag and removed the silverware.

"That's certainly what you seemed to be doing," she said, "except that I didn't see the computer. There was absolutely nothing in front of you, and you were typing on the tray table. You reminded me of my grandson. He strums away on nothing and says he's playing 'air guitar' while he listens to that loud music of his."

George laughed. He'd only had the VR portable a few months, and he enjoyed explaining his new toy. "I suppose it does look weird when you put it that way," he said. He removed the glasses and cuffs from his pocket. "These are what we call 'magic glasses.' The name is a joke; they aren't really magic, of course. They're linked by infrared, like a TV remote control, to a small workstation in my briefcase. They measure my head and eye positions, and they draw full-color three-dimensional images directly in my eyes with small diode lasers built into the frames. The laser beams bounce off the inner surfaces of the lenses and write with light directly on the retinas of my eyes." He didn't mention that the thing was also a top-of-the-line ultra-high-capacity Unix workstation and that its price had removed a big chunk from his Department of Energy research contract funds.

"Isn't that dangerous?" the woman asked. "I thought one needed eye protection around lasers."

"Correct," said George, "but these are very low-power lasers that scan very fast. Even in the worst case, they wouldn't have enough power to damage a retina. And if a malfunction was obvious to me, all I'd have to do would be to close my eyes and take off the glasses."

She looked interested. "They look like my variable density sunglasses."

"They're similar," said George. "The lenses are variable density like your sunglasses and they're nondistorting, so I see the real world through them. I can use the liquid crystal effect to eliminate outside light, but I had them set for full transparency."

"What do you see when you're wearing them?" she asked. "Is the picture small?"

"The computer images are superimposed on external surroundings, so I can see both the real world and the computer world at the same time. The picture is as big as you want it to be. It can fill your whole field of view, if you want. I was looking at a fairly simple picture, just a standard word-processing display screen and a keyboard. My computer can make far more complex three-dimensional images with the right programs, but this is all I need for word processing."

She considered this. "But you were typing. You were behaving as if images drawn by the computer can be treated as real objects. As if, with your magic glasses, you could reach into the television, snatch the game-show prizes, and deal severely with the irritating host."

George laughed. "That sounds like fun. Perhaps I should try it sometime. Perhaps I didn't explain the hand part of the eye-and-hand operation." He held up the flesh-colored objects in his lap. "These are data cuffs. They go around my wrists and measure my hand and finger positions by monitoring the movement of tendons in my wrists with Doppler-shift ultrasonics. They send the information to the computer over another infrared link. The glasses were making the image of a keyboard on the tray table. When I typed, the cuffs detected my finger motions, the computer correlated them with the locations of the keys it was drawing, and the words I typed appeared on the computer screen that I saw on the seat back."

She thought about this as she pulled the strip of a small red cheese. "It seems like a lot of trouble to do a simple thing," she said. "Why don't you just use an old-fashioned laptop computer?"

George smiled. "Good question. My computer is a new model intended for high-resolution interactive graphics and complex data analysis. It can also be used for other purposes, for example, providing maps and navigation information when you're driving a car. Using it for word processing is like using a jet engine as a hair dryer. However, it's convenient to use it in a cramped space, and airline seats seem to get more cramped every year." He picked at the complicated foil wrapping on the butter pat until it opened, then applied some of the good Irish butter to his roll.

"That's very interesting," she said. "What is it you were writing?"

"I'm a physicist. I'm just returning from a trip to the CERN laboratory in Geneva," he said. "I was writing a report on what I learned there about radiation-hardened electronics. It's useful for the physics experiment we're presently doing at the Superconducting Super Collider in Texas. I'll finish the report with a bit more work, and then I'll connect into the plane's Airphone system and send it to my colleagues, using the Internet.'' He looked at his watch. ''It's a bit after 9 A.M. on the East Coast, so some of them will be able to read it even before we land in Seattle.''

She brightened at the mention of the Internet and began to tell him about the Web forum she belonged to that focused on medieval cuisine and recipes.

The meal finished, George put the glasses and cuffs back on. He called up the LEM handbook. The glasses darkened, and a bright multicolor image of the great detector hung in the dark volume of space before him.

He reached out and lifted off the top of the detector, then gestured to expand the cutaway image. It grew until it had an apparent size greater than the airplane. George reached out and touched a region near the center of the image. The small region brightened, and the rest of the image vanished.

Before him was the vertex detector, a barrel-shaped object that was shingled with small slabs of silicon. Wires and fiber-optic cables snaked away on both sides. George enlarged the view until it was approximately true size, then he touched one of the control spots on the right edge of the display. It was as if the device had contracted a disease. Bright purple spots appeared at random places on the shingled surfaces.

These were the failure points, the places where the tiny transistors created on the silicon surface with large-scale integration had failed and died in the hail of charged particles and gamma rays from the SSC's ultra-relativistic proton-proton collisions.

Perhaps looking at the thing one more time would give him an idea. It was worth a try. George looked for a pattern but could see none. Perhaps there were more dead transistors at the central region of the device than near the edges, but the effect was not striking.

It was a fucking disaster, he thought. The fact was that the transistors were dying, more every day, and there was apparently nothing the LEM group could do but tear the detector apart, at great expense and downtime, and replace the silicon slabs with improved ones, at even greater expense, some millions of dollars. There were lots of better things to do with that money. And there was no expectation that the replacements would work any better or live any longer.

George blanked the display and called up the handbook's index, then selected the section on radiation damage. There, in beautifully typeset mathematical equations, were the calculations on which the design of the pixel detector slabs had been based. ATLAS's pixel detectors worked, and LEM's died. Both designs were based on the same measurements, the same equations. What the hell was the difference? George banged his fist on the tray table, erasing the image before him and bringing questioning looks from his fellow passengers. He inhaled, taking deep measured breaths until his composure returned. Conceding defeat, he put the finishing touches to the radiation damage report, linked to the Airphone, and sent it on its way on the Internet.

With a gesture he called up the book reader and mounted a detective novel set in Seattle, a ROM-book he'd picked up at the HUB branch of the University Bookstore just before leaving Seattle for Geneva. He would let J. P. Beaumont do the detective work for a while. George did not feel capable of solving any problem just now.

• 7

THE CONCANTATION OF INDIVIDUALS WAS ENDING NOW. TUNNEL Maker watched as the Individuals exited the enclosure of meeting. In the low gravity of this part of the Station some rolled, some flowed, some floated, and some undulated, depending on their individual perceptions of taste, style, and convenience. The variety of sizes, shapes, and metabolic support systems of the Individuals did not seem unusual to Tunnel Maker. The extreme conservatism of their decision did.

Perhaps Tunnel Maker should have expected this outcome. Many of the Individuals had their own programs and projects that competed for resources, and some resources were in short supply at this remote outpost, so far from the Makers' Sun. The Concantation had not been convinced by the evidence that he had been able to marshal. A vocal minority had favored no action at all until there was more conclusive data. But the majority had preferred a middle course.

The consensus had authorized the opening of a Bridge to the neighboring Bubble, but it would be only a microscopic one. If the proton-size ultra-high-energy concentration that had been detected, it was argued, was truly the product of a high technological civilization, then the microscopic Bridge should, with a high probability, be sufficient to attract their attention and accomplish the initial contact at a moderate cost in resources. Even if no contact was established through the initial Bridge, it could at least be used to accumulate more data that could be carefully weighed before considering the expenditure of additional resources needed to expand the Bridge to macroscopic dimensions.

As Tunnel Maker floated to the equipment enclosure in which he would prepare the Bridge, he felt disappointment and frustration. He thought of the more compelling arguments that he might have made but had not. He had argued that the occurrence of the regions of ultra-high-energy concentrations in the other Bubble had been very erratic. If the signals stopped altogether, it would be impossible to establish a Bridge. Therefore, it was important to establish contact at the next opportunity.

He had argued that by hoarding resources that were presently available, the Concantation was risking the very possibility of contact. He had pointed out that contact was extremely important to the progress and prosperity of the Maker civilization as well as to the civilization that was to be contacted. After all, the Makers had originally learned to *Read* and *Write* from another civilization that had been reached through such a contact, using such a Bridge.

Some Individuals countered with the argument that if the signals should stop as Tunnel Maker had suggested, there would be no need to protect their originators from the Hive. They also argued that, since seventeen civilizations in other Bubbles had already been contacted, the benefits to the Makers of a new contact would, in all likelihood, be minimal.

Tunnel Maker had not argued forcefully enough against these points, and now he regretted it. He might have reminded the Individuals that only a dozen gross of orbits ago the Makers had themselves been isolated, and by today's standards had been impoverished, both technologically and culturally. The paradox of the extreme rarity of the occurrence of intelligent life in the universe had at last been understood. Intelligent life was extremely rare and precious. Most Bubbles probably had none at all.

The Makers were unique and alone, isolated by vast distances within their Bubble. Inhabitable planets around well-behaved stars were a gross of light orbits away, and the speed of light was an insurmountable barrier. Their ancestors had despaired of ever being able to realize the dream of escaping the confining boundaries of their own planetary system or the dream of contact, of meeting and exchanging ideas, information, and techniques with another intelligent species that had evolved and developed through completely separate evolutionary processes and local conditions.

The Makers had simultaneously pursued other investigations, including the exploration of the realm of extreme energy densities and the search for new particle species that are the building blocks of matter and the keys to the fundamental forces. That investigation, most unexpectedly, had led to the breakthrough of contact.

Another intelligent and advanced species, the Rovans, residing in a separate Bubble Universe, had used a region of ultra-high-energy density produced by the Makers' experiments to open a Bridge to the Makers' world. The result was an ongoing revolution of ideas and technologies that had now been rolling forward for a dozen gross of orbits and showed no signs of slowing down.

The Maker culture, having first learned the techniques of Bridge-making from the Rovans, had proceeded to use the technique to contact the Baltrons, from whom the all-important genetic skills of *Reading* and *Writing* had been learned and adopted by the Makers. The Makers had taken in hand their own biological evolution, which had previously been governed by random chance, and had placed it under the control of intelligence for the first time. They had subsequently located and contacted seventeen other civilizations in seventeen different Bubbles of the Cosmos. Each new contact had produced its own revolution in thinking and technology.

And then they had been contacted by the Hive, and everything had changed. It had been a desperate time, a time when his race had come very near to destruction. If one Individual had not *Read* the initial Hive probe when that contact had been established, the entire Maker civilization would have been destroyed, taken over by cunning Hive nanomachines designed to convert whatever they found into another Hive world. Their world would have become a new Hive Bridgehead in a new Bubble, which could then initiate new Bridges of its own.

The Hive War had been brief. The Makers used an enormous allocation of resources to enlarge the Hive's Bridge to large macroscopic dimensions, something the Hive apparently did not know how to do, and, with tragic losses and heroic sacrifices, had sent through Individuals and Similarica who had completely destroyed the Hive's Bridge-making apparatus before retreating and sealing their universe off from further incursions by the Hive. Aside from that which had been *Read* during the initial attack, the Makers knew very little about the Hive. In subsequent contacts with other intelligent species, however, they had discovered that the Hive was continuing to use the Bridge-making process to systematically reach emerging civilizations and destroy them. To the Hive, this was simply a form of reproduction. It threatened every Bubble in the Cosmos as newly emerging civilizations were systematically located, contacted, and destroyed.

The Maker civilization and some of its contact allies had effectively frustrated this Hive practice by mounting a systematic program of contacting each emerging high civilization before it was reached by the Hive. It was Tunnel Maker's job to accomplish this for the Makers. And he was now expected to accomplish it without the optimal resources that were needed.

He pushed his resentment to the back of his sensorium and busied himself with preparations for making the Bridge. For producing even a microscopic Bridge it would be necessary to accumulate a large quantity of antimatter in the storage receptacles, an operation requiring a time period of at least half a dozen rotations. When the antimatter energy level was sufficient, the waiting for another ultra-high-energy concentration would begin. The apparatus would trigger on the next occurrence of a sufficiently large concentration in the target Bubble. When this happened, an unimaginably powerful stroke of topological lightning would flash between the universes, and a new Bridge between Bubbles would emerge from the quantum vacuum.

● PART II
May 29, 2004

February 14, 1987

[The SSC is] the most challenging and exciting scientific project which this nation has ever undertaken on the surface of the earth . . . Give our physicists the tools, and they will do the work.
—Congressman Robert Roe (D.-N.J.)

April 2, 1987

Particle accelerators . . . have spent [pause] meant so much to our economic growth.
—President Ronald Reagan in a radio address

August 24, 1988

I want to be "Robin" to Bush's "Batman."
—Senator Dan Quayle after receiving the Republican nomination for Vice President

November 15, 1988

[The SSC] is the most important scientific project that will be built anywhere in the world in the last quarter of the twentieth century.
—Senator Phil Gramm (R.-Texas)

Let's find the Higgs boson for the Gipper!
—a Senate staff member

• 8

ROGER STIFLED A YAWN. HE HAD BEEN IN TEXAS FOR ONLY TWO days, and the jet lag from the shift of seven time zones was still with him. He had been looking forward to attending one of Bert's famous Texas-style barbecues, but at the moment his body wanted desperately to be in bed sleeping. He'd met so many people here that their names and faces were beginning to blur into one another. He walked away from the gathering around the barbecue pit. Perhaps some exercise would help him to wake up.

Once, when he was perhaps ten, Roger's school class had toured the Pinewood Studios near London and had visited a Western movie set there. Bert Barnes's "ranch" reminded him of that outing. The ranch house certainly looked authentic. Perhaps it was, although it had clearly been extensively remodeled and fitted with insulation, double-pane window glass, and central air-conditioning. The interior walls were well-varnished knotty pine decorated with cow horns, deer skins, branding irons, antique guns, serapes, and Remington prints.

The barn was new but looked old. A veneer of silvery-gray weathered wood, perhaps scavenged from some decaying local wooden structures, had been carefully attached to all exterior surfaces of a modern steel-frame building. Its interior was more like a laboratory than a barn. It smelled of plastic and disinfectant, not cow manure.

The fence rails of the corral also looked authentic from a distance, but close up it was clear that they had been made in a factory from pressed wood chips and plastic overlaying a steel core. Their artfully formed "irregularities," knots, and sweeps of grain could be seen to repeat from rail to rail, and at the ends the steel cores were visible.

Bert strolled over while Roger was inspecting the fence. He clutched a longneck bottle of Pearl beer in his plump hand and gestured with it, like a baton. "Roger, my lad, this is a party," he said. "You're here to meet people, not fence posts. As the most eligible bachelor in my group, you have, um, certain obligations and responsibilities to fulfill. Come on over to the grill. There are some folks I'd like you to meet." Bert led the way behind the ranch house. Roger noted with interest Bert's Stetson, his Western shirt with pearl snaps for buttons, his factory-faded and softened broad-cut jeans, his coordinated silver and turquoise bolo tie, belt buckle, and cuff links, and his high-heeled rawhide boots, complete with silver spurs. Bert did nothing in half-measures.

He walked up to a pair of attractive young women who were standing beside the stone barbecue pit. One of the women was tall and blonde, a slimmer version of Bert with the same narrow nose and rounded forehead. The combination looked much better on her. The other was shorter, with high cheekbones and long dark hair that glistened in the twilight. "Ladies," Bert said, "I'd like you to meet our new arrival from CERN. This is Roger Coulton. He's already one of the leading theorists of his generation, and he's just getting started. He's a bachelor and a Brit: Harrow, Oxford, Cambridge, and all that. But don't worry, ladies. I'm told he likes girls, despite his education."

Roger blinked.

"He works in my group at the SSC, and he's absolutely brilliant. Had to be, or we wouldn't have hired him. And if he doesn't stay brilliant, we'll kick his ass out. Right, Roger?"

"Of course," Roger said smoothly and smiled, feeling an inner twinge of anxiety that Bert might know about the recent problem with his new approach. The women looked at him appraisingly, he noticed.

"Roger, this is my daughter, Virginia, and this is her best friend, Susan Elliott. They were roommates in college. Virginia teaches history at Brown, and she's here for a short visit. Susan is a molecular biologist. She now works for a molecular bioengineering company in Dallas."

As they shook hands, Roger, instinctively veering away from a potentially awkward entanglement with the boss's daughter, smiled at Susan. "Molecular bioengineering," he said, elevating his eyebrows. "What firm?"

"Not one you'd have heard of," Susan said. "I work for the Mitocon Corporation. It's a small start-up company put together five years ago with venture capital by some very sharp people from the M. D. Anderson Cancer Center in Houston. I've been there for two years."

Roger nodded. She had bright greenish-hazel eyes that flashed when she talked, and she was quite beautiful. "And before that?"

"I got my Ph.D. at Hopkins with Marcel Perez, and I did a postdoc at Stanford with Helmut Rohrlich. My specialty is the synthesis of neural proteins.''

Roger revised his estimate of her age upward by five years. She must be almost his age, he decided. Out of the corner of his eye, Roger noticed that Bert and Virginia were moving off to join another group. He didn't mind at all. "I really know very little about molecular biology," he said, looking into the wide hazel eyes. "But I'd like very much to learn more about it." He smiled.

• 9

ALICE LOOKED AROUND THE RENTED APARTMENT THAT HAD BEEN her home in Tallahassee for the last three years. With her books, papers, and file cabinets moved to storage, three years of clutter disposed of, and newly cleaned curtains on the windows, it looked like a different place. Through the Florida State University housing office she had been able to sublet it to a visitor to the university for the two summer months she would be away in Texas.

She had never really liked this apartment. She hated the color of the tile in the bathroom, and the ceiling in the living room was cracked. Also, her furniture was showing serious signs of wear. Three years here was quite long enough. It occurred to her that when she returned from Waxahachie she should plan to move to a nicer apartment and buy new furniture.

She had come here, fled here, really, after Steve's death. She had decided to quit her job with the *Democrat* and sell the house with its bittersweet memories and big mortgage payments. On her tight budget she hadn't been able to afford the high-rent district, so she brought the remnants of her old life to this new home. She considered the years she had lived here. It had been a time of healing. There had been good times here, parties and friends, a lover once or twice . . .

She picked up the silver-framed picture of Steve shown roped to the rock wall of *El Capitan* and confidently waving. He'd been such a self-centered jerk sometimes . . . She sniffed, wrapped the picture in a pillowcase, and placed it carefully into the cardboard box from the liquor store that now held some of her possessions and memories. She sealed the box, carried it to her car, and slammed the lid of the trunk, perhaps a bit harder than necessary.

She suddenly felt good, released from a burden. She was, she decided, pleased to be shedding, for the moment, her frugal Tallahassee apartment and lifestyle, the shrunken fragments from the split chrysalis of a dormant creature that was about to spread its new wings and fly away.

Quitting her job at the *Tallahassee Democrat* and becoming a freelance writer had at first been very appealing. It released her from the burden of dealing with the bad assignments, the routine, the unforgiving deadlines, the jerks and the lechers at the *Democrat*, and also it offered the advantages of not being tied to a particular city, a particular job, of being able to live and work anywhere she wished, anywhere in the world. She had always liked to travel and had looked forward, in a year or so, to spending a season in London or Paris, a month writing on a Greek island or on the Costa Brava of Spain or in the South of France, or doing a few weeks of research in Hong Kong or Tahiti or Rio while she worked on a new book.

It hadn't turned out that way. For the past three years she had been securely bound to Tallahassee by the realities of economics. Her equity in the house had not been large. It, along with Steve's insurance money and the small income from her first books, had been barely enough to support her, even in this part of Florida, where the cost of living was among the lowest in the nation. She had been tied here as securely as if she had been under house arrest.

But now the economic equations were changing, and her writing career was finally taking off. A year ago the advance for *Earthworms* had been only $20,000, but the recent advance for *Fire Ants*, based on the first chapter and an outline, had been a promising $40,000. She was proud that she had half of it still in her savings account. Now *Earthworms* seemed sure to earn out its advance with another month of sales. Her agent, who up to now had been conservative but surprisingly accurate in his educated guesses, was predicting that in the coming year she would be getting more royalties from the unexpectedly large sales of *Earthworms* and the boosted sales of her previous books that were still in print. He was even suggesting that if *Fire Ants* was good enough when she turned it in, he might be able to negotiate a multibook contract for her next three books with a ''mid-six-figure advance,'' as they say in *Publishers Weekly*.

Alice was finally rising above the poverty level, and it felt damned good. Perhaps Waxahachie was not a Greek island, but it was a good start.

She checked the contents of her suitcases, still open on the floor. Everything she needed was packed. She made a final check of the closets. They were empty for the first time in three years. Deciding what to take in the car had been a watershed. What she didn't think enough of to take, she didn't need. She had stored some years' accumulation of clothing. When she returned, she might donate the things to local charities. Her accountant had said that the donations might make a nice tax deduction to offset the taxes on her increased income, if her agent's predictions came to pass, if the *Fire Ants* book she hadn't written yet was good enough.

She would go to Waxahachie, she would write the book, and it would be a good one. The opportunity was there within her reach, and she would snatch it. She must.

She smiled, imagining a slim silvery lighter-than-air craft dropping ballast in preparation for free flight. She was ready to fly. She snapped her suitcases shut and carried them to the car.

• 10

GEORGE GLANCED AT THE TIME READOUT HANGING IN MIDAIR AT THE top of his field of view. It read 05/31/04, 11:32 CDT, LEM AUDITO-RIUM, SSC, TEXAS. He mentally translated the time as 9:32 A.M., Seattle time. He still had almost two hours before he had to disconnect and teach his 11:30 class. He was bored and becoming slightly irritated. Larry's rambling "ten-minutes" talk on the status of the data compression software had now been going on for almost half an hour and showed no sign of concluding. George heard his remote's motor whirr softly as he turned to look at Jake, who sat in his special chair against the wall at the front of the auditorium. Jake's eyes were hooded in thought, and his ivory hands were in his lap with the fingertips together, making a horizontal steeple.

He turned toward Wolfgang, who sat in an aisle seat in the LEM auditorium, next to the spot where George's remote was parked. "Jake is a ticking bomb," George whispered to him. "Watch. He'll go off any second now."

As if responding to the cue from George, the spokesman and absolute monarch of LEM, Harvard University Professor Jian-Kwok "Jake" Wang, stood up. "Enough," he said and paused, his head tilted slightly backward, staring at Larry. George was familiar with that Stare. All too familiar.

Larry looked toward Jake. "B-but I wasn't quite finished," he said.

"Time is short," said Jake. "LEM is running, and data are coming in at this very moment. Many of us have shifts that will start soon. If you have more to tell us, Larry, you may continue at another group meeting." Jake consulted the list in his hand. "Next," he said, "George Griffin, who was at CERN last week and is now back in Seattle, will tell us about radiation damage and vertex detectors."

Larry stood bewildered at the overhead projector for a moment, then attempted to collect his numerous scattered transparencies. About half of them slipped from the pile and skittered across the floor. A few in the audience of about three hundred people gathered in the LEM auditorium laughed nervously, but most sat quietly in sympathetic silence.

George's remote whirred up to the podium and with a robotic hand he expertly scooped up the loose transparencies in his path. The robot arm telescoped outward, offering them to Larry, who snatched them and retreated to the back of the auditorium in disarray, arms crossed over the transparencies and notes clutched against his chest.

George's remote turned off the overhead projector and activated the projection monitor system. Through electronically tracked camera eyes George looked out at the large group. "First," he said, "I want to introduce a visitor who is newly arrived from CERN, Dr. Wolfgang Spiegelmann, a distinguished physicist, a microelectronics specialist, and a valued member of the ATLAS collaboration." At George's urging, Wolfgang stood, turned, and nodded to the audience. "Wolfgang will be working with our group for the next month," George continued. "His stay with us is relevant to the present discussion because he's an expert on radiation damage in pixel detector microchips."

George looked at a sensitive spot in his field of view and blinked, and his first figure appeared on the screen. It showed a cylindrical device with flat black surfaces on its sides. "I'll keep this short," he said, "but I want to start with a bit of orientation for the new students. This is the vertex detector for the LEM experiment. It's placed as close as possible to the point where the two proton beams collide, and the emerging particles reach it first. It's made of five concentric layers of slabs of silicon containing several million tiny pixel detector elements, along with some of their associated electronics." He blinked again and a second figure appeared. "A pixel detector is a square of silicon twenty microns on a side that gives a current pulse when a charged particle passes through it." His pink wireframe hand appeared in the projection and pointed at the dark square area on the diagram. "These pixel detectors and their electronics are made directly on a slab of silicon, using the same fabrications processes used to make integrated circuits for commercial electronics."

George blinked, and the picture changed to a display of curving colored tracks. "The vertex detector provides some valuable information for LEM. Using all of the pixels together, we get a close-up image of the charged particles from the collision. We're able to track some of the secondary products of short-lived particles from the collision and establish the location where their breakup occurred. This helps in following the production of strange and charmed quarks in the collision. The secondary vertex particles, as we say, have strangeness and charm."

Another blink, and the picture changed again, displaying the vertex detector now mottled with damage points shown in purple. "Now the problem is that we've been running LEM for less than a year, not even at full luminosity yet, and we're already losing pixels from the vertex detector due to radiation damage. We were expecting to be in our present state of radiation damage after perhaps two or three years of operation at full luminosity, not after six months at low luminosity. So we've got a problem."

"We all *know* we have a problem, George," Jake interrupted. "Do we have a *solution*?" He stared across the room, seeming to focus his gaze several yards behind George's remote.

George noticed that Jake's famous Stare was less intimidating through a telepresence remote. The remote's motor whirred as he turned. "Patience, Jake, patience," he said with a grin. "*First* the problem, *then* the solution. It's important to do these things in the proper order." A few in the audience laughed appreciatively. Fewer than would have liked to laugh, George suspected. As a full professor with tenure, George had little to fear from Jake, but others here were not so fortunate.

He blinked his next figure to the screen, a diagram of an electronic circuit. "This shows one pixel detector and its associated on-chip electronics. We made some tests with our probe station of a few of the radiation-damaged chips that were replaced last month. The good news is that it is not the pixel detectors themselves that are failing. Even in the failed units, the detector leakage currents are staying low." He gestured and two areas of the circuit became circled in red. "The bad news is that there are two key components that are failing: the first FET of the input stage and the power-drive junction transistor of the output stage. What we've learned so far, Jake, is that with no input and no output you don't get much data." Again there was scattered laughter from the group.

"We did a lot of radiation damage testing of vertex detector prototypes several years ago, and we never saw such problems. So the question is: Why are these components failing now? The answer is: We don't know . . . yet. It could be an undetected beam halo from the SSC. It could be some subtle impurity in the kind of silicon we're using. It could be the on-chip layout of the integrated circuit components, which is slightly different from the layout we tested. It could be the design of the circuit itself, also slightly different. It could be some glitch in the details of the fabrication process. It could be a lot of other things.

"Fortunately, we have a way of finding out which it is. Our European competitors at the LHC were very accommodating during my visit last week in sharing their experience. In their ATLAS detector at the LHC they have a similar vertex detector with very similar on-chip electronics. Moreover, because of the LHC runs at a lower energy, the radiation damage at full LHC luminosity is about the same as ours at reduced luminosity. And, as Wolfgang will tell you in a seminar scheduled for next week, their vertex detector is performing above their expectations. It has not had the radiation damage problems that ours is suffering. The question is: Why not?"

George's remote held up a small plastic box with its right robot arm. Something wrapped in pink polyethylene was visible inside. "This is one of the spare silicon chips from the ATLAS vertex detector that Wolfgang brought us. He brought a dozen more of them and also some electronics and components. We're going to test their chips along with ours and find out why theirs live and ours die. That's about all for now. Thanks for your attention.''

He stopped, turned to look at Jake, and nodded, indicating that he was finished. There was scattered applause.

Jake stood and leveled the Stare at George's remote for what must have been a full minute. ''This is not satisfactory,'' he said finally. ''We should not humiliate ourselves before our competitors by admitting our failings and begging their help. We should go to CERN to discuss our victories, not our defeats.''

George shook his head, producing a whirr. ''First we have to *have* victories, Jake,'' he said with a twinkle, drawing more laughter from the group and discharging the tension that had been building a moment before. ''Our resources in this experiment, as you know better than anyone else here, are very limited. If we can shortcut many man-months of work by getting assistance from CERN and directly comparing a chip that works with one that doesn't, then the effort saved can go elsewhere. I'm just goddamned glad that the ATLAS people were willing to provide us with spare chips and expertise. I think we would have done the same, if the circumstances were reversed. At least, I hope we would have.'' He stared back at Jake. He was certain that Jake would never have diverted any LEM resources to help AT-LAS with their problems.

Jake made a dismissive motion with his hands, a gesture that one might use to send away a servant. George rolled the remote back up the aisle and positioned it next to Wolfgang's seat. Jake could be such a jerk sometimes, he thought.

Jake peered at his notes. ''The next speaker,'' he announced, ''is Pierre Barbotin, who is in Nantes at the moment. Pierre will tell us about the performance of the straw tubes.''

Wolfgang looked at George's remote inquiringly.

''Welcome to the LEM collaboration,'' George whispered.

ALICE PRESSED DOWN THE DICTATION BAR AND HELD THE RECORDER
near her mouth, speaking loud enough to be audible over the car noise.
She held the steering wheel steady with her other hand. "PARA-
GRAPH," she said to the recorder.

*"The heifer edged down the slope and into the ravine, loose clods
dislodged by her hooves tumbling down the slope ahead of her. Then
she trotted to the place she had seen from above, a spot where tall
grass grew in the shade of the overhang. Ignoring the unfamiliar
musky smell that permeated this place, she began to crop the lush
grass. It was good, and she ate it contentedly.*

"PARAGRAPH

*"There was a dry rustling noise behind her. She turned a wide
brown eye toward the sound. A large insectoid head was framed by
a shadowed hole in the wall of dirt, sharp pincers extending toward
her hindquarters. She uttered a high shriek of primal fear and moved.
But it was too late, as she felt the cruel pincers grip her shank . . ."*

Alice paused and released the DICTATION bar, placing the small
recorder on the seat beside her. Should it be "primal fear" or "pri-
mordial fear"? The trouble with trying to write while you were driving was that it was just you and the recorder, with none of the
electronic aids of a writing workstation available. The scene she was
working on was not going well. It sounded too much like a B-grade
horror movie. Perhaps she should work on the plot continuity and
save the scene writing for later, when she could run the recording
through her workstation's speech-to-text program and have what she
had dictated directly on the screen in front of her.

Through the windshield she could see that she was approaching the
state boundary, as denoted by state-shaped concrete monuments and
large signs beside the highway. Alabama was giving way to Louisiana,
white oak and hawthorne woods to palmetto wetlands. YOU ARE LEAV-
ING ALABAMA, THE HEART OF DIXIE. Y'ALL COME BACK AND SEE US
REAL SOON! and WELCOME TO LOUISIANA, THE PELICAN STATE. CALL
1-800-33-GUMBO FOR TOURIST INFORMATION.

Alice considered picking up her cellular phone and doing just that, but raised the small recorder instead and squeezed. "NEW PAGE," she said. "HEADING *Plot line for* UNDERSCORE *Fire* UNDER-SCORE *Ants*; SUBHEADING *Problems*." She relaxed her grip on the RECORD bar, took a deep breath, and thought about the many problems with her plot so far. The basic idea was that the fire ants burrow into the SSC tunnels, are exposed to radiation, and mutate into giant ants that attack the countryside. Her research had turned up a few problems with this plot concept.

First, the mobile ants, the one that were likely to be exposed to radiation, were workers. The queens and drones, the ones who reproduced and were the ones that mattered genetically, tended to stay in the anthill except for a brief trip to the outside world for a mating flight. She would have to have some special scenario that exposed a queen or drone to radiation. A queen would be better, she decided. She pressed the RECORD bar and spoke. "BREAK *Problem* COLON *Radiation exposure* BREAK *Find a way to expose a queen to radiation.*"

The depth of the SSC tunnel would also be a problem. The accelerator and the radiation that went with it were buried in a tunnel as deep underground as a thirty-story office building is high. Ants never burrow more than a few feet below the surface. How were they supposed to get down to where the radiation was? She pressed the RECORD bar again. "BREAK *Problem* COLON *Depth in ground* BREAK *How does queen get down to radiation?* QUESTION, BREAK *Elevator?* QUESTION," she said.

Another problem was that ants, and insects in general, were not very susceptible to radiation-induced mutations. Irradiated animals almost always died or became sterile instead of producing mutated offspring. A particle has to break both sides of just the right DNA strand in the same place and the broken ends have to oxidize before they rejoin, a Florida State University biologist had told her, and that was very unlikely. If you really wanted mutations, he'd said, it was far easier to produce them with certain organic chemicals than with radiation.

When she thought about it, however, this wasn't a problem for her novel. Her readers *believed* that radiation easily produces mutations— everyone *knew* it was true. So even if it wasn't, it didn't really matter, at least for the purposes of her novel. She felt a guilt twinge and pushed it aside. She was writing a book to be read for entertainment, not a textbook.

She was approaching a tall advertising sign featuring a giant hot dog that was mounted atop a fast-food place near the upcoming freeway exit on the right. Giantism was a similar kind of problem. If you took a creature like an ant and made it bigger, its weight increased faster than its strength did, and its breathing and metabolism also got out of whack. The biologist had tried to explain it by talking about surfaces and volumes and scaling laws, but she hadn't really followed the details. However, his conclusion was clear. Scientifically speaking, you couldn't make a big ant by, say, boosting the quantity of growth hormone in a small ant. Even if it magically grew to the desired size, it wouldn't be able to stand up and would probably die on the spot.

However, this probably wasn't a problem, either. There had been innumerable sci-fi movies and books about giant insects, so her readers *knew* that giant ants were possible, and they wouldn't be dissuaded by the quibbling of a few scientists.

Alice put the recorder back on the seat, considering what she should do next. Perhaps she should dial 1-800-33-GUMBO and ask what they knew about giant mutant fire ants.

• 12

GEORGE PUT THE BRIEFCASE DOWN ON HIS DESK AND WALKED TO the window of his office in the physics-astronomy building. Beyond the south campus of the University of Washington he could see the morning boat traffic on the Montlake Cut waterway. Farther on, the Roosevelt Bridge connecting the northern and southern halves of Seattle across the Ship Canal stood erect as a two-masted schooner and three smaller boats moved westward under it in the direction of Puget Sound. It was a clear day, and there was a nice breeze from the northwest. Ideal weather for a bit of sailing, he decided.

George thought of his neglected sailboat, tied up over at Shilshole Marina, ready to take him out to the beautiful hidden coves and island beaches of the Sound. He sighed. Not today, too much to do. He glanced at his watch. It was 8:45. There was enough time for a little virtual excursion before he had to prepare the graphics for his 10:30 class. This was his first opportunity to have a closer look at the new results from the radiation damage tests.

He walked across his office to the Swedish black leather recliner next to the tall bookshelf. The recliner, which he used for teleoperation, was his own. It was quite comfortable, unlike the standard university issue.

Switching on the graphics processor, George lifted the data cuffs from the wire-mesh bin beside the recliner. He put on the flesh-colored bands that always reminded him of the wrist weights used for exercise. With duly cuffed hands he lifted the magic glasses to his eyes and adjusted them for a snug fit at the nose and temples. Unlike those he had used on the airplane, these were the ''full-view'' model that resembled wraparound sunglasses. They fitted tightly against his forehead, cheeks, and temples. The glasses were in transparent mode, and he had a clear view of the room.

With the smooth coordination of long experience, he moved his hands through the standard cuff calibration gestures: point index finger, thumb up, thumb down, clench fingers over thumb, clench fingers thumb up, spread fingers, extend arm, touch nose with fingertips, touch top of head with palm, and so on. His gestures followed graphic cues provided by the glasses. Then he inserted the molded sound tubes in his ears and rotated his head up, down, right, and left in response to more calibration cues.

Finally he leaned back in the recliner, adjusting the chair so that it gave his back good support while leaving his head free to ''look.'' He blinked twice, and the glasses switched opaque. Involuntarily his eyes moved from side to side, seeking to penetrate the near total darkness. He relaxed in the dark, considering what should be done next, feeling a slight warmth as the infrared beams of the glasses scanned his eyes, locating his pupils.

He blinked his eyes three times in rapid succession, and the darkness vanished. He hung above a landscape. To the east he could see a mountain range, and to the south a vast desert. He turned his head. Northward was a lush green forest, and to the west a broad body of water. This virtual reality desktop had been done by a Berkeley programmer with too much time on his hands. To some extent it reflected his Northern California worldview. Even at this distance George could see stylized whales, sea monsters, and the suggestion of an island in the blue water, several pyramids and a green palm-ringed oasis out in the desert, smoke rising from the chimney of a cabin in the forest, and a Gothic castle perched high atop one of the tall mountains.

George knew intellectually that the scene was only an electronic illusion that was being painted directly on his retinas by the quick color-modulated laser beams of his glasses. But the illusion was so seamless, so well synchronized with the motions of his head, so vividly *there*, that the vision center of his brain had already been taken in and was completely convinced. He could not doubt that this world *existed*, within some immediate definition of existence.

He raised his hand before his face. His right hand, as represented by a structure of pink shaded polygons, hung before his field of view, drawn in considerable detail and texture but supported by an arm that was shown only in pink wire-cage outline. Since he did not expect to meet anyone else here, he usually saved processing power by not "wearing" much of a body in virtual space. He pointed his index finger toward a gleaming white building far to the south where the desert joined the green plane below, touching his thumb to his middle finger to control his speed.

The flight took him above a meadow dotted with clumps of wild-flowers. He dived until he was very close to the surface of the meadow and could examine the flowers as they passed by. They were generated with some fractal algorithm, and each flower was distinctly different in its intricacies.

George found this exhilarating, almost as if he were really flying. He loved paragliding and flying rigid-wing gliders. Since moving to Seattle he had spent many hours searching out the powerful updrafts in the foothills of the Cascade Range. Now he angled downward toward the white building, watching as it grew in size and complexity. He halted on the green lawn before the entrance and looked upward.

The Palace filled the scene before him, unchanged and unchanging. He tilted his head back, looking up at the magnificent edifice. On the foundation of massive gray rough-hewn stone blocks stood an edifice of tall grooved columns of grainy milk-white marble that supported a high pedimented roof. The vast construction stretched away to a hazy vanishing point in the desert to the south. Over the arched entry, engraved in majestic gold letters, were the words:

LEM DATA ANALYSIS SYSTEM
VIRTUAL DESKTOP—VERSION 2.1A
GIVE UP ALL SLEEP, YE WHO ENTER HERE

George pointed upward and flew inside the Palace, moving smoothly up the broad marble stairway, pausing for a moment on the floor of broad milk-white marble slabs veined in brown and black. The many-hued statues stood before him like a vast army, rank upon rank, file upon file, and each was different. Some of them were of abstract shapes that teased the eye with their curves and intersections, some showed graceful or warlike human figures, some depicted fabulous monsters or human forms with the heads of beasts, some depicted fairylike creatures embodying a standard of beauty beyond the compass of the human form.

George loved the Palace. It was like having your own Uffizi or Louvre to work in. Pietro, LEM's VR programmer and the "architect" of the Palace, was another computer jock with a hyperactive imagination, but his aesthetic sense was on the mark. The Palace was great human engineering. Pietro had found a holo-ROM containing three-dimensional representations of the world's greatest statuary and had used them to produce the icons for the Palace. The result was user-memorable and certainly aesthetically preferable to the comic-book VR scenes that other SSC groups used, and the flat desktops and primitive directory tables preferred by some of the more backward members of his own group.

The fourth row of statues consisted of icons related to LEM tests and checkout procedures. George flew along the row until he came to a white marble statue of a beautiful woman with piercing eyes and trifold tentacles where her arms might have been. It was a suitable symbol for the death of electronics under mysterious circumstances.

George made a gesture, and a glowing three-dimensional network appeared in the air before him, a lacework of interconnected solid icons labeled with short phrases. He reached out with yellow-sheathed hands and turned the network until he found the symbol he was seeking. He touched it with a yellow fingertip, and it expanded to fill his universe.

The members of George's vertex detector group at Waxahachie, working with Wolfgang, had been busy. Test pixel detector slabs of the LEM and ATLAS designs had been mounted in approximately the LEM geometry at a test station at the west campus where surplus beam from the SSC injector synchrotron was available for testing equipment and components. Collisions were occurring, particles were passing through the detectors, and data was accumulating.

George examined the poster-size blowups of two detector slabs suspended in the space before him. One was a LEM design and the other was from ATLAS. Both had a few dead pixels, random failures of the intricate fabrication process. But as a function of time there was no increase in dead pixels in either device. The problem that was plaguing LEM was not being reproduced in the test setup.

Interesting, George thought. It was not just radiation damage, then.

"George," said a smooth synthetic female voice. "Your class begins in one hour. This is your first warning."

"Damn!" said George. This was his last lecture of the quarter, and he wanted to make it a good one. He made a gesture in the air, and the Palace vanished.

It was replaced by the user interface for the interactive graphics application he used in his teaching. He began selecting multicolor illustrations and equations from the electronic version of the textbook used by his graduate class, modifying them to emphasize the points he would make in the lecture, and adding new diagrams and material.

Not radiation damage, he was thinking. What, then?

PART III
June 4, 2004

January 15, 1989

The SSC is another Spindletop oil gusher. With the oil running out, Texas is going to leapfrog into another economic revolution by exploring the frontiers of knowledge and producing high technology. We call it "High Tex."
—Senator Phil Gramm (R-Texas)

February 3, 1989

[The SSC] represents a national commitment to excellence and leadership in research . . . [The Space Station] is an investment in neither excellent science nor excellent technology . . . It is the past brought forward.
—George "Jay" Keyworth, the Hudson Institute, former Reagan Presidential Science Advisor

April 7, 1989

If [the SSC] is worth $5 billion to us, then the innovative technology that would flow from it should be used to the benefit of Americans and not given away to other countries.
—Representative Bryant, Texas State Legislature (R.-Dallas)

• 13

ALICE STOOD IN THE FRONT YARD OF THE FURNISHED HOUSE SHE HAD rented sight unseen before leaving Tallahassee, a Waxahachie ginger-bread belonging to an SSC physicist who had gone on leave for two months to organize a summer physics workshop in Aspen, Colorado. She liked the house; after three years in a small apartment, she enjoyed the extra space. It was turning out to be a pleasant environment for her writing, too.

She held her notebook in one hand, surveying the roofline of the house for sagging gutters or loose shingles. She had heard about the sometimes spectacular weather patterns of Central Texas and did not want any roof water leaking on her computer equipment and papers. The house, however, appeared to be in good condition.

"He'p you, ma'am?"

Alice turned and saw a man leaning on the white picket fence that separated her house from the one next door. He was about her age, tall and slim, his pleasant face crowned with a shock of unruly white-blond hair.

She smiled. "Hello," she said. "I'm Alice Lang. I'm a writer. I've rented this house for two months. Are we neighbors?"

"Sure are, ma'am," the man said. "I'm Whitey Buford." He indicated the building behind him. "I was born in that there house, and m' grandma and I still live here. I'm a master electrician. Been workin' at the Super Collider for the last few years."

Alice looked at him with interest. He wore soft jeans and a Western shirt. He held himself like someone in a Frederic Remington painting, and his speech pattern was a distillation of the local Texas dialect she'd been immersed in since her arrival. She noticed that his pale blue eyes had a hidden glint of sharp intelligence. "I'm very pleased to meet you, Mr. Buford. I'm doing a story for *Search* magazine about the people who work at the SSC. I'd like very much to interview you for my story." She meant it. In the past she'd gotten some of her best material from smart folksy locals, and Whitey seemed to be another one.

"Call me Whitey, ma'am. Everybody does." He suddenly looked

shy. "Don't know what I could tell you, though, compared to all those scientists out at the site. They're the ones that know what's goin' on. They tell me what needs to be done, and I do it."

Alice nodded. She had planned to see more of the laboratory before she began interviewing the Waxahachie townspeople, but Whitey was a source worth cultivating. "So, Whitey," she said, "you're from around here. What are the good restaurants in the area? You know, where one might go for a special occasion?"

Whitey stroked his sideburn. "Well, now," he said, "there's the Texas Choice Steakhouse on the left side of Interstate 35 north o' town near De Soto. They have pretty good steaks and barbecue. The K-Bob Steakhouse in town ain't bad, neither. It's part of a chain. The little Café on the Square has real good chicken-fried steak. And that fancy restaurant at the Denim Ranch Inn is supposed to be good. Never been there myself.

"Course, if you want the real fancy eatin' round here, you have to drive up to Dallas. There's just no end to how much money you can spend on food up in Dallas. They have cooks there that came from France and waiters that wear those tuxedo suits, like they was in a weddin' or a funeral. Saw a friend of mine in the oil bidness pay two hundred dollars for a bottle of wine once in Dallas. For wine! Can ya feature that, ma'am?"

Alice shook her head in mock incredulity, thinking of the special bottle of '82 Château Margaux still lying within its protective wrappings in a box in her living room. She paused. "And what's a good place for having a few drinks and perhaps some dancing? Know any good places for that?"

Whitey looked at her appraisingly. Then he smiled slyly. "Well, ma'am, you have to understand that you've plunked yourself smack in the middle of Dry Country here. There's lotsa Hardshell Baptists in these parts who don't take to drinkin', except maybe behind the door, and who don't want nobody else drinkin', neither. And that goes for dancin', too. But it's a free country, you know, and everybody understands that, so around here we have what's called the Local Option."

Alice blinked. Yesterday she'd been at a nice restaurant in Dallas that sold wine and mixed drinks, and she hadn't noticed anything unusual about it. "How does that work?" she asked.

"Well, ma'am, any votin' unit . . ."

"Wait, Whitey," she interrupted. "What's a voting unit?"

"You know, like a city, or a county, or a town, or a local improvement district. Any group of a few dozen folks that live in the same area and know how to do the paperwork. A votin' unit can pass their own liquor laws. Make it wide open, or tee-totally dry, or anything in between. Mostly in these parts, though, they're either completely dry or they just allow drinkin' at private clubs."

"What's a private club?" Alice asked. "You mean like the Elks or the Moose or some country club?"

"Well, there's them." Whitey nodded. "But there's also the little ones out in the country and the ones that the restaurants run. Like, say, you was up at the Texas Choice Steakhouse up on the Interstate, and maybe you wanted to have a nice cold bottle of Lone Star with your dinner?"

Alice nodded.

"Well, real sorry, ma'am, you just couldn't have it. It'd be against the law. But suppose you told the waiter you had a mind to join their private club, and you paid him five dollars? Then he'd write your name on a little membership card that'd be good for a year and give it to you, and then it'd be okay. You could have your cold beer and buy one for your friends, too. They'd be your 'guests' at your 'club,' y'see? That's the way it works round here."

Alice closed her mouth, which had been gaping open. "Why, that's simply incredible!" she said. "They make laws against drinking alcohol, and then they leave huge loopholes so anyone can get around them for five dollars. Why would the voters put up with such a stupid hypocritical system?"

Whitey grinned. " 'Cause they like it, ma'am," he said. "The Hardshells like it 'cause they've voted against drinkin', just like their ol' preacher told 'em to last Sunday. The restaurants like it 'cause they get their membership fees, and their club members keep on comin' back again and again once they've joined. And the drinkin' folks like it 'cause they get their beer, and it's kinda exclusive and high-tone, you know, belongin' to a private club? So everybody's just as happy as pigs in shee-it. And the outta state folks that are just passin' by on the Interstate, well, they pay their five dollars, and they don't vote anyhow. Ya understand, ma'am?"

"You should call me Alice, Whitey. 'Ma'am' sounds like my

grandmother. I wonder how the physicists and engineers at the SSC like it,'' she said.

"Not very damn much," said Whitey. "They complain a lot. But then, they don't have no votin' unit, Miss Alice, so it don't matter."

Alice thought about that while she made notes.

"As for the dancin'," Whitey continued, "there's the Gaslight Inn up toward Dallas, but there's mostly just kids there, and anyhow the music's too damn loud. Maybe you'd like P. J.'s better."

"P. J's? What's that?" asked Alice.

"It's a little private club, what you might call a waterin' spot," said Whitey. "It's in a kinda trailer near the north end of the ring, over by Palmer. P. J. is the lady that runs it. She's got a jukebox and places where you can sit indoors or outdoors and have an ice-cold beer, and there's a little dance floor, too. The local folks like it, and some of the SSC people go there, too. Has what you might call 'local color.' There's lotsa little beer joints like it all over the county, but I kinda like P. J.'s best. It really jumps on Friday and Saturday nights. They's a few fights now and then, but they don't amount to much."

"That sounds interesting," said Alice noncommittally, wondering how many trucks were found in ditches near P. J.'s on Sunday morning. "Perhaps I'll try it sometime."

Whitey looked at her inquiringly, his eyebrows raised.

"Sometime when I'm not so busy," she added. She was quiet for a while as she wrote rapid notes. Then she turned to a fresh page in her notebook. "Whitey, when they were first building the SSC, there were some news stories about the problems with imported fire ants. Are they still a problem?"

"Hope ta tell ya they are," said Whitey. "Those damn little bugs are the ruination of Texas. Get into ever'thang. When my daddy was in the oil bidness, he had no end of trouble with them damn fire ants. He'd set up to drill a well and bring in his trailer and equipment. If he put the trailer over a fire ant mound, the things 'ud start chewin' into the trailer insulation, then they'd get into the wirin' and the plumbin'. The next thing you know, you'd wake up with fire ants in the damn bed with you."

"Can't you spray them or something?" asked Alice.

"They sell lots of sprays around here, there's long shelves full of 'em at the stores, but they just don't do much to fire ants," Whitey answered. "I think they're protected by the EPA or somethin'. When Daddy was drillin' a well, ever' once in a while he'd drive down to Mexico and buy some insecticides down there that would kill the damn things. Was against some damn law, but it sure as hell killed the fire ants."

"Can't the Texas government do something?" asked Alice. "With all the genetic engineering and biotechnology, I would have thought they could deal with a few ants."

"The Texas Department of Agriculture has sure tried," said Whitey. "Still tryin', I guess. They got them bug scientists over at Texas A&M University to raise some fire ants of their own, and they fixed those boy ants to make 'em, you know, impotent?"

"You mean sterile," said Alice, suppressing a smile.

"Yes'm, sterile, I guess. Anyhow, they turned thousands of 'em loose when the fire ant queens was supposed to be, you know, a-swarmin'." He grinned. "But it didn't do no good. Guess they couldn't fool them queens with impotent boy ants. There's as many fire ants as ever."

Alice scribbled in her notebook. "Do they ever get into the equipment at the SSC?" she asked.

"Well, they sometimes get into our wirin' in the surface buildings. Lotsa relays and contactors and transformers have burned up because of the damn fire ants. Keeps me busy fixin' 'em. Now the SSC has a whole crew of bug experts that goes around in special bugproof suits, spraying 'em and digging 'em outta the ground.

"But the big ring is way down under the ground, two or three hundred feet down there, and them ants don't like to dig down that far. Oh, sometimes they crawl down a conduit pipe or something, but it don't amount to much. Never caused any real problems down in the ring tunnels."

Alice nodded. "Thanks, Whitey," she said. "I have to go do some unpacking now. I really appreciate the information. Hope I'll see you again soon." She gave him a big smile.

Tonight after dinner, she decided, she was going to write another scene for *F as in Fire Ants* before going to sleep. She looked back at Whitey and smiled as she climbed her porch steps. He's going to make a very good character for the book, she thought.

• 14

TUNNEL MAKER DREW THE DATA STREAM INTO HIS SENSORIUM AND examined the pattern of its time fluctuations with anticipation. The detections of ultra-high-energy concentration in the neighboring Bubble had reappeared five rotations ago, then stopped again. There seemed to be a pattern to the recent stops and starts. If the pattern held, the ultra-high-energy concentrations should start again soon.

He was excited at the prospect of making his first Bridge. Three orbits ago he had been designated Creator of Bridges. Now, at last, he could practice the craft that was the basis of his current assignment.

Tunnel Maker examined the long chain of energy storage receptacles that stretched off into the distance in the station bay. They were vessels for storing antimatter, essentially pure energy. The receptacles assigned for his use had been steadily filling with antimatter for half a dozen rotations. He noted with satisfaction that they were nearly at maximum capacity.

The Bridge-making apparatus occupied most of the next station bay, a massive engineering work of energy-flow channels, field generators, and particle directors. Carefully Tunnel Maker activated the diagnostic network. The neural diagnostic nodes indicated no problems. He initiated a dynamic test procedure to verify the status of the device, but he had no real doubts. All was ready for the next occurrence of a trigger.

The third station bay contained the tools that he and some collaborating Individuals would use after the microscopic Bridge had been created. The initial aperture of the Bridge, the Bridgehead, would be only a few atomic diameters, just sufficient for manipulation with a beam of coherent light or a stream of charged particles.

Light was preferred because massive particles significantly altered the energy balance between the two Bridgeheads, the station end gaining energy with each passing particle and the Bridgehead in the other Bubble losing a corresponding energy. This could build up to the point of instability, when it became necessary to annihilate or create dark matter at the Bridgeheads to redress the energy balance. The same effect occurred when light passed through the Bridge, but the size of the effect was much smaller. He practiced with the coherent light manipulator, *Writing* the assembly of a simple nanomachine from the molecules of the station wall, then *Reading* it to verify the accuracy of the process.

Satisfied now, and with a rising sense of excitement, Tunnel Maker touched the central neural node, activating the trigger mechanism that would initiate the complex Bridge-making process.

Extrapolations of the periodic structures found in recent recordings from the new Bubble indicated that a concentration of energy sufficient for a Bridge trigger might be expected to resume in one or two rotations. It was now only a matter of time. Feeling simultaneously proud and impatient, Tunnel Maker set himself to wait for a trigger.

• 15

ALICE FOLLOWED THE VISITOR INFORMATION signs dotting the SSC west campus, finally parking her car near the entrance of a low building with a geometrical roof. She recognized it as one of the "architectural statement" variety, although she could not quite make out what the statement was supposed to say. She wondered if the convoluted roof was watertight in a good Texas rainstorm. In her experience there was a good correlation between architectural masterpieces and leaky roofs. As she stepped out of her air-conditioned car, the wall of Central Texas heat hit her like a physical blow. She was feeling a bit nervous and hoped she wouldn't start to sweat.

She walked through the wide door marked SSC ADMINISTRATIVE OFFICES and up to the broad counter. The air-conditioning felt wonderful. A woman behind one of the desks rose and walked over. She was tall and thin, pretty in a sharp-featured way, with dark eyes and long wavy black hair. She wore a low-cut white blouse with a necklace that featured several crystals of different colors with a central double-fish astrological symbol as a pendant. "May I help you?" she asked.

"Yes," said Alice. She held out her press credentials. "I'm Alice Lang. I'm a journalist with *Search* magazine. I have a 1 P.M. appointment with Dr. Roy Schwitters, the SSC director."

"Oh, of course," the woman said. "I'm Belinda. Welcome to the Super Collider." She smiled. "I'm very sorry, Ms. Lang, but Dr. Schwitters's schedule has slipped a bit today. He's still busy with Dr. Wang right now. Perhaps I could arrange for you to talk to somebody else."

Just then a tall woman with gray hair done in a bun entered the building.

"Oh, Dr. Troy!" Belinda called.

The woman turned and walked to the counter.

"Dr. Troy, I'd like you to meet Alice Lang," Belinda said. "She's a reporter from *Search* magazine, and she's here to do a story on the Collider." She turned to Alice. "And Alice, this is Dr. Edwina Troy. She's the SSC deputy director for operations. She headed the group that designed the SSC and now her group runs it."

They smiled and shook hands.

"Do you have time to talk to me now, Dr. Troy?" Alice asked.

"Call me Edwina," said the other woman. "I'd be delighted to talk to you about our accelerator. I could tell you some good stories about how we designed and built it. But I'm afraid this isn't a good time. I have to get ready for a presentation."

Alice made an appointment to interview her the following day, and Edwina left.

"She's a very nice person," said Belinda. "Too bad she couldn't talk now. I'll try to find someone else." She took some papers from a plastic rack on the counter. "You need to do a little paperwork, so we can get you the proper access cards for the experimental areas and you can visit the experiments and interview the scientists. It's not a big thing, but to keep the Washington crowd happy you'll have to provide us with some information and sign a few release forms. Then we'll get you your SSC press credentials, your access cards, and your radiation badge."

"I'll need a radiation badge?" Alice asked. She wasn't sure she liked the implications of that.

"Oh, don't worry," Belinda said, smiling. "You won't be exposed to any radiation made by the Collider. Nobody is, because it's turned off whenever we go near it. But everyone who enters an area where there might be the possibility of increased radiation is required by federal regulations to carry a radiation badge. It's just a sensible precaution. To get access to the places where the physicists work, you'll need a radiation badge like the ones they carry. Okay?''

Alice nodded, still feeling a bit apprehensive.

Belinda's ''little paperwork,'' as it turned out, consumed the better part of half an hour. Alice was just finishing the last form when a manlike machine rolled up to the counter. It was about the height and size of a man's torso, a rectangular box with rounded corners, apparently propelled on cleated rubber tank treads. Atop the contraption was a curved full-color image of a man's face and head. The head glowed with an eerie light, like a television screen that had been transformed into a head. The head was that of a rather good-looking man with blond hair, a darker blond beard streaked with gray, and ruddy cheeks. The man's eyes looked unnaturally bright and sparkling, as if concealed lights were illuminating them.

''Hi, Belinda,'' said the machine.

Alice watched the machine suspiciously. Was this some kind of joke they played on visitors?

''Hello, George,'' Belinda replied. ''Where are you? Seattle?''

''No,'' the machine said. ''I'm just over at LEM. This is finals week at the University of Washington, but I gave my students a take-home final last week and got away early. My grades are all turned in, so I'm here for the summer.''

Belinda turned. ''Alice, I'd like you to meet Professor George Griffin.'' She seemed amused by Alice's bewilderment. ''George, this is Alice Lang. She's a reporter with *Search* magazine, and she's just arrived here. She's doing a story about the laboratory.''

Alice wondered if she should offer to shake hands with the machine, then noticed that it didn't have any hands.

There was a whirring sound as the head swiveled in her direction. It smiled. ''I'm delighted to meet you, Alice,'' it said in a rich baritone voice. ''Have you ever interacted with a remote before?''

''N-no,'' she replied, feeling unsure of what to do. ''Are you some kind of . . . of robot?''

Belinda and the machine laughed. Then the face of the machine looked embarrassed. ''I apologize for laughing, Alice. No, I'm not a robot. I'm a human being of male persuasion who is presently sitting in a recliner a few miles away, conducting my business at the SSC office using telepresence. This machine is a telepresence remote that belongs to the laboratory. It's a brand-new technology that was developed here.''

At the mention of the word "telepresence," Alice smiled. That was a newsworthy detail that she could use in her *Search* story, and maybe in the novel, too. She looked with new interest at the little machine.

"It allows me to go about the administration building and talk to people," George said, "just as if I were physically present here. Rolling into an SSC functionary's office and demanding some action works better than a phone call or a fax, I've found. Present company excluded, of course. Even over the telephone I can sweet-talk Belinda into almost anything.''

Belinda laughed and threw a wad of paper at the machine.

"Uh, you can see using closed-circuit TV?" Alice asked.

"Not exactly," the machine said, "although TV cameras are involved. I see you in full color and three dimensions and hear you in stereo, just as if I were standing in the room with you, and when my head turns, my camera eyes and microphone ears turn also. In fact, I have a better illusion of presence than you do because the remote I'm using is a cheap model. It doesn't provide a very good representation of me as a real person. But as far as I'm concerned, I'm standing right in front of you.'' The head pivoted with a whirr, looking her up and down.

Alice noticed that a pair of camera lenses, spaced about as far apart as human eyes, were mounted on the head unit and moved with it.

"Uh, George," Belinda broke in, "would you perhaps have time to show Ms. Lang the LEM experimental area? She's just arrived, and she needs to be shown around. She has an appointment with Dr. Schwitters, but he's tied up in an emergency meeting with Dr. Wang.''

"Indeed," said George, "a meeting from which I very much appreciate being absent.'' The face smiled. "Jake has gone off on another of his personal crusades. He's mounting an attack on some imagined beam degradation that he thinks is coming from the SDC.'' The head swiveled in Alice's direction.

Alice looked interested. "What's SDC? Sounds like a designer drug," she said.

George laughed again. "SDC stands for *Solenoidal Detector Collaboration*. It's one of the many acronyms used around here, acronyms that you'll have to get used to. SDC is one of two half-billion-dollar experiments presently going on at the laboratory. The other experiment is LEM, the one I'm working on.''

"Are the experiments nearby?" she asked.

"Some of the smaller experiments are not far from where you're standing, in the west campus of the ring," George said. "Their buildings are part of the SSC campus, just a short walk from here. But the two big detectors are both located off at the east campus. That's on the far side of Waxahachie, about a forty-five-minute drive from here. What would you like to see first? Do you want to see LEM right now?''

Alice looked at her watch. It was almost 1:30. This looked like a good opportunity, so she might as well go for it. She considered how she could work this telepresence thing into her novel. "Sure, if you have the time," she said.

"Okay. I have a couple of hours before I have anything scheduled." George's headscreen swiveled toward Belinda. "Tell Roy that Ms. Lang will return around four. Jake should be finished chewing on his leg by then.

"And before I forget, what I came here about was a little project for you, Belinda. KIRO-TV in Seattle wants to do a news spot for tomorrow's seven o'clock news about how people in the University of Washington's particle physics and microgravity biology groups are using telepresence remotes at the SSC and on the Space Station. I think they're looking for a contrast between the science done at Department of Energy projects and at NASA projects. I almost feel sorry for NASA. They always make the DOE look good by comparison.''

Alice looked at George's expression and opened her notepad. "Telepresence: DOE vs. NASA, KIRO-TV/Seattle, Conflict!" she wrote.

"One of my biology colleagues and I went over to their studio and did an interview last Thursday," George continued. "Now they want background. Could you find some stock clips of the SDC and LEM experiments and put them on the satellite feed? Preferably clips showing some mix of the University of Washington people and remotes swarming over one of the LEM subsystems. They'd like to have it sometime tomorrow morning, Seattle time. Noon at the latest. Okay?''

"No problem," said Belinda. "That's just the kind of thing our video database was designed to do. And we're always delighted to give NASA another object lesson in how the technical support of science should be done.'' She grinned.

The head and upper torso of the remote swiveled toward Alice with an audible whirr. "Do you have a car, Alice?" George asked.

"Sure, it's just outside," Alice said. She glanced downward to the bulky rollers on the base of the remote. "However, I don't think you'd fit." She was beginning to enjoy her conversation with the little machine. It was like being Dorothy in Oz, talking to the Tin Woodsman or the Tick-Tock Man.

"Not a problem," said George. "Belinda will give you a map, and I'll meet you in the reception area of the LEM building on the east campus."

Alice looked down at the little machine. "You're going by a different route?" she asked.

George's face registered a smile. "You might say that, Alice," he said. "It will take you about twenty minutes to drive to LEM. While you're in transit, I'm going to park this remote in a charger bay, disconnect, and eat my sack lunch in my office here. When you arrive at the LEM building, I should be waiting at the front door."

Alice blinked. "This is like a *Star Trek* rerun," she said. "You're going to beam over to the other building."

"In a manner of speaking," George agreed, "except that I'm already here, or should I say 'there'?"

Alice took her little digital still camera from her purse and took several shots as the image of George winked at her. The remote pivoted sharply to the right and whirred away down the corridor.

Just then a familiar figure in blue coveralls strolled up to Belinda's desk. "Belinda, you sweet thang, would you mind callin' me a shuttle?" Whitey said. "I need to go over to the LEM buildin' on the east campus."

"Hello, Whitey," said Alice. "I was about to drive to that very place. Can I offer you a ride? You can show me the way."

• 16

ALICE FOLLOWED THE CURVING TREE-LINED SSC CAMPUS ROAD TO the point where it exited to a farm-to-market highway.

"Go that way, ma'am," said Whitey. "Goes through the middle of Waxahachie, but it should be quicker this time of day."

She turned on the road he had pointed out. "You have work to do on the LEM detector?" she asked.

"No, ma'am," he said. "They want some more wirin' done down in the ring, and the LEM buildin' is the closest access point. There's a fast little monorail down in the ring that I could ride over on, but drivin' across the middle of the ring in a car or riding the SSC shuttle bus is faster. Somebody borrowed my truck for another electrical job, or I'd drive myself."

"How long have you been an electrician, Whitey?" Alice asked. She was glad to have another chance to interview him without being too obvious.

"Got m' trainin' in the Marine Corps," he said. "I was a demolition expert and did a lot of wirin' that way. Of course, my daddy was an Oil Man . . ."

Alice could hear the capital letters.

". . . and I did electrical wirin' for him sometimes when I was in high school, but I didn't get real good at it till we was down in the Persian Gulf. After they let me out of the Marines, I got a job with a construction company when the SSC was being built, and then got a staff job with the laboratory. Been here ever since."

"How old were you when you joined the Marines?" she asked, interviewer style.

"Oh, I was about nineteen," he said. "It was summer, and I'd just graduated from high school. I'd played football for the Waxahachie Indians, but I hurt my knee when we was playin' the Italy Gladiators, so I didn't get a college scholarship. I was plannin' to go to Texas A&M anyhow, but Daddy was goin' bankrupt. So I made a deal with the Marine recruiter to get electrician trainin' if I joined up. Guess it worked out pretty well for me, though I near got myself killed once or twice down in the Gulf, defusing Iraqi booby traps at the Kuwaiti oil rigs and around Ol' Saddam's hidey-hole in Baghdad.''

"Your father had problems in the oil business?" she asked, remembering the stories she had heard of the high rollers. She hadn't seen much evidence of Big Oil since coming here. Despite what one might think from the old *Dallas* TV series reruns, she had learned that most of what remained of the Texas oil industry was concentrated in Houston, while the Dallas–Fort Worth economy was driven primarily by aerospace, biotechnology, banking, and insurance.

"Daddy was an independent Oil Man, a wildcatter," said Whitey. "He did pretty well for a while. Did lots of drilling. Had him a fine cable-tool rig on the back of a truck."

"You mean you can drill for oil from the back of a truck?" asked Alice. "I thought it took a big steel tower and massive machinery."

"Well," Whitey said defensively, "it was a pretty big truck. You see, he wasn't runnin' one of those giant oil companies. My daddy was a wildcatter."

"How does that work, being a wildcatter?" Alice asked.

"Well, he'd buy hisself an oil lease on some land. Where it looked like there might be some oil? Then he'd round up some investors. They's folks in the East and in California that just love to put their money into the oil bidness. 'Investing in our Energy Future' they call it. It's one of them tax shelter things. Daddy'd take the money and hire himself some roughnecks and go out and drill for the black gold. Can take a year or so to drill a well, and of course they's lotsa expenses while the drillin's goin' on. He never had much of the investment money left by the time the well was done. So when it came in a dry hole, he'd just have to send out the telegrams to his partners telling that they'd had some bad luck. After that, he'd go out and buy another lease and line up some more investors."

Alice looked across at him penetratingly. "It sounds like an interesting life," she said. "His, uh, living expenses were paid from the invested funds?"

He turned to her with a look of indignation. "No, ma'am! He wouldn't take nothin' for himself from the expense money for drillin' the well. Daddy was an honest bidnessman, not a damn crook! Only money he got was his standard salary, just like it always said in the investor's prospectus."

"How much of a salary did he get?" she asked.

"Hardly nothin', ma'am. Just two or three thousand a week. Real piddlin', compared to what the big Oil Men pull down.''

Alice raised her eyebrows. She didn't need a calculator to understand that Whitey's father had been paying himself around $150,000 a year for bringing in dry holes. "So what went wrong, Whitey?" she asked. "It sounds as if your father had a permanent livelihood. Surely he couldn't have run out of dry holes."

He turned toward her again with a look of narrow-eyed suspicion. Then he said slowly, "As a matter of fact, Miss Alice, runnin' out of dry holes is exactly what my daddy did do. Y' see, he struck oil with his little rig. He drilled right into this great big old salt dome that nobody had even suspected was down there. It came in a real gusher, squirted oil fifty feet in the air. The black crude was all over the damn place. Daddy like to never got the smell outta his Cadillac.''

"Your father struck oil?" She glanced at him to see if he was making a joke, but his expression conveyed despair, not humor. "Surely that must have brought him much more money than he'd have made from drilling another dry hole."

"Of course it did," he said. "Millions. Trouble is, my daddy's way of handlin' money had always been to spend it all. So that's what he did. Gave hisself a big raise in salary for bringing in a gusher. Bought his bidness some more cars and trucks and a jet airplane. Bought hisself a big house in Highland Park in Dallas and another in River Oaks in Houston. He'd fly me and Grandma over to Vegas or Reno once in a while; he made lotsa friends there. Had him a hell of a time, just like one'a them big Oil Men.''

"Sounds very nice," said Alice without enthusiasm. She never enjoyed hearing about other people doing stupid things.

"Trouble was, the damn investors expected to be paid. That'd never happened to Daddy before. Always before he'd send them the telegrams tellin' about the dry hole, and that'd be the end of it. But this time they wanted more than telegrams. They wanted their money, and they sicced their fancy New York lawyers on to him.

"Skinned my daddy good, they did. He had to file for bankruptcy. They took his cars, his jet plane, his houses, his boat. They took away the red Corvette he'd bought me. They took every damn thing but my grandma's house, the one next to where you live? They even took away his drillin' rig, so he couldn't even drill no more wells to pay 'em back. I was a senior at Waxahachie High when it all hit the fan. I was plannin' to go to A&M and study petroleum geology and help

Daddy in the bidness when I graduated. But I decided to join the Marines instead. Some people thought it was real funny when we lost our money.''

Alice nodded. ''Small towns can be cruel,'' she said.

''My daddy never recovered,'' Whitey continued. ''By the time I was back from the Persian Gulf, he'd got himself drunk as a skunk and killed himself in a car wreck.'' Whitey's voice sounded constricted. ''Guess it was just as well,'' he said finally. ''Ain't no wildcatters left in the oil bidness anymore anyhow. My daddy was the last of 'em. Texas is pretty much out of oil, at least oil that can be got out of the ground for less than you can sell it for.''

They were both silent for a while. Then ahead on the right she saw what looked like the stone walls of a medieval city, with many-colored pennants fluttering from the peaked watchtowers and battlements. There was a parking lot beside the place filled with cars, and she could see people, some in bright costumes, walking in and out of the arched sally ports. ''What in the world is that?'' she asked.

''Oh,'' said Whitey and laughed. ''That's the Scarborough Faire. It's kinda hard to explain, but they have all these buildings made of plaster and plywood that are made to look like real old castles and things. Like in the Middle Ages? Every year about this time they have a sort of medieval folk festival that lasts all of the month of June. They get actors who pretend to be medieval characters, and they have archery matches and jousts and sword fights and things. They have pony rides for the kids. They sing and dance and roast pigs and have a great time. Folks come from all over the state to go to the Scarborough Faire. Some say they like it better than the big Texas State Fair in Dallas.''

As they passed the Scarborough Faire, Alice shook her head in wonder. What a lovely setting. It wasn't at all what she would have expected to find along a rural Texas highway. And it was marvelous for her purposes. She could just see the giant mutant fire ants doing battle with medieval knights in armor. She would write the scene tonight.

Whitey pointed to the large building looming on the horizon. ''That there's the Ellis County Courthouse. Have you had a chance to look at it yet, Miss Alice?''

"I'm afraid not," she said. "It's on my list of things to do, but I've been too busy so far."

As they entered Waxahachie, the red and white stone courthouse loomed ever larger. In a few minutes, as she was curving around the courthouse square, she got a close look at the building. Its details, as they became clearer, were hard to believe. There were watchtowers and balconies, columned belvederes and pediments. It looked, Alice thought, like the opium dream of a Victorian building contractor.

"See those red stone carvings above the doorways?" Whitey asked. "They hired some Italian stone cutters to come over here and make them. And one of them fell in love with the town librarian. Daughter of the woman who run the boardin' house where they was stayin'? That fella must have really loved her. He carved her picture all over the buildin'. And he started out carvin' her real sweet and prettylike. But after a while they must not of got on, ya know? 'Cause the last carvings he did showed her old and kinda strict-lookin', with real hard eyes. They say he just went on back to Italy, poor guy. Hope he did better there."

Alice smiled. "That's a wonderful story," she said. She had already read it in a brochure and planned to work it into her novel somehow. Perhaps the giant mutant fire ants would invade the Ellis County Courthouse and eat a tour guide in midspiel.

They were heading east out of the town now, and both sides of the highway were lined with cultivated fields. "I noticed that some of the farmers seemed to be raising crops right on top of the ring," said Alice.

"Sure," said Whitey. "Ain't no radiation, it's so deep down. The state bought the land and gave it to the U.S. government. The DOE leases it back to the farmers to raise crops on, if they want to. Farmers don't like that much, though, 'cause they can't drill water wells near the ring, and the SSC health people get on 'em when they try to poison the cotton."

"Poison cotton?" Alice echoed.

"Yes'm," said Whitey. "This here is black-dirt cotton country. In the olden days Waxahachie used to be a rich boomtown, the cotton capital of East Texas. All those nice gingerbread houses in Waxahachie was built then. When the cotton plants are full growed, you can kill 'em with plant poison. That way you can harvest the cotton in time to plant a second crop in the same year. The plants die and dry out in a hurry, the bolls open up, and it's easy to pick the cotton quick and send it off to the gin. If you look way over there, you can just see the big cotton gin at Palmer. It's too early in the year for them to have any cotton bidness, though.''

Out her left window Alice could see a corrugated tin structure in the distance. "The SSC people don't like the plant poisoning?"

"No," said Whitey. "The spray fumes was gettin' into the ventilation system, they said, and makin' their people sick. Got them EPA inspectors after the farmers, and they made them stop. Now the cotton farmers get only one crop a year. They say the SSC cut their income in half for no good reason, though they still look pretty well off to me.

"But I hear they're startin' to use some new poison that's okay, some plant hormone stuff that makes the cotton plant kill itself. Like commitin' suicide? I just hope it don't do that to the SSC folks." He grinned.

Alice smiled back. This had definite possibilities as an explanation of the origins of the giant mutant fire ants, she thought. Plant hormones plus radiation . . . She nodded to herself.

"Now we're over the SSC ring on the east side," Whitey said. "See where the Interstate crosses that highway? The green stripe on the highway marks where the ring goes underneath, and that white building over there is one of the service buildings for cry-o-genics and pumpin' and things. They got 'em all around the ring."

She nodded, stopping at the intersection. "Where to now?" she asked.

"Turn south, Miss Alice," said Whitey. "The east campus begins right up ahead."

She turned and accelerated. "I've never been over here before," she said.

Whitey nodded. "If you was to keep driving south on this road," he said, "you'd come to the SDC building. The other big detector? And farther on down south is the town of Ennis. Settled by Czech people in the 1880s. If you like to do the polka, Ennis is the place for you. It's still mostly Catholic, and at the eatin' places in Ennis you can get beer and wine with your dinner. Even farther on down the road is the little town of Alma. Now it's *real* wet in Alma, a regular oasis. You can get anything in Alma." He looked across at her, then blushed. "Anything to drink, I mean, ma'am."

• 17

THROUGH THE WINDSHIELD ALICE CAUGHT GLIMPSES OF A LARGE blocky building. They came to an intersection marked by a neat sign pointed to the right branch of the road. It bore the inscription U.S. DEPARTMENT OF ENERGY, SUPERCONDUCTING SUPER COLLIDER, EAST CAMPUS NORTH.

"That's where we're goin'," said Whitey.

Alice followed the road, which led to the large hangarlike building she had seen from a distance. It looked like one of the large NASA assembly buildings at Cape Canaveral. It was flanked by a smaller office building.

She drove into the parking lot and found an area labeled VISITORS next to HANDICAPPED and DR. J-K WANG. As she opened her car door and left its air-conditioned interior, the afternoon Texas heat struck her again like a warm damp slap. Whitey headed off to the large open building, and Alice strode up the walk to the office building's reception area, already regretting her panty hose and white business suit.

The digital clock at the reception area read 2:23. The building was blessedly air-conditioned. Standing beside the desk was a tall man with sandy blond hair and a darker beard. Alice put out her hand. "Hello, George," she said. "My, how you've grown since I saw you last." She wondered how old he was. Perhaps a vigorous forty-five or so? She decided she liked him, perhaps even felt a certain attraction.

He laughed as he took her hand. "The telepresence remotes they have at the SSC administration building are the cheaper model that doesn't have hands and doesn't provide an adjustment for individual height differences," said George. "It's a bit disconcerting at first to have to look up at everyone. But perhaps it promotes humility. We physicists could use more humility, I'm told.

"Over here at LEM we use models that have adjustable height with arms and hands. Perhaps there's also a certain symbolism. In the administration building one needs to talk. Over here there's work to be done, so we need hands." He gestured with his hands, as if to illustrate.

Alice nodded. "Your office is here?" She found that she was distracted, watching his hands and imagining them replaced by metal robotic manipulators.

"Yes," said George. "All of us working on the LEM detector have our offices here. There's a building like this for each pair of experiments."

"Pair?" asked Alice. She told herself to focus on what the man was saying so she could ask intelligent questions instead of parroting a word or two.

George walked to a large diagram of the SSC complex on the wall and pointed. "See the two beam paths—here and here?" he said, indicating places on the flat sides of the ring where the red line of the beam split into two. "The machine is designed so that there are a pair of side-by-side experiments that can alternate using the beam. The experiment on one path uses the beam while the experiment on the other path is setting up. Here on the east side of the ring the bedrock under the tunnel can support the most weight, so the biggest experiments are placed here. The west side of the ring has the SSC campus with the administration building, the smaller experiments, and the injector complex. Our experiment and SDC have been designated 'primary' by the program advisory committee so we share the same beam leg and get 80 percent of the Collider beam time. Experiments EA-3 and EA-4 are set up on the other leg—here. They're considered 'tertiary' and get about 20 percent of the available beam. We share the LEM building with the EA-3 people."

"So the same beam goes through LEM and SDC?" Alice asked, focusing her camera on the diagram. "Doesn't one experiment interfere with the other?"

George laughed. "That's why your interview with Roy was delayed. One experiment isn't supposed to even notice that the other experiment is there. But Jake Wang, the spokesman for our collaboration, is absolutely convinced that the SDC people have done something that has degraded the beam we get, and he's been hassling Roy about it. I think Jake is wrong, but nobody has asked for my opinion in the matter."

Alice was surprised at the frankness of his comment. There must be some tensions in the LEM group, she concluded, storing that fact away for later use. She looked at the diagram again. "What experiments are over there by the campus?" she asked.

"That's called the west experimental campus," said George. "The 'secondary' experiments WA-1 through WA-4 are located over on the west side of the ring." He pointed to the place on the left side of the diagram where the red line split into two paths. "They each get 50 percent of the beam, more or less."

Alice pointed to two circles near the split. "Where are these?" she asked.

"That's the injector system. We accelerate protons, first with an RF quadrupole, then with a linac, then in this small magnet ring, and then in the intermediate one, until finally they get up to sufficient energy to be injected into the main SSC ring. We inject half of the protons so that they go clockwise, with the other half going counter-clockwise, and then we bash them together. The SSC's injector system is about the size of the old Fermilab accelerator in Illinois. That used to be the largest accelerator in the world, back in the 1970s. As we say in particle physics, 'Yesterday's premier accelerator is tomorrow's injector, yesterday's Nobel prize-winning discovery is tomorrow's background.' "

Alice smiled as she took notes. "And will there be an even bigger accelerator that will use the SSC as an injector?" she asked.

George shrugged. "Almost certainly not," he said. "Perhaps when we get better at building superconducting magnets the SSC might be eventually upgraded with new magnets that make higher fields. That might boost the energy by a factor of two or so. But if particle physics continues to be a hot field and some next-generation accelerator needs to be built, it would probably have to use a new and presently un-developed technology like plasma waves or laser acceleration, and it would probably be arranged in a straight line rather than a ring."

"Not a ring?" Alice felt disappointed. Accelerating particles in a circle seemed right somehow.

"For the past sixty years the highest-energy accelerators, from the Berkeley Bevalac and the Brookhaven Cosmotron of the 1950s to the CERN LHC and the SSC of today, have always been synchrotron rings, large circular rings of magnets in which the particles travel in a closed path while the magnetic field is gradually increased as energy is added and they're accelerated. The SSC, with its fifty-three miles of ring and eighty-six hundred dipole magnets, is probably the end of that line of development. It's the last of the giants." He looked solemn for a moment, then grinned.

"Or perhaps not. I'm not much of a prophet. At any rate, the SSC is presently the world's biggest accelerator, and that statement will remain true for at least the next ten years.''

Alice looked at the diagram and pointed to an area near the bottom. ''Isn't that a lake?'' she asked. ''Can you dig a tunnel under a lake without water leaks?''

''That's Lake Bardwell,'' said George. ''It's down near Ennis. The tunnel goes right under it. Before the tunnel was dug, them DOE geologists swore the Austin Chalk was gonna be watertight, but they were wrong. The tunnel leaked lake water and ground water here and there. It cost the DOE a pretty piece of time and money to fix the leaks, but it's okay now.''

Alice made more notes.

George turned from the diagram. ''But you're here to see the LEM detector. Let's go have a look at it.'' He led her down the corridor to another door and down a ramp. Adjacent to the office building was a big open building, like an airplane hangar.

''This is called the LEM detector building,'' said George. It was a long rectangular metal structure with a huge corrugated door at one end. A semi was parked at the big door, and a forklift was creating a huge stack of large cardboard boxes marked SUN MICROSYSTEMS, COMPUTER EQUIPMENT, FRAGILE!

As they entered, Alice realized that it felt more like a cathedral than a hangar. It was *big*, noticeably cooler inside, and the sounds reaching her ears were accompanied by vast hollow echoes. It seemed to be mostly empty space. George led her forward across the concrete floor of the loading area to a railing.

''Look down,'' he said.

Alice looked down and was immediately hit by vertigo. They stood on the edge of a vast pit. It plummeted, level after level. Each level was brightly illuminated by floodlights mounted at the edges of the vast open area. At the bottom of the pit was an enormous pile of equipment. Looking carefully, Alice could just make out tiny moving figures, people and remotes so reduced by the distance that they looked like . . . like ants.

''There it is,'' said George. ''The LEM detector.''

''I don't understand,'' Alice stammered. ''I thought a detector was a crystal that makes light flashes or something. What I see is a giant irregular mound of equipment.''

''The mound is the detector,'' said George. ''It's very big.''

"What's that white column over to the side, with all the wires going to it? It looks like a stack of white bricks."

"That's the electronics stack," said George. "Each of those 'bricks' is a house trailer. That's where we keep most of the electronics for the LEM detector. It's stacked up that way to simplify the ducting for the air-conditioning and power wiring."

"But I count six layers of 'bricks.' That means it's at least six stories high," Alice objected.

"That's right," said George. "This is a damn big experiment. It's at the bottom of a shaft two hundred feet deep, it's as tall as an eight-story office building, weighs fifty thousand tons, cost five hundred million dollars to build, and keeps a thousand scientists busy full-time.

"The particles that come out of that collision have large energies. They're hard to stop. They don't bend much in magnetic fields. They'll travel large distances through anything, depleted uranium or steel or concrete, creating showers of lower-energy particles as they go. We need thick walls of heavy metal to slow them down and contain them. The detector is so big because it needs to be."

"And why is the hole so deep?" asked Alice.

"Because the SSC is two hundred feet below ground level here, and the detector has to be at the same level as the accelerator. Also, the depth makes for better shielding."

"Why is there no shielding up here?" Alice asked, watching as the beam crane lowered a large piece of steel into the pit.

"The radiation goes away when the SSC is turned off, so there's no problem working on the detector now. And when the SSC is making collisions, only remotes are allowed in the pit and we clear the area over it, except for quick looks."

"Then the machine must be off now," said Alice. "I see people down there."

"Indeed," said George. "The next beam cycle starts tomorrow night. We're making preparations for it now. Let's go down and see what's going on." He turned and led the way to the elevator.

As they descended, Alice leaned back against the wall and scribbled detailed notes. Then she glanced down, carefully examined the floor of the elevator car, looking for crevices where an ant queen might be able to hide.

18

ALICE SAT ON THE LEM COUNTING HOUSE SOFA, SIPPING FROM A
can of Diet Coke and reading over her notes. She had followed George
around the enormous LEM detector for almost two hours. It had been
interesting, but now she felt tired.

The room was a typical temporary office module: vinyl tile floor,
diffused-fluorescent ceiling lights, and textured plastic workspace partitions. But it was filled to overflowing with computer displays and
electronic equipment which, she now understood, consolidated a minute distillation of the vast information processed in the multistory
pile of electronics trailers that comprised the electronics stacks down
below.

She sucked at the straw and turned as George, across the room, put
away his cellphone and walked toward her.

"Roy's done with Jake, but he apparently has another emergency,"
he said. "Belinda suggested that you come to her office tomorrow
morning, so that the two of you can work out your interview schedule
and probably get in to see Roy. Is that okay?"

Alice nodded. "Sure," she said, "no problem. I'll be in Waxahachie for a while. I've rented a house there for two months. I'll spend
a couple of weeks here at the SSC doing interviews, then write the
Search article and perhaps work on a book project, too." And I'll
finish the damned thing before I leave, she thought.

"Very good," said George. He seemed pleased.

"I've been reading over the notes I made while you were telling
me about the reason for building the SSC," Alice said. "Can I check
them with you to make sure I have it straight?"

"Sure," said George.

Alice flipped pages in her notebook. "Okay, you people in high-
energy physics are not satisfied with this QCD theory you presently
use, what you called the 'Quantum Chromodynamics Standard
Model,' even though it works well, because it relies on too many
arbitrary numbers. Did you say that it has twenty-three adjustable
parameters?"

"Yes," said George, "the quark masses, the lepton masses, some mixing parameters, the interaction strengths, and some other things.''

''And you need data from collisions at high energies, which should lead you to a new theory that will explain where the masses and strengths come from. You think that the SSC will provide that data because . . .'' She frowned at her notes. ''I'm not sure I caught this part. Something about GeV temperature and boiling water and a change of 'phase,' whatever that is.''

George smiled. ''In high-energy physics we measure temperatures in energy units like GeV instead of Celsius or Fahrenheit. There's a special temperature, which we believe is around four hundred GeV— four hundred billion electron volts—where space itself changes its properties in a second-order phase transition, going from the 'normal' vacuum of the early Big Bang to a frozen-out vacuum condensate where particles have the masses we measure. 'Phase transition' just means space changes its properties, like ice melting or water boiling. The 'second-order' business means the change is very smooth, with no conspicuous jumps or bumps.''

Alice nodded, reading her notes. ''And you believe the universe made this change early in the Big Bang, after the first millionth of a millionth of a second, and that the SSC will get you to the same temperature.''

''Yes,'' said George, ''exactly!''

''What I don't understand,'' said Alice, ''is why you need the SSC data. If the theory tells you so much about what you're going to measure, why don't you just calculate it?''

George laughed. ''You sound like a member of the SSC program advisory committee. The scenario I just told you comes from an analogy with the theory used in condensed matter physics to explain superconductivity and related phenomena. In principle, particle theorists could use the same theory, except for a few 'minor' problems. They don't understand the nature of what is being 'condensed' from the vacuum, or the underlying forces, or the correct mathematical formalism to use. Therefore, anything they do is a stab in the dark. They need data to set them on the right path. Until we get that data here at the SSC, or perhaps at CERN, we're stuck where we are, with a paste-up theory that doesn't really explain the fundamental nature of the universe.''

Alice nodded as she wrote. ''And why is it important that it be done now, instead of, say, waiting ten or twenty years until we have better technology and can better afford the expense? As I recall, that's what some congressmen who opposed the project were suggesting.''

George pursed his lips. ''You reporters ask nasty questions,'' he said. ''When the SSC construction was started in 1988, there was a team of people available to build it who had experience from Fermilab and SLAC and Cornell and were ready to move on to the new project. Building accelerators is an art. If you wait ten or twenty years, it becomes a lost art.

''The same can be said for the people like me who build the detectors and analyze the data. The manpower for the enormous effort needed to successfully build a detector must come from somewhere. That manpower and expertise has been built up in this country since the 1950s, and if Congress had inserted a ten- or twenty-year delay, that would have been lost. The trained people would have gone elsewhere, done other things. They would have been unavailable, perhaps retired or even dead, by the time they were needed.''

Alice frowned. ''You believe that the SSC could not have been built at all, if it had been delayed and hadn't been started until, say, 2010?''

George shrugged. ''I told you I'm not a very good prophet. All I can say is that the hypothetical people who would start to build the SSC in 2010 would not be the same people who actually built it, and they would surely have far less experience as accelerator builders. There were enough design glitches and start-up problems with the SSC as it was. I'm sure that, starting the project in 2010, there would be a lot more.''

George paused while Alice wrote in her notebook. He smiled, then looked at his watch. ''I'm afraid I have to attend a meeting in about fifteen minutes,'' he said. ''Anything else I can tell you about?''

''Yes,'' Alice said. ''Next question. I gather that the SSC laboratory has invested quite heavily in telepresence and has some leadership in that field. Why?''

''Well, let's consider my own case,'' said George. ''The SSC laboratory is three thousand kilometers from my university. In the old days, if I wanted to do physics here, I'd have to pack up and come with my colleagues, graduate students, and postdocs and either live here most of the year or make nearly weekly trips here. I'd have to spend many days just flying back and forth between Dallas and Seattle, and even more in residence here, away from my classes and

most of my students. There was no real alternative. The cost of large
particle accelerators is so great that there can be only a few of them,
and those who want to use them must rearrange their lives accordingly. My wife divorced me a few years ago because she didn't like
the rearrangements and finally couldn't tolerate them.''

Alice noted that detail. ''Like the astronomers who used to travel
to Australia or Chile to use telescopes that could study the Southern
sky?'' she suggested. She had interviewed some Florida State University astronomers for the *Democrat* some years ago.

''Exactly,'' said George. ''Fifteen or twenty years ago, no one
thought the situation would ever change. But then came the miracle
of bandwidth.''

''Bandwidth?'' asked Alice. ''That has something to do with communication frequencies and TV channels, doesn't it?''

''Indeed,'' said George. ''Over the past few decades the bandwidth,
the range of frequencies available for communications and the transfer
of information, has been increasing by a factor of ten every five years.
There's a principle that enough small quantitative changes can become
a big qualitative change, enough small improvements can add up to a
technological revolution. That's what's happened with bandwidth. It
started with TV conferences. We'd link into other laboratories to listen
in on their seminars and group discussions. But as the bandwidth got
better and we got fiber-optic links that eliminated the satellite-link
time delays, we developed telepresence. Instead of watching on a TV
monitor, you can go there with telepresence and experience what is
happening on the spot. You can walk into somebody's office and ask
what's going on. We even have some electronic blackboards where
you can scrawl equations and diagrams by telepresence or use robot
hands and arms to do the same thing.

''If you had walked into my office several hours ago,'' George
continued, ''you would have seen me sitting in a black recliner wearing what look like wraparound sunglasses. We call them 'magic
glasses.' Lasers from the sidepieces bounce off the front lenses and
draw pictures directly on the retinas of my eyes. The unit also has
sensors that detect my head and eye movements and points the cameras on the remote accordingly. Because the cameras move when I
turn my head, my eyes see just what they would if I were looking at
the same scene directly. The vision center of my brain is fooled into

thinking it's all real, and I get an amazing feeling of 'presence' that has to be experienced to be appreciated.''

''But if you're wearing glasses, why did I see your face on the remote without glasses?'' Alice asked.

''There's a TV camera mounted above the couch that scans my face and head, and the magic glasses monitor my eye and eyelid positions. A computer synthesizes a representation of my face from the data and reproduces my features on the remote's headscreen, with the magic glasses electronically removed. That way the people I'm talking to can see my lip movements, my eye motions, and my facial expressions and react to them. I get 3-D stereo sound from the earpieces, and I wear data cuffs that detect my hand and arm movements. The cuffs buzz when I put my hand through a 'solid' object, and I'm now conditioned not to do that.''

Alice heard soft footsteps to her right and turned. A well-dressed man with Oriental features stood next to the sofa. ''George, have you seen Hans?'' the man said. ''I think he's hiding from me.''

Alice had a roommate in college who was addicted to the Taiwanese cinema, and she recognized the man's guttural vocal mannerisms as those of a Chinese alpha male ''bossman.'' She smiled and looked closely at the newcomer.

''We saw him down in the electronics stack an hour ago, Jake,'' George said. ''Why don't you just call him? He always carries a cellphone.''

''I was about to have Sally do that,'' said Jake, ''but I will bet you that he doesn't answer. Do you know what he did? He told SDC people that they could tune a test beam through our detector tonight.'' Jake took a cellphone from his pocket and dialed. ''Sally? This is Jake Wang,'' he said into the telephone in a completely transformed voice, urbane and courteous. ''Would you please try to reach Herr Doctor Professor Hans Koch? Tell him that he is urgently needed in the LEM counting house. Thank you very much, Sally.'' He hung up.

''I don't think it matters if they tune through our detector, Jake,'' George said. ''The end calorimeters are rolled back, and we could use a little beam down the pipe to check the veto system.''

Jake froze and seemed to grow larger. ''What?'' he shouted. ''Just who took out the end calorimeters?'' He looked upward, as if seeking the source of his cruel fate. ''Who gave permission to roll back the end calorimeters! Do I have no one but fools and charlatans working with me on this experiment? Can I not turn my back for one fleeting moment without having someone roll back the end calorimeters? George, I thought I could trust you. What could have possessed you to allow these imbeciles to roll back the end calorimeters?''

Alice turned her head away, suppressing a snicker. She found it hard to believe this performance had not been staged for her benefit, perhaps to deceive her into believing that mad scientists could be found outside late-show sci-fi flicks.

"Jake," said George, "didn't anyone tell you that the protection diodes needed to be changed in about a thousand of the calorimeter scintillators?''

Alice noticed that George's voice was now unnaturally soothing and well-modulated. He sounded almost like a funeral director.

"I'm sure it was reported in the setup group meeting yesterday," said George. "We can't start the new run until the diodes are changed, and that means rolling back the calorimeters and working on them. That is what's going on now."

"I see," said Jake. "Somebody must have told the SDC people that our calorimeters were rolled back. That explains a lot. Why can't my people keep their mouths shut? Why don't they ask me before talking about our private affairs to other groups? How can I run this experiment when nobody asks me before they do these things?'' He gestured again, but the aura of high drama was rapidly dissipating.

"By the way, Jake," George said, "there's someone here that I'd like you to meet."

Jake halted in midgesture and pivoted toward George, then toward the sofa where Alice was sitting. Alice suddenly felt uncomfortable in his gaze.

"Alice," said George, "I'd like to present Professor Jake Wang. Jake, this is Alice Lang. She's a professional science journalist here to do a cover article for *Search* magazine on the important new physics being done here at the SSC."

Alice started to protest that she was only a freelance writer and had no reason to believe that her story would be a cover article, but she didn't have the chance.

Beaming, Jake strode around the sofa and took her hand. "Miss Lang!" he said. "I am an avid reader of *Search*. We are so delighted and honored to have you pay us a visit." He turned his head sideways and gave her a long look. "Can you keep a secret?" he asked.

"Uh, why, of course!" Alice said, confused by Jake's sudden focus on her.

"You have come here to visit us at a time that must have been arranged by the Fates. We are on the brink of the most momentous discovery of our new century. The Higgs particle, the very mysterious and elusive boson that breaks the symmetries that make our wonderful universe what it is, this magical particle is about to reveal itself to us. The great detector below us, which I personally designed, will deliver this new key to understanding God's Creation into our hands. It must be of great significance that you have come here at just this time, this turning point in the history of science."

Jesus, thought Alice, he's trying to write my story for me, right here on the spot. She imagined the reaction of the *Search* editors to Jake's hyperbole "That's quite fascinating, Professor Wang," she said sweetly.

"Call me Jake, please," he said.

"Okay, and I'm Alice," she said. "Uh, Jake, I heard what you said about, um, disclosing information. I hope you won't mind if I interview some of the scientists working on your experiment in the next few days. I can assure you that I'll treat anything I learn as privileged. I'll also be sure to check the scientific details for accuracy and sensitivity with you before I use them in my article for *Search*." Saying this made her feel deceitful, but it was nevertheless true as far as it went.

"Alice, we have a deal," said Jake, smiling, and took her hand in his very dry cool one. Then he turned, walked over to a man wearing yellow coveralls, and began an animated conversation about computer chips.

Alice looked at George. "Wow," she said, "so that's Jake Wang." She was considering how she could work him into her novel, perhaps in a personal encounter with a giant mutant fire ant.

George nodded, then looked at his watch. "One more thing before I go off to my meeting. Would you be interested in having dinner with me tonight? I'm getting a bit tired of SSC cafeteria food, and I was thinking of finding a nice thick Texas steak."

Alice pursed her lips and thought for a moment. She was here under false pretenses and should keep her distance. On the other hand, she liked George. "Sure," she said finally. "I'd enjoy that."

19

ALICE FELT EXHAUSTED BUT SOMEHOW FULFILLED. IT HAD BEEN A long day, during which she had gathered a lot of valuable material, but the sheer visual complexity of the SSC laboratory and the LEM detector had brought her to the brink of sensory overload. Now it was time to relax and chill out after the afternoon heat of Central Texas. She inhaled the delicious smell of steaks grilling on an open fire, leaned back in her chair, and looked up at the building's barnlike structure. She liked the large overhead wooden beams and ranch-style decor of the Texas Choice Steakhouse.

She looked closely at the fine print on the membership card that George had received from their waiter in exchange for a five-dollar bill. It stated that whereas George Griffin was an official and honored member of the Texas Choice Club, he or she was therefore entitled to all the rights and privileges conferred by this exalted status. Among these rights and privileges was that of ordering longneck bottles of ice-cold Lone Star. George took a long pull from that benefit of his new status and smiled contentedly.

Considering that George must make frequent trips to the SSC, Alice was surprised that he didn't already have a Texas Choice Club membership. He must not go out very much. Come to think of it, neither did she.

Alice cut another chunk from the thick medium-rare steak, wondering if she'd be able to finish it all. She glanced at George. Might as well get on with the relationship probing, she decided. "You mentioned that your wife divorced you," she said.

George's eyes widened momentarily, as if he'd been discovered doing something forbidden. "That's right," he said. "Grace, who is British, decided to put herself in competition with physics for my attention, and physics won. She's gone back to the U.K. now, and I hope she's happier there."

Alice nodded. The message that George's work was more important than the wishes of his ex-wife came in loud and clear. "As a writer, I've been around scientists enough to know that their work requires a large amount of time and effort. Most of them seem to be workaholics who love what they're doing. Didn't she understand that?''

"Not really," said George. "After I landed the faculty job in Seattle, she developed the Oxfordesque vision of me as a university don,
tutoring students, attending faculty assemblies, arguing with colleagues over fine points of philosophy, and writing an occasional mon-
ograph containing my great thoughts. She simply never understood
how things work in experimental particle physics. She had never
imagined, she told me once, that such a large group of people would
choose to work so hard, for so long, and spend so much money to
accomplish so little.''

Alice grimaced. "Did you have any children?" she asked.

"No," George answered. "We held off at first because our finances
were very tight. Then in Geneva we discovered that Grace had, as
they say, a problem. We could have used one of those microsurgical
fertilization techniques, but about then we began having disagreements
about my working hours, so it seemed prudent to wait. I suppose we
avoided many complications, as it turned out." He stared bleakly at
the table for a moment and then looked up at her. "How about you,
Alice? Married? Or otherwise involved?''

"I'm a widow, actually," she said, feeling suddenly trapped into
unfolding a story she would rather keep packed away. "Steve and I
were married for six years. Happily married, I guess you could say.
We met as students at Florida State in 1992 while we were both
working on Bill Clinton's unsuccessful presidential campaign. After
graduation, I got a job as a reporter with the *Tallahassee Democrat*
and supported both of us while he was finishing law school. When
Steve graduated, he got a job with a good law firm in Tallahassee,
which is the state capital. Two good jobs, many good friends, a wonderful life, a nice house. We were active in politics, and Steve was
planning to run for the state legislature when the time was right. We
were both too busy to contemplate dealing with children. And then
he was killed in a mountain-climbing accident." She paused and swallowed.

George said nothing, so finally she continued. "Steve had grown
up in Montana, and he was a climbing nut. Once or twice a year we'd
go off to Switzerland or Colorado or Alaska to climb mountains. I
learned enough to keep up with him, most of the time. It was good
healthy exercise, and it kept us in top condition. We were at Saas-Fee
when I suddenly came down with the flu. Steve decided to take the

opportunity when I wasn't along to do something more challenging. He hired a Swiss guide and set out to climb the Eiger. There'd been an unusually heavy snowfall that winter, and it was warming up. And, to get to the point, there was an avalanche where there had never been one before. The guide came back, but Steve didn't. It them took two days to find his body.''

George said nothing, but he squeezed her hand.

''The insurance money and the sale of our house in Tallahassee provided me with enough financial independence so I could do free-lance writing instead of working for the newspaper. I've been a full-time writer ever since.'' She hadn't intended to talk so much about it, but George didn't seem to know what to say. So she had babbled on, hoping that her anger at Steve for getting himself killed hadn't been too obvious.

She glanced out the window. The sun was low and red over the Texas prairie. ''I'm glad it's flat here,'' she said finally. ''I don't much like to look at mountains anymore.''

George took another sip from his longneck beer bottle and swallowed. Twice. ''I'm really sorry, Alice,'' he said at last. ''I'd forgotten that someone could be so charming and so vibrantly alive and still have deep sorrows beneath the surface.''

She wiped her eye at the inside corner. ''I think it's time to change the subject,'' she said in a low voice. Talking about Steve made her recall the pit of depression that had trapped her for so long, that she had struggled so hard to climb out of. ''I'd like to see your experiment when it's actually running and collecting data. So far, all I've seen are the preparations.''

George stroked his beard. ''They're almost finished with the present machine development cycle,'' he said. ''We expect to have beam available sometime tomorrow night. My next shift at LEM starts at 10 P.M. and ends at 6 A.M. How do you feel about staying up all night?''

''Actually, it sounds great,'' she said, feeling her spirits lift. ''I'm rather a night person. When I'm working on a long piece of writing, I tend to write all night and sleep all day. In Tallahassee it's quieter and cooler at night, and the work goes better.''

''Okay,'' said George. ''You're on for the Tuesday night shift. I hope you don't bore easily. Experiment runs are usually structured as many hours of routine checking when nothing much is happening, punctuated by an occasional fifteen minutes of panic and confusion when something goes wrong.''

Alice smiled. ''Perhaps I'll be lucky, and disaster will strike while I'm there.''

PART IV
June 8, 2004

July 5, 1989

Building the Super Collider would be a Super Mistake.
—Congressman Dennis Eckart (D.-Ohio)

So the question becomes: Is the SSC the kind of good science we most need right now?
—Congressman Sherwood Boehlert (R.-New York)

September 1, 1989

Mars is essentially in the same orbit [as Earth]. Mars is somewhat the same distance from the sun, which is very important. We have seen pictures where there are canals, we believe, and water. If there is water, there is oxygen. If oxygen, that means we can breathe.
—Vice President Dan Quayle

September 8, 1989

What a waste it is to lose one's mind—or not to have a mind. How true that is.
—Vice President Dan Quayle

• 20

WOLFGANG WAS SITTING AT THE CONSOLE OF THE SCANNING TUN-
neling Microscope when George walked in. "Sorry I'm late," he said.
"The trigger group meeting ran way overtime." George felt guilty
about being late. Wolfgang must have been here for almost an hour
and had the STM in full operation. The display showed what looked
like the gate region of a failed field effect transistor.

George walked forward and peered through the thick glass window
of the instrument's sample holder. The silicon slab they had brought
was clipped to a complicated positioning mechanism. The interior was
close-packed with unfamiliar shapes, but George imagined that he
could make out the needlepoint probe of the STM as it scanned a few
atomic diameters above the surface of the silicon, measuring the electrical conductivity of the tip-to-surface gap on an atom-by-atom scale.
The display screen showed a colorful contour map depicting a lumpy
mountainlike terrain. "How's it going, Wolfgang?" he asked.

"*Schlecht*," said the other man. "It's clear that your FET gate
pinched off destructively for some reason, but its geometry is not
significantly different from its neighbors, and also no different from
the ones we used in the ATLAS detector." He gestured at the colorful
display.

George looked at the structures on the screen. The p-type and n-
type regions of the silicon differed in elevation by a few atomic layers,
enough to show up clearly on the STM. The gate region, which should
have had an hourglass shape, was instead two separated clumps with
no connection between them. Around the region where the connection
channel should have been George noticed several clusters of white
dots. "What are these?" he asked.

"Those speckles?" said Wolfgang. "I don't know. There seem to
be clusters of them near the gate region. Perhaps they are small particles made during the gate failure, debris from the catastrophe. There
must have been some energy dissipated when the semiconductors decided to rearrange themselves."

"Perhaps so," said George. "Can we look at some gate that didn't
fail?"

"Of course," said Wolfgang, typing into the keyboard of the STM control computer. The scene on the display began to shift to the right as the piezoelectric needle-position mechanism was given a new bias voltage. The stratified terrain passed by until an hourglass shape appeared on the screen.

George studied it closely. "I see a few of the clusters near the gate region here, also. There are fewer of them, though, and they seem to be lined up along the gate channel, like spectators along a parade route," he said. "Was there anything similar on the ATLAS chips?"

Wolfgang shrugged. "I don't think so," he said. "I think we would have noticed."

"What's the scale here? A few microns?" George asked.

Wolfgang typed a command, and a graduated scale appeared along the lower part of the display. "*Ja*, the clusters are perhaps a micron across," he said.

George thought for a moment. He had an idea. "The superconductor metallurgy group has a scanning electron microprobe. It scans an energetic electron beam over a surface, and records the X rays produced at each spot. It can label any feature of a scan picture with its chemical composition of elements. Maybe we can schedule some time on it to find out what the clusters are."

Wolfgang pursed his lips and nodded. "*Ja*, good idea." he said.

George took out his cellphone and called Jerry Walton, the superconductor metallurgy group leader. George reserved two hours of microprobe time in the next blank spot in the schedule, Friday, June 18. It was frustrating to have to wait more than a week, but there were no openings sooner. Jerry promised to call George or Wolfgang if anyone canceled.

They spent the rest of the afternoon moving the STM probe around on the micro-landscape of the detector, finding other blown FETs and clusters of speckles but learning nothing more.

At the end of the day, after a quick meal in the cafeteria, George returned to his room at the SSC hostel feeling depressed. He spent the evening watching second-rate movies on the room's TV wall-screen.

21

ROGER STROKED HIS CHIN AGAIN AS HE STUDIED THE PAPERS AND diagrams on Susan's laboratory desk. Susan was very excited about her work, and her enthusiasm had caught him up, too. And it was interesting. He thought about the implications of her neuroprotein. If it worked, it could change the world. Again he felt the dull ache in the pit of his stomach, an ache related to how badly his own work had been going lately. Her protein, when it was available, could even change theoretical physics, he thought. It could change *his* theoretical physics.

Susan laughed.

Roger looked up inquiringly. Had he done something amusing without realizing it?

"You always stroke your chin when you're thinking hard," she said. "Elvis seems to be imitating you. Perhaps he's considering going into particle theory."

Roger walked over and looked in at Elvis, the rhesus monkey in the laboratory cage on the cart in front of Susan. "There are some fairly odd animals in the field already," he said. "I suppose we could accommodate one more." He wondered if imitating humans was an indication of intelligence. He watched the movement of Elvis's eyes, studying Roger, then flicking away. He could believe there was intelligence behind those eyes.

Roger turned to Susan and again felt the pull of her attraction. He liked her very much. After a pleasant Tuesday evening dinner at the Four Seasons in Dallas, they had driven the short distance to her laboratory at Mitocon. Susan had told him that she was concerned that the person on the evening shift had called in sick, and she had decided to give Elvis his next shot and checkup herself. Roger was pleased to finally get a look at her laboratory and at Elvis, one of her favorite topics of conversation. He had been seeing a lot of Susan in the past week and a half, but this was his first visit to her lab.

"I wonder . . ." he said, watching Elvis and thinking again about what Susan's drug might do for humans. "Do you have any quantitative measure of how much this new protein has improved his intelligence?'' he added lamely. He didn't want to bring up the topic of human experimentation again. He had already heard Susan's strict views on the subject.

She removed a felt-tipped pen from the pocket of her white lab coat and scribbled on a pad. "It's a matter of interpretation," she said. "I have superconducting magnetometer measurements showing a significant increase in electromagnetic brain activity after we gave him synaptine, but there's no way, at present, to relate that to intelligence. His reactions are faster. His basic reaction time is down to about 70 percent of what it was before the treatments.''

Roger nodded and inserted a long cylindrical greenish "monkey chow'' pellet into a mesh opening of Elvis's cage. The animal snatched it to his mouth with a lightning-fast motion.

"There are also the sequence learning tests,'' said Susan. "Before we started him on synaptine, it took about four repetitions before he learned a new sequence. Now he always gets them after the second repetition and often after the first. Is that a 100 percent increase in IQ? Or a 50 percent increase? Or is it nonsense to apply a one-dimensional measure like IQ to a characteristic with as many independent variables as intelligence seems to have? All I can say is that I'm sure Elvis is much brighter than he was a few weeks ago.''

Roger nodded. "How long does a dose of synaptine last? Or is it permanent?''

"The protein is metabolized, so it has to be replaced. With Elvis an intramuscular dose lasts about twelve hours. But there's some evidence of residual benefits that last much longer. With the rats it's more difficult to tell, because the effect is so much smaller.''

"Smaller in rats . . .'' Roger mused, trying to recall what she had said about the tests. "Oh yes, you were doing trials with rats until a few weeks ago, weren't you?'' If the increase in intelligence is small in a rat and bigger in a monkey, what would it be for a human? he wondered.

She nodded. "That series was disappointing. Synaptine didn't do much for rats, for some reason,'' she said. "In low doses it made them meaner, and in large doses it gave them seizures, but the effect of what should be a normal dose was only a slight improvement in their T-maze running performance.''

"Any theories as to why?''

"We did some autoradiographs of brain tissues with carbon-14-

labeled synaptine. The stuff is quite selective. It's active mainly in the prefrontal brain areas of primates, and rats don't have any prefrontal development to speak of. Probably there are different versions of the same basic molecule that operate with different types of neurons.''

Roger peered closely at Elvis again. ''Any evidence of side effects with this guy?'' he asked, walking around to the side of the cage. Untested experimental drugs could be dangerous, he knew.

''Nothing obvious, certainly,'' Susan answered. ''His weight has been a constant six kilos, his appetite is good, and his coordination, like his reaction time, has improved. Synaptine is a natural protein, if a rare one. Primates already have some quantity of it in their brain tissue, so raising the concentration wouldn't be expected to do unpleasant things, unless the dose was very large. That's the argument we're using to persuade the Food and Drug Administration, so they'll approve our application for preliminary human trials to try small doses on certain retarded children, Alzheimer's patients, and others that show evidence of a synaptine deficiency.''

Morons and the hopelessly senile, he thought. What a waste. ''Is it going to be expensive as a drug?'' he asked.

Susan grinned. ''All the market will bear, as we money-grubbing biotech business folk say.'' Then she grew more serious. ''In my experience, Roger, you physicists with your big federal grants don't have much appreciation for the realities of commercial research. We have a huge research overhead here''—she gestured at the long racks of electronic and chemical equipment in the laboratory—''which has to be supported from the profits of our relatively few commercially successful products. If we can't do that, we go out of business, and the research stops. Mitocon has made it as a successful business so far. We've survived two biotech shakeouts in which many similar companies were liquidated or bought out. Appropriately enough, biotechnology is a very Darwinian business.''

''I think it also helps to have an instinct for the jugular,'' said Roger, looking at her. It helps in theoretical physics, too, he added silently.

''Perhaps,'' said Susan. ''Since you asked, the actual production costs of synaptine will be fairly low. For a neuroprotein, it isn't very complicated. A good solid-phase synthesizer could sequence a batch of it in a few weeks if necessary, but we have better ways. We've already located the coding sequence in human DNA and inserted it into *e coli* bacteria. If necessary we could produce it by the ton. Synaptine is very stable at room temperature and doesn't even need to be refrigerated. There are none of the usual storage problems, which lowers the cost.''

She picked a vial of bright yellow liquid from a nearby rack half-filled with similar ones and held it up to the light. "Now I'm going to give Elvis his booster shot."

Roger walked over to the rack. There were many vials there.

"By the way, Roger," Susan said. "Would you count those vials for me? A new batch arrived just before quitting time, and apparently the carton had been dropped in shipment. A number of the vials were smashed. My technician cleaned up the mess, but he didn't have time to do a new inventory before he had to leave. Just write the count here." She indicated a clipboard on the table, pointing to a blank line on a printed form.

"Glad to," said Roger. As she worked, he moved between her and the long rack of synaptine vials. "And you discovered synaptine? Yourself? I'd wager there's a good story there," he said. His index finger moved along the rack as he counted.

She smiled. "Perhaps," she said. "I owe it all to your fellow countryman Francis Crick, actually. I'm sure you must know about neural networks. Uh, the electronic kind, I mean." She removed a very thin disposable syringe from a drawer, stripped off the sterile wrapper, attached a needle, and inserted it in the pink top seal of the synaptine vial.

"Of course," said Roger, writing a number on the clipboard. "The computer that doesn't need a program. Our experimenters at the Super Collider have trained neural nets to distinguish good data events from garbage. The circuits have solved many problems of pattern recognition in situations where conventional computers have failed miserably. And I seem to recall that molecular biologists trained them to predict protein folding." He watched as she withdrew about half a milliliter of the vial's contents. "Doesn't take much," he observed.

She nodded. "Some years ago when neural nets were first being investigated, Sir Francis Crick of DNA fame publicly objected to calling them 'neural' networks. He pointed out that the electronic 'neural networks' were using an external procedure to adjust the transmission weights between the connections of the net depending on the net response to a stimulus, the so-called back-propagation algorithm, and that there were no similar processes in natural networks of real neurons.

"Since the two types of networks obviously operated on different principles, Crick contended that it was misleading, even intellectually dishonest, to call the electronic device a 'neural' network, which carried the implication that it was an electronic model of the brain." She slipped the needle beneath the skin of the animal's pink buttocks. Elvis squealed in protest, but it was a mild protest.

"I perhaps read that somewhere," said Roger. "But I suppose the terminology was too firmly entrenched by the time Crick complained. People still call them neural networks."

"So it seems," said Susan. "For a long time I've been interested in brain function, and occasionally I've thought about Crick's argument. A couple of years ago, while I was driving along the Nantucket coast after a conference, I happened to consider it from a different perspective. I had a wonderful insight." She smiled and seemed to be recalling the thrill. "Electronic neural nets work very well. If the method of weight adjustment they employ is so useful," she said, raising her eyebrows and looking inquiringly at Roger, "why doesn't nature use a similar process in real neurons?" She smiled at him, waiting for his answer.

Roger rubbed his chin. "Tricky question . . ." He paused. "Perhaps there wasn't an evolutionary path that could lead . . . No, wait a minute . . ." He stopped, then grinned at her. "Maybe there *is* such a mechanism in real neurons, but no one had found it yet, so Crick didn't know about it."

Susan grinned back and kissed him on the cheek. "Very good for an amateur!" she said. "That's exactly what I concluded. So I decided to look more carefully to see if I could localize an agent that might be enhancing changes in the synapse transmission strengths. I was able to use some new tricks, real-time MRI microimaging, for example. And I found that in primate brain tissue whenever the synapse connections showed large changes in their transmission strengths, a certain protein was always present.

"That's how I found synaptine. It's the protein agent that provides Crick's missing mechanism. It enhances adjustment of the connection strengths at synaptic junctions, just the way the back-propagation calculations do at the connection nodes of a neural network."

Roger, whose hands had been behind his back, brought them forward and grasped both of hers. "That's a great story. You're wonderful," he said and kissed her slowly and purposefully. As they kissed, he could feel the four slim glass cylinders he had slipped into the tight back pocket of his slacks pressing against his buttocks. He'd stolen the drug from Susan. *Stolen* it! When the act of theft had occurred, it had been very smooth, as if he were watching someone else, some skilled thief who had effortlessly pocketed the vials and made the bogus entry on the clipboard. He could still slip the vials back in the rack, he thought, but he made no move to do so. He recalled the time in King's Lynn when he'd been caught stealing a sweet at the grocer's. He'd been perhaps seven at the time, but the shame of being caught still brought a flush to his cheeks.

Was he crazy? Yes, he did seem to be rather crazy just now. He *needed* the synaptine, and Susan had so much that she would never miss what he had taken. If this was a crime, it was one that lacked a victim. Roger's feelings of guilt were not diminished by this rationalization, but he decided, guilt or no, that he was keeping the drug. He had to. He kissed Susan with rising urgency, guilt transmuting to desire.

They left soon after and, with some haste, returned to Susan's apartment.

Two hours later the empty laboratory was very quiet. Elvis was feeling very strange. The street sounds that came to his ears seemed to have dangerously sharp edges. The light from the window seemed to have an aura of fruity taste about it. The familiar smells of the laboratory seemed each to have an individual musical ring. He began to shake, then to rock slowly back and forth.

He fell to the floor of his cage, his back arching, his mouth stretched in a rictus grin. An electrical fire danced in his brain.

Elvis was having his first *petit mal* epileptic fit.

22

GEORGE LOOKED AT THE LARGE WALLSCREEN DISPLAY MOUNTED ON the SSC counting house wall. The beam luminosity was stabilizing nicely. The SSC beam had been late in the ramp-up on Tuesday evening and was not at full energy until well after midnight. LEM had limped into operation but now was finally recording data smoothly.

He glanced over at Alice, who was seated at a nearby table, busily transcribing handwritten notes into her laptop workstation. It was almost 3 A.M. She seemed to be holding up very well. He realized that he really liked having her here with him.

He looked at the colorful flatscreens of the LEM counting room. The data acquisition computers continuously sampled the data stream and selected a few of the events for display. All events were also recorded on ultra-high-density holographic optical platters for later analysis.

The displays showed several views of the LEM detector and the paths of the reconstructed particle tracks that signaled the occurrence of a head-on collision between two 20 TeV protons, particles so highly accelerated that their rest mass represented only a part in twenty thousand of their mass-energy. The beam monitors showed that tonight the twin proton beams had been ramped to a new SSC record for luminosity.

A brushlike fan of varicolored particle tracks from a new event was traced on the screen, while numerals below the picture indicated the quantities of energy deposited in the various calorimeters. George smiled. The LEM experiment, constructed with the efforts of almost a thousand physicists and perhaps two thousand technicians, for once seemed to be functioning properly.

He seated himself at one of the consoles and studied the oscilloscope traces of signals from electronics units thirty stories below that were processing the massive flow of data from each event. Everything seemed okay.

He directed the signals from the vertex detector into the analog signal bus and checked the overview monitor of the pixel detectors. The number of dead pixels from radiation damage had increased slightly since the beam had come on. Well, at least the chips should be usable through the end of this data collection period.

Without warning, the digital oscilloscope signal trace changed. The smooth up-and-down bump of a single particle passing through the detector was replaced by a rise to the saturation level of the amplifier chip, as a section of the pixel detector was overwhelmed with ionization and charge.

"What the . . . ?" he said aloud. The numerical display showing the number of tracks in the detector, which normally registered the few hundred tracks from a normal event, was now registering over a thousand. And from the tracking display, most of them were not coming from the vertex of the collision. One particle, indicated in purple because of its heavy ionization, traced across the detector in a path that was almost undeflected by the 2 Tesla field of the toroidal magnet. Emanating from this particle were jets of secondary particles that seemed to occur every centimeter or so along the path.

George glanced at the numerals along the bottom edge of the display. The calorimeters were indicating an impossibly high energy. They had received far more energy than could be supplied by any proton-proton collision, more even than from several superimposed collisions.

"What the hell is that?" George demanded in a loud voice. The dozen physicists and technicians also in the counting room all reacted at once.

"Holy shit! Was that a spark?"

"Could that have been a computer glitch?"

"How did it get past the fucking trigger?"

"You should have seen what the straw tubes just did!"

George blinked. He was sure that this had not been a detector failure. He was all too familiar with detector glitches and knew how they looked. This was not a glitch. He had just witnessed the law of conservation of energy being violated with extreme prejudice.

He walked to the central console, sat down, and began to write in the logbook. Then he looked across the room. "Ralph," he said, "run the diagnostics! Quick! If that was an equipment glitch, we need to know as much as possible about what happened." The technician strode to an equipment rack and began to move switches.

Alice was suddenly beside George. "What just happened?" she asked.

"As Lewis Carroll might have put it, Alice, we just saw a Snark,'' he said. "An impossible event. Something just lit up the LEM detector in a way that, according to our conventional wisdom, could not, should not have happened. The collision event, according to our readouts, had more energy, more momentum, and more particles than the laws of physics can allow. It could not have happened, yet it did.''

"Was it some kind of breakdown of the equipment?'' she asked.

"Perhaps,'' he said, "but I doubt it. Except for the obvious problems with violated conservation laws, it behaved like a real event. I saw a particle producing a huge ionization and with more momentum than both beam particles put together. It made a jet of particles every few centimeters. It was like a machine gun that was spitting quarks.''

Several people had gathered around George as he talked. "But if it's real . . .'' said a graduate student.

"Even if it's real, folks,'' said George, "there isn't much we can do about it tonight. It must have been a rare event. It isn't likely to repeat soon, and unless it does it's an unpublishable fluke, a glitch in the apparatus due to causes unknown. We should examine it carefully and train the trigger net to watch for more. For now, I want everyone who noticed something unusual to write an entry about it in the logbook and sign their entry. We'll discuss this with the next shift at the 6 A.M. run meeting. Before that, we need everything that everyone observed written out in full detail.''

As the crew members dutifully wrote their entries, animated discussion erupted among the physicists. They batted about speculations and ideas on what they had seen, what it might mean, and how they might analyze the data from the event. Finally, however, the discussion deflated from lack of focus. As it tailed off, one by one the participants drifted back to their consoles and workstations.

Alice stood by George for a moment longer, smiled, then walked back to her lapstation. She began to type very rapidly.

It was going to be a long night, George thought, but he was glad she had been here for the excitement.

• 23

WHEN THE SUMMONER HAD ACTIVATED, TUNNEL MAKER HAD BEEN deep in transtemporal meditation. He hurried out of his personal enclosure, hurled himself down a deep inertial shaft, and accelerated through a maze of access conduits to the enclosure of the Bridge Generator.

A glance told him that there had been a massive discharge. The energy receptacles in the long row had been fully drained of their antimatter and stood cold and empty. He accessed the data stream from the nearest neural node. His sensorium translated along the time axis until he came to the discharge event.

A feeling of relief overlaid with deep satisfaction suffused his emotion center. The apparatus had performed flawlessly. A microscopic Bridge with the right characteristics had been snatched from the quantum vacuum, establishing a connection between his universe and a point of ultra-high-energy density in the target Bubble. The Bridge Generator had successfully brought the new Bridge to a stable energy balance.

He studied the data stream further. The Bridgehead had appeared in the new Bubble while traveling at a high velocity relative to the matter medium there. It had appeared in a vacuum, passed through a region of pure element 4 and several layers of element 14, then moved to a gaseous medium consisting mainly of element 10, with traces of elements 1 and 6. It had traveled some distance in that and various solid media, which analysis showed to consist of layers of elements 14, 26, 29, 82, and 92. A momentum flow through the Bridge consisting mainly of massive neutral dark matter particles, with a few quarks entrained, had been established and used to decelerate its Bubble end until it had come to rest. The Bridge had stopped in a medium made of elements 82, 14, and 8. The ambient temperature of the medium was between the freezing and boiling points of water. The data on the medium made of element 92 were particularly interesting. It was essentially pure isotope 238, with only faint traces of the other expected isotopes.

The message implicit in these data was very good news. The new

Bubble was an accessible matter universe. The combination of materials encountered was clearly a product of technology. Element 10 was an inert gas and was never found naturally in high concentrations.

There was also a puzzle. The isotopic composition of the element 92 medium through which the Bridgehead had passed was difficult to explain. Element 92 was the most massive and highly charged of the stable chemical elements, with good structural properties, and so it was a commonly used material. That much was to be expected. Because of its high nuclear charge and mass, it was excellent for slowing or stopping charged particles. But why did the medium consist of pure isotope 238, with only parts per hundred thousand of the other two stable isotopes? Isotope separation was technologically very difficult, particularly for so massive a nucleus, and there seemed little point in it.

Was it possible that the processes of nucleosynthesis in the new Bubble were sufficiently different as to suppress the natural occurrence of the other two stable isotopes of element 92? Tunnel Maker had no idea. The Individuals specializing in astrophysics and cosmology should be alerted immediately to these data. Perhaps when contact was established, they could learn the answer by asking.

• 24

ALICE HAD LEARNED THAT THE SSC CAFETERIA, ALONG WITH THE SSC visitors' center and science museum, was perched atop a small artificial hill made of dirt that had been excavated from the tunnels during the construction. On the flat Central Texas landscape it seemed to be the highest viewpoint for three hundred miles. Her gaze swept across the golden prairie and the blue and gold sky. They had arrived while the fading colors of a spectacular sunrise were still visible.

Alice felt exhilarated. Although she had been up all night, she didn't feel tired. She could not recall when she had felt more alive. "George," she said as they sat down at a window table for breakfast, "I still don't understand. If what we saw this morning was some unprecedented new physical phenomenon, why isn't that important news, a big scientific breakthrough?"

George shrugged as he cut a piece of ham. "Because we can't explain it, we can't reproduce it, and we can't eliminate the possibility that it was the result of faulty equipment. Therefore, we can't publish it. It will have to remain as a big one that got away."

"You said something like that at the run meeting," she said, "but you can't just ignore what happened."

He chewed thoughtfully for a while. "Let me recall a little piece of physics history for you, Alice," he said finally. "There is a might-be particle called a 'magnetic monopole' that was suggested by certain theories of Dirac and others but had never been observed. It's supposed to be a fundamental particle like an electron or a proton, except that instead of having an electric charge, it's supposed to have a 'magnetic' charge, like the north pole of a bar magnet that has been cut off and isolated, with the south pole completely gone."

From force of habit Alice took her notebook from her purse and began to take notes.

"In the early 1980s," said Professor George, slipping into lecture mode, "a physicist at Stanford named Blas Cabrera designed and built a very clever detector for finding magnetic monopoles using some tricks involving superconductors. And a few months after he turned on the apparatus, on Valentine's Day, February 14, 1982, nature sent Cabrera a special valentine. In the middle of the night the apparatus recorded the perfect signal of a magnetic monopole passing through the sensitive volume of the detector."

"That sounds like our Snark," said Alice.

"Actually, his situation was a bit better than ours," said George. "He had a fairly respectable theory that predicted the particle he had apparently detected, right down to the observed signal. And so, with considerable fanfare, he published a paper describing his monopole observation in a very prestigious journal. Cabrera's paper produced a kind of physics gold rush. Dozens of laboratories set up various types of monopole detectors. Cabrera himself received a big National Science Foundation grant and built a much bigger version of his original detector. And they all waited . . .

"That was over twenty years ago, and for all I know they're still waiting. Because neither Cabrera nor anyone else has yet detected another believable signal of a magnetic monopole. And if they did see another one today, they'd have trouble getting the result published, because the physics community now 'knows' that there are no magnetic monopoles. The current standard model of cosmology, the inflationary scenario, now explains why there are none."

Alice wrote rapidly. "But what *did* Cabrera see?" she asked finally.

"Nobody knows," said George, taking a sip of orange juice. "I guess he saw a Snark, just as we did last night."

"This is new to me," said Alice. "Does this happen all the time in science? Are there desk drawers full of unpublished data on spectacular measurements that only happened once and can't be reproduced? It sounds like a dirty little secret of the field." Maybe she should do a *Search* article about it, now that she had her foot in that magazine's door. But she had to finish her *Fire Ants* novel first. Nobody can make much of a living writing freelance articles for science magazines.

"Perhaps it is," said George. "When I was an undergraduate at MIT, I had a very good course on the philosophy of science. I did a paper on a famous essay by the French philosopher-scientist Poincaré. He was an excellent physicist, but he had the problem that he was also a devout Catholic. Poincaré was deeply concerned about the implicit conflict between divine miracles and the laws of physics. So he considered a hypothetical phenomenon that occurs, like a miracle, *just once* in the history of the universe. He argued convincingly that science has no way of dealing with a one-shot physical phenomenon. They have to be reproducible. Poincaré believed that scientists would tend to ignore one-shot events, might even pretend that they didn't exist."

"It would seem, George," said Alice, "that Poincaré's dilemma has been dumped in your lap. What are you going to do with it?" She smiled. She enjoyed listening to him talk and particularly enjoyed skewering him with his own logic.

He winced. "Dammit, Alice," he said, "the paper I wrote for that class challenged the professor on that point and argued against Poincaré's conclusion. The Big Bang seemed to me to be a good counterexample of a one-time event with great scientific significance. I guess that, basically, it goes against my grain to ignore data, particularly interesting data. But after what happened this morning and considering the alternatives, I must concede that perhaps Poincaré had a good point."

"You can't just drop it!" said Alice. Her investigative nature was offended by the thought that she might never know what they had seen.

George inhaled deeply and sighed. "Believe me, Alice," he said, "I won't drop it. After I get a few hours of sleep, I have lots of work to do on the Snark. I have to study its kinematics. I have to find out if we've previously recorded anything similar that we didn't notice. But as long as it's just one event, it's not going to be of much interest to my LEM colleagues."

"Well, *I'm* interested," she said and meant it.

• **25**

GEORGE LOOKED DOWN ON THE PALACE FROM ABOVE, CONSULTED an index that hung in midair before him, then pointed his pink wire-frame hand in a direction that led along a diagonal track that led deep into the Palace. He sped above the endless rows of statues, past pools and stairways and atria, until he arrived at the icon that he had re-served as a repository for anomalous events recorded by LEM, a goat-headed figure with a male human body.

Just before eight this morning, he had returned to his room at the SSC hostel, but after about four hours of sleep he had come wide awake with an irresistible compulsion to know more about the bizarre event that had occurred in the LEM detector. Lying in the narrow bed, he had used his briefcase workstation to connect to the SSC network directly from his room. Now he was about to have a closer look at the Snark.

Months before, George himself had set up this system for identi-fying anomalous events selectively. Jake and most of the other prin-cipals of LEM were not particularly interested in anomalies. They had a clear vision of the object they wanted to find. It was the Higgs vector boson, the theoretically predicted mediating particle that, in the early universe, had split the strong interaction off from the electroweak interaction. The Higgs had a theoretically predicted range of possible masses centered around 200 GeV and a definite signature in the LEM detector that was clear and unambiguous. The whole idea of LEM, and indeed of the SSC, was to discover the Higgs and collect the Nobel prize.

Therefore, most of George's LEM collaborators did not welcome any distractions from the unexpected. George, a maverick as usual, felt as a matter of principle that the whole point of experimental physics was to discover the unexpected, not to confirm the predictions of some theorist. Therefore, he had the anomaly territory all for himself.

"Output summary, please," he said to the goat-headed statue. A cube appeared in the air before him. Its sides contained multicolored lists summarizing the progress made, enumerating the events scanned and recorded, tabulating and plotting their characteristics.

George reached out and turned the cube, studying the list of events that had satisfied the trigger criteria of LEM but showed anomalous behavior when processed by the analysis programs and categorized by the LEM neural network.

He quickly found the Snark event from this morning. He gestured in the air, there was a *pop* sound, and he was in darkened space. He floated in darkness before an intricate self-luminous structure, a multicolored starburst pattern of gently curved arcs emanating from a central vertex point. He reached out and touched a green-hued line that radiated upward from the vertex. It dimmed to a dotted line, retaining its place but revealing behind it a more complex structure. A violet line speared outward from the vertex, punctuated at almost regular intervals with clusters of red-fingered jets, like a straight vine with red blossoms.

So many jets. George had never seen anything like it. His fingers made a gesture and a column of figures appeared to the left of the structure.

The very heavy ionization of the undeviated particle was noted, along with the unusual production of jets. Interesting events usually showed one to four jets, always coming from the vertex. But the summary list showed that this event had twenty-nine jets, none from the vertex! That, of course, was not possible. Even with 40 TeV in the center of mass and colliding particles with forty thousand times the proton rest mass in available energy, there simply wasn't enough energy to break loose twenty-nine quarks or gluons, to make twenty-nine jets.

George scanned the summary table more closely. There was also a problem with the momentum balance of the event. Usually jets, clusters of particles emitted in the same direction, are emitted nearly back-to-back because of momentum conservation. But these jets were systematically emitted in nearly the same direction that the massive particle was moving, almost as if they were being emitted to slow it down. In the process there was an apparent violation of the law of conservation of momentum, even if one left out the momentum of the heavy particle.

George shook his head in wonder as he orbited the structure, viewing it from above, from below. With another gesture he quadrupled its size. He pointed and flew to the starburst, then moved into it. Radiating lines seemed to pass through his wireframe body. George placed his eye at the vertex and sighted out along the long violet trajectory of the Snark. It showed no curvature at all in crossing the 2 Tesla toroidal magnetic field.

What if . . . ? With quick motions he bracketed the violet structure and its jets, shaping the boundaries of the surface around it with his hands until only the violet line and its attendant red blossoms were within. Then he gestured and the envelope was empty, the violet structure gone.

The column of figures reappeared. After correction for the energy and momentum removed by expected but unobserved neutrinos, the laws of conservation of energy and momentum had been reestablished. The violet line and its jets were the problem.

A double hit? George wondered. He gestured and the violet line reappeared. Once again he expanded the starburst. And again. And again. Then he propelled himself close to the vertex, the center from which all the lines radiated. Within the position resolution of the detector, the violet line came from the vertex. There was no hint of an offset that might indicate event pileup.

Finally George scanned the database for other similar events that might have been previously recorded but overlooked. There was not much there. A couple of events showed unusually large missing mass and momentum, probably from very energetic neutrinos. A few were obviously the result of electronic glitches in the detector. He deleted these, implicitly telling the neural net that similar ones should, in the future, be recognized as uninteresting.

This would require further thought, he decided. He gestured for hardcopy of the characteristics of the Snark, the output directed to the color laser printer in the hostel lobby, then gestured again and the starburst vanished.

He was standing before the goat-headed form. Under the event serial number engraved on the pedestal he added new text, writing with a white-hot finger. He carved SNARK → TALK TO JAKE! into the milk-white marble. Another gesture sent him into blackness. He was lying in bed in his room at the SSC hostel.

He removed the magic glasses and data cuffs and put them into the briefcase beside the bed, then walked through the dimness to the room window and raised the blackout blind installed for day sleepers like himself. He blinked into the early afternoon sunlight that now streamed through the window. Then he stretched, took off his pajamas, and went to the bathroom for a shower.

The warm water felt wonderful. He turned his body slowly under the stream, thinking. He would need to talk to someone about this Snark thing very soon. Alice was fine, it had been nice having breakfast with her and discussing the Snark. She was excited and acted almost proprietary about the thing, and she was going to come to his office this afternoon to discuss it further. And they had another dinner date for tomorrow night. But at the moment George needed to talk to someone who knew some physics. Preferably, more physics than himself, which narrowed the choices considerably. Who . . . ?

Then he remembered Roger Coulton, the new member of the SSC Theory Group who had just arrived from CERN. Roger had struck him as a person who had the flexibility and playfulness to be interested in a problem like this. The theory building wasn't far from the hostel. Yes, he'd look up Roger as soon as he dressed and grabbed a bite of lunch.

• 26

AN UNDULATING SURFACE OF MANY BLENDED COLORS WAS DISplayed in 3-D on the workstation screen, a fairy landscape of red-topped broad rolling hills and blue-violet shadowed valleys. Toward the right end of the slowly changing surface, however, it disintegrated into a jungle of wild fluctuations. Roger stared at the screen of his workstation and pounded his desk. The damned perturbation series had diverged again. Surely God must have it in for QCD!

The basic problem with quantum chromodynamics, the fundamental theory of quark behavior, was that the forces were simply too strong. All the mathematical tricks developed by generations of theoretical physicists, all the dodges and gimmicks and workarounds that had worked with weaker forces, were useless. The color force was the strongest in the universe, and it stoutly refused to be perturbed.

While he was still at CERN, Roger had invented a new approach, a convoluted expansion based on canonical variables that became smaller as the strength of the force increased. He had been so sure that it was the key to making reliable QCD predictions. But the lousy series wouldn't converge!

The calculation on the screen had been his final hope, one last straw to be grasped at. Several months of work were down the drain. It *should* have worked, dammit. He couldn't understand why it hadn't. He combed his fingers through his thick brown hair. The trouble with taking on difficult problems that no one previously has ever been able to solve, he thought, is that you feel like such a fool when you can't solve them, either.

Roger's father had been a baker in King's Lynn. It had been his custom to spend much of his free time and earnings at the corner pub near their terrace house. Roger had three older sisters, and it seemed that the family had never had enough money. At least, many an evening he had fallen asleep listening to his mother and father arguing about it.

Roger's grandmother, he learned later, had intervened to change his life. She had never approved of her daughter's marriage and had always kept her distance. However, she was fond of Roger, whom she said resembled her late husband. She had recognized his intelligence and arranged for him to take competitive examinations that had won him a generous scholarship to Harrow. When he was admitted, she had arranged to pay for his uniforms and the other costs out of her modest savings.

When Roger went up to Harrow, it had seemed a miraculous escape from a dreary and constricted life. For the first time he had classmates with interests somewhat like his own. Classmates who read books. Who, when they weren't yammering about sports, could talk intelligently about astronomy and rockets and chemistry and electronics and computers and particle physics, all in the course of an evening. Harrow had computers and an enormous and venerable library. For the first time in his life Roger found that he had more interesting books available to him than he could read.

Of course, there were the "initiations" and the bullying and the snobbery. Roger had been tall for his age, but painfully thin. It was well known at the school that he was one of the "dole" students, there on charity because his working-class family could not afford the standard tuition. And there was also his East Country accent, which marked him as different more clearly than a brand on the forehead. Several bullies among the older boys had turned some of their attention in his direction. At first he had accepted it as inevitable unpleasantness and had learned to avoid certain people and places and times.

But then one rainy evening Greg Rutlege, a senior boy who was on the school rugby team and who seemed to have it in for Roger, had caught him as he was leaving the rooms of his math tutor. Roger was carrying a beautiful book on projective geometry, just lent to him by his tutor. It contained vivid pictures, along with the equations for projecting any three-dimensional object onto the two-dimensional plane of a computer screen. Roger was hurrying back to his quad, his head full of ideas that he wanted to try, when he found Greg blocking his way on the dark path. Greg had shoved him several times and then knocked the book from his hand. It tumbled with a splash into a puddle.

Roger became very, very angry. Through a red haze of rage he saw that he was now holding a brick from the walkway in his hand. It was as if he was watching from a distance the actions of someone else, someone who was bent on homicide. That person fully intended to kill his adversary. However, due to a general lack of coordination, he managed only to place a three-centimeter split in Greg's scalp, just above the hairline.

It was sufficient. The quantity of blood was most impressive to both of them. So were the six stitches that were used to close the wound after Roger had helped Greg to the infirmary.

Roger had been quite surprised when the other boy had calmly explained to the school physician that his good friend Roger had been demonstrating a new wrestling hold when they slipped, so that he accidentally banged his head on the stone portal of the quad. The doctor was skeptical, but he finally entered the explanation in his report.

Later Roger carefully cleaned the book with a towel and sponge, put blotting paper between the wet pages, and even ironed them to remove some of the swelling and wrinkles. But despite his best efforts, the book looked terrible. His tutor, however, seemed not to take much notice when Roger sheepishly returned the book, perhaps because the man was so fascinated by the graphics program that Roger had made using the equations in it.

After that incident, the older boys had called him "Killer Coulton" for a while, but had kept their distance. The "Killer" nickname had stuck, but it took on a new meaning during his years at the public school. Roger became an academic aggressor.

The red-lit image of a brick raised high in the act of braining the enemy, within the convoluted pathways of Roger's cerebral cortex, had somehow been transmuted into a strategy for success. He sought out what were considered the hardest subjects, particularly in the sciences and math, then ferreted out the tricks and gimmicks that would allow him to understand them better than his classmates, to bludgeon his way to the top of the heap. He consistently outscored the others on examinations, sometimes by such a large margin that it was embarrassing.

The scholarship to Oxford had followed, almost as his due. It was not until he went up to Oxford that he finally managed to shed the "Killer" nickname. Oxford had been good for him in other ways, too. He had learned enough about physics and women there to know that he simply had to learn much more about both.

He set about doing so. He had somehow intuited, through the haze of academic self-satisfaction that overlay the British academic scene, that diversity was important and that the inbreeding he saw around him might be avoided by moving to another institution where the learning might be different enough to cover the gaps that he sensed in his present state of understanding of physics.

Lincoln Jeffries, his Oxford tutor, had been annoyed when Roger announced that he had decided to take his Ph.D. at Cambridge. Old Linc had carefully explained that such a switch was the sign of a misfit, and that it would seriously compromise Roger's chances of securing a permanent position at either institution. Linc's implicit assumption that the life of an Oxford don represented the pinnacle of

Western civilization had convinced Roger, as much as anything else, that he was making the correct decision.

Roger had put his Cambridge thesis supervisor, a Nobel laureate, on notice from the start that he intended to do a first-rate thesis in theoretical particle physics. And it had happened just that way. Roger had stumbled onto a subtle aspect of quark-gluon interactions that no one had ever looked at before in the right way. His omnivorous plundering of the literature had turned up enough seemingly unrelated clues to show him the direction he needed to proceed. He could actually have finished his thesis in two years, but some unfinished business with a certain young lady who was doing her thesis in medieval history had made him decide to stay the extra year and to do a more thorough job.

The thoroughness had paid off. His thesis research became two papers in *Physics Letters*, a long review article in *Physics Reports,* and three invited papers, special invitations to present his work before large audiences at physics conferences at Snowmass, Catania, and Les Houches. These had made something of a splash. Roger had turned down several job offers, including an assistant professorship at Princeton, to take a postdoc job in the CERN Particle Theory Group. And that, along with the other theoretical triumphs which followed, had led to his present job at the SSC, presently the premier high-energy physics laboratory in the world.

Which, the way it looked now, might be as high as his rocket would rise. Roger looked around his new office, the walls already decorated with colorful graphs, cartoons, and travel posters. What the hell was he going to do? This was Wednesday. He was supposed to give a particle theory seminar on Thursday afternoon describing progress on his brilliant new approach to QCD, the technique that in the past weeks had turned to ashes. He had nothing to discuss except a handful of mathematical tricks that hadn't worked. As he thought about it, he realized that in truth he hadn't really had a workable idea in many months.

He was *good*, dammit. He knew that he was good. He was now supposed to be at the peak of his creativity and intellectual power. He was working in theoretical particle physics, the toughest, most competitive, fastest-moving, most intellectually demanding field of endeavor in the history of the human race.

But somehow his timing was off. Of late the ideas that his instincts told him were good, after months of effort, had turned out to be blind alleys. Other ideas that he'd originated and then rejected as obviously flawed had been reinvented later by others, and often those ideas had brought them recognition and even fame.

This job in the SSC Particle Theory Group was supposed to be his stepping-stone to a secure tenured faculty position at a top-of-the-line university or institute in the United States or Europe. But his stepping-stone was rapidly sinking into a quicksand bog.

He looked again at the broken surfaces on his workstation screen. The bloody thing refused to converge. There had to be some way, another trick, if only he were smart enough to find it.

His eyes drifted to his open desk drawer. He could see the black plastic box there. In it he had placed disposable diabetic syringes and the four vials of synaptine. Last night he had on impulse taken them ... correction ... *stolen* them from Susan's laboratory. Even as he was doing it, he'd felt rather surprised at himself, as if it was someone else performing the act. Someone less honest than himself. He wasn't in the habit of stealing from his friends, after all. He was bloody well not in the habit of stealing from anyone.

But Susan had discovered a drug that promised to significantly raise the level of human intelligence! And she was planning to squander it for years to come on the treatment of hopelessly retarded children and Alzheimer's patients. She and her colleagues would administer the drug and take careful note of whether the poor souls that received it remembered not to pee their pants or drooled less or recognized one of their relatives unexpectedly. And meantime the rest of humanity, which was barely clever enough to find its shoes in the morning and keep from annihilating itself in the evening, must muddle along as best it could.

He now knew Susan well enough to understand that she was a very stubborn and dedicated woman. There was no way he could persuade her to let him test synaptine on himself as a ''volunteer.'' He'd hinted at this and had encountered a stone wall, receiving a canned lecture on medical ethics and the strictness and fairness of the rules concerning experimentation on human subjects.

He looked at the black box again. In most human endeavors high intelligence was useful but not really essential. Motivation and persistence worked almost as well, sometimes actually better. Roger remembered the friend at Cambridge who got rent-free rooms for serving as part-time manager of a block of flats. Once he'd had to pick a new maintenance person for the complex from a large number of applicants. So he'd given them all intelligence tests copped from the Psychology Department and selected the applicant with the lowest score. Claimed the person had made the best maintenance super ever.

But in theoretical physics, if you weren't the brightest chap in the quad, the cleverest, trickiest, sharpest, most imaginative bastard in the business, then you were the dog's breakfast. The difference was just a bit of extra intelligence, just enough to put you out in front of the pack. You knew it when you had it. And he'd had it, dammit. Before he'd left Geneva for Waxahachie, he'd had it.

But here, now, he was definitely the canine's morning repast. And perhaps he would remain canine cuisine. From now on . . .

Perhaps he'd simply set his sights too high. Only one person could be the brightest particle theorist of the generation. Perhaps, after all, it wasn't him. Perhaps he could go back to England and get a nice faculty job at some redbrick university with large teaching and administrative responsibilities and less pressure on research. He could become a gentleman lecturer who met with fawning undergraduates over coffee each afternoon to discuss the Nature of Structure. Roger grimaced, recalling a few of those.

Or perhaps he could get a well-paid programming job and move east to Wall Street or west to Silicon Valley, as some of his friends at Cambridge and CERN had done when they couldn't make it as particle theorists. He thought of the prospect of driving his Porsche for an hour on the San Jose Freeway or the Long Island Expressway to a job where he made clever improvements to programs that drew better pie charts for business leaders.

No, by God! He'd rather die than do that. He had to wield the brick again, he needed to pound on a first-rate new problem, beating on it with an avalanche of ideas until it yielded results that came so fast he hardly had time to write them down. He had to.

Roger got up and closed the door of his office. He pulled up his trouser leg past the knee. Then he took the black plastic box from the drawer and placed it on the desk. He knew well what needed to be done. One of his girlfriends at Cambridge had been a diabetic, and many times he'd watched her give herself an insulin injection as she explained how it was done.

Susan had given Elvis an intramuscular injection. The protein was stable enough, she said. The effect lasted longer if it was injected into muscle tissue rather than directly into the circulatory system. He stripped the wrapper from the hypodermic, fitted on the needle, selected one of the vials, and punctured its latex cap.

Then he paused. Susan had used half a milliliter on Elvis, he recalled. Should the dose be scaled by body weight or cortex area? That determines if I should use half a vial or the whole thing. Better play it safe and use cortex area, he thought, drawing half the contents of the vial into the syringe. Using his left hand, he wiped a patch on the inside of his left thigh with alcohol, then injected the protein. It was done. He withdrew the needle. A yellow droplet beaded its tip, a red droplet dotted his thigh. He wiped the spot with alcohol again and rolled down his trouser leg.

Roger breathed a sigh when his paraphernalia were safely placed in the black box and locked in the lower drawer of his desk. He sat, considered what he had done. He had injected himself with an untested experimental drug with completely unknown side effects. He could feel a slight tingling sensation spreading upward from his left thigh and minute twitchings of the muscles near the injection point.

Suppose he had an adverse reaction, perhaps convulsions requiring hospitalization. He could visualize them carrying him out of the building on a stretcher while his colleagues looked on. He could not tell them what he'd done. He'd been very stupid to inject himself with a drug that had only been tried on rats and monkeys. Perhaps he was feeling a bit ill. He extended his hand and studied it to see if it was shaking. It was, a bit.

There was a knock at his closed office door. Roger jumped, feeling he'd been caught in some unclean act. He glanced at his watch. It was 1:50. Who could it be? He stood, now feeling a bit shaky, and walked to the door. He opened it carefully, hoping that he looked more calm than he felt.

Roger was surprised to see George Griffin, the chap he'd met at CERN a few weeks ago. They'd had lunch at the CERN cafeteria and later gone to dinner at the Pizza d'Oro in Meyrin. They had ended the evening trading beers, jokes, philosophy, and personal histories.

George was an experimentalist with the LEM collaboration here. He was older, perhaps forty-five, and had held a string of research positions at CERN and Fermilab before he landed his present tenured faculty job at a big university somewhere on the north Pacific coast of the United States. Was it Oregon? Roger couldn't remember. "Hello, George," he said more cheerfully than he felt. "Good to see you again."

"Good afternoon, Roger," said George. "Welcome to Waxahachie. How do you like the New World?"

"I like it well enough, so far," said Roger. "How are you? We must do a bit of pub crawling soon, assuming we can find crawlable pubs in this arid landscape."

"My informants tell me," said George, "that in Texas pub crawling is called 'juking.' It has to do with moving from one juke joint to the next until you must stop because you either run out of quarters or can't make it back up on your horse." He grinned.

Roger laughed. He had difficulty in imagining George sharing the same roof with a functioning jukebox.

"But actually, Roger, I dropped by to ask you a theoretical question. Is this a good time?"

Roger glanced quickly at his desk drawer. Yes, it was indeed closed and locked. "Of course," he said and stood aside to offer George a chair. He glanced at his workstation screen. "Actually, I've just finished a project." As Roger sat at his own desk chair, he noticed that the tingling feeling had migrated from his thigh up to the base of his spine. He could feel the twitching of muscles in his buttocks. He looked across at George. "What's up?" he asked.

"I've only had about four hours' sleep since my night shift, but I need to talk to someone. I've been puzzling over a very peculiar collision event that the LEM detector recorded in the wee hours this morning," he said. "It cannot plausibly have been produced by the usual suspects, event pileup or equipment failure, yet it violates several of my favorite laws of physics. It seems to be legitimate."

Roger rubbed his chin. "So the laws of physics were overthrown overnight?" he said. "I hadn't heard, George. You must tell me about it." The twitching sensation was moving progressively up his spine. But now it felt rather pleasant, like a back rub.

George described the LEM event and showed Roger the colorful hardcopy details of the event's characteristics, graphs, histograms, tables.

Roger thumbed through the sheets of printout. It was very complex, and the format was unfamiliar. But somehow he was able to grasp the densely packed information on each page almost at a glance. As he did this, a remote corner of his consciousness was considering model after model that might explain the data and rejecting each in turn as inappropriate. It was quite enjoyable. Roger was beginning to feel very good as he warmed to the task.

There was a multitude of models to sort through. Three generations of particle theorists had made it their business to fill the physics literature with every possible twist on what at any given time was called "the standard model." Every conceivable variation that could be wedged into an unoccupied corner of "theory space" had been published and promoted by its progenitor. It had been a gold rush of ideas. The losing theorists had their papers published, perhaps had their ideas tested against reality by some hyperactive experimental group, and usually had their work listed a few times in the *Citation Index*. The winners, those with enough of "the right stuff" to hit upon a combination of theoretical ideas that happened to map, at least momentarily, into the actual structure of the physical universe, became famous, received Nobel prizes, were given endowed chairs in physics, and were asked to sign numerous petitions expressing outrage at or support for various social and political issues and causes.

But the forward march of particle physics had left in its wake a vast array of theoretical ideas and formalisms that were relegated to the limbo of untestable theories. These were neither confirmed nor falsified, neither accepted nor rejected because, at any given time, there was no feasible way to test them. It was these theories that Roger was somehow dredging up from his voracious reading of the physics literature, was comparing one at a time to George's event, and was tossing aside, one by one.

Finally Roger paused. "Perhaps your collision event only acted as the trigger for something else," he said quietly. "Perhaps it was a stimulated emission."

"Stimulated emission?" George said. "You mean like a laser?"

"Yes," said Roger. "In a way. To make a laser work, you have to create a population inversion, to kick most of the available atoms up into an excited state where they hang, all ready to emit a photon. Then, if a photon like the ones that the atoms are trying to make happens to pass by, it triggers some atom to emit and you get a second photon. And the two of them can trigger more, and so on.

"What I was thinking is that your event, assuming it isn't some detector fluke, may have triggered some otherwise exceedingly rare process that made the track with all the jets. Your collision didn't *make* your peculiar massive particle. It only triggered the process that created it, perhaps out of the vacuum itself.''

George frowned and was silent for a time. "Okay," he said at last, "but I don't see how that solves the problem of violating energy and momentum conservation. You're saying that the energy came from the vacuum?"

Roger shrugged. "If you didn't know the population inversion was there in a laser, the photons would seem to come from nowhere and you would think that energy conservation was being violated. Do you recall how Pauli deduced the existence of the neutrino?"

George shook his head.

"In the 1930s measurements of beta decay processes seemed to be indicating violations of energy conservation, momentum conservation, and spin conservation, all at once. So Pauli invented the neutrino, a neutral particle that carried off the missing energy, momentum, and spin, and at a stroke fixed all the conservation laws.

"Now, Pauli's neutrino was in the final state. Suppose there's something large, neutral, and energetic, perhaps dark matter, hanging there in an initial state. Your central collision, with its enormous energy density, triggers that system into emitting your particle."

"Really?" said George. "Is there any theoretical basis for such an object?"

Roger laughed. As he did so, he felt his neck and back muscles twitch again. "Surely you jest," he said. "I could reel off a dozen hypothetical particles that could be pressed into service. It's definitely strongly interacting. From the jets it's producing it must be producing color ionization, kicking loose quarks as it goes by the way a charged particle kicks loose electrons with its electric field.

"But some wild-eyed theoretical speculation is not what you need at the moment. You can't support a half-baked experiment with a half-baked theory. You need to find more events with the same signature. If you can show that it happens more than once, you might be able to attract a few believers. Perhaps even me." He looked sharply at George.

"You're not convinced?" said George.

Roger studied the brightly colored representation of the event. "It's beautiful data," he said, "and I'd love to believe it was the first inkling of some brand-new physical phenomenon. But my good sense tells me that it's far more likely to be some fluke or glitch in the equipment. You need more evidence, George.''

"I've already looked for similar events in our data. There are none. What if this stimulated emission process of yours is very rare? What if it only happens once in ten years? Or a hundred?''

"Then you're well and truly screwed,'' Roger said. "Unless . . .'' An interesting idea had suddenly popped into his head.

"Unless . . . ?'' said George.

"Unless your mystery particle is stable. Perhaps a quarter of the hypothetical particles that I could conjure up for you from the dregs and leftovers of theoretical physics are simply too weird to decay into normal particles, so they must hang around. They possess conserved quantum numbers that they can't easily get rid of.''

"Then,'' said George, "the damned thing could have stopped somewhere in the LEM detector and still be sitting there . . .''

"Or in the walls of the tunnel, or on the dome of the Ellis County Courthouse, or it could be well on its way out of the solar system,'' said Roger. He was beginning to develop a nasty headache. "Anyhow, do some kinematic reconstruction. Assume that your particle has a Planck mass. About a microgram, say. Assume it's losing energy like mad, perhaps in the color ionization that's producing all those jets. From that energy loss and your time of flight information you should be able to roughly estimate how far it's going to travel. Or perhaps check your detector for any odd instrumental behavior along the flight path of your mystery particle.''

Roger winced as his headache intensified. As he had been talking to George, he realized, several new approaches to his QCD perturbation problem had occurred to him. One of them was so radical and beautiful that it hurt him to think about it. But it was a pleasant pain. He stood up. "I'm afraid you'll have to excuse me now, George,'' he said. "I'm much in need of some aspirin for a roaring headache that just came on.

"And I have a load of work to do. I have to prepare for my particle theory seminar tomorrow afternoon. I've just given birth to a brand-new and very beautiful brick of an idea, which I'm going to use to bash out the brains of my colleagues.'' He was amused by the thought.

GEORGE BLINKED AND TURNED HIS HEAD TO THE RIGHT, HEARING AS he did so the motor whirr of the remote he had just linked into. He recognized his new location as the charging dock of the LEM counting house. He looked in the wall mirror, saw his own familiar features on the headscreen, and adjusted the height of the remote to one hundred eighty centimeters, matching his own. Across the room he could see Jake Wang, impeccably attired in a pearl-gray business suit. He was talking to and gesturing at Murray, clad as usual in yellow SSC coveralls.

"You have to get those new transputer chips for us, Murray," Jake said. "There's no alternative. The machine people are improving the luminosity, and as the data rate goes up, we're getting more and more dead time. It would be a great embarrassment if I had to ask them to turn down the luminosity to keep our electronics from hanging. We *must* have those faster transputer chips."

"Sure, Jake," said Murray. "Maybe I should call up the Secretary of the Navy and tell him that his jets don't need fast transputer VLSIs in their radar. Maybe . . ." He stopped talking and looked thoughtful. "You know, I do have a friend in the testing and quality control department at Inmos. We used to work together at Motorola. Last time I talked to him, he was complaining about how much trouble they were having with testing their new transputer chips for radiation damage. Their sources weren't hot enough or didn't have the right spectrum or something. Maybe we could, uh, volunteer to help him out with some of the testing. Any transputer chip that can survive in the middle of the LEM detector should have no problem at all in a nuclear war."

Jake paused and seemed to be absorbing the idea, then grinned. "Superb thinking, Murray," he said, clapping him on the back. "Do it! I'll check with you later." He turned to the remote. "Hello, George," he said. "You were on the owl shift last night, and I didn't expect to see you until tomorrow. You should be sleeping. Where are you?"

George wondered if Jake had heard about the Snark event yet. He put on what he hoped was a charming grin. "I'm upstairs in my office," he said. "I'll sleep later, Jake. I was giving Ms. Lang a demonstration of the use of remotes, and I found you here. Jake, I need to talk to you about an event we recorded early this morning. It's now our leading candidate for weird event of the year," he said.

Jake frowned. "Weird in what way?" he asked.

Apparently the news hadn't reached him, George thought. The students and postdocs were afraid of Jake and didn't talk to him if they could avoid it. "Well," he began, "in most ways it's a normal collision. The Fermi motions of both interacting quarks must have boosted the collision energy a bit, but otherwise it's very much like our other central collisions, except for one thing. There's an extra particle coming from the vertex. A most unusual extra particle."

"Unusual?" Jake said. George noticed that the brightness of his brown eyes seemed to intensify. He was interested. "Exactly what kind of unusual particle, George?"

George gestured with the remote's right arm and metal hand. "First, it's not a Higgs, Jake," he said quickly and watched as the brightness faded. "It's not any particle that you could hang a theorist's label on. It came straight out of the vertex, leaving a huge ionization trail but not a trace of any deflection in the magnetic field. It made a new jet every few millimeters, twenty-nine jets in all, and all of them pointing roughly forward in the momentum direction of the particle. But the inner time-of-flight system claims the thing was only moving at about 2 percent of the speed of light when it went by. It has to be massive as hell."

"Couldn't you get its mass from the missing energy?" Jake asked.

George shook his head, hearing the remote's motors whir as he did so. "No missing energy, Jake. The event conserves energy and momentum only when the extra particle is removed from the analysis."

Jake stared in George's direction for a moment, then broke into a peal of ironic laughter. "You mean . . ." he said, then stopped to laugh again. "You mean that you've not only discovered a new particle of great mass, George, but you've also discovered a violation of energy conservation! And momentum conservation, too, no doubt!" He lapsed into laughter again, stopped abruptly to frown at George, then turned on the Stare.

Then, quite abruptly, the Stare was transformed into a broad smile.

"We shall call a press conference immediately to announce your great discovery, George. We must give a name to this remarkable new particle of yours. I know! We'll name it after you! We'll announce to the assembled multitudes of reporters that you've discovered the"— he broke into laughter again—". . . the George-on! Or wait! Perhaps it's neutral. We could call it the George-ino!"

He turned the Stare on George again, his gaze seemingly focused some distance behind the remote's head. This lasted for what seemed a full minute.

George waited for what he had learned was the appropriate length of time, enduring the Stare as he patiently monitored the seconds on the telepresence chronometer floating at the upper right of his field of view. Finally he spoke. "You're the LEM spokesman, Jake," he said quietly. "You need to look at the data on this thing yourself. If you don't, you aren't doing your job."

Jake's frown deepened. "George, you're wasting my time," he said. "You're looking at a cosmic ray or a fission fragment or some glitch in the detector electronics and trying to make it into something important. Face it, George. If it doesn't conserve energy, it isn't physics."

"At least think about it, Jake," said George. "Let's not get too hung up on conventional wisdom. There is a possible mechanism. I have a theorist friend who suggested . . ."

"George . . . No! You're wasting my time," Jake said, his voice smooth but very deep and low.

"Okay, Jake," said George, "but I think it's important. I'm going to follow up on it, and I'm going to use LEM resources."

Jake uttered a deep sigh. "Just what do you want to do with this wonderful magic event you've discovered, George?"

"I'll use processor time to do a detailed scan of all the event tapes to see if there are any more like it that the anomaly system missed. And I want to retrain the neural net of the event-trigger to be more sensitive to anything similar in the next run. Jake, I have a feeling about this event. It's important."

Jake frowned. "You don't have enough to do already, George? You're in need of new projects? You don't have enough to do in discovering why our vertex detector is dying? The tens of millions of dollars invested in that vertex detector are going down the drain while you pursue fantasies. You need to retrain the trigger, too? That's a month's work, George. Every time we try to retrain that trigger net-work, it does ugly things to us. It's working now, George. Leave it alone!''

"Jake," said George, "I want you to look at this event. Please. It's important.''

"No!" Jake shouted. "Absolutely not. I have better things to do. You have better things to do. The whole damned experiment is col-lapsing around us, and you want to repeal conservation of energy. Get some sleep, George. Tomorrow this will all seem like a bad dream.''

Jake looked at his watch, then moved his hand in a dismissive manner. "I must go, George. I have to go talk to Roy again. Now those SDC imbeciles have done something to the sextupoles that is destroying our beam quality. We have the next group meeting on Monday morning, George. Be there, with your report on your progress toward understanding and fixing the pixel problem and without this event you found in the garbage can." He spun on his heel and stalked out of the room.

George angrily wheeled the remote, its motors howling, to the near-est charging dock and disconnected.

• 28

ALICE REMOVED THE MAGIC GLASSES THAT HAD BEEN PATCHED INTO George's, placed them in their holder, and looked across the office at him.

His face was red, and he seemed to be breathing deeply. "That was Jake at close range," George said finally.

Alice had been a passive participant in the confrontation. She was embarrassed at what she had just witnessed. She didn't understand why George had approached Jake as a remote when he had such an important matter to discuss, or why he had included her as an ob-server. During the past few days, she had interviewed a number of physicists from LEM and other groups at the SSC. She'd found a wide range of viewpoints on many topics. But about Jake there were only two common views: Jake was a great world-class physicist who would soon win a Nobel prize, or Jake was a madman who was leading his group to disaster. She nodded finally. "Is he always like that? How do you stand it?"

"You have to understand the culture of particle physics," George answered. "We're probing the most fundamental aspects of nature, and the intellectual appeal of that attracts some of the best minds in physics, as well as some of the strongest personalities. There are many differences of opinion about how the physics should be done, many violent disagreements. Over the years a method of resolving differences has evolved, a way of making a firm decision on what path to take, so we can put that decision behind us and move forward. It's called the 'shoot-out.' "

Alice laughed with delight. "Like the Old West. It sounds quite appropriate for Texas," she said. Had George deliberately provoked this shoot-out with Jake? Had he expected to win? He certainly hadn't gone about it in the right way, if he had wanted to win Jake over. Perhaps he had wanted to get Jake to take a position against investigating the Snark.

"We even do it in Geneva, California, and Illinois," George said. "It is a bit like the Old West, except that the shooting is done with ideas and logic instead of bullets. When there is a controversy, the laboratory director will call a big meeting. The groups in contention select spokesmen who present their best arguments in support of their case. The physicists in the audience ask questions, often very nasty ones. This can go on for many hours or even days. Finally the director, sometimes with the advice of an executive committee, makes the decision. After that decision is made, the question is considered settled, and work goes on."

Alice was puzzled. "I don't see what that has to do with Jake and what I just saw," she said.

"I was coming to that part," said George. "What you must understand about Jake is that he is the absolute master of the shoot-out. He's extremely intelligent. He can go into a library with absolutely no knowledge of a technical subject and emerge a few hours later with complete mastery of it. His presentations are flawless. After the first minute, he'll have an audience of tough-minded physicists eating out of his hand. His responses to hostile questions are lightning-fast and subtly calculated to make the questioner appear absurd, but without any appearance that Jake has ridiculed him. Most of Jake's adversaries in shoot-outs never know what hit them. Sometimes it's a few days later before you realize that the other guy in the shoot-out perhaps had a pretty good idea. And by then it's too late.''

"I don't understand," said Alice. "Why don't the others see through Jake's tricks?'' Had George provoked the confrontation in private to see what Jake's response would be?

"Because they are not tricks," said George. "Jake really does want to do the best physics in the world, and he'll sift through the best ideas available, borrowing or stealing where he can, originating where he must, to come up with the best course of action. He's really good, Alice. That's why I and the others put up with the personality quirks that come in the same package with his talents.''

Alice began to see the story possibilities in this revelation. "How did Jake get that way?" she asked.

George smiled. "I've known Jake a long time," he said. "We were at SLAC when the SLC was just coming into operation.''

"SLC?" said Alice.

"The SLAC Linear Collider," said George. "That was an American attempt to do some quick physics with Z and W bosons and skim off the cream before the LEP Collider at CERN started running in the late 1980s. That didn't work, but it did get Ph.D.s for me and Jake.

"Anyhow, we knew each other at SLAC. Jake grew up in Taiwan. His family was large and not particularly well off. As a kid he'd collect junk machines and electronics, take them apart, and use the pieces to make things. He liked to make weird electronic gadgets, radios and motion detectors and spark generators. He managed to slip into the United States somehow while he was still in high school and went to the University of Minnesota on scholarships while working at odd jobs in Minneapolis for extra support.

"To understand Jake, you have to realize that a certain style of argumentation involving very fast interchanges is considered a high art in Taiwan. It's a kind of verbal karate. Jake was probably the smartest kid in Taiwan when he was growing up, and he naturally learned how to outargue anyone he encountered.

"When he was doing his Ph.D. working at SLAC, it must have been a terrible culture shock for him. His haranguing tricks from Taiwan, his oratorical style, and his histrionics didn't work at SLAC. Everyone just thought he was a crazy Chinese guy and paid no attention to him. But Jake is not stupid. Over a period of time he watched the masters carefully and discovered the key to winning arguments at

SLAC, and he began to gain recognition and move up in the pecking order."

"And what was his trick?" asked Alice. "It sounds useful."

"The key to winning arguments at SLAC," said George, "is to always be right. And to be able to prove that you're right so conclusively that no one can prevail against you."

"Oh," she said, disappointed. That didn't sound like a useful trick at all. "But if he's always right, why do you argue with him?" she asked.

"Because," said George, "the only time Jake is consistently right is when he's making a public performance. The rest of the time he's often wrong. He learns to be right by soliciting arguments from people who, at the time, know more than he does."

"Then I don't understand what your argument with him was about," she said. "It wasn't a public performance, and he was wrong."

"With Jake," said George, "it's an iterative process, like breaking a horse. You always lose the first argument. But you have to introduce him to the idea and give him time to get used to it. He can't stop me from looking at the Snark, but I had to let him know about it and that I intend to investigate it, whether he likes it or not."

"Oh," said Alice, feeling confused. George lost, but he won?

"Jake isn't our problem," said George. "The Snark is. Roger Coulton suggested that the thing might still be around, and now I need to figure out where it might have ended up. Want to watch?"

"Sure," said Alice.

• 29

ALICE PUT ON THE MAGIC GLASSES AND SETTLED BACK IN THE RE-cliner. "I think this 'telepresence' business is all just a ruse to allow you to lie around on a soft couch all day while you're pretending to work," she said.

"You're not the first person to suggest that," said George's voice in her earphones.

She was getting the hang of adjusting the glasses. George had explained that she would have an independent "body" in the interface, but that her position would be servoed to his so they would move together.

As her eyes adapted to the lower light level, she saw that she was standing at the corner of a magnificent building, a Greek temple that appeared to be filled with amazing statues. She was reminded of the Loggia dei Lanzò on the Piazza della Signoria in Florence, but this building was huge. It stretched away as far as the eyes could see. Curiously, over the entry stairway were carved and gilded architectural letters that read LEM DATA ANALYSIS SYSTEM☐VIRTUAL DESKTOP— VERSION 2.1A, followed by a modified quotation from Dante.

George's voice spoke next to her. "Alice, can you hear me okay?"

"Sure," she said and turned to see that a wireframe figure with George's face stood next to her. "Where are we? What is this place?"

"Oh," George said, laughing. "I should have explained. This is our 'desktop,' our locational interface. Pietro, one of the programmers, had a dual college major in computer science and classical art history. One morning I connected to the system, and here it was in all its glory. He took statues from a giant classical sculpture database and used random combinations of statue elements filtered by an 'aesthetics' expert system developed by the Harvard Department of Fine Arts."

"It's beautiful."

"As it turns out," George continued, "associating computer files and operations with physical locations in the Palace does seem to make a good computer-human interface. The operations and locations feel very natural and stick in the memory. Pietro claims the interface is based on a classical scheme for memory improvement developed by the Greeks."

"Are there more of these locational interfaces?" asked Alice, wishing for her notepad. "I've never heard of them before."

"As far as I know," said George, "it's unique to the SSC. But it's become rather a local fad to see who can come up with the most bizarre locational interface. The SDC programmers designed one based on the works of Lewis Carroll, and I'm told there's a new one at the EA-4 experiment that's supposed to be derived from the H. P. Lovecraft mythos."

The view of the Palace began to change. They were moving through the vast building. The statues were passing faster now. So fast that she could not comprehend one before the next appeared. They passed gardens, open areas, belvederes, glittering fountains, and elaborate staircases leading up or down. Finally the view stopped before a goat-headed man. Alice noticed that the words SNARK → TALK TO JAKE! were carved in neat architectural letters into the white marble pedestal of the statue.

"Here we are," said George. "This is the icon for the event I need to measure."

Alice saw George's phantom hand, a representation of curving connected yellow polygons and lines, reach out and touch the pedestal. The words TALK TO JAKE vanished from the inscription. Then the hand moved to touch the foot of the statue . . .

. . . there was a *pop* sound and she floated in a black night illuminated by a spiked flower pattern constructed of many-colored curving lines.

"This is the Snark event," George said. "Its collision products passing through the LEM detector made this pattern."

"It's like a neon-tube sculpture I saw once," she said. As she watched, the phantom hands dimmed each colored line of the pattern until only one remained. It was a straight line that glowed with a violet color, and at random intervals along its length were blossoming bunches of shorter red lines.

"Here," said George, "is our Snark. It has a large electric charge and a very large mass. It came out of the vertex, but it took no energy or momentum from the collision." The phantom hand touched one of the bunches of red along the violet line. "See these? They're called jets, bunches of energetic particles that are made when a quark or a gluon is ejected by a collision."

"I've read about them," said Alice.

"They always come from the point of collision. *Never* are they found at random spots along a trajectory like this."

"What? Never?" Alice quoted.

"Well, hardly ever," George responded.

She imagined that he must be grinning.

"Roger Coulton suggested that they're from a process he called 'color ionization.' Somehow the Snark is losing energy by separating quarks and antiquarks along its path and making them into forward jets, just as a normal charged particle loses energy by separating electrons from atoms."

A frame of yellow lines, which Alice took to be an outline of the LEM detector, now surrounded them, and they swam in the space it enclosed. "What I'm trying to do," George said, "is estimate where in the detector the Snark stopped. Ah!" A region at the edge of the detector suddenly contained a sprinkling of colored line segments. The viewpoint shifted until Alice could see that one of the segments, a fat red line, was a direct extension of the violet line that still glowed near the center of the device. A dashed yellow line winked on, connecting the violet line to the red.

"That," said George, "means the Snark went through the inner slab of the depleted uranium absorber, made a big flash of light in this lead glass scintillator, but never made it to the outer muon detector. It stopped somewhere in here. A column of green numbers appeared momentarily above the place where the red track ended."

The field of view expanded and grew more detailed. Alice could see structures within structures within structures.

The hand gestured again, and a bar with a hexagonal cross section lit with a violet glow. "Jackpot!" said George. "The Snark hit this lead-glass scintillator unit, and the thing is still scintillating, half a day later. I think our Snark must be embedded in it." The hands made another gesture . . .

. . . and Alice found herself before the statue of the goat-headed man.

"Okay, I have the Snark's coordinates," George said. "Now we know where it's hiding. So we need to figure out how to get to it."

They moved off through the forest of statues at a dizzying speed.

• **30**

ROGER GLANCED AT HIS WATCH. HE HAD BEEN TALKING FOR ABOUT forty-five minutes now. The seminars of the SSC Particle Theory Group were supposed to last an hour, but that rule was frequently breached by long-winded speakers. At the rate he was going, however, he would finish easily with some time for questions. That was fine, because his headache was intensifying again. "So," he said, "last night I set up the problem on my workstation to do a preliminary evaluation of the perturbation series, using the formalism outlined on the previous transparencies. Here's what Mathematica gave me. It's a standard 3-D plot of generalized isospin against flavor, treating both as continuous variables for the purposes of the minimization, with mass as the altitude on the vertical axis.'' He placed the color transparency on the stage of the overhead projector. It was a brightly hued two-dimensional surface that showed the gentle rolling hills of the surface, punctuated here and there by deep depressions.

Roger ran the red spot of the laser pointer over the numbers near the depressions. "As you can see, the minimization gets the masses of each of the ground-state mesons to better than 1 percent. I think that can be improved, but it's fairly good as it stands. I haven't had time to investigate the baryons, but I see no reason why it should not do as well for them.'' He paused and massaged his temples. His forehead was pounding. The bright colors of the slide seemed to bring with them peculiar individual odors. He turned toward his seated colleagues. "Well, that's about all. This formulation is only one day old, but it shows, as they say, initial promise. In fact, I think it looks quite lovely! Thank you.'' He nodded to the group to indicate he was through and switched off the projector.

The applause from his theoretical colleagues, usually somewhat perfunctory and reserved at the end of an informal theory seminar like this one, was thunderous. Roger smiled. He knew that he had done well. They had understood the complicated ideas that he'd presented, and they were delighted with his new approach.

"Questions?'' he said quietly, and a dozen hands shot up. As he turned to point to a postdoc in the front row, he was surprised by a sharp peculiar odor. He stared in bewilderment at his audience. Each person seemed to have a bright coruscating aura around his head. Roger could feel the points of each aura like sharp individual pinpricks. Their faces were weirdly distorted, and they were attempting to speak to him in sibilant glottal languages that he could not comprehend.

The sharp smell intensified, and his ears filled with a high-pitched warbling susurrus that seemed to whisper hints of forbidden knowledge. A vast enveloping darkness closed in about him, and he could feel himself falling out of the world . . .

• PART V
June 11, 2004

January 15, 1990

*The only way to keep the cost of the SSC at $5.9 billion would
be to seriously reduce its capabilities . . . We considered whether
there are cuts that would allow substantial savings . . . restored
later. We found none.*
> —report of the Drell Panel on the SSC

*It's important that we not end up with a Cadillac but with a
Chevrolet . . . I'll help Congress get over the sticker shock, and
you'll have to make sure of a sturdy and reliable Chevy.*
> —Senator Phil Gramm (R.-Texas)

May 10, 1991

[The SSC costs are] on the road to a bottomless pit.
> —Congressman James Sensenbrenner (R.-Wisconsin)

February 7, 1992

*Exotic luxuries like the Space Station and the Super Collider
perhaps ought to be put off or canceled until we can shore up
our faltering economy.*
> —Senator Robert Byrd (D.-West Virginia)

May 1, 1992

We told [the other congressmen] that the DOE had blown the $5 billion budget cap [voted by the House in 1990], that we were not going to see the $1.7 billion in foreign contributions, and that they wanted to balance the budget. It's an easy case to make in fifteen or twenty seconds.
—staff aide to Congressman Sherwood Boehlert (R.-New York)

July 1, 1992

This place [the SSC] attracts scientific genius the way the Dream Team attracts autograph seekers.
—President George Bush

• 31

Tunnel Maker floated into the instrumentation enclosure and connected to a neural node. He felt anxious. It had been more than two rotations since the Bridge had been established and there was still no indication that the Bridgehead had been noticed. The instruments recorded that it remained at rest in the same medium of elements 82, 14, and 8 where it had been stopped. Occasional short-duration flashes of light were observed. These occurred at very regular intervals. They were perhaps part of a testing process but were definitely not a signal.

Tunnel Maker's apparatus continued to send light-coded messages through the Bridge. These used the time-tested codes that had been successful in other contacts. They had now been transmitted many times over the past three days, but with no response.

Tunnel Maker considered his options. He could continue on the present course. He could try other more energetic transmissions, bursts of positrons, muons, gamma rays, or antiprotons that might attract attention to the Bridgehead. Or he could notify the Concantation of Individuals that this attempt to establish contact with a microcsopic Bridge had failed and that the time had come to enlarge the Bridge to macroscopic size and perhaps send an Emissary through the Bridge aperture.

It was clear that he must allow more time before approaching the Concantation. And increasing the energy of the signals had its dangers for the inhabitants of the other Bubble, who might be damaged by the radiation. He would save it as a last resort. He decided that he must be patient. Experience with other contacts indicated that communication often required a dozen or so rotations.

Tunnel Maker resolved to wait for at least another dozen rotations before taking any further action. The waiting vigil was the most difficult part of contact.

• 32

GEORGE SAT IN THE THIRD ROW OF THE SSC'S LARGE LECTURE THE-
ater. The room was about one-fourth full. The speaker was a distinguished theorist, a Nobel laureate and holder of an endowed chair on
physics at an Ivy League university. He waved the laser-spot pointer
at the diagram projected on the tall screen at the front of the room.
He was discussing the Energy Desert and once again raising the possibility that particle physics, as practiced at the SSC, was about to
come to an end.

George had heard this argument before. The progress of particle
physics had been driven by a succession of ever more powerful accelerators beginning with E. O. Lawrence's original cyclotron and culminating with the SSC. The field had advanced in a series of carefully
orchestrated leaps, quantum jumps from each particle accelerator to
the next new and more powerful one. And like clockwork, again and
again new phenomena, completely unexpected discoveries, had appeared when each new accelerator began to produce its higher-energy
particle beams. One of the wisdoms of science is that to see what
none have seen before you must look where none have looked before.
That maxim was epitomized by the unbroken chain of remarkable
discoveries that had emerged from experimental particle physics from
the 1930s onward. But the chain could break.

The pessimistic argument that the speaker was presenting was that,
in his esteemed judgment, the chain of new discoveries was indeed
about to break, the series was about to terminate. With the wisdom
of hindsight, one could see that the great discoveries of particle physics had all been consequences of the fundamental underlying structures of matter, the quarks and leptons and the "carrier" particles that
mediated the fundamental forces. The set of these particles now
seemed almost complete. All the expected quarks and leptons had
been found, culminating with the discovery of the top quark at Fermilab in 1994–95. The Higgs particle, presently being sought in different ways by several experimental groups at the SSC, might be the
last piece in the cosmic puzzle. The next generation of particles might
lie vastly higher in energy, at the Planck scale, the mass scale set by

the smallest possible black holes, the domain where gravity and the three other forces of nature must unite into a single force.

If that was so, the SSC was the end of the line for accelerator-based particle physics. There was little point in building an even more powerful machine. From the SSC at the edge of the desert a vast energy wasteland stretched from the Higgs to the Planck scale, a great energy region where nothing of interest would happen, where no new particles would be discovered. Where the dance of theory with experiment to produce new knowledge was about to come to an end.

The QCD Standard Model worked too well, the speaker declared. There would be few surprises in the energy region that the SSC had opened to exploration. Experimental particle physics was reaching its logical conclusion. He advised the younger physicists in the audience to begin preparing for an alternative career.

George thought of the violet track with its twenty-nine clusters of jets, and he laughed. Others near him glanced curiously in his direction. He knew something that the speaker had come to doubt. The universe is indeed a far stranger place than is dreamed of in our philosophies.

George's cellphone made a chirp. It would have to be of some importance, he thought, because he had set the threshold at a fairly high urgency level. As unobtrusively as he could, he squeezed down the aisle past several sets of knees, shrugged at the speaker in apology, and walked up the aisle to the rear door.

When he was in a quiet place, he pressed the receiver button of the device. "George," said Wolfgang, "I wanted you to know that there was a cancellation in the superconducting metallurgy group's schedule. We have time on their X-ray fluorescence microprobe on Monday morning at 7 A.M. Is that okay with you? If it is, I will prepare an insert now, so it will be ready to go on Monday."

"Monday morning is fine," said George. "I could even have some results in time for the group meeting at 10 A.M. I'm scheduled to report on our progress then. I just hope this works, Wolfgang. If those speckles on the pixel chip aren't the problem, we'll have to go back to square zero."

"Just one step at a time," said Wolfgang, "as they used to tell us in the East German Army."

ALICE AND GEORGE RETURNED TO THEIR TABLE AT P. J.'S, REJOINING
Roger and Susan. Alice seemed happy and a bit out of breath. George
was glad that his initial performance as a dancer to country and western music had been at least adequate.

He had never been to P. J.'s before, although he'd heard about it from
the students. He was glad that their table was well away from the jukebox,
permitting some conversation. George looked at Roger. He was looking
pretty good, considering. "How're you doing, old friend?" he asked.

"Fine," Roger said. "It was a bit disconcerting to have a seizure,
particularly when I'd never had one before, but there seem to be no
lasting effects. I slept eight hours last night, woke up feeling fine, and
I've felt unusually relaxed all day."

"Yes, he's fine," said Susan, apparently speaking with some authority.

"So you think you know where your Snark-thing stopped?" Roger
asked. "That's exciting."

"Maybe," said George. "We tracked it to a particular lead-glass
scintillation counter. The slow-control archives show that about the
time of the Snark event, that unit started drawing excessive photomultiplier string current and has been doing so ever since. It could be
that the Snark is embedded in it and is making it scintillate continuously. It could also be that the Snark or something else caused the
unit to develop a light leak.

"In any case, the unit is drawing excess current and needs to be
replaced. I'll do that as soon as there's a shutdown. That will be when
the next maintenance cycle starts and the circulating beam in the ring
is dumped, maybe in a week. Then we'll see."

Roger nodded sagely and patted George on the shoulder. "Retain
your faith, my son," he said. "Everyone must believe in something.
In my own case, I believe that I'm ready for another Lone Star. Anyone else want one?"

Alice and Susan both nodded.

"Sure," said George. "Western dancing promotes a powerful
thirst."

Roger disappeared through the crowd in the direction of the bar.

*   *   *

"Well, look who's here," said a voice.

George turned to see Belinda walking toward them, accompanied by a man who looked familiar.

Belinda was wearing a flowery low-cut dress, her astrological jewelry setting off her cleavage. She smiled at George. "Hello, Dr. Griffin. I'd like you to meet my friend Whitey," she said. "How are you, Miss Lang? We spotted you folks over here and came by to say hello."

"George, Whitey is my next-door neighbor," Alice said.

George shook hands with Whitey and introduced Susan. "It's a small world. And I'm George, not 'Dr. Griffin,' " he said. He gestured to a pair of chairs at the table. "Why don't you two join us?" He recognized Whitey now. The man had a reputation as an electrician who was smarter than he looked and could deal with the tricky problems.

"Surely would like that," said Whitey, and they sat down. Conversation was becoming difficult as the music increased in volume. Finally Whitey turned and said, "Alice, I was wonderin' if you would do me the honor of a dance."

"Of course," said Alice. They walked toward the dance floor just as Roger was returning with four longneck bottles of Lone Star. George introduced him to Belinda and explained that Roger was a new arrival from CERN.

"How do you like Texas, Roger?" Belinda asked. Roger looked around the room. "I'm liking it more and more," he said. "It has its own unique flavor, and I seem to be acquiring the taste. You have good people here."

Belinda nodded. "Did you know," she asked, "that a lot of famous Americans originally came from Texas? Like George Washington?"

George saw that a tall Texas tale was coming and smiled.

"George Washington came from Texas?" asked Roger, looking skeptical. "Are you sure?"

"Oh yes," said Belinda, smiling. "The story goes that little George got a small hatchet for his eighth birthday, and he went outside the ranch house and cut down his father's favorite mesquite bush with it. When Father Washington came home from rounding up his herd, he noticed that his mesquite bush had been cut down, and he became very angry. 'Who in the Hea-yul cut down mah mesquite bush?' he demanded. George walked bravely up to his father and said, 'Father, I cannot tell a lie. I did it with my little hatchet.' Father Washington scowled down at his son for a long time. Finally he came to a decision. 'George,' he said, 'you go on in and pack up your saddlebags. Tell your ma we're movin' to Virginia. You're sure as Hea-yul never gonna make it in Texas!' "

Alice and Whitey returned to the table while the others were still laughing. "It's a wonderful coincidence that we met you here," she said to Belinda.

"It's particularly nice because Whitey's on the night shift this week and he was scheduled to work tonight," Belinda said. "He was supposed to be doing wiring at the lab all night, but one of the ring quadrupoles quenched. They had to rearrange the schedule and let him off, so we decided not to let a perfectly good Saturday night go to waste."

George looked up in surprise. "The ring is down?" His thoughts were shifting rapidly, formulating a plan.

"Sure is," said Whitey. "Hell of a mess. Gonna be down till they change out that quad. They sent all the operating crews home for the weekend."

George abruptly stood. "Then I'm very sorry, but Alice and I have work to do. We're off to hunt a Snark." He looked at Susan and Roger. "Sorry. I'd planned to do this next week, but if the ring is down now, we'd better take the opportunity."

"I completely understand," said Roger. "I hope you find something."

"Good huntin'," said Whitey.

• 34

ALICE FOLLOWED GEORGE OUT OF THE ELEVATOR TO THE LEM PIT
floor. She'd been rather annoyed by George's abrupt announcement
that they were leaving P. J.'s. But she also realized that she would
have asked to come along, if he'd consulted her.

It was cool in the pit. George had given her a white lab coat to
wear over her dress, for which she was grateful. A few lights supplied
illumination, but most had been turned off when the crew left, and
George had not turned them back on. She sniffed the now-familiar
smells of machine oil, electrical insulation, and cleaning solvents, and
the mustiness of the underground installation. Farther down the tunnel
she heard a click, and puffs of steam began to billow outward. Cryogenics, she thought.

George consulted a printout. "This way," he said. They rounded
the corner of the giant detector and stepped into a shadowy region.

It was spooky, Alice decided. This would make a good set for a
horror movie. In fact, it was just the place for an attack of giant mutant
fire ants.

"Here's where it is," said George, looking up. He walked to a
rack, typed something into a keyboard mounted there, and flipped
several switches. "Do you know how to operate a beam crane, Alice?"

"Sorry," she said, shaking her head, "they didn't have many of
those in the newsroom."

George smiled and shrugged. "Okay," he said, "you can watch
and call for help when the experiment falls on me." He walked to
the wall and removed a control box on the end of a long wire. He
pressed a button. The relative silence of the pit was broken by the jolt
and hum of electrical machinery going into operation. A long horizontal steel beam rolled out from the wall along parallel rails until it
was directly overhead. He touched another control and a squarish assembly at one end of the beam rolled in their direction, a hook dan-
gling below it by several cables.

George wheeled a tall stepladder over to the detector, climbed it
with the control box under his arm, removed a cover plate, and very

slowly, with occasional adjustments of the crane, slid a long tray out of the detector, so that its outer end was supported by the crane hook. Alice could see that the tray contained a row of long slabs encased in black plastic, stacked like fallen dominoes or shingles on a narrow roof. The "shingles" were studded at their upper ends with silver plates trailing bundles of electrical wires.

Carefully, George removed the electrical connectors from one of the units and slid it out of the array. He slowly descended the ladder holding the unit in the crook of his elbow and placed it carefully on a workbench. Then he opened a cabinet and removed an identical unit. "We have spares," he said, "and that one needed to be replaced anyway." He climbed the ladder, slid the new unit into its place in the array, connected the wires, slid the tray back into the detector, and replaced the cover plate. He descended, restored the switches to their original positions, and typed commands into the keyboard and studied the screen. "Everything is back to normal," he said, picking up the unit he had removed, "and the other scintillators are much happier with this one gone."

George walked to a tall blue cabinet that stood back against the gray concrete wall and removed a small instrument. "This," George said, holding up the instrument, "is a radiation survey meter for checking radioactivity." He placed the round end of the survey meter against the unit in his hand. The instrument chirped every few seconds, and a digital readout on its face read 0.1MR/H. Then he slid the device along the length of the unit. As he neared the far end, the chirp rate increased sharply, and the readout changed to 1.3MR/H. "I'll be damned!" he said. "It does seem to be a bit radioactive."

"Isn't that what you expected?" Alice asked. "Isn't that what this was all about?"

George turned, smiling. "Sure, but it was only a wild idea," he said. "I didn't really expect to find anything. Chances were, this thing had only developed a light leak. There's almost never any measurable radioactivity from events in the detector after the beam goes off. But the Snark made jets all along its path from ejected quarks and gluons. If it could do that, it might disrupt normal nuclei and make them radioactive, so I thought it was worth checking the level of radioactivity."

He walked to the cabinet, replaced the meter, and closed the door. He took a small knife from his pocket and cut at the black tape on the outside of the unit. It peeled back, to reveal a transparent crystal interior.

In the dimness of the area Alice could see that a blue glow illuminated the crystal inside, and that the glow was centered at the tiny blue point near the end of the bar. "Is that the Snark?" she asked, feeling a rising excitement.

"It must be," said George. "It has to be! We did it, Alice. We've captured our Snark!" He placed the glowing scintillator bar on the workbench, slowly gathered Alice to him, and kissed her. She was surprised but responded with some enthusiasm, and they stood together for a long time.

Finally they walked to the elevator. George held the glowing barlike object in one hand and Alice's hand in the other.

• 35

DEREK INCHED ALONG THE CATWALK, PULLING THE STIFF CRYOGENIC hose after him. Below Patricia moaned softly as she retreated to a corner, where she was hemmed in by the tall racks of electronic equipment. The train of giant fire ants, their clattering venom-wet mandibles extended, clamored toward her.

She lifted a heavy piece of equipment from a table and hurled it at the giant insect at the head of the line. It caught the object in its jaws, then flung it aside with a twist of its giant head. It paused, as if studying her with its jet black compound eyes, then brushed its mandibles with its forelegs.

"Patricia," Derek called from above, "turn your back on them and cover your face with your arms. I'm going to try something." She looked up at him, then turned as he had directed. She was sobbing softly to herself, waiting for the mandibles to dig into her back, waiting for death.

Derek twisted the valve at the end of the long corrugated hose. A jet of clear, steaming liquid nitrogen leaped forward and cascaded downward, producing great plumes of vapor as it fell. Derek played the stream directly on the head of the first fire ant. The insect stopped in midstride. He could hear a cracking, popping sound as the insect froze solid. It did not fall over, but stood rigidly frozen in a six-legged midstride.

"It's working," he called down to Patricia. She seemed to be shivering, perhaps from the rapid drop in temperature. He pulled the hose backward now and directed the stream at the other ants in the column. Through the heavy work gloves he wore the back-splatter of the liquid nitrogen was slowly freezing his fingers . . .

Alice stopped typing, yawned, and decided to save the file and go back to bed. An hour ago she had come wide awake and had decided to work on her novel for a while. She shut down the lapstation, turned off the dining room light, opened the door, and padded barefoot back into the darkened bedroom. She dropped her robe on the floor and crawled slowly back into her big bed. She stretched and pulled the sheet over her nakedness. She felt wonderful.

She could hear George's soft breathing beside her. She looked at him, sleeping peacefully with a contented smile on his face, and she thought about recent events. He was wonderful. She thought perhaps she was in love with him. It had all been very exciting. It had been romantic, too. His delight at finding the Snark had turned to passion. It was fun while it lasted. But realistically, it couldn't last much longer.

She had to earn her living by finishing *Fire Ants*. A great deal of money was at stake. Their lovemaking had inspired her to write a great new scene. But when George found out why she was really studying life at the SSC so closely, the chances were he would want to have nothing more to do with her. She had come here to Waxahachie under false pretenses, and that fact was likely to sour their blossoming relationship. Nevertheless, she had to tell him. Soon. She sighed and snuggled against him. But not yet.

Out of the corner of her eye, she saw a flash of light from across the room. She rolled over, facing the dresser. George had placed the scintillator bar on the dresser, its open end toward the wall. In the mirror she could see its blue glow. It was flashing. But just as she focused her attention on it, the flashes stopped and there was only the faint and continuous blue glow. She waited, drowsy now. Perhaps she had dreamed the flashes.

Then, as she was almost dozing off, they came again. Flash-Flash. Flash-Flash-Flash. Flash-Flash-Flash-Flash-Flash. Flash-Flash-

Flash-Flash-Flash-Flash-Flash. Flash-Flash-Flash-Flash-Flash-Flash-Flash-Flash-Flash-Flash-Flash . . . This went on for a while and then stopped again.

She waited, wide awake now. In a few minutes the flashing began again. This time she counted flashes. 2–3–5–7–11–13–17–19–23–29–31–37. Then it stopped. Twelve numbers. Something was familiar about their sequence. When she had worked as a reporter for the *Democrat*, Alice had interviewed some Florida State University astronomers about their research. They had been using the Arecibo radio telescope in Puerto Rico to search for extraterrestrial intelligence, SETI they had called it. They were searching for radio signals that might have been sent by some hypothetical alien race that lived in another star system.

After the usual jokes about picking up alien game shows on TV and whether that could be construed as intelligence, Alice had asked about strategies for making the initial contact. How could they be sure that a message they received was not random noise or some natural phenomenon? Or, to put it the other way, how would they send a simple radio signal that was clearly a product of an intelligent species? One answer had been to send a sequence of prime numbers, numbers that had no integer divisors. She was sure that the first few primes were 2–3–5–7–11–13. The Snark, Alice decided, was trying to send a message. The Snark wasn't an exotic particle. It was . . . something else . . . something much more important than that.

She shook George awake.

• 36

ALICE GLANCED AT THE WALL CLOCK AS ROGER COULTON ARRIVED at George's LEM office. It was just after nine o'clock on Sunday morning. Roger looked a bit hungover as he stood in the doorway, unfocused and rather disheveled. He absentmindedly rubbed a spot on the inside of his thigh.

"Good morning, Roger," said Alice. "Sorry we had to abandon you at P. J.'s. I presume George told you about our successful Snark hunt last night." She didn't want to advertise the fact that she had been in bed next to him when George had made the call.

"He certainly did," Roger said. "Hours ago." He yawned. "So you two have actually managed to isolate George's mystery particle, which is now embedded in a scintillation counter. And you've discovered that it gives off a blue glow."

Alice pointed to the unit on George's desk. The scintillation cylinder now had a light-tight metal cap mounted on its narrow end. "A blue glow that flashes," she said.

"A single wavelength blue glow that flashes," George added. "I decided we might get a clue from the optical spectrum of the glow, so this morning we looked at the light with a small grating spectrograph. That turned out to be interesting. The thing has only one spectral line: bright blue, with a wavelength of 439.7 nanometers, if I did the calibration right."

"What atomic transition makes such a line?" asked Roger.

"I don't know," said George. "I tried looking it up on the Web in an atomic physics database, but there was no match."

"Curious," said Roger.

"It gets even more curious," said George.

"Curiouser and curiouser," Alice added.

George frowned at her, then smiled. "To come to the point, Roger, the thing flashes. And this morning we discovered that even when the blue light seems to be continuous, it has a time structure. It's sending binary code at about ten kilohertz," he said.

"What?" Roger turned, studying the two of them. "Is this a joke?"

"Perhaps it is," said George, "but I assure you that it isn't *my* joke. Alice first noticed that the flashes came in groups with the sequence 2–3–5–7–11–13–17–19–23–29–31–37, the first 12 prime numbers. And the binary stream gives the first 144 prime numbers in binary code."

Alice suddenly had a terrible thought. What if *all* of this was a joke, a joke on her? Perhaps they had found out that she was here under false pretenses and decided to teach her a lesson by preparing an elaborate hoax to make the woman science reporter look foolish. It wouldn't even have to be all that elaborate, a simple battery-powered microprocessor concealed in the scintillator thing to make the blue light flashes under the control of a program. George and Roger could both be in on it, and maybe others, too. Perhaps even the Snark event had been staged for her benefit.

She thought more about this possibility, then began to relax. They'd have to be awfully good actors, she decided. And how could anyone know that she would notice the flashes last night? No, it's probably not a hoax, she decided. In any case, she had no choice but to go along with the thing for the moment, play her assigned role, and watch carefully.

Alice looked closely at Roger, who had been silent for a while. He now looked much more alert, she thought. Apparently he had recovered from his hangover.

"Can I have a look at the time structure?" he asked finally.

"Thought you'd never ask," said George. He showed Roger a sheet containing several parallel traces of rectangular peaks and valleys. "I synched this plot at what I think is the starting point. The ones and zeros below the trace are a rendering in binary and hex. That's the preamble. After the primes, it goes into another mode that we haven't been able to penetrate.

"The overall pattern is that it makes the flashes, then the binary primes, then followed by the other stuff. That sequence repeats about every five minutes. The stuff that comes after the binary primes is different each time, though it may repeat, too, after a while."

Roger smiled. "It's very likely that the 12 and 144 carry the implication of a base-12 number system. But . . . what the hell could this Snark thing be?"

George turned to Alice. "You discovered the flashes, and you've had as much time to think about this as I have. What's your guess as to what the Snark is?"

Alice was caught by surprise by the question. "Calling on the students, Professor George? I detect your academic tendencies surfacing," she said. She opened her notebook and flipped pages. "But, okay, if you want class participation, here's my list of what we know about the Snark. It came out of an energetic particle collision. It seemed to bring along its own energy. Its ionization track shows that it has a big electric charge, and its lack of magnetic deflection indicates that it's very heavy. It spits quarks as it goes along, which has something to do with color. At rest it emits blue light at a single frequency. It flashes and it sends a series of prime numbers and a lot of additional code. Did I miss anything?"

"You're doing fine," said George. "I might add that the Snark is much more massive than any known particle, but nevertheless it seems to be stable. Continue.''

"From the flashes I must assume we're dealing with a signal," said Alice. "I once did a story on SETI. The claim of the experts I interviewed was that the sequence of primes indicates a message generated by intelligence rather than some product of a natural phenomenon. Okay?''

George shrugged. "We'll accept that as at least a working hypothesis," he said. "Keep going.''

"Okay," said Alice. "The first possibility, it seems to me, is that the Snark might be a tiny mechanism for playing back a prerecorded message.''

"Wait a moment," said Roger. "Do we know how large this thing is?''

"Small," George said. "We tried looking at it this morning with a good optical system, but all that could be seen was a diffraction-limited blue spot. It's certainly smaller than the dust grains the system was resolving.''

"We know it induced those quark jets," said Roger. "That suggests to me that its size is probably subnuclear. So it can't be a playback device," he concluded.

Alice frowned. "How do you know that, Roger?" she asked.

"Any message must be stored in the form of structure," he said. "And a structure must be an arrangement of components. What, then, are the components? Atoms? Much too big. Nuclei? Neutrons and protons? Or perhaps quarks or leptons? What forces could possibly fix them in such a structured arrangement? Or read them out and produce a playback? There are no forces that could do that. Conclusion: There is no such structure.''

"For an open-minded theorist, I fear you may be verging on the dogmatic, Roger," said George. "We're dealing with a new phenomenon here, and we can't absolutely rule out previously unknown forces. But I agree with the sense of your conclusion. It seems unlikely that the Snark could be a self-contained playback device.''

"And I suppose," said Alice, "that the same argument also applies to my second alternative, which is that the Snark is a self-contained intelligence that's trying to communicate with us.''

"Indeed," Roger said. "That would require even more structure.''

"Any other possibilities on your list?" George asked.

"Just one," said Alice. "The Snark might be a link to an intelligence located elsewhere. It might be the equivalent of a tiny radio receiver."

"That requires structure, too," said George, "but not as much. An optical fiber is considerably less complicated than a compact disc player. Or the musicians who made the music recorded on the CD."

"But," said Roger, "isn't your Snark a bit, uh, short for an optical fiber link?"

George spread his hands. "Who can say? At any rate, I agree that a communications link hypothesis is more probable than your other alternatives, Alice. But is it for one-way communication or for two-way communication?"

Roger scowled. "Surely," he said, "two-way communication is not a serious possibility. If the Snark was a link to an extraterrestrial intelligence, which I, for one, am not yet willing to concede, such an intelligence would have to be very far away. Hundreds of light-years, perhaps thousands or millions. Even if you did send a message that they were able to receive, you, and perhaps our whole civilization, would have died before the reply message came back. Remember your relativity, people. You can't beat the speed of light!"

George looked directly at the theorist and grinned. "Roger, that's all very logical, but I have a hunch you're wrong. We have, as they say, a significant difference of opinion. So I'm willing to wager, say, five hundred dollars that two-way communication is possible using the Snark. You may accept my wager at whatever odds you consider to be fair and equitable. Interested?"

Roger looked flustered. "Uh, five hundred dollars? Let me, uh, think about that for a while, George," he said. "Your intuitions have a certain reputation around here."

"Two-way communication?" said Alice softly. "I hadn't thought of that. How would you do it?"

"Well," said George, "our Snark, by dumb luck, is already mounted in an almost ideal system. That lead-glass crystal is optically coupled to a photomultiplier light detector for receiving signals, and it has an onboard light-emitting diode system that makes light flashes in the scintillator for testing. We can use the LED system to transmit light pulses back to the Snark."

"If you were going to send the Snark a message, Roger, what would you send?" Alice asked.

"Hmmm," said Roger. "The conventional wisdom is that you should send back the same message you received. In this case, though, that might not be such a good idea. It could be interpreted as just a reflection. I'd say, send back a string of primes, perhaps at a different transmission rate, and don't stop at prime number 144.

"But I think we must wait a bit before trying to communicate back. There are profound implications of that which need to be considered. I think there are even protocols established by the United Nations for communicating with alien species that should be observed."

George turned to the theorist with a look of mock disappointment. "Do I take it then, Roger, old sport, that you don't want to bet against me?"

• 37

GEORGE YAWNED AND LOOKED AT HIS WRISTWATCH. IT SAID JUNE 14, 2004, 06:55 A.M. After the excitement of the weekend, he was glad that he had remembered the appointment to use the microprobe.

The SSC's superconducting metallurgy research laboratory was on the west campus, just across from the administration building. Wolfgang had arrived early and was already securing his prepared sample of two chips on the polished metal surface of the scanning microprobe stage when George arrived. They had received a brief lesson in how to use the device the previous Friday, and Wolfgang now had the system almost ready to go.

"Which chips are we testing first?" George asked. He considered the importance of this measurement. It could provide the key to their radiation damage problems, or it could be another blind alley. In either case, at 10 A.M. he would have to make a report on their progress. He hoped there would be something to report.

"One is from the new batch that just arrived from the chip foundry," said Wolfgang, "and the other is one of our problem children. I thought we might learn something from a comparison." George placed a loop of soft ductile indium wire on the lower vacuum flange and Wolfgang lowered the counterweighted upper part of the apparatus down to meet it. Together they began to clamp down on the flanges, compressing the indium to form a metal-to-metal vacuum seal.

"Is the bad one the same chip we looked at with the STM?" George asked as he worked.

"Unfortunately, no," said Wolfgang. "The STM probe did some surface damage to that one, and I thought it would be better to start fresh. However, this chip was mounted near the other in the pixel detector and shows exactly the same symptoms." He moused START PUMPDOWN on the microprobe control computer's screen. The roughing pump below the apparatus made a chugging sound as it removed air from the microprobe's inner chamber.

As they waited for the vacuum to improve, George, still feeling the excitement of the weekend's developments, began to tell Wolfgang about his recent Snark hunt. Wolfgang seemed interested at first and asked about the tracking and kinematics of the peculiar object. But when George began to describe the repetitive flashes and prime number sequences, Wolfgang's attitude changed. He looked uncomfortable, as if George were describing something private and personal that he did not wish to hear about. Too bad, George thought, considering Wolfgang's reaction. He had been hoping to recruit him to help with their Snark investigations.

Wolfgang got up, tapped the mechanical vacuum gauge unnecessarily, moused around the computer screen, and announced that the vacuum was now down below the top operating limit and the microprobe was ready. George nodded and Wolfgang started the imaging sequence. The scanning microprobe produced a beam of electrons that were scanned in a tiny raster pattern across the sample. The viewing screen of the device was scanned with the same raster and modulated in brightness by a current of scattered electrons received on one side of the device. The result was a startlingly realistic and sharply focused microscopic image of the scanned area.

The sharp image quality of the microprobe, however, was not the reason George and Wolfgang were using it. The scanned electron beam which the device used was unusually energetic, and when it struck individual atoms, it sometimes knocked out their inner-shell electrons, causing them to produce X rays with an energy characteristic of the producing atom. These X rays were detected by the device, and their energies used to color the microprobe image that appeared on the screen.

"Let's find one of the destroyed FET gates on the bad chip," said George.

Wolfgang moused a slide bar on the control screen, and the picture blurred, then stabilized. There was less magnification than the STM had provided, but the gate region was visible. Wolfgang found a gate where the characteristic hourglass shape had been distorted into two separated pink clumps. Around the ruined gate were clusters of green speckles.

"Green," said George. "What does that mean?"

Wolfgang used the mouse to make a box around one of the larger speckles, then clicked on a control. A new window appeared. It showed the black points of the measured X-ray spectrum, a smooth variation ending in a series of spikes, overlaid in green with the matching reference spectrum that the computer had fitted to it. The graph label in the lower right of the window showed the green line of the fit with the symbol *Cd.*

" 'Cd,' that's cadmium," said George. "What the hell would cadmium be doing on that chip?"

Wolfgang scanned other regions of the chip and found similar green speckles. He set a cut so the microprobe responded only to the cadmium X rays and backed off the magnification. A pattern became clear. Near the end of the chip where the tiny gold connection wires were attached there were concentrations of the material. He panned over to the new chip. No such areas were present. "It must have come from the manufacturing process used in that particular batch," Wolfgang said.

"I doubt it," said George. "Remember the tests we did on unused chips? I think this cadmium contamination must have something to do with the way they were mounted in the pixel detector's holder. Let me try a long shot."

He pulled his cellphone from his pocket and dialed. "Hi, Murray," he said, "George Griffin. I'm glad you're in already."

"Hi, George," Murray's voice answered in the earpiece. "Yeah, I had to come in early today to get something ready before a contractor crew arrives. What's up?"

"Murray," George said. "What do you know about how the chip connections were made on the pixel detector? Were we using any new techniques or materials? I'm particularly interested in soldering or spot welding."

"Hmm," Murray said and paused. "Yeah, I remember. We had some problems with cracked solder joints due to the flexing of the thin beryllium frame, so we went to a new more ductile solder alloy. I think it came from Japan or somewhere. Sony had been using it in some of their LCD processes."

"Do you have a spec sheet on it?" George asked.

"Yeah, lemme see here . . ." George could hear the sound of typing as Murray interrogated the LEM materials specification database. "Aha! Here it is. What did you want to know?"

"Is there a breakdown of the metals used in the alloy?" George asked.

"Um, yeah. It doesn't give percentages, that must be proprietary info, but it says that in descending order of concentration it contains tin, lead, silver, cadmium, and indium."

"Bingo! Thanks, Murray. I think you've just solved our pixel detector problem." George felt a great wave of relief. The problem that had been plaguing him for months was probably solved.

He hung up and turned to Wolfgang. "There's cadmium in the solder they were using for mounting chips," he said.

"*Ja*," said Wolfgang, "so . . . ?"

"Cadmium has a low vaporization temperature. It gets spread around easily, and can migrate on a substrate in the presence of electric fields. And it selectively absorbs neutrons and makes betas and gamma rays. It's used as a neutron-eater to control nuclear reactors. That's harmless in a normal environment, but near the SSC beam there are great floods of neutrons traveling along the beam line. That's what's killing our detectors. We've been poisoning them with cadmium-based solder."

"*Ja*," said Wolfgang, "and ATLAS wasn't using such solder, so it had not the problems. I see. *Sehr gut*, George. We must test this theory, of course."

"Of course," said George, "but at least I have some progress to report at the group meeting this morning. I'll need some hardcopies of those images showing the cadmium spots."

Wolfgang set about capturing the microprobe images they had produced as image files.

George's cellphone beeped. He excused himself, walked across the room, and pressed the RECEIVE button. Must be Murray calling back, he thought.

"Hello, George." It was Roger. "I've been working all night on our little problem. I understand the message!"

"You do?" George said. "That was fast. Tell me all about it." Roger sounded very alert for someone who had been up all night.

"The 12 primes and 144 primes were the key," Roger said rapidly. "The following bit-stream is a set of pictures. The resolution matrix is 1728 by 1728. That's 12 to the third power, 12 times 144."

"Excellent," said George. "And what are the pictures?" He was feeling a rising excitement. This was starting out to be a very good day.

"There are twelve pictures in all," Roger said. "I don't understand all of it yet, but I've made some progress. It seems to be a tutorial in elementary science, very graphic and with a minimum of symbols. You know the bit. The periodic table, the structure of matter, and so forth."

"That doesn't sound very informative," said George, feeling a slight disappointment. Roger seemed to be building up slowly to . . . what?

"Just wait," said Roger. "Then it gets into general relativity and cosmology. And then it comes to the punchline. George, the Snark isn't a particle. It's the mouth of a wormhole!"

"A wormhole?" George exclaimed. "Do you mean an Einstein-Rosen bridge?" He paused, struggling to recall the concept. "That can't be right, Roger. When I studied general relativity at MIT, my prof was very fond of the idea of Einstein's bridges, of curving space into a shortcut between two distant locations.

"But, as I recall, the things are dynamically unstable. They have the annoying tendency of winking out of existence so rapidly that one can't even shoot a photon through. And besides, an Einstein-Rosen bridge should have a lot of space curvature and a mass comparable to a black hole, shouldn't it?"

Roger laughed. "You were at MIT a while back, my friend. In the late '80s Kip Thorne at Cal Tech discovered that, theoretically at least, a wormhole can be kept open and stabilized in several ways, all involving a bit of negative mass-energy. And as for the wormhole mass, it can be anything from a Planck mass upward. A Planck mass is only a microgram. I don't think you know for sure that your Snark isn't that massive."

"A microgram?" said George. "That's much too large. If it started at 2 percent of the speed of light, it would never have come to rest in the detector.''

"Perhaps the chaps on the other end helped to stop it," Roger said. "Perhaps that's what all of those jets were accomplishing." George could imagine Roger's grin.

"Does the message say where they are? Where the other end of the bridge is located?" George asked.

"Yes," said Roger. George waited, but Roger said nothing else. He seemed to be playing for dramatic effect.

"So where are they? Is it a nearby star system? How many light-years?" Damn the man and his cute games, George thought.

"It's not that simple," Roger said quietly.

"What do you mean, it's not that simple?" George was growing exasperated. "Roger, where in hell are they?"

"Not in hell," Roger said. "A place that's harder to reach than that. They're in another universe, George."

- # **PART VI**
June 21, 2004

June 15, 1992

The truth is, I don't think there is a single person in this body who has the scientific background to know for sure whether [the SSC] is the greatest investment ever or the worst . . .
—Congressman Newt Gingrich (R.-Georgia)

June 20, 1992

High-energy research with particle accelerators has resulted and will result in plastics for medical use, solutions for DNA research and . . . maybe even for AIDS . . . nuclear waste disposal . . . pollutant removal . . . , location of oil deposits, creation of integrated circuits . . . studies of water tables . . . cryogenic engineering, tumor and body chemistry detection . . . ultra-fast computers . . . and lots, lots more . . ."
—Congressman Bob Livingston (R.-Louisiana)

They have already, as a result of this program, developed cancer technology, developed treatment of tumors, developed advanced plastics that can be used in hospitals to reduce hazardous wastes . . . The SSC is almost driving supercomputer technology, and supercomputers are what has made the United States an advanced technology [leader] in lots of areas.
—Congressman Sam Johnson (R.-Texas)

What will happen once [the SSC] is finally completed? It deals with compressed energy. Scientists say they will be able to have enough energy to run an automobile . . . In the medical profession, they will have a machine that [can] find any tumors or cancer in your body, never using a knife.
—Congressman Bill Sarpalius (D.-Texas)

• 38

THE TIME HAD PASSED SO RAPIDLY. ALICE COULDN'T QUITE BELIEVE that it had only been nine days since they had isolated the Snark. She recalled how George had commandeered a new laboratory room for them to work in and set up the recording and display hardware, how Roger had quickly scanned electronic conference proceedings, identified SETI experts on alien contact, and persuaded them to come to the laboratory, how the subtleties of the Snark's pictorial messages had slowly been decoded. It seemed like months of events compressed into a handful of days.

She looked around SSC's large lecture theater. It was absolutely packed. Alice suspected that its occupancy probably exceeded the fire code limit by 25 percent. The front row was occupied by the laboratory hierarchy, with Roy Schwitters, the SSC director, seated in the center. Jake Wang sat immediately to his left and occasionally delivered a whispered comment in the director's ear. Also scattered along the first and second rows were the group leaders, Nobel laureates, and distinguished physicists that Alice had come to know and recognize in the past two weeks.

George had wanted Alice, as a participant in the Snark discovery, to sit on the front row also, but as a reporter she had preferred to sit halfway back in the lecture theater, where she could experience the reactions of the audience around her. She had arrived forty minutes before the seminar was scheduled to begin, and she was glad that she had. Late-arriving graduate students and others sat on the floors, filling the aisles and the space on the floor in front of the first row of seats. Both walls were lined with remotes. Alice had heard from some of the late arrivals that all the telepresence units and couches in the laboratory had been commandeered for the special seminar, bringing all interactive data analysis at the SSC to a dead stop.

George had been speaking for over half an hour and was now getting to the final conclusions of his talk, which had been designed to provide an overview of the past week's work on the Snark. The seminar schedule, projected at the beginning, had indicated that George would speak first for forty-five minutes, followed by a question period and a break, followed by thirty-minute talks by four other speakers. Roger Coulton, seated now at the far right of the front row next to his boss, Bert Barnes, would discuss the twelve Snark diagrams and their interpretation. Professor Angelo Axel, distinguished cosmologist from the University of Chicago, would discuss inflationary cosmology and bubble universes. Professor Rudyard Horne of Cal Tech would discuss general relativity and quantum gravity as applied to stable microscopic wormholes. And Professor Wilson Mulligan, George's friend from the University of Washington Astronomy Department and a longtime leader of SETI efforts in radio astronomy, would discuss strategies for establishing two-way contact using the Snark.

There had been some discussion of coupling the seminar to a press conference, but George had vetoed that idea, preferring to wait until the two-way contact attempt had been made. Alice was delighted with this decision. She had a major news scoop, the discovery of the Snark, ready to break to an unsuspecting world later this afternoon. Alice took digital camera shots of the arrangement on the front row and made detailed notes of everything. She was thinking of the news release, the *Search* article she would write on the Snark, and the popular-level science book that would follow it. The Snark was a historic event, and she was in a unique position to write its history.

George started his talk by projecting several multicolored and rotating views of the now-famous Snark event on the large computer-driven flatscreen at the front of the room. He mentioned several important features of the LEM detector that had been essential in discovering the event. He graphically traced the path of the Snark through the various layers of the detector, projecting diagrams that showed in detail the region where the Snark had stopped. He then described how he and Alice had come in the middle of the night and removed the scintillator bar containing the Snark from the LEM detector. He held up a unit like the one they had removed.

Alice smiled. George made it sound as if their actions that Saturday night had been a thoroughly planned course of action, a careful set of logical steps, rather than the slightly beery culmination to an evening of dancing at P.J.'s. And he didn't mention that after they'd found the thing, they'd gone to Alice's house and screwed like demented weasels. He seemed to imply that at least half of the insights that had led to finding the Snark had been hers. George was a gentleman, but he was unduly generous. She felt embarrassed, thinking about her half-finished techno-disaster thriller.

George showed a close-up image of the lead-glass scintillator that held the Snark, made at a sufficiently low light level that the blue glow was visible. This was followed by graphs showing the wavelength spectrum of the light and its time structure. Then he described the encoded message, including all twelve of the bit-map images it contained. Finally George described the plan for transmitting a message in the other direction, mentioning that one of the following speakers would describe the plan in more detail.

There was thunderous applause in the auditorium as George concluded. The SSC director stood and asked if there were questions. Alice shifted in her seat, wondering what the question period would bring. She could see that Jake was holding his hand stiffly in the air.

The director called on the first questioner, a theorist in the front row who asked a detailed question about the energy and momentum balance in the reconstruction of the Snark event. George answered the question and projected a new diagram that provided additional information.

Another questioner, an experimentalist for the LEM group whom Alice recognized, asked skeptically about the mass and charge of the Snark and how these related to its stopping power. George quickly admitted that there was a problem here and projected a graph showing an analysis of the Snark's ionization track in the various parts of the LEM detector. He followed this with a graph of the time-of-flight analysis of the Snark event. "If we assume the Snark is an object having a Planck-scale mass with a velocity of beta equals point-oh-two," he finished, "then the observed ionization should have been insufficient to bring it to rest. We suspect that the previously unknown color ionization process, the process that produced the twenty-nine jets we saw, also served to decelerate the Snark. Roger has suggested that there may have been neutral particles involved in the deceleration, which we wouldn't track. We would be interested in other suggestions bearing on this issue."

The third questioner, one of the accelerator engineers, wanted a more complete explanation of what had been learned from the bit-map diagrams. In particular, what could be learned about wormholes and about the location from which the message was being sent? "First let me deal with the wormhole question," said George. "The wormhole, or 'Einstein-Rosen bridge' as we used to call it when I was in graduate school, is almost as old as Einstein's general theory of relativity itself. The mathematics of general relativity indicates that when space becomes sufficiently curved and distorted, a three-dimensional tube can form that connects one region of space-time with another, a sort of spatial shortcut.'' George projected a diagram of a surface curved back on itself, with a tube connecting one region of the surface to another.

Alice was amused. George had spent long hours fetching papers on wormholes from electronic preprint databases, studying the papers in great detail, complaining about the unintelligible math, and bombarding Roger with questions. Now, a week later, he sounded like an expert who had been working in the field for years. Perhaps he had learned something from his association with Jake.

''In 1962,'' George continued, ''Fuller and Wheeler showed that a wormhole is so dynamically unstable that it would pinch closed before any light, matter, or information could pass through it. Then in 1988, Morris, Thorne, and Yurtsever demonstrated that a Casimir-effect capacitor could stabilize a wormhole, preventing its pinch-off. Subsequent work of Visser and others demonstrated that the same stability could be achieved in other ways. From what we now gather from the Snark diagrams, there are ways of stabilizing a wormhole that we had not previously considered. Professor Horne will discuss this later.''

''But what's at the other end of the wormhole? In particular, what's this 'other universe' business you mentioned?'' the questioner persisted. ''Are we talking Everett-Wheeler probability branches or shadow-matter worlds or what?''

''None of the above,'' said George. ''Professor Axel will address the cosmological aspects of the Snark message later today, but let me attempt a lowbrow experimentalist's answer to your question. The 'inflationary scenario' describing the early history of the Big Bang is a synthesis of cosmology and particle physics. But up to now, there seemed no hope of attempting any experimental verifications of its predictions. The scenario described the very early universe as a region of expanding space saturated with an almost unimaginably large quantity of energy. As that space expands, a local irregularity occurs, perhaps around a single magnetic monopole, and a sort of bubble forms. Inside that bubble is what we would call normal space, while outside is the energy-saturated space in which the strong, electro-weak, and gravitational forces are indistinguishable. The walls of the bubble, driven by the energy liberated in this transition from one kind of space to another, move outward faster than the speed of light. That bubble of space is what became our universe. We and all the space we can reach, all the planets, stars, galaxies, and galactic clusters are inside it. But a larger megauniverse, the true cosmos, remains outside the bubble.''

Not bad, thought Alice, taking notes. Now George is an expert on cosmology, too.

"The inflationary scenario," George continued, "allows for the possibility of many such bubble universes, each isolated from the rest, each walled off in its own pinched-off isolation from the others and from the greater megauniverse in which they all exist. It now appears that through the Snark, we are receiving a message from intelligent life that inhabits another bubble universe. Apparently it's easier to contact intelligent life in other universes than it is in your own. That's the conclusion we've reached from studying the Snark diagrams. Inflationary cosmology seems to have been experimentally confirmed.'' The questioner nodded and sat down.

Alice observed that there were fewer hands raised now; the audience must be running out of questions. The director called on Jake. He stood and slowly turned to face the audience. "There is a time to push your own work, to toot your own horn," Jake began. "This, however, is not such a time. A leading member of my LEM team, my friend and colleague Professor George Griffin has made a momentous, unprecedented, and completely unexpected discovery. A discovery which, as he has graciously pointed out, was made possible because of this great accelerator and because of the remarkable sensitivity and measurement capabilities of our LEM detector. I would like to congratulate Professor Griffin on his work. Two weeks ago he tried to interest me in this Snark event, and I blush to admit that I dismissed it as uninteresting background.'' He turned to the stage and smiled at George.

"And background it is, in a certain sense," he continued. "The Snark is not a fundamental particle, not an object of the kind this great facility was built to study. It is something unique, something far stranger. It is an alien artifact, an object whose very nature we can only guess at from the meager clues that their messages have so far provided.''

I can't believe it, Alice thought. Jake is actually being magnanimous. Could he have had a personality transplant over the weekend? But what did he mean about the Snark not being the kind of object the SSC was built to study?

"Some might argue that Professor Griffin's discovery lies outside the realm of particle physics. That it more properly belongs in the domain of astrophysics, SETI studies, or even extraterrestrial biology." Jake paused and looked at the audience.

Okay, here it comes, Alice thought.

"But I feel that this great discovery was made in this laboratory and it should remain in this laboratory. I would like to suggest to the SSC director and the SSC executive committee, with all due respect for their prerogatives, that they should create a Snark task force to investigate this new phenomenon as fully and rapidly as possible, that significant laboratory resources be committed to this project, that additional external support be immediately sought from the funding agencies and foundations, and that Professor Griffin be asked to take a leave of absence from his university so that he can head this task force and devote his full effort to this project." Again he turned to George. "And I want to congratulate Professor Griffin again for his remarkable achievement."

Facing George, Jake began to clap, and soon the audience of the entire auditorium rose in a standing ovation.

The director strode up on the stage and warmly shook George's hand. "We'll take our break now," he said into the microphone.

When she could get George's attention, Alice, balancing her coffee cup and cinnamon roll, said quietly to him, "Was that really Jake Wang who said those things? Or was this a changeling swapped for Jake in the night by the elves?"

George laughed. "You have to be able to read your Jake," he said. "Allow me to interpret. First, he saw no way of blocking work on the Snark, so he got out in front to lead the parade, radiating whatever reflected glory he could in the process. Second, he claimed as much credit as he could for the LEM detector as a device for discovering wormholes, and I'm sure he'll continue to do so with rising intensity for the indefinite future. Third, he has effectively moved all work on the Snark as far from LEM as possible, sending me with it. And finally, he's suggested that general laboratory funds and external funds be used to support whatever work is done on the Snark, meaning that LEM funds will not be spent on it. Understand now?''

''He's moved you out of his road, so he can get on with discovering the Higgs?'' Alice asked.

''Exactly,'' said George. ''I suppose I might have done something similar in his place.'' He winked at her.

A tone sounded in the hallway, indicating that the second part of the seminar was about to begin. Together they walked back into the lecture theater.

• **39**

THE DISTINGUISHED VISITORS WHO HAD PARTICIPATED IN THE SNARK seminar this morning stood clumped together, their attention directed at the large flatscreen mounted on the Snark laboratory wall. It displayed the bit-stream from the Snark, rendered as a 1728 by 1728 pixel bit-map image. The display changed as the bit-stream came in, cycling through the same twelve images every two hours. A nearby oscilloscope showed the changing waveform of the transmission.

Alice leaned against the wall opposite the flatscreen. She had seen the images enough times to have memorized them all by now. She was growing impatient.

On the lab bench rested the now-famous Snark scintillator unit. It was connected to several cables that led to an electronics rack standing beside the bench. The electronics provided the signals and protocol for connecting the device to the local area network. As far as the network was concerned, the Snark was now just one more node.

George sat at the old-fashioned computer terminal, looking up at Roger.

''What are you waiting for, George?'' Alice asked. She had a sense of being present at a historic moment. She thought again about the Snark book she intended to write and wondered what kind of advance it might bring.

''This is the moment of truth, Roger,'' he said. ''When I hit this computer key, we will have done something irreversible. We will have revealed ourselves to an alien civilization that must be far more advanced than we are. We'll signal them that we exist and wish to communicate. Once I hit the key, the world becomes a different place. Do I really want to do it?''

Alice made rapid notes, not wanting to miss anything.

Roger looked at George. ''Your options are very limited, I'm afraid. The rumors of our work have been going out like a tidal wave. Many people in other places attended the seminar this morning using remotes, and the computer mail is flying. I predict that by tomorrow there will be an Internet discussion group devoted exclusively to speculations and news about the Snark. I predict that soon an army of reporters will converge on the laboratory, with bureaucrats from a whole array of federal agencies not far behind. I think there are only two choices. You can initiate communications right now, or you can let a bunch of State Department or military bureaucrats do it. Your choice, George.''

George bit his lip and shook his head. ''Shit!'' he said and hit the RETURN key.

''That may become a famous quote, George, like 'Damn the torpedoes—full speed ahead!' or 'One small step for a man . . . ' '' Alice said, writing more in her notebook.

''Let the record show,'' said Roger, ''that George said, 'I initiate this contact in the name of all humankind,' before he hit the final keystroke.'' He grinned.

The message that Roger, Wilson Mulligan, and their rapidly assembled team of SETI experts had prepared began to flow into the Snark. It had not been necessary to prepare it from a cold start. The community of radio astronomers, mathematicians, psychologists, and others interested in the search for extraterrestrial intelligence, despite their battles with former Senator Proxmire and other members of Congress, had been refining a basic strategy for establishing contact with an alien civilization for the past four decades. Parts of that plan, of course, were irrelevant. There seemed little point in communicating to residents of another universe the coordinates of pulsars near the solar system, for example. But most of the approach was directly applicable to the problem of contact: the sequence of smooth transitions from mathematics to physics to chemistry to biology to language to culture. A distillation of this approach, distilled to a bit-stream, was now flowing down the cables and through the Snark, to emerge in another universe.

Alice backed away from the wallscreen and studied it. There was no change in the sequence of diagram. It was presently tracing the last few lines of the Snark version of the periodic table of the elements, one of the diagrams it had repeated in roughly two-hour intervals for the past week. The nuclear chemists were fascinated by this diagram, which extended to element number 128, some seventeen positions beyond the place where our own periodic table of known elements terminated.

Perhaps, Alice thought, Roger was right and the communications link, if one were possible at all, would require months or years, even centuries to establish. How short could a wormhole path be that connected one entire universe with another? This could be a long wait.

The periodic table diagram on the flatscreen had just completed. Alice watched it, anticipating that the next diagram, which depicted atomic orbits and transitions, would be displayed. But the flatscreen remained unchanged, with no update trace proceeding across the top, and the oscilloscope beside it now showed a green blur. Alice glanced across the room to the electronics rack. Angry red lights were flashing from the data-processing modules there.

"What the hell?" muttered one of the electronics technicians as he punched at the controls of an oscilloscope. The screen of the scope flashed green and fluttered, then stabilized in a fixed trace. It showed a sequence of up-and-down rectangular traces. At the left of the screen the square-cornered swings were widely spaced, but as they progressed across the screen they grew closer and closer together until they merged into a continuous blur of blue haze.

"That's a different pattern," Alice said, remembering the sequence of regularly spaced ones and zeros that the Snark had been producing for the past ten days.

"Yes," said George. He turned to Roger. "It's a good thing you wouldn't bet with me," he said. "We've made contact. They're obviously telling us to transmit faster."

IT HAD BEEN A BUSY WEEK FOR ALICE, GEORGE THOUGHT. SHE HAD backed up the SSC laboratory's press release about the Snark discovery with her personal account, which had been distributed internationally by Associated Press. At the press conference the day after the seminar, she had been designated as pool reporter to feed new information to the reporters who had converged on the laboratory to cover the story. And her *Search* article on the Snark discovery had been the magazine's featured cover story for the week.

George had framed an enlarged copy of the *Search* cover. It now hung on the wall of the Snark laboratory opposite him. In the bookshelf below it was a copy of *Time* bearing its own cover heralding the discovery. He noticed that Alice was thumbing through a similar copy of *Newsweek*.

"How did *Newsweek* treat us?" he asked.

"Not bad," she said, "but they did garble a few key points. They seem to think that Roger is also a member of the LEM collaboration. By the way, how is Roger? Any news?"

"I called the hospital this morning," said George. "He's at his apartment resting now. The doctor told me that his second seizure was worse than the first. I'm very worried." Roger's brilliance had been essential to the Snark contact. The doctors seemed to be having trouble establishing what his medical problem was.

George stroked his beard as he studied the terminal display. The Snark was simultaneously communicating with him, racing like a wildfire from database to database on the Internet, asking a continuous string of questions to various experts, and filling the latest in a series of ultra-high-density one-terabyte holographic optical platters.

The first level of the Snark download, about a terabyte of easily decoded information on the science, mathematics, biology, culture, arts, history, and philosophy of the race of Makers, had already been transmitted and was being widely distributed and analyzed. Now the second-level transmission was in progress. More detailed information about the Makers' culture and science, along with information about the other civilizations that the Makers had contacted, was being received. The SSC data analysts on Team Snark were processing these new tapes off-line and making the information they contained available on the Internet as quickly as they could, which was not nearly fast enough to satisfy the information-starved world tied into the network.

George pressed a switch and spoke into the microphone before him on the desk. "Tunnel Maker?" he said.

"I'm here, George," the voice from the speaker on the desk, the voice they had come to identify as that of Tunnel Maker, said.

"I see you have been making good use of the Internet," George said.

"Yes," said Tunnel Maker. "Our historians have been studying your recent history, and they unexpectedly cleared up a nuclear astrophysics mystery that had been puzzling us."

"Really?" Alice, standing behind George, said into the microphone.

"Yes," said Tunnel Maker. "When our Bridgehead was moving through your detector, we noticed that it passed through a region of almost pure element 92, isotope 238—what you call uranium-238, I believe. The mystery was: Why was there almost no trace of isotopes 234 and 235, which should be present in small concentrations? There were speculations that nucleosynthesis somehow worked in a different way in your universe than in ours."

"We use depleted uranium in the LEM detector," George said.

"So we deduced," said Tunnel Maker. "We studied the history of your Manhattan Project and later nuclear weapons and nuclear reactor programs and concluded that the uranium-238 in your detector must be what was left over when the lighter isotopes were removed for bombs and reactor fuel."

"Exactly," said George.

"Your species has never made nuclear weapons?" Alice asked.

"No," said Tunnel Maker, "we have weapons and conflicts, but nothing quite like yours. However, you have emerged from a very dangerous period, and you are to be congratulated. It appears to us that the enormous destructive power of the weapons you developed held your great nations in place without major conflicts long enough for the inherent problems of some of your political systems to become obvious even to their adherents. Our historians find this very interesting."

"Yes," said George, "we do live in interesting times." He had decided that Tunnel Maker should be told about the impact his contact was having. "You should know that you're creating a lot of new problems here," he said. "There's been a stock market crash in the high-technology and manufacturing sectors. The U.S. Congress is now debating a bill that would expropriate our Bridgehead and place it at Livermore, behind a wall of high security. Other countries are threatening censures, boycotts, and even military action if that is done. And our 'open' SSC laboratory has become an armed camp, with DOE security guards brought in from all over the country to protect us from the news media, the industrial spies, and the curiosity seekers. We on Team Snark have had to move our base of operations twice so far. We've now relocated belowground in a side tunnel of the ring."

"It's also been very exciting," Alice chimed in. "There has been enormous coverage of your contact with us in the news media. I've become the 'pool reporter' for every news organization in the world."

"You should not concern yourselves unduly about these problems," Tunnel Maker said. "Change is always somewhat painful. This difficult initial phase is about to reach its successful completion."

Alice blinked. "What do you mean?" she asked.

"We have almost completed the transmission of the second-level information. In about one more rotation of your planet our transmission stream will conclude, except to answer questions you may wish to ask us. But now I must ask you to help me. Our Concantation of Individuals is pleased with the way things have gone so far and has reached a consensus. I am authorized to proceed with the second phase of our contact."

"What is the second phase?" asked George.

"In a manner of speaking, I'm coming for a visit," said Tunnel Maker. "You will need to find a quiet place for the first part of it, well away from the busy environment of your laboratory."

"A visit?" exclaimed George. His mind raced, trying to imagine how that might happen.

"Wow!" said Alice and began to type into her lapstation.

"Just how do you propose to do that?" George asked. "Do you plan to come through the wormhole?"

"Pick up the scintillator unit and look underneath," said Tunnel Maker.

George stood, reached out, and picked up the black object. Beneath it a cavity had seemingly been carved out of the plastic and pressed wood of the desktop. In the cavity was a small white sphere about the size of a large marble. He studied the underside of the scintillation bar. There was a small hole there, just over the place where the cavity and egg had appeared, and a thin beam of blue light emerged from it. "What is this white sphere on the table?" George asked. "Where did it come from?"

"That is my Egg," said Tunnel Maker. "I produced it by manipulating atoms with coherent radiation. In a sense, I am contained in that Egg. Pick it up, please."

George did so. The object had a slightly rough surface and felt warm in his hand. "I see you used our tabletop in your molecular rearrangements," he said.

"Yes," said Tunnel Maker. "I hope the object that provided the donor atoms was not of great value to you. It was necessary to damage it, in order to produce the Egg. You must now take the Egg and follow the instructions I will give. The survival of your species depends on you. I hope you believe this."

George looked at Alice, then at the small white sphere in his hand. "What is it you want us to do with this thing?" he asked.

"The second phase of contact involves teaching you new skills. This cannot easily be accomplished through a microscopic Bridge. The Egg you hold, if placed in the proper environment, will grow to become a Maker Emissary, a temporary replica of me, complete with my mental processes and memories. I have designed the Egg to grow in an environment that is common on your planet, a body of water that is rich in minerals and marine life. I believe you call it an 'ocean.' Ours is a race of amphibians, and this seems natural to us. You should take the Egg to such a body of water and select a relatively private place. For your own benefit, it should be well away from what you call the 'news media.' You should place the Egg into the water and wait twenty-four hours. At the end of that time, our Emissary will emerge at the same location where the Egg was placed."

"You want us to drive to an ocean and drop in the Egg?" said George. "Why? Why did you make the Egg so that it needs an ocean? Why do we need privacy?"

"I did what I could do quickly with the resources available to me," said Tunnel Maker. "The environment of privacy is best for the communication and learning that must take place. I hope you trust me. I mean you only good, and time is short, for reasons that you will learn about soon.''

"It goes against my judgment to blindly follow orders," said George.

"I understand," said Tunnel Maker, "but I urge you to at least find a place such as I suggested while you are considering your proper course of action. It would be better for you to be in a place that is less public than your present location.''

George frowned.

Alice pointed at the Egg and nodded.

"Okay, dammit," said George. "We will do what you ask, at least the first part. What about this communication apparatus?''

"It will continue in operation," said Tunnel Maker. "I believe there are others of your Team Snark who can see to its operation. But it would be better for the two of you to take the Egg and leave now.''

"Okay," said George. He took a large sheet of laboratory tissue, folded it around the Egg, and slipped the packet into his jacket pocket. Then he began stuffing papers into his briefcase.

Alice folded her lapstation and prepared to leave.

George called for replacements from Team Snark, giving the excuse that an unexpected emergency in Seattle had come up. Then together George and Alice walked through the limestone tunnel to the elevator.

When the elevator doors opened at ground level, there was Roger, who had been waiting to descend.

"Roger, you're supposed to be at home resting," said George.

"I'm all right," said Roger. "Where are you going?''

He was wearing his perennial backpack. George noticed how pale and weak he looked. George was silent for a moment and looked inquiringly at Alice.

She nodded.

"Walk with us to the parking lot, and I'll explain," said George. He told Roger about the Egg and Tunnel Maker's instructions.

"I'm going with you," Roger said abruptly as they reached Alice's car.

"But you can't, Roger," Alice objected. "You're ill. You should be home in bed.''

"I owe you an explanation about that," said Roger. "Let's drive.''

"Where?" asked Alice.

"Hm," said George, taking a Texas map from the glove compartment and studying it. "I think we should go to Interstate 45 and head south to the Gulf Coast area beyond Houston. The Gulf of Mexico is the nearest piece of ocean. Do either of you need to pack clothes or anything?"

Roger shook his head. "I can make do with what's in here," he said, patting his backpack.

"Reporters' habits die hard," said Alice. "I always keep a jump bag packed and ready in the trunk of my car. What about you?"

"I'll buy some things when we get there," said George. "Let's go."

Alice headed south on I-45. As she drove, Roger told them the tale of synaptine and his experiments with it. "Synaptine is wonderful and deadly," he concluded. "Under its influence, I've been able to understand its actions far better than Susan had. It does create a kind of back-propagation loop in the human nervous system. And it also does other things. Have you ever wondered why large brains and intelligence are not more common in the animal kingdom?" He looked across at George and Alice.

"I suppose because it took time to evolve them," said George.

"And then there's the business of the head diameter and the birth canal," Alice added.

"Which is nonsense," said Roger. "Nature is extremely good at duplicating or enlarging an organ if it proves useful for survival. One can find thousands of examples of that in evolutionary biology. But only humans, dolphins, and whales have large brains, and in the latter two the brain structure seems more devoted to signal processing than intelligence. But, George, what happens when you make a neural network too big or give it too many layers?"

"Oh!" said George. "It goes unstable."

"Exactly," said Roger. "It has become clear to me that the problem with making big brains is not in producing them but in stabilizing them. It took nature a long time to evolve the stabilization mechanisms of the human brain. And it's still not highly stable, as any psychiatrist can testify. We teeter at a delicate balance point on the edge of stability, and some of us fall over the edge into obsession, paranoia, manic-depressive cycles, or epileptic fits."

"And synaptine affects that stability?" asked George.

"Yes," said Roger. "I've been having epileptic fits of increasing severity. During the last one, my heart stopped, and an emergency team had to use an electric jolt to restart it. Susan's rhesus monkey, Elvis, died last week of a similar seizure.''

"What about antiepilepsy drugs?" asked Alice.

"My condition isn't really epilepsy. That's only a convenient label. The standard antiepileptic drugs like ritalin have no effect on the problem and produce some really unpleasant side effects. I've tried them. I've been having about one seizure per week. The last one was a couple of days ago. I think the next episode, or perhaps the one after that, will probably kill me," Roger said calmly.

"But why don't you just stop taking synaptine?" asked Alice.

"A large concentration of synaptine was the trigger, not the ongoing cause," said Roger. "Once the seizure syndrome is established, withdrawal of the drug has no effect. Besides, I've needed the intellectual boost I get from synaptine to understand the Snark problem. And I have a bit of it left. Perhaps I'll need it again."

George patted his pocket, where the Egg lay nested. "Perhaps you will," he said grimly.

• 41

ROGER HUNCHED HIS SHOULDERS AND STRETCHED. ALICE HAD driven south from Waxahachie on Interstate 45. After several hours of rural Texas cropland and an hour of threading past the strip-mall suburban sprawl of Houston, they had crossed the long causeway beyond La Marque and entered Galveston onto Avenue J, otherwise known as Broadway, the backbone arterial of the island city. Broadway was lined with tall palm trees and knife-leafed oleanders adorned with pink and white blossoms. Even with the car windows closed and the air conditioner running, Roger could detect their oversweet scent.

Roger consulted the screen of his lapstation, studying the detailed street map provided by its holo-ROM-based world atlas and travel guide. "Rosenberg Avenue is coming up," he said to Alice. "I think you should turn right there, drive to the beachfront, and make another right along West Beach." They were passing the long blue awning of the EZ Pawn pawnshop. At the intersection Alice circled a monumental female figure brandishing an ivy-covered sword commemorating the Heroes of the Texas Revolution. The pawnshop awning bore the inscription LOANS—GUNS—TOOLS—STEREOS, while the monument was carved with the words PATRIOTISM—COURAGE—HONOR—DEVOTION. There's a moral there somewhere, Roger thought.

Alice followed the trolley tracks south to the Galveston seawall and the Gulf of Mexico. Roger opened his backseat window, inhaling the salt smell of the Gulf and getting a better view of the wheeling gulls above the gray-green water. He read aloud from the travel atlas entry on Galveston. " 'On September 6, 1900, a major Gulf hurricane hit Galveston, flooding the island, destroying much of the city, and killing five thousand people. Up to this time, Galveston had been the largest city in Texas, but the flood ended the city's role as a major Gulf seaport. A second flood on August 17, 1915, killed two hundred and seventy-five people. The citizens of Galveston responded to these disasters by constructing a long seawall along the side of the long island fronting on the Gulf, with elaborate jetties and breakwaters to tame hurricane-driven waves. Galveston has survived *subsequent major hurricanes* without significant damage.' "

Roger clicked on the atlas hyperlink SUBSEQUENT MAJOR HURRICANES and continued reading. " 'The major Gulf hurricanes that have impacted Galveston, Texas, since World War II include Hurricane Audrey in 1957, Carla in 1961, Beulah in 1967, Camille in 1969, Celia in 1970, Allen in 1980, Alicia in 1983, and Barry in 2001.' "

"Goodness," said Alice. "I've been through more than my share of hurricanes in Florida, and I don't need another one. Remind me to watch the weather reports while we're here. With satellite pictures we'd have plenty of time to evacuate."

"Oh, I don't know," said George. "It might be fun to watch a good hurricane from a vantage point on the beach and experience the forces of nature at firsthand." He grinned at her.

She turned west on Seawall Boulevard at the beachfront. The seawall overlook provided a nice view of the now-tranquil waters of the Gulf. In the distance several ships could be seen heading for the eastern tip of the island and the Port of Galveston inlet beyond. Alice drove west, with the ocean on the left and beachfront shops, restaurants, and luxury hotels on the right. Finally the tourist-oriented businesses thinned and the highway, now called Termini Road, veered away from the ocean as the seawall ended. On the left was a strip of land overgrown with tall weeds that ended at the beach.

"Coming up is a cross-street called 8-Mile Road," said Roger. "From the satellite map it looks as if it might have some beachfront houses on it." As they approached the intersection, they saw a prominent FOR RENT sign. Closer to the beach was a cluster of houses, all built atop tall poles. "Stilt houses!" said Roger. "One of the paintings that inspired Mussorgsky's *Pictures at an Exhibition* was based on a Russian folktale about the hut of the witch Baba Yaga. It was built on stilts in the form of giant chicken legs, and the hut could walk around, carrying the witch across the countryside. I wonder if these houses can walk." He grinned.

"Only during hurricanes," said Alice, turning the car left toward the beach. "You'll notice that they're all relatively new. There are no old houses fronting directly on the Gulf. Hurricanes scrub the beaches clean every decade or so."

They found the rental office, and George paid two weeks' rent in advance for a furnished two-bedroom beachfront stilt house that was well separated from the neighboring houses. He gave the real estate agent a personal check for the rent and deposit. Then they drove back to the Food King store on Rosenberg and Avenue P½ and bought a good supply of food and other items. At a hardware store across the street, George bought a large blue plastic tarp to cover Alice's car. They parked the car under the house between the stilts and Roger and George carefully covered it with the tarp to protect it from the salt spray, but also to conceal its conspicuous Florida license plates.

Alice watched the ocean through the picture window that looked out over the beach and the ocean. The waves broke and rolled up onto the sand and into the wave-barrier rocks, making a soothing rush-and-flow sound. Gray-winged gulls wheeled overhead, sometimes diving into a wave and emerging with a fish. In the distance a white pelican flew east. This view must have looked much the same for a million years, she thought.

She looked across the room. On the coffee table in its nest of white laboratory tissue lay the Egg. George sat on the couch, studying its rough surface as if looking for hidden meanings. The tension was thick in the room. The sound of the ocean's roar and hiss from outside did not have the usual calming effect.

"It's clear enough," said Roger. "We throw the Egg into the water, wait twenty-four hours, and go back to the same spot. Sounds rather like a fairy tale, doesn't it?''

"Too damn much like a fairy tale," said George. "What if the thing carries a virus or something that infests the Gulf of Mexico? The Makers could be bent on taking over or destroying our planet."

"It could just as well be an airborne virus that has infested the planet already from Waxahachie," said Alice.

"Exactly," said Roger. "If Tunnel Maker and his people wanted to do us ill, they would not have needed to enlist our cooperation to do so. Your Egg could just as well have been a flock of nanomachines for converting the planet to gray goo, or into a new race of Makers. They are up to something else, and they are trying to minimize the impact of implementing it. I'm sure that's why they wanted us away from the laboratory and out of the media spotlight. I'm convinced that we have to trust them, George. I see no alternative."

George looked at him closely. "If you don't mind my saying so, Roger, you're dying anyway. Perhaps you're more inclined to take risks than the rest of us."

"George!" said Alice, shocked by his insensitivity.

Roger raised his hand. "No, Alice, it's all right. George is correct, in a way. In my present condition I am perhaps a bit more inclined to take risks. My previous gamble with synaptine could certainly be taken as evidence of that. But I assure you, George, I would not be willing to gamble with any life except my own. I believe our only rational course of action is to follow Tunnel Maker's instructions. If there is a danger, it isn't from him and his people."

George stroked his beard for a time. "Okay, dammit," he said finally. "I suppose you're right. In fact, I have a gut feeling that you're right. I just needed to make sure that we had thought it through."

"Maybe Tunnel Maker just wants to introduce himself to us, before revealing himself to the rest of the world," said Alice.

George picked up the Egg from its nest on the table. "So let's get it over with." He headed for the door.

"George," said Alice as they were walking back from the beach, "we need to talk."

For a moment George's face took on a deer-in-the-headlights look. He took a deep breath and said, "Sure, Alice. What about?"

"I need to tell you about the kind of books I write, about the book I'm working on now," said Alice.

George looked relieved, if a bit puzzled. "Books?" he said. "I don't understand."

Alice told him about her pseudonym, about her previous books, about *F as in Fire Ants*, and about how she had come to be commissioned by *Search* magazine to write an article on the SSC. She allowed him to read parts of *Fire Ants* from her laptop.

"The business with the press credentials was pretty devious, Alice," he said with a look of dismay. "Sneaky, even."

"I know," she said. "At the time I thought it was necessary. How would you have reacted if I'd approached you for information and told you I was working on a novel about giant mutant fire ants attacking the SSC?"

"I can't say," said George. "I might have been willing to help, but it would clearly have been lower priority than helping you with an article for *Search*." He was quiet for a while and finally said, "You know, when I think about it, our current situation is probably a lot more bizarre than anything you might have put in your *Fire Ants* book. Fiction has been outweirded by reality." Then he looked closely at her. "What I don't understand is why you choose to write bug-disaster novels, Alice. Somehow you don't seem the type."

She looked at him and smiled. It was going to be all right, she thought. "I suppose I wandered into it, George. In my view, most mainstream literature is an extended and depressing description of losers in the process of losing. I never saw the point of that kind of writing, aside from the fact that it's currently fashionable and 'literary.'

"When I made the decision to produce a book, I seriously considered doing investigative reporting and making that into a book, perhaps an exposé of the Florida drug-money laundering scene. However, my late husband was against that because it might offend—or possibly even expose—some of his clients.

"Then I realized that I liked reading bug-disaster novels, as you call them, and that I would enjoy writing one. I sat down and analyzed why it was that I liked them. And I found the answer.

"It's because they're actually about *change* and how people react to it. In all of these novels something terrible happens, some unpleasant change occurs, and the people in the novel must deal with it. Some of them simply give up, lie down, and die. Some of them react, but they do all the wrong things, and they die, too. But some of them, either through cleverness or instinct, somehow do the right things, successfully deal with the problem, and survive. Those are the characters we identify with, and when they get beyond their problems, we feel good about it. In some measure we adopt their attitudes, so that when we come to a real problem in real life, we're perhaps better prepared to deal with it.''

George looked thoughtful and nodded.

''There's also another aspect of my bug-disaster novels,'' Alice said. ''Some of the themes I've used in my novels are real problems, like the overuse of chemical fertilizers and pesticides and their effect on the environment. I've fictionalized the problems and exaggerated their effects, but the problems are nonetheless real. My bent for investigative reporting has been put to good use in developing that part of my books. And I think it's had an impact. My paperbacks are read by far more people than any fancy hardcover work of investigative nonfiction would have been.

''That's what I like to think people get from my books. They learn about real problems, and they learn how to deal with change in their lives in better and more effective ways. I'm not ashamed of what I write. I'm proud of it, and I'm delighted that people are willing to pay for it.''

George looked closely at her. Then he kissed her. ''That's wonderful,'' he whispered.

Alice looked up from her lapstation, then saved the file she had been working on. This had been a long and trying twenty-four hours. Between eating, sleeping, and lovemaking, Alice had continued to work on her manuscript and now had a nearly completed first draft. She hadn't slept much, and she felt tense and strung out.

Roger had retreated to a big chair in the corner, using his lapstation to go over the Snark data stream and to read one textbook holo-ROM after another. He read at an amazing pace, turning a page every few seconds.

At last George's alarm watch beeped. ''Showtime!'' he announced. Alice followed the two men outside to the beach, feeling a rising excitement.

The bright summer day was cooled by a breeze from the ocean. Alice squinted into the light after the dimness of the cottage. There was a sharp salt smell in the air, and seagulls wheeled overhead. The tide was coming in, the gray-green waves lapping progressively higher on the beach. She could see children playing in the surf far down the beach, but no one was close by.

George led them to approximately the spot from which he had waded out into the surf and thrown the Egg, and they looked out to sea. In the far distance Alice could see an oil tanker moving past at a stately pace, probably heading for a refinery in Baytown or Texas City. They waited.

She thought she was the first to notice the disturbance in the water. There was a small turbulence almost directly in front of them, about forty meters out in the water. Then a blonde head broke the surface, moving in their direction.

Alice couldn't quite believe what she was seeing. The Botticelli-perfect young female face smiled at her, streaming water from nostrils and mouth but not seemingly bothered by this. White shoulders appeared.

George and Roger stood frozen, watching. A wave broke over the child's head, but she came on unperturbed. The waterline was down to the chest now. Her form was subtly female, but there were no breasts, only small pink nipples. The golden blonde hair reached to her waist. A flat belly appeared, complete with a small belly button. Then the crotch, with a labial cleft but no sign of pubic hair. Definitely female. Finally her thighs and legs. Emerging from the water was a young prepubescent human female who looked perhaps ten years old.

The child waded toward them through the water and stopped on the beach. She paused to study them with arrestingly blue eyes, and without a word took Alice by one hand and George by the other. Alice could feel a subtle electricity in the child's damp grip. They walked away from the ocean. Clearing her throat and ejecting some water, the child said distinctly in a low voice, "I am in need of shelter to provide temperature stability. Can we use the structure before us?"

42

ALICE GOT THE CHILD INTO THE HOUSE AND INTO A WARM SHOWER
as quickly as possible. There was probably no question of catching a
cold, but she decided not to take chances. She had shown the child
how to wash away the saltwater, how to shampoo and condition her
hair, how to dry it with the hair dryer. She was amazed that she had
anything to teach the alien. She had given the child her robe to wear
and combed her long blonde hair. Finally they emerged from the bathroom.

Roger and George were waiting quietly on the couch. They appeared to be somewhat dazed by what had happened. Alice and the
child joined them. The child took the armchair next to Roger and
moved about experimentally in it, apparently exploring her first sen-
sations of sitting. Alice sat in the chair opposite.

"What shall we call you?" George began. "Tunnel Maker?"

The child smiled. It was like the sun coming out. "In a sense,
Tunnel Maker was my father. I was him, but I am him no longer,
although we are in communication. Since I am now separate from
him, it would be appropriate for me to have a new name. I have
studied your mythology. Perhaps you could call me Iris after the female messenger of your Greek gods. Would that be acceptable?"

"Yes," said Alice, remembering that Iris was also the goddess of
the rainbow, the bridge between Olympus and Earth.

"Of course," said Roger, "but may I ask why you are a child and
a female? Is Tunnel Maker also a young female?"

Iris laughed, a pleasant tinkling sound. "The concept of male and
female is no longer appropriate for the Makers and has not been for
over a thousand years, since we learned to *Read* and *Write*. The age
of Tunnel Maker is half a gross of orbits, about seventy-two of your
years. He is not particularly old, but neither is he young. You should
understand that I could have emerged from your ocean in any form I
chose: a goddess, a monster, a bird, a giant, a dragon. I could even,
with minor modifications to accommodate the local environment, have
emerged in the form of the real Tunnel Maker. However, if I had, all
of you would have run screaming from the beach. I chose to be a

young human female, in order to be as nonthreatening to your race as possible. You find humans most familiar, children less threatening than adults, and females less threatening than males.''

"You said that your race had learned to *Read* and *Write*," Alice said. "Those words occurred occasionally in our conversations with Tunnel Maker, but he was evasive in explaining what they meant. It is clear, however, that they mean more in your world than simply learning symbolic language skills.''

Iris nodded. "One of the reasons I have come into your world is to teach you three, as representatives of your race, to *Read* and *Write*. These are skills that we learned through contact with another race, the Baltrons, who reside in another Bubble. In a way, Alice, it does involve learning some symbolic language skills. But the language is the genetic code, and one must *Read* and *Write* in the media you call DNA and RNA.''

"I don't understand," said Roger. "Surely DNA genetic coding is not a universal language that extends from one bubble universe to another, from one species to another that evolved separately. Surely the genetic patterns of your race have nothing to do with ours.''

"There is more similarity than you might think," said Iris, "but you are partially correct. Your language of English differs greatly from Russian or Sanskrit, yet knowing one language makes it is easier to learn another. For carbon-based life-forms the proteins are much the same from one evolved species to another, and therefore the DNA that controls protein synthesis is also very similar. There is less variation in the separate carbon-based genetic codes than in human languages. The coding details may differ, but the basic underlying principles for carbon-based life-forms are always the same, from species to species, from Bubble to Bubble. We have found no violations of this principle.''

"But, in a sense, we are already *Reading* and *Writing*," said George. "Our molecular biologists over the past decade have extracted the coding of the human genome. It now resides in a huge computer database and is being intensively used to develop drugs and to combat genetic diseases. We can also do genetic modifications, using synthesized retroviruses. Isn't that what you are talking about?''

Iris smiled again. "We too were doing such things before we contacted the Baltrons. The difference is, we now can *Read* and *Write* in a natural way, within ourselves. Each Individual can do it. We do not require machines to assist us. In fact, *Writing* has become our way of making machines, and we use *Reading* and *Writing* to control and communicate with them." She held out her hand to Roger. "I would like to *Read* you now," she said.

She took Roger's hand. He sat passively, gazing at the silent child. His face had been looking more and more haggard with each passing day. Alice wondered how long it would be before he had another seizure, how much longer he might live.

Finally Iris spoke. "You have a very high level of intelligence for your race, and you are particularly adept at abstract thinking, perhaps less so at focusing on concrete objectives. Your vermiform appendix is subject to infection, and perhaps it has already been removed. The dynamic range of your vision is peaked toward focusing on nearby objects. I presume that is why you suspend artificial lenses before your eyes."

Alice smiled. The child sounded like a fortune-teller.

"Your mother had blue eyes," Iris continued, "but yours are brown. Your father became bald, starting at the crown of his head and progressing. You will begin to do the same in a few years. You have a tendency toward cancer of the colon. You . . ." Her eyes widened. "Your life is severely threatened by a series of seizures, and you will die soon. I did not *Read* that from your DNA, but from some messenger RNA that I came across almost by accident. Were you aware of this, Roger?"

He nodded. "I took an experimental drug, a neuroprotein that increases intelligence. The seizures are an irreversible side effect."

She looked closely at him. "I believe I should correct that condition immediately. Do you agree?"

Roger swallowed hard, then managed to say, "Yes!"

Iris placed her index finger in his mouth and seemed to be concentrating and breathing hard. "There. It is done," she said. "You will have no more seizures."

Alice felt a wave of relief. Her concern about Roger's condition had been like a weight, dragging down her usually optimistic outlook.

"I corrected the neurostability problem," Iris said, "and also increased the natural supply of the neuroprotein you wanted. Your neural processes will henceforth function at the level you wanted, but without the side effect. Is it usual for your race to accept such risks for such a purpose?"

"Roger is rather special and unusual in that regard," said George. "How were you able to do that?"

"It is the product of what you would call genetic engineering," said Iris. "My body, this body, has special chemical receptors and manipulators in the hands that can isolate and read DNA and RNA very rapidly. My brain has a special pattern-recognition section devoted to decoding the information received and reconstructing what the implications of that coding are for the organism from which it comes. You might call it on-line genetic modeling. That is what we call *Reading*. It feels quite natural to me. It's really no more difficult than the pattern recognition done by your vision centers. It is only pattern recognition applied in a different domain."

"And *Writing*?" asked Alice.

"It's the reverse process. If you understand how an organism works, you can see how to change it for the better or to accomplish some particular purpose. The manipulators in my hands can produce DNA, RNA, or retroviruses that can alter the genetics of an individual or produce a new organism or nanomachine with the desired characteristics. It's a little harder than *Reading* and takes more training and concentration, but it works the same way.

"I should add that there is a strong compulsion that comes inextricably with these abilities. When you use these skills, you will always feel compelled to do good for the target organism involved, never harm. That's quite inconvenient on some occasions, but it is for the best." She smiled.

"A wired-in Hippocratic oath," said Roger, who now looked more relaxed.

"And you're going to teach us to do these things?" asked George. "Why?"

"There are two reasons," said Iris. "First, *Reading* and *Writing* are gifts of contact that we received from the Baltrons and that we are obligated to pass on. When your race has received these gifts, you will incur the same obligation."

"We are the first race in our universe, our Bubble, that you have contacted?" asked George. "That seems strange. Surely there are other intelligent species here, and many of them must be doing something equivalent to high-energy physics."

"There are no others that we have detected," said Iris. "Intelligent life is extremely rare. We know of no other intelligent species within our own Bubble, for example, and our exploration probes have been investigating other star systems for many dozen gross of orbits, thousands of your years.''

"How can that be?'' Roger asked. "Surely life is not so rare.''

"Primitive life is common, but intelligence is rare,'' said Iris. "The process you call evolution usually moves forward only slowly and spasmodically. Even the achievement of multicellular life takes a long time. Species evolve to fill the available ecological niches and then stabilize. It requires a dramatic climate change or some disaster to disrupt that stability and restart the evolutionary process. Your scientists have described this pattern as 'punctuated equilibrium.' ''

"Disasters drive evolution?'' Roger asked.

"In part,'' said Iris. "Your solar system contains a giant planet, Jupiter, and a belt of asteroids in the next inner orbit where a planet might have formed. In that asteroid belt are certain empty zones where the orbits become completely chaotic from the influence of Jupiter.''

"Ah yes, the Kirkwood zones,'' said Roger. "Asteroids there would have orbit periods that are integer ratios to the orbit period of Jupiter, like 3:1 or 5:2.''

"This structure in your solar system is like a weapon that about every twenty million years sends a large asteroid to collide with your planet. This produces a sequence of disasters that have driven forward the evolution of life on your planet. The solar system of our world has much the same arrangement.''

"Like the asteroid that killed the dinosaurs sixty-five million years ago,'' said Alice.

"But surely,'' said George, "there must be other star systems where similar structures exist, and where the evolutionary process is driven even faster.''

"Yes,'' said Iris, "but there is an optimum rate. If the disasters, the 'punctuations,' occur too often, there is not enough time for recovery from the previous disaster. If they occur too slowly, the organisms are too firmly embedded in their ecological niches and cannot readily adapt to the changed conditions. In your world and ours, the rate of disasters from asteroid collisions is near the optimum, and intelligence has evolved. In most star systems in most universes, the conditions are wrong, and this does not happen.''

Alice had been trying to take notes, and she was becoming impatient. "I'm getting confused,'' she interrupted. "Let me try to summarize what you've said so far. Your race uses wormholes to contact other intelligent species, which are rare. You had two reasons for coming to our world to teach us to *Read* and *Write* the genetic code. First, you are obligated to pass on this skill. I've been waiting to hear the second reason, but you haven't mentioned it yet. Or did I miss it?''

"No, I hadn't come to it yet," said Iris. "I must teach you *Reading* and *Writing* so that your species can defend itself. The ultra-high-energy collisions that you have recently been producing are generating signals that echo throughout the Cosmos. They attracted our attention and resulted in our contact, but they are also likely to attract the attention of a less benevolent species, the Hive. The Hive is the only example of which we are aware of a social insect species, similar to your ants, bees, and termites, that has achieved intelligence. Their intelligence is collective, each Drone, Worker, Soldier, and Queen united through electromagnetic links as components of an overall Hive Mind.

"Your world is presently in great danger from this species. With your Superconducting Super Collider in operation, it is only a matter of time until you attract the notice of the Hive. You have at most a few years, perhaps much less time to prepare yourselves. They may already have noticed your signals. Even now they may be preparing their response."

"I don't understand," said George. "You're suggesting this Hive might attack the Earth? This sounds like something out of H. G. Wells."

"The Hive was unknown to us until the last four gross of orbits, excuse me, until about six hundred years ago. Their form of contact is to establish a Bridge, then use coherent light beamed through the Bridge to manipulate atoms and construct nanomachines in the contacted universe. The Hive nanomachines then reprocess any matter they find into Hive components: Workers, Soldiers, and Flyers. After a short while, perhaps three of your days, when they have reached the critical number of components, they produce a Hive Queen. At that point, the new Hive Mind becomes conscious.

"Their species has in the past few centuries been attempting to reproduce and spread in this way by colonizing other universes. They have had some successes. They attempted their trick with our world, but one Individual *Read* the initial contact nanomachines and 'improved' them so that they became benevolent. He saved our species.

"We destroyed their Bridge-making apparatus, but they built more. We have formed an alliance of intelligent species that has resolved to stop the spread of the Hive. We want to prevent it from infesting your world. Some of your race, at least, must learn to *Read* and *Write* as soon as possible. Then, if and when the Hive arrives, you will be able to deal with them."

"Why don't you simply sabotage the SSC? Wouldn't that stop the signals?" asked Roger.

"That would be intrusive, and also unwise. Over a period of time we have developed a technique for isolating each universe from the Hive by capturing the Bridgehead they send before a Hive Mind has formed and using the Bridge against them. We cannot be absolutely sure that the Hive has not already established a Bridgehead here. However, from past experience with them, that would be unlikely. When they do arrive, we must be ready. And then your SSC may be useful."

"Why do you think it's unlikely they're already here?" Alice asked.

"In all Hive attacks in our experience," said Iris, "the hyperdimensional signals were produced by the target species for about one of your years before the Hive attempted to establish a Bridgehead. It appears that they must devote considerable time to making preparations before they can act."

"Wait a minute," said George. "The LHC at CERN has already been operating for more than a year. Doesn't it send the same signals, attract the same kind of attention?"

"It's a matter of the energy threshold," said Iris. "The collisions of the other machine are 'silent' because they are below the critical energy level, while the SSC collisions are above it. Your machine's energy was perhaps an unfortunate choice. But, of course, you had no way of knowing that."

George stroked his beard, frowning. "What did you mean about using the SSC?" he asked.

"We might defeat the Hive with a time vortex, and if we did the high concentration of electric power of the SSC would be useful. However, that is a desperate measure with consequences for you and us that we wish to avoid. But the SSC also has another use. We have found that the captured Bridgehead can be placed into a focused particle beam and given a very high electric charge, then accelerated with a machine like the SSC to a near light-speed velocity and held there for a time, a few days or weeks. Then relativistic time dilation produces a time shift in the Bridgehead's time frame. The existence of such a time-shifted Bridgehead makes it impossible for the Hive to establish another Bridge into your universe without forming a catastrophic time vortex. You would be permanently protected from them.''

"In this context, I'd like to understand more about how you establish a wormhole, what you called a Bridge," said Roger. "Can you connect to anywhere?"

"We can only make a new Bridge to a locus that has reached the critical energy density," said Iris. "And we are careful only to Bridge to a single location in another Bubble and never within our own. To do otherwise would be extremely dangerous."

"Dangerous how?" George asked.

"Again, there is a danger of accidentally creating a time vortex. It is a rather complex subject, but I can explain it now, if you like."

"Later," said Alice, "I'm sure there will be time enough for small talk about physics. What I want to know is: When do we learn to *Read* and *Write* and how can we use the skills to protect humanity against the Hive?"

"We could begin now," said Iris. "I must *Write* a retrovirus that will modify your genetic code and also *Write* several different nano-machines that will alter your body and your brain, installing receptors, modifiers, nerve paths, and creating new brain centers. I will introduce these into your bodies. You must rest for about two rotations, forty-eight hours, while your bodies are changed to accommodate your new capabilities. After that, I will give you instructions in how to use the skills."

"Does it hurt?" asked Roger.

"There would be some pain if nothing were done to counteract it. However, part of the process involves the generation of endorphins that nullify most of the painful effects. You will not, however, be particularly mobile or comfortable. It will be like having a bad case of influenza, but without the fever and congestion."

"Okay," said Roger. "I'm ready now."

"Me too," said Alice, feeling some anxiety as she spoke.

George looked irritated and uncomfortable. Finally he said, "Okay, dammit. I suppose I might as well join this stampede of the guinea pigs."

43

ALICE WOKE FIRST. SHE FELT WEAK AND VERY HUNGRY, AS IF SHE had been ill for a long time. She vaguely remembered recent periods of dull aches, sharp pains, and strange dreams, as if her mind and body had been dissolved and reassembled.

She struggled out of bed and stood. As the initial dizziness cleared, she glanced across the bed at George. He did not look ready to face the day, she decided. She quietly closed the bedroom door and tiptoed to the bathroom. After a quick shower, she felt better and returned to the living room.

Iris was sitting in a chair by the window where she could see the ocean. She seemed to be using Roger's lapstation, rapidly reading page after page of dense text and arcane mathematical equations. The plastic case of a textbook holo-ROM lay nearby. Its title was *Advanced Quantum Gravity Theory*. The child was wearing a frilly pink dress that Alice had not seen before.

"That's a very nice dress," said Alice. "It adds to the effect you were trying to achieve. Where did you get it?" Alice felt almost as if she were seeing double, viewing Iris simultaneously as a mysterious alien and as a beautiful and charming child. She began to appreciate the subtle power of the alien's choice of body forms.

"I grew it," Iris said. She led Alice into the backyard. A large plant was growing there. Hanging from a pair of its larger branches were two long pods. The pod walls were translucent, and Alice could see that one contained something yellow, the other something blue.

"These aren't quite finished," Iris said, "but they will be by this evening." She pointed to another plant across the yard. "I have underwear growing there," she said.

"The world of women's fashion will never be the same," said Alice as they returned to the house. She went to the kitchen and rummaged through the food supply, finally deciding to cook up a big pot of spaghetti. She explained the fine points of cooking spaghetti and making sauce to Iris as she thawed a package of ground beef in the microwave. She thought how strange it was to be teaching cooking to a being who could grow her own underwear.

Iris touched the meat. "Oh yes," she said, "I had forgotten. You still eat the flesh of animals. Is this what you call a cow?"

"Yes," said Alice as she dropped clumps of the meat into the oiled frying pan and sprinkled it with garlic salt. "I'm afraid we're still rather primitive in our sources of food. Over the centuries we've selectively bred animal species that we feed on grass and grain and then kill for meat. No one who has thought much about the practice is particularly happy with it, but as a species we're genetically programmed to enjoy eating meat."

Iris sniffed. "It does smell good," she said. "I hadn't expected that."

Roger poked his head out of his bedroom door. "What's that I smell?" he asked. "Spaghetti sauce with lots of garlic?"

"Good nose," said Alice. "Might you perchance be hungry?"

"I feel as if I were in the last stages of terminal starvation," said Roger. "I hope you made a lot."

"It may not be up to the highest standards of gourmet cuisine, but there's plenty of it," said Alice. "Why don't you see if George is ready to join the living?" She rested her right hand on the soft flesh of her left armpit as she talked and noticed a peculiar sensation. There was an electric tingle under her arm, and she felt she was looking at herself in an unfamiliar way from a long distance off. She looked at Iris. "I just touched my body and experienced a strange sensation. Was I *Reading*?"

"Yes, I think perhaps you were," said the girl. "Learning to *Read* yourself is the first step in the process you must learn."

George, looking pale and disoriented, walked out of the bathroom and sat at the dining table. The others came to join him.

Alice served up plates heaped with spaghetti, sauce, and hand-grated parmesan. Then she poured red California jug wine into glasses. Holding out a glass, she turned to Iris. "This is red wine, a beverage made from the juice of a kind of fruit, grapes, which has been fermented by yeast cells. The fermentation converts sugar into alcohol, which when ingested has some interesting effects on the human nervous system. In small quantities we find it relaxing, but too much can be harmful and disorienting. Normally we do not serve wine to children. What should I do about you?"

Iris put a fingertip into the glass and looked thoughtful. "Fascinating," she said. "Sugar, alcohol, tannic acid, and a whole array of complex long-chain molecules. Your species seems to have evolved specific genetic programming to deal with this substance, and it has some benefits. I think I should try some." She took the glass. "I'll synthesize an enzyme to aid me in dealing with the psycho-physiological effects."

As Alice began to eat her own meal, she noticed that Iris was sipping wine and watching each of them intently, but not eating. She looked down at her plate self-consciously, then looked up. "Are you going to eat?" she asked Iris.

"Yes," said the child, "but the process looks complicated, and I'm attempting to understand it. Roger rotates his fork against his spoon, rolls up the long strands, and moves the fork and spoon to his mouth together to transfer the food. George cuts the strands into small lengths and eats them with his spoon. You rotate your fork against the plate and bring the fork to your mouth, sucking in the loose ends. Why does each of you use a different method?"

"I suppose it's a matter of how we learned to eat spaghetti as children," said Alice. "Perhaps there is no good and proper way to eat spaghetti, so we each use a different awkward way."

Alice carefully demonstrated her method to the child, who successfully transferred a roll of spaghetti and sauce to her mouth. She tasted it thoughtfully. "That is very interesting," she said, taking a drink of water. "It is sweet and hot and salty and a bit bitter, all at the same time. In a human body the sensation of eating is very different from that of the Makers. It's a very pleasant sensation." She began to eat the spaghetti with some enthusiasm.

After they had finished off all of the spaghetti, they had more wine and Iris commenced the *Reading* lessons.

"You must understand," she began, "that I will only be able to teach you a few basic skills now. The arts of *Reading* and *Writing* require lifetimes of work and discovery. You are at the starting point of a very long road. You must not expect too much too soon. But let us begin."

As Alice had done by accident, they were instructed to place their right hand in contact with the soft flesh under their left arm, close their eyes, and concentrate.

After the electric sensation that Alice had experienced previously, the *Reading* commenced. Alice became aware of her own body in a way she could never have imagined. She could see clearly the small miracles of its operation, the cycles and processes she took for granted or was simply unaware of. She could see the tendencies to accumulate fat in the wrong places, the muscle tone that was withheld unless pounded in with physical exercise. She could see the programming associated with aging, the withdrawal of hormones and collagen replacement, the cross-linked proteins that were allowed to accumulate, the wrinkles, sags, and crow's-feet that were the consequence. She could see the wired-in hair-graying cycle, the biological clock ticking toward the onset of her menopause.

She could also see the outright defects, the tendencies toward breast cancer, arterial plaque, and calcium loss that were part of her genetic heritage. "That's awful!" she said aloud and looked around. George and Roger lost their self-absorbed expressions and looked at her, nodding in agreement.

"To me," said Iris, "all of you *Read* like untended gardens that have been allowed to go to seed and decay. Now that you see the problems, perhaps we can begin to work on the solutions. Let me give you an example." She swiped her index finger across each of their palms. "*Read* that," she said.

Alice concentrated on the area of her right hand that Iris had just touched. Somehow she could see that it was a virus. She focused on it, wondering what its function was. Suddenly the answer popped into sharp focus. It was a retrovirus designed to transcribe itself permanently into a human cell nucleus as a small loop of DNA that coded for a specific enzyme.

What did this enzyme do? She considered this, and the answer became startlingly clear. In normal cells each strand of DNA had a special noncoding segment on each end, like the plastic tips of a shoe-string. She could see that each time a cell divided this special end segment became shorter. And finally, when the segment length went to zero, the cell could not divide again, the natural cell renewal processes stopped, and the body began to age. The new enzyme systematically restored the end segments to human DNA. It did not require cells to divide, but it allowed them to when the body's repair mechanisms made the request.

"Wow!" said Alice aloud. "It's the Fountain of Youth!"

44

WOLFGANG STOOD AS GEORGE WALKED INTO THE UNDERGROUND laboratory that now housed the Snark. "Well," he said, "welcome back. It looks as if your vacation did you good. You look very healthy." They shook hands. Wolfgang looked down at his hand as he withdrew it.

"I had to make a quick trip over to Seattle," said George. "Not particularly restful."

"I must go to Seattle sometime," said Wolfgang. "You look ten years younger."

"Perhaps it's the coffee," George said. "How has our Snark been behaving while I've been gone?"

"*Schlecht*," said Wolfgang. "The day after you left, the second-level transmissions from the Makers stopped. Tunnel Maker is still talking to us, but he's been rather evasive about further large transmissions. He says they have come to the end of their prepared downloads. From now on we should ask questions or request specific information. On the other hand, his end is still downloading massive quantities of our data from the Internet, the Web, the NSF net, and various proprietary databases that they have bought access to, using the bank account we provided. I've watched it on the monitor. There is no subject, from pornography to pet grooming, that has escaped their notice."

"Hmm," said George. "What happens when you do make a request for further information?"

"When I've tried," said Wolfgang, "Tunnel Maker has usually given me a reference to data that we've already downloaded. It's certainly true that it's going to take us a long time to digest all the information they've already provided, but surely that's not all there is. It seems the equivalent of giving a child a set of encyclopedias instead of educating him."

"What about this end?" asked George.

Wolfgang gestured toward the equipment racks. "We made many equipment changes. I think we've reached some limit to the transmission rate. We're up to two hundred megabaud now, and it seems difficult to go higher.''

"Any problems with outside interference?''

"We had an official visit. Your SSC director showed up here with a big group of 'interested parties' from various of your government agencies. There were people from your DOE, FBI, CIA, NSA, and some military officers in uniform. The military people said their experts had been studying the downloads and had some questions about the Hive species mentioned in them. They were once again threatening to take the Snark and move it to a secure site, but we convinced them that as long as the data was streaming in from the Makers, we shouldn't change anything. I don't know how long that will last.''

"Okay, Wolfgang, thanks for all your effort here,'' said George. "I can take over now, if you've got things to do. I need to talk to Tunnel Maker. Perhaps I can get a clue as to what's going on.''

Wolfgang looked relieved. "I'm glad you're back, George,'' he said. "I've been practically living here, and my wife is beginning to complain.''

As they shook hands again, George looked at him closely. "You don't look so well, Wolfgang,'' he said. "Perhaps you're coming down with some virus. I've heard there's a new flu strain going around. Perhaps you should take a few days off.'' He wondered how Wolfgang would react when he began to *Read*.

Wolfgang blinked, surprised. "I feel well enough,'' he said as he left. "But I'll be careful. *Danke*.''

After checking the door, George triggered the microphone connection. "Okay, Tunnel Maker, we're back. We hatched your Egg in the Gulf of Mexico. Your daughter, Iris, is a lovely child. We like her very much.''

"Yes,'' the voice of Tunnel Maker came from the speaker, "I am in contact with the one you call Iris. I am aware of your progress.''

"She told us that you were in contact, but I don't understand that,'' said George. "I thought such communication between Bubbles was only possible through a wormhole.''

"Once a Bridge, what you call a wormhole, has been established, it is not difficult with our technology to cause it to divide, to become two instead of one. It can be dangerous to have more than one Bridge connecting between Bubbles, should a time shift between them occur, but in this case there is no problem. The Egg contained a new Bridgehead, which is now inside the head of Iris. We use it to communicate.''

"Iris has told us about the race she calls the Hive and the danger they present. She thinks that we have perhaps a year to prepare."

"Yes," said Tunnel Maker. "There is a certain risk until we can train you to be fully prepared to deal with a Hive incursion. Fortunately, you probably have some time to prepare. You will need to construct a permanent network of sensors around the SSC ring to detect such an incursion. You must make preparations for capturing the Hive Bridgehead, for using the SSC to process it, also certain other backup preparations.

"But for the critical next few days, while these steps are in progress, you must make certain that no Hive Bridgehead is already here. You must begin a survey of all the beam intersection points around the ring, using handheld Bridge detectors. Iris can assist you in producing them. If you should detect another event like the one you call the Snark event, if another Bridge has been produced, it must be captured immediately."

"That sounds okay," said George. "I've been given a team of scientists assigned to work on the contact with you, and we can train them. What you describe can be taken on as a subsidiary task. But suppose we did detect a Bridgehead? What could we do about it?"

"First, isolate it as you did the Snark particle. Second, immerse the Bridgehead and its immediate surroundings in liquid helium. No incursions by the Hive would be possible in such a low temperature and inert gas environment. Iris can provide details."

"If we do detect a new Bridge, how long would we have to deal with it?" asked George. "What you describe would certainly take some time."

"From our past experience with the way the Hive operates, it takes some time before they have produced enough Workers, Soldiers, and Flyers to form a Hive Mind. We can be sure that you would have at least two of your rotations to deal with the problem. Perhaps longer, but it is important to detect their Bridgehead as quickly as possible. After the Hive Mind becomes conscious, their incursion cannot be contained."

"And the consequences if we fail to contain it?" George asked.

"Your world, your universe, would be assimilated by the Hive. Or perhaps destroyed with a time vortex to prevent this."

• 45

THE BRIDGE DETECTOR THAT IRIS HAD PROVIDED LOOKED LIKE A plain white bar of soap with a dark blue dot on one end. At some level, Alice could understand saving the universe while wielding some gleaming sword or high-tech laser bazooka, but a bar of soap? The whole idea seemed absurd. She had protested to Iris, but the child had not understood her objection.

This morning she, George, and Roger had each gone to one of the three SSC beam intersection points on the west campus to check for Hive incursions. They had found none, but it was good practice. Now they were doing the same thing for the east campus. George was surveying LEM, she was doing the SDC, and Roger was surveying the east test area used primarily for beam diagnostics.

She adjusted her grip on the detector carefully. The thing, in addition to being a sensitive detector of Bridges, contained a cutting laser that could be useful or dangerous. Its control system was crafted to interface with her new *Reading* skills. Variable molecules on its surface fed information through the molecule-sensing areas of her fingers and into the new molecular pattern-recognition centers of her brain. She somehow perceived directly what the Bridge detector sensed. At present there was no real signal from the detector, but there was perhaps a faint sniff of something as she walked toward the SDC office building.

Inside, Alice located the reception office. "Hello," she said to a secretary there, "I'm Alice Lang. I'm looking for Daniel Warren. I have an appointment."

The secretary consulted a list before her. "Oh yes," she said, "Dan said he would be waiting for you in the data analysis room. It's just down the hall to your right."

Alice found the room and entered. The inside was a mixture of conventional graphics workstations and VR-equipped recliner chairs, about half occupied by physicists wearing magic glasses and data cuffs. A tall thin man sitting at one workstation rose as she entered. "Alice?" he inquired.

She nodded.

"Hi," he said, "I'm Dan. After you called, I looked through our collection of oddball SDC events. I found something that might interest you. Have you ever used our VR gear, Alice?"

Alice assured him she had. Soon she was seated in one of the recliners and wearing magic glasses and data cuffs. She lay back, went through the calibration ritual, blinked three times, and . . .

. . . found that she was slowly falling down a deep well, the sides of which were lined with cupboards and bookshelves, with maps and pictures hung on pegs.

"Don't worry," said Dan's voice at her right ear.

She turned and could see Dan, now wearing a yellow wireframe body, falling with her.

"This is the Lewis Carroll positional interface that our SDC systems people developed," he said. "Sometimes I wonder if they actually spend any of their time trying to write useful programs, rather than amusing themselves. Watch the things on the wall as they go by. Each item is different every time."

Alice watched and wondered at the complexity of detail. Finally the fall stopped, accompanied by an appropriately loud crash from the sound system, and Alice looked around. She seemed to be standing in a heap of sticks and dry leaves. The figure of a white rabbit wearing a checkered vest was just disappearing down a passageway.

Dan's wireframe hand gestured, and they moved down the same passageway and turned a corner. Alice could see now that they were in a long low hall lit by a row of lights hanging from above. The room contained several glass and wooden tables and a great many doors. "Just how far did your programmers go in following Lewis Carroll?" she asked.

"You don't want to know," said Dan. "Don't touch anything labeled 'Drink Me' or 'Eat me." There's supposed to be a Mad Hatter, a March Hare, a Dormouse, a Caterpillar, a Cheshire Cat, a Walrus, a Carpenter, and a Mock Turtle down here somewhere. The SDC users seem to like it, but if these programmers were working directly for me I'd have packed them off to Walt Disney World long ago."

They came to an elaborately carved round door that bore the words UNUSUAL EVENTS in elaborately serifed letters. Dan's wireframe hand opened it, and they entered . . .

*   *   *

. . . and Alice found herself suspended in darkness.

"This is an event that we recorded three days ago," Dan said. "It bears some similarity to your Snark event. Here it comes . . ."

The darkness filled with the wireframe outline of a massive barrel-shaped object that Alice recognized as the SDC detector. Multicolored curving tracks emanated from a point at its central region. One track, colored a deep blue, came straight from the vertex point with no evidence of curvature and passed in a nearly horizontal trajectory through the outlined wall of the detector.

"What have you learned about this event?" asked Alice, feeling some alarm. Three days ago! That's too long. If this is the Hive's Bridgehead, it may already be too late!

"We wouldn't have paid much attention to it before we heard about your Snark," said Dan. "The blue track is very highly charged, judging from its ionization, but doesn't curve at all in our 2 Tesla magnetic field. The event's energy and momentum balance only if we exclude it. It went right through the iron-stopping wall of our detector, leaving a track in the muon counter as it passed through, and probably went into the tunnel wall. It didn't make any jets, though."

"The SSC beam is still off, right?" Alice asked. She was trying to remain calm. She remembered Iris's assurance that they would have a year before the Hive attempted a Bridge.

"Yeah," said Dan. "At last report, they're almost finished fixing the dipole in the north segment of the ring that quenched last night. They should be starting another ramp-up cycle soon."

"Could we go down to the SDC detector, then? I need to have a look at the place on the wall where that track would have hit."

"Sure," said Dan. "I can assure you there's nothing to see on that wall, but you might as well have a look at the detector itself while you have the chance. When they get the dipole fixed, they'll turn on the beam again, and there'll be no access for many days."

Alice tried to call George, setting the urgency level to maximum, but got no answer. He was probably down in the tunnel at the LEM detector, where his cellphone wouldn't work. She recorded a message telling him where she was going and suggesting that he link to an SDC remote and join her.

Ten minutes later Alice stood with Dan in the vast SDC experiment cave. Beside them was a tall remote. George had received her message, finally, and linked to an SDC remote. He said that Roger and Iris were with him, watching. His bearded face was visible on the remote's headscreen.

Dan consulted a printout and reached up to touch a spot on the wall of the concrete-lined cave wall. "As nearly as I can tell," he said, "that blue track should have hit the wall about here." He took a felt-tip pen from his pocket and drew a red x on the wall.

Alice had been getting weak positive signals from the Bridge detector ever since she had stepped out of the elevator. Now she stood on tiptoes and held the soap-bar device up to the spot. It produced a remarkable sensation. As it moved it closer to the mark, she could "see" that there was indeed a Bridgehead behind the wall. "It's here," she said, turning to the remote, "about five meters in. It must have been here for several days. What should we do now?"

The image of George on the headscreen frowned. "Hell, I guess we'll have to bore into the concrete and limestone. That won't be easy. It will interfere with accelerator operation and make a big mess next to delicate equipment. Hold on a minute. Let me ask Iris."

"I wonder if . . ." said Alice. She walked to a nearby tool board and returned with a medium-size ball-peen hammer. She began to tap the wall, starting well away from the spot of interest and working her way toward it. As she approached the red x, the tapping sound changed from a dull *thunk* to a more resonant hollow sound.

Dan looked surprised. "Let me try," he said. He took the hammer from her hand. She was too startled to protest.

"Dan, wait! . . ." said George, looking up to realize what was happening.

Dan struck the x a solid blow, and the wall crumbled like a broken eggshell, falling away to leave a jagged hole about forty centimeters across. Behind the hole was darkness.

Alice realized that Dan had never heard of the Hive. He had no idea that there was any danger.

Dan pulled a small flashlight from his pocket and shined it into the hole. He leaned forward, inserting his head in the opening. "I don't see anyth . . ." he began, and then screamed. His whole body lurched forward, and he was pulled through.

The mechanical arms of George's remote reached for Dan's feet, but missed. The remote, its work lights beaming forward, its tractor treads spinning, thrust itself into the hole after Dan. A shiny gray cylindrical pseudopod snaked out of the hole, wrapped around the remote, and pulled it inside.

"Dan! George!" Alice shouted, stepping back. It had all happened so fast. She looked around for help. There was a red alarm button on the wall nearby, and she pressed it. In the distance an alarm signal began a slow whooping sound.

She heard a loud electric-motor noise and turned. Behind her another remote was driving in her direction on an electric vehicle containing a large cylindrical gray tank. As the vehicle stopped before the hole, she recognized the face of George on the headscreen.

"I switched to another remote," he said. "Dan is dead. Cut to pieces and dissolved into the floor, along with my remote." The remote rolled around the tank and uncoiled a long steel-mesh-covered hose. "Liquid nitrogen," he said. He rolled to the hole and began to direct a stream of the clear cryogenic liquid inside. Alice had a feeling of *déjà vu*.

Clouds of steamlike condensed water vapor poured out of the opening, obscuring Alice's view. She held out the Bridge detector. The Bridgehead was still in the place where she had first detected it. "George," she said, "can you tell me what's going on?"

"The Hive sent a Bridge through the SDC and planted it behind the cave wall. By manipulating through the Bridge, they've put together nanomachine assemblers, and they've had several days to build Hive Workers. Iris thinks there's a good chance that there hasn't been enough time for the Hive Mind to become conscious. Something grabbed Dan and my remote and disassembled us for molecular spare parts, but perhaps that was an automatic response of the nanomachines. I didn't get much of a look before the remote link broke, but there are structures in there and what look like folded-up dormant insects."

"Perhaps those are the Workers," said Alice.

"I'm hoping this liquid nitrogen will lower the temperature enough to immobilize the nanomachines," George said. "It's our only hope of stopping this. Alice, you'll have to help. I can't use a Bridge detector through a remote. I want you to go down the cave about fifty meters to the left. When you come to a sign on the wall that says 'Cryogenics,' there should be a cabinet with some cryo-protection suits and respirators. Put on a cryo-suit and come back here as quickly as you can."

Alice raced down the cave. She returned wearing a silvery cryo-suit. The remote, the headscreen now dim, was frozen in a fixed position, still hosing liquid nitrogen into the hole. Another remote bearing George's image on the headscreen stood near a smaller cryogenic dewar. It was swinging a sledgehammer to enlarge the opening, which now looked like a tunnel.

"Now," said George's voice from the remote, "we're ready to try. I'll go in first. However, you'll have to use your Bridge detector. What you have to do is find the Hive's Bridgehead and tell me where it is, so I can put it into this liquid helium dewar. If we can do that, everything will be okay."

"Okay," Alice said doubtfully. The remote turned off the flow of nitrogen, approached the tunnel, and rolled inside, carrying the small liquid helium dewar with it. Alice followed, crawling carefully through the rough opening, her one ungloved hand holding the Bridge detector before her. Once inside she was able to stand. It was hard to see much because of the mist of condensed water vapor left by the liquid nitrogen, and her ungloved hand felt very cold. There was a huge rounded area behind the wall lined with strange organic-looking structures. Along one side Alice could see the huge dormant insectlike creatures George had mentioned. They seemed to be frozen in place. The floor felt yielding, jellylike. Alice touched the floor and *Read*. She realized that the surface was lined with tiny molecular machines programmed to disassemble whatever they met and reconstruct it into something else. They had been shut down by the low temperature. These things had killed and dissolved Dan. She felt sick at the thought.

Alice crawled forward to a rough stone extrusion that extended up from the floor like a stalagmite. Scanning it with her detector, she sensed the Bridgehead just within its tip. "It's here," she said, pointing. "Now what?"

"Okay," said George, "lock the laser cutting beam in the 'on' state and hand me the Bridge detector. Then move back."

She activated the cutting laser in the Bridge detector, carefully pointing the intense blue beam down the tunnel, and held it out. George's remote took the device from her and extended its jointed arm to the stalagmite, using its other arm to hold the mouth of the liquid helium-filled dewar just below the point that she had indicated. The bright blue beam began to slice into the limestone, making white sparks. Suddenly a blinding green flash overwhelmed the blue of the laser. Alice was flung back by the shock wave.

"Shit!" said George's voice. "The thing was booby-trapped." As her eyes readjusted, she could see that both of the remote's arms had been burned off, the detector was gone, and the dewar lay broken and steaming some distance away. "It's a trap!" said George. "The Hive Mind is conscious. Get out, Alice! Run!"

As she backed out of the tunnel, she could see that the insectoid forms along the wall were beginning to move. Outside the opening she grabbed the hose of the liquid nitrogen tank and shoved it into the hole, cranked the valve to full open, then tore off her respirator hood. Should she shed the rest of the suit? Her eyes caught movement from the tunnel. She glanced around for another possible weapon, but saw none. George's last word finally connected with her legs and she began to run for the elevator.

Halfway there, she turned for a quick look. The scene evoked images from a Hieronymus Bosch painting she'd once seen in Madrid. Emerging from the tunnel were a hellish variety of shapes and forms that walked, flowed, squirmed, flew, rolled, and slithered from the opening. Prominent among them were large black insectoid forms with sharply spiked bodies and large cruel pincer jaws. Somehow she knew that these were Hive Soldiers. They ran toward her on six legs, with two smaller legs extended forward, grasping strange tessellated objects. Another remote with George's image on the headscreen darted out from a charger bay and tried to intercept them. One insect grasped the machine in its jaws and tossed it sideways. The remote hit the wall with a loud crash and was still.

"I can't believe this," Alice she said to herself. "This isn't happening." She kicked off the clumsy boots of the cryo-suit and ran barefoot across the painted concrete floor.

She had almost reached the sanctuary of the open elevator door when the Hive Soldiers caught her.

• 46

WHEN GEORGE HAD RECEIVED ALICE'S MESSAGE, HE, ROGER, AND Iris had rushed to the LEM data analysis room so that he could connect to an SDC remote and they could watch.

Now Roger tore off the glasses and stared at the others in horror. "My God! They've killed Alice!" he said.

"Yes, she's dead," said George. "There was nothing I could do." He put his hands over his face.

Roger straightened slowly, struggling to calm himself after the grisly spectacle he had just witnessed. He walked across and placed his hand on George's shoulder. "We understand, George," he said. "We were watching. There was nothing more you could do."

Iris walked over and put her hand against George's cheek. Roger wondered if she was doing something to calm him. "The Hive Mind was just reaching sentience," she said. "We almost succeeded. It's a tragic loss, George, but only the first of many millions. We Makers were naive to assume that we had a year to prepare before the Hive arrived. They modified their tactics, probably in response to our previous successes. On your planet, we have failed to stop the Hive incursion. The Hive will now assimilate your world."

"We need to warn people," said George, taking out his cellphone.

"That would be futile," said Iris. "The entire human race will be dead by tomorrow. Warning your people would have no effect."

"But surely there must be a way to stop it," said George. "Suppose a hydrogen bomb were detonated at the SDC site . . . ?"

"It would have little effect," said Iris. "A Bridge is a topological defect in space itself, and it represents a Planck-scale concentration of energy. It cannot be removed by some minor energy discharge at the nuclear scale. Moreover, by now the Hive Mind has surely dispersed itself far enough to withstand any local act of destruction." She paused, her head cocked to one side as if listening, then spoke slowly and deliberately. "There is one further thing we can attempt that might stop the Hive. We had expected to have more time. We've made no preparations for it, and it is at best a desperate measure. It will require a very large electrical power source."

"How large?" asked George through gritted teeth. He was crying. Roger fished a handkerchief from his backpack and handed it to George, frustrated that this was all he could do.

"In your units of energy flow, perhaps two hundred megawatts at a bare minimum," said Iris. "We have studied the design of the SSC and have determined that there is such a power source associated with it."

"Yes," George said in a choked voice. "That's about the size of the magnet power supply for the injector synchrotron." He wiped his eyes with Roger's handkerchief, blew his nose, and sniffed.

"Then we must go to it immediately," said Iris. "The Hive tends to ignore mechanical infrastructure in its initial attack, but we must get there while the power supply is still operating."

"The problem is," said George, straightening, "we're here on the east campus of the ring and the injector is in a tunnel at the west campus. We'll have to drive across."

Roger shouldered his backpack and led the way as they walked quickly to the lobby of the LEM building. His car was just outside in the parking lot. But before the wall of glass in the building lobby he halted abruptly. Looking south toward the SDC building, he saw that the air around it was a dirty gray. In the distance large dark shapes were moving. Outside the glass they could see small metallic-looking flying insects landing on the concrete and shrubbery.

"Pandora's box has been opened," said Iris. "The Troubles are abroad in your world. Those creatures are Hive Flyers. The assimilation of your world is beginning. Their touch brings instant death."

"Could we make it to the west campus in my car through that?" asked Roger. He doubted it.

"No," said George, suddenly alert. "I have a better idea. Come on." He led them to the building's deep elevator. Inside the car he pushed the button that would take them down to the LEM detector itself, two hundred meters below the surface. "We can reach the west campus through the ring," he explained.

"But that would take all day," Roger objected. "The circumference of the ring is eighty-six kilometers. Halfway around is forty-three kilometers, a good day's hike."

"Yes," said George, "and because it's so far they have a fast little monorail system to take the engineers and technicians and hardware around the ring when the beam is off. We can use that."

The doors opened to reveal the LEM detector. George's access card got them through three security doors and into the SSC tunnel itself. Not far away a yellow vehicle, like a wheelless pickup truck, hung from a siding rail mounted on the ceiling. They climbed in, and George engaged the drive mechanism and swerved out onto the main railing. The vehicle began to move backward, truckbed first and passenger area behind. It accelerated until it was backing up at about 70 kilometers per hour.

"We're going by the north side of the ring, in the direction that avoids the SDC detector area," George said.

Roger nodded.

"Okay, Iris," George said, "we have about half an hour before we get to the other side, assuming the power stays on. You'd better explain your plan to us. What is it you want to do?"

The beautiful child smiled. "We will try to deliberately create a time vortex, what your quantum field theorists call a 'timelike loop' or a 'Cauchy horizon,' " she said. "The vortex will destroy your present universe, unravel it to a point in the past, and produce a new history in which the Hive does not create a Bridge and your world is safe."

"Do you mean you want to build a time machine and change the past, to rewrite history?" said Roger. "I thought that was . . ."

". . . impossible?" Iris finished. "In a way, it is. Creating a time vortex produces a catastrophic condition that is usually considered unacceptable. It destroys the part of the universe in which the loop is created."

"How can that be?" asked Roger.

"You are a field theorist, Roger," said Iris. "Surely you know about path integrals."

Roger nodded. "Only too well," he said.

"What happens when the space-time interval along the path goes to zero?" Iris asked.

"Oh, you mean the self-energy term," said Roger. "That's certainly a problem. It makes a singularity. The energy goes to infinity. We've learned to renormalize the theory by subtracting those infinities away. I should add that we always feel uncomfortable about doing that, but it works."

"You subtract the singularity for a particle acting on itself, with zero interval between the particle and itself," said Iris. "But suppose there was also another path that had a zero interval, a net zero space-time distance. What would you do then?''

''Another? There can't be, because . . .'' He stopped. ''Oh, I see. With a wormhole back through time, you can make the negative time-like part cancel the positive spacelike part, so the net interval goes to zero. That would produce a very nasty singularity that probably couldn't be disposed of by subtraction.'' He smiled with the pleasure of a new idea, then frowned. ''You're suggesting that the resulting singularity destroys the universe?''

Iris nodded. ''It does indeed. We Makers have done it. Fluctuations in the vacuum are amplified and build up until all paths within the timelike loop acquire arbitrarily large energies. The part of the universe that is threaded by the loop is destroyed. History is nullified and must form again from the earliest point of the loop. That is what a time vortex is.''

''Hold it,'' said George. ''How can you destroy only part of a universe?''

''I suppose 'destroys' gives the wrong impression,'' said Iris. ''Perhaps 'unraveled' provides a better metaphor. Or consider it as the 'rewind and restart' of a recording. All events related to the existence of the time vortex are nullified, as if they never happened, and are replaced by new causal sequences that do not contain the loop.''

''You mean that we can go back to a time when Alice is still alive?'' George asked. He looked a bit wild-eyed, Roger thought.

''Yes,'' Iris replied, ''of course.''

''Wait a moment,'' said Roger. ''Are you talking about moving back to some alternate-branch Everett-Wheeler universe?''

Iris laughed. ''Since we established contact with your culture, many Individuals of our world, particularly our science metahistorian specialists, have derived great amusement from your quantum mythology, that area which you call the 'interpretation of quantum mechanics.' They were particularly amused by your Copenhagen interpretation, with its state vectors that are altered by the thoughts of intelligent observers, and by your Everett-Wheeler interpretation, with its splitting and resplitting into multiple universes. In this regard, your culture is unique among those that we have encountered. No other has provided such a remarkable demonstration of fertile creative desperation in seeking to understand physical behavior at the quantum level. We find these myths of yours quaint and charming.''

"In other words, 'wrong'?" asked Roger.

Iris looked troubled. "No more wrong, say, than your Greek or Norse myths. Your excursions of scientific fantasy are an interesting manifestation of your culture, but they are not an accurate portrayal of the behavior of the universe. Human observers, for example, are not demigods with the ability to collapse a wave function with an act of measurement or of insight. It is better that they are not, believe me."

"I'm not sure where this is leading," said George, "or what it has to do with our present predicament. I gather that you were in the process of saying that there is a way of—how did you put it?—nullifying the Hive's discovery of our universe."

"Pardon me, George," said Iris. "Yes, that's what I was saying. This universe, all Bubbles individually and all of them together, moves forward in time at the quantum level by a chain of handshakes between past and future. The psi-star time-reversed wave functions of your formulation of quantum mechanics, though you have never realized it, represent the future reaching back to make an accommodation with the past that allows a quantum event to happen, to become reality. Each quantum event emerges into reality as the result of a feedback loop between past and future. These are allowed timelike loops that bring the universe into being.

"If we create an artificial timelike loop back to some point of spacetime within the negative light cone of the present, we create a condition that nullifies all of those handshakes, those transactions between future and past. The events within the loop are in effect erased or unraveled and the universe starts over from the first instant where the forbidden loop would have begun to exist. The universe is wounded and heals itself with a new set of handshakes that do not bring a timelike loop into being. Nature, as your ancient Greek natural philosophers might have said, abhors a time machine.

"We will attempt to create a time-hole back to an era from which you can prevent the SSC from being built. If we can achieve that, then your world, your Bubble, will be safe from the Hive."

"Why do we need to stop the SSC project?" George asked. "If the universe really reforms without the timelike loop, why do we need to do anything more? Won't the universe heal itself to take care of the Hive problem?"

"Not necessarily," said Iris. "There are many paths that could lead to the absence of a timelike loop. For example, your SSC is built and the Hive discovers your world, but we do not."

"Does this time vortex thing really work?" asked Roger. "You've actually done it before?"

"We have been making contact with other Bubbles for a dozen gross of orbits, over seventeen of your centuries. For about the last half of that period, we have had to deal with the Hive civilization. In our last eight contacts, we were able to provide isolation from the Hive in five cases, and we had to create timelike loops in two cases. The other case was lost to the Hive altogether."

"I don't understand," said George. "How could you know that you created the loop if it erases its own existence? Wouldn't it erase its traces in your world, too?"

"Excellent question," said Iris. "As a part of the process of creating the loop, we transmit a complete record to our past. In this way we know what has happened and also preserve all the new information we gained from the contact."

They had come to a maintenance station, and their way was blocked by another vehicle on the rail. George brought their truck to a stop, and they got out.

"Well, if it ain't George and Roger," said a voice. "Howdy!"

George turned.

It was Whitey, dressed in blue SSC coveralls and carrying a tool-box. "You folks have any idea what in God's Creation is goin' on round here?" he asked. "The diagnostics say that all hell is breakin' loose on the east side of the ring, and nobody will answer my phone calls."

"Hell is indeed breaking loose," said George. "Poisonous insect things have invaded the ring and the above-ground area too. The people that don't answer your calls are probably dead. Alice is dead, too. We're trying to get to the west campus to try to do something about it."

"Alice is dead?" Whitey exclaimed. "What . . . ? How . . . ?" His face turned the color of his pale blond hair, and he seemed to shrink.

"Here, let me," said Iris. She stepped forward and placed her right hand on Whitey's cheek. His dazed expression slowly vanished, to be replaced by a look of calm determination.

"The Hive has invaded your world," said Iris.

"Yes'm," said Whitey.

"We are trying to stop this."

"Yes'm."

"We would like you to help us, if you're willing."

"I surely am, ma'am," said Whitey. "Just tell me what to do."

"We need to get to the injector synchrotron power supply complex," said George. "We need to get there fast."

"Then follow me," said Whitey. He led them to his monorail vehicle, which was pointed west. The truckbed was loaded with supplies, including cans of solvent and steel industrial gas cylinders in a variety of colors.

As they were climbing into the service vehicle, Roger glanced up the vertical shaft leading to the surface. "Look!" he said and pointed. At the top of the shaft, illuminated by floodlights, was a gray haze. A cloud of Hive Flyers was just entering the upper part of the shaft.

Whitey moved the controls, and the vehicle moved rapidly down the tunnel.

"Those Flyer creatures are spreading fast," said Roger, looking back. "How many more maintenance stations do we pass before we reach the west campus?"

Whitey consulted a diagram on the dashboard. "Two more to go," he said. "No, hold on. There's a branch beamline tunnel leading up to the injector. We can stop there and walk up the tunnel. That means we only have to pass one more maintenance station."

• 47

BELINDA STROLLED ALONG THE BANK OF THE LITTLE BROOK THAT meandered through the SSC west campus. She had worked with the architect who designed the campus and had watched him lay out the path of the brook on a CAD machine. She had transmitted the work order to the company that dug its path and lined it with fieldstones. She knew at one level that this was a man-made "amenity" of the landscape design, no different from a streetlight or a parking lot. Nevertheless, it certainly looked and felt natural and wholesome, and she always felt refreshed when she walked along it at lunchtime.

She climbed the spiral path of the cafeteria hill. The building was perched atop a grassy knoll, also artificial, that overlooked the rest of the campus. The place was less busy than usual. Just before her lunch break started, Belinda had heard that there was some problem at the east campus. The phone lines were down or something. Perhaps some of the people who usually ate lunch here were off working on the problem.

At the salad bar Belinda assembled a tall creation in the boat-shaped bowl and anointed it with low-cal dressing, extracted a Diet Coke from the refrigerated case, and paid the cashier. Looking around the table area, she didn't see any of her friends, so she selected a small table against the broad window that looked east across the campus in the direction of Waxahachie. It was a clear day, and she could make out the courthouse tower and two church steeples on the horizon.

As she ate her salad, she thought about the recent events at the SSC laboratory. The Snark business had made a lot of extra work for her, with news media calling every day wanting more information. She had been transmitting dozens of video clips per day for a while. She had even arranged a press conference in which reporters had interviewed the Tunnel Maker creature through the wormhole itself. But now the media interest in the Snark seemed to be dying down, and she was glad. Alien contact had been exciting for a while, but she would be glad to get back to the routine of high-energy physics, which was the real business of the laboratory.

A bright flash on the horizon attracted her attention, and she looked up. The sky had turned a dirty gray in the direction of Waxahachie. The courthouse was no longer visible, but dark shapes seemed to be moving against the background of the darkening sky. The delayed *whump* of something like a thunderclap rattled the glass cafeteria walls. Was a storm front approaching? It didn't look like any storm she had ever seen.

Belinda touched the crystal pendant at her breast. Her horoscope in the *Dallas Morning News* this morning had warned her to expect an unpleasant change. She wondered what was happening out there.

Suddenly the public address system in the cafeteria came on. It was carrying a radio news broadcast apparently in progress. Belinda glanced around the large room. Everyone in the cafeteria had stopped eating and talking and had turned in the direction of the wall speaker. She heard the familiar voice of the radio news reporter who usually reported on the freeway traffic from a helicopter. The clacking of the helicopter engine could be heard in the background. "We still have no reports from the ground of what is going on," the reporter was saying. "Communications with the Texas Ranger we were interviewing at the I-45 roadblock have been cut off.

"To recapitulate for those of you who may have just tuned in, a problem of unknown origin has developed south of Dallas along the I-45 corridor. It seems to be localized in the Palmer-Waxahachie-Ennis area. An expanding gray cloud is hovering over the whole area. Speculations of a chemical spill are being denied by chemical producers in the region that could be reached. No traffic is emerging from the problem region, no radio or telephone communication inside the region can be established, and the Texas Rangers have set up roadblocks in the major arterials to turn back traffic attempting to enter the area until the problem is identified. We are told that there is no cause for alarm, but that Interstate 45 is blocked in both directions and plans to drive into the area south of Dallas should be postponed. Please to not attempt to use your telephone to call people you know who live there. The telephone lines are already overloaded, and we have determined that calls do not go through due to some problem with the telephone system."

Belinda noticed that several people stood and walked quickly to the wall telephones in the lobby.

"Here's a bulletin. The Texas Rangers report no, repeat, no evidence of radioactivity or dangerous chemical agents at the edges of the problem area. Reports that the Superconducting Super Collider has exploded are also being denied."

Belinda blinked. Somebody thinks the SSC exploded? The office telephones must be ringing up a storm. I'd better get back to the office, she thought. She quickly finished her salad, gulped down the last of the Diet Coke, and slid her tray into the rack. As she walked toward the exit along with several other people, she noticed that the gray cloud from the east seemed nearer.

"Here's another bulletin," said the reporter. "The governor has requested that all members of the Texas National Guard in the Dallas-Fort Worth area report to their headquarters units immediately."

Belinda stopped by the cafeteria exit and listened. Others pushed past her and hurried outside.

"Okay, folks," said the reporter, "we've finally received authorization from the D/FW air traffic controller to fly over the problem area and have a look-see. Here we go. I can see down below us that the traffic on Interstate 45 is completely stalled. There are stopped cars all over the freeway and many collisions. Some of the cars are burning. I can see some bodies. None of them are moving. There seem to be some large black things moving among the cars.''

What in the world is it? Belinda wondered. Some kind of nerve gas attack? It sounds worse than what happened in Bangkok last year.

''We're flying toward the densest part of the gray cloud now,'' the reporter said. ''It seems to be centered north of Ennis. Something is hitting our front window now. They seem to be small silvery objects with wings, perhaps flying insects. Maybe I can catch one. They . . .''

The voice stopped, and shortly afterward the helicopter engine noise halted. Another voice came on the radio. ''We're having technical difficulties. Please stay tuned,'' it said.

Belinda hurried through the cafeteria door and walked rapidly down the walkway, away from the parking lot where others seemed to be hurrying. Along the gravel path by the brook something was rustling in the trees. It looked like a swarm of metallic insects. One of them landed on her arm. Belinda reached down to brush it off and froze in midstride.

She fell into darkness.

• 48

ROGER HAD ARGUED WITH THE OTHERS ABOUT HOW TO APPROACH the last maintenance station. He and Whitey wanted to blast through at top speed. George suggested approaching more slowly. Iris favored George's strategy and finally convinced Roger and Whitey. When they reached the station, Whitey turned off the vehicle's running lights and eased the truck forward at low speed, listening.

As they reached the edge of the shaft, Roger heard a buzz. Looking upward, he saw a new swarm of Hive Flyers, these much lower. The maintenance truck moved slowly across the open area beneath the shaft. Near the top of the opening, Roger could see large dark shapes moving down the walls of the shaft. He thought of Alice, and felt a sinking fear.

The Flyers ignored them at first. Then, as if reaching some consensus, the swarm began to drop down the shaft. Whitey pushed the accelerator control all the way forward and the vehicle began to pick up speed.

George took the Bridge detector from his pocket and pointed it like a weapon at the wall above the double line of long cylindrical dipole magnets that made a two-layer stack on the right side of the tunnel. The bright blue cutting beam sprang from the device, and he slashed it downward, first through cryogenic plumbing above the magnets, and then through the thin-walled magnet cylinders themselves.

The magnets of the great accelerator contained large reservoirs of cryogenic liquids, a reservoir of liquid helium encased in a blanket of liquid nitrogen. The ultra-cold fluids exploded outward into the tunnel behind the speeding vehicle. Roger looked backward at the steam clouds of condensed water vapor produced by the outpouring of ultra-cold. Through the steam clouds he could see the Hive Flyers hit the wall of ultra-cold gas and drop to the floor of the tunnel. "The SSC will never be the same," Roger said.

In another ten minutes they had reached the injection line branch, where the beam from the injector joined the main SSC ring. Whitey halted the vehicle, and they climbed out. He looked back down the tunnel. "Those damn critters will be here soon," he said. "I'd better wait right here and stop 'em." He walked to the back of the truck and began to unload gas cylinders.

"You can't do that," said Iris. "Their merest touch would be fatal. There's nothing you can do."

Whitey smiled. "Oh yes there is, ma'am. I was a demolition specialist in the Marine Corps durin' the Gulf War. I know how to blow the hell outta things better'n just about anybody. These gas bottles are full'a hydrogen, oxygen, and methane. And the truck carries big cans of acetone, xylene, and alcohol. For solvents, y'know? Just give me a few minutes, and I can rig a pretty nice reception for those Hive critters when they come down the tunnel. I'm just sorry you folks can't stay to enjoy the fireworks. But you'd better get on with your bidness and leave me to do mine.

"Go on now. Get on up that branch tunnel. Time's a'wastin'."

They shook hands with Whitey, and George led the way up the sloping tunnel. Finally they reached the injector itself, which was buried in a curving tunnel at a higher level. George led the way along the curving walls to the injector power supply room, a stubby cylinder carved into the Austin Chalk stratum.

He pointed to the large motor-generators that towered above them, making a high whining noise as they spun. "These," he said, "turn huge vacuum-enclosed flywheels. The SSC injector is made of normal nonsuperconducting magnets that receive the beam and dump energy from the flywheels to the magnetic fields as they ramp up to accelerate it. Then they eject the beam and ramp back down, putting most of the stored energy from the magnetic fields back into the flywheels. The energy flows back and forth like that, with new energy from the power lines brought in continuously to make up for the losses due to bearing friction, coil resistance, and eddy currents. You'll find more electrical energy available here than anywhere else in the whole accelerator, even though this is only the injector part. Most of the rest of the power goes into the cryogenics distributed all around the ring."

Iris held her fingers about two centimeters apart. "I will need a gap about this size across which the electrical energy will flow," she said above the whine of the generators.

George nodded and led the way across the room to an area that was surrounded by a wire fence. His blue laser beam chewed through the lock on the gate. Inside the gate he moved a long aluminum shorting pole out of the way and walked to the back wall of the enclosure. "This is the area," he said, "where, in case of an electrical emergency, the total electrical energy of the machine can be dumped into a dummy load, a large tank filled with water that is vaporized by the dumped energy and vented off. If I cut here and here"—he indicated two thick copper bus bars—"and bend them to form a gap, you'll have what you want. See the button over there?" He indicated a large red button with a glass cover outside the cage. "It triggers thyristors that will dump all the power here. Shall I do it?"

Iris nodded. George cut the copper bars with the laser, then found a large wrench and bent them until their shiny cut surfaces were separated by about two centimeters, held at that gap by a scrap of plastic insulation.

Then he walked outside the cage to the red button. He removed the plastic cover so that the button was exposed. "We need a way to push this to dump the power."

"Do not concern yourself. I will deal with that," said Iris.

As she spoke, there was a very bright flash of light, followed shortly by a deep and very loud *whump* sound from the branch tunnel.

"Whitey was a good man," said Roger.

Iris walked to the distorted bus bars, and her face contorted. She extracted a small pink sphere from her mouth. It seemed to have flecks of bright red blood on it. "This is the Bridgehead I have carried," she said. "My contact with the Makers is broken for the first time. It is very strange to be so alone. You humans must be very strong to bear it continuously." She placed the sphere on the block of plastic in the gap.

"Now let me explain," she said. "When you trigger the discharge, this Bridgehead will momentarily expand. At the same time, its twin Bridgehead in the scintillator unit on the other side of the ring will be connected to a new fluctuation Bridge extracted from the quantum vacuum of your Bubble, a Bridge selected because it spans an interval about seventeen of your years into the past. The two Bridgeheads in the Maker Universe will be joined and their connection with the Maker Bubble released. This will be done all in one operation.

"The result will be the creation of a Bridge that makes a timelike loop, one Bridgehead here and the other about seventeen years in your past. This Bridgehead here will expand and dissipate as the singularity forms and goes to completion. During this process, because the singularity annihilates the intervening space-time, both Bridgeheads will momentarily be in the same place. If we succeed, since the present no longer exists, you will be propelled back through the Bridge to the beginning of the loop, to the site of the Bridgehead in the past."

"You say 'you,' not 'we,' " said George. "Aren't you coming with us?"

"I cannot," said Iris. "This body is a temporary thing, and its processes were regulated through the Bridgehead that I carried. That link is now broken, and I am dying. It is well. I would not be able to bear this isolation if I could not see its end approaching. If you stand close to the Bridgehead, within about five meters, you should be projected through the time-hole. I will go and press the red button that starts the process." She turned and walked toward the fence gate.

"But," Roger objected, "we're a hundred meters underground. If we arrive at a time where there's no SSC tunnel down here, we'll be trapped in solid limestone."

Iris stopped. "The other Bridgehead will not be located here," she said. "I suggested to our engineers that the Bridgehead in the past should be located at the site where you hatched my Egg. We have good coordinates for that location. You will be deposited above the water there and will have to swim to shore.''

''I'm not a great swimmer,'' said Roger, ''and the water will ruin my computer. Let me make a float.'' He raced across the room, grabbed a large plastic garbage bag from a workbench, and returned to the enclosure. He removed his backpack, placed it in the bag, and knotted the end, trapping considerable air inside. He held this to his chest.

''Then prepare yourselves,'' said Iris. She walked to the gate, then paused by the door. ''I hear something outside.'' She moved closer to the closed door and stood listening. ''Hive creatures,'' she said.

As Roger watched, the door seemed to melt. Behind it was a gray fog. Hive Flyers and a myriad of other creatures began to fly or crawl into the room. ''I cannot destroy them, but perhaps I can delay them,'' Iris said. ''I am sorry, but one of you will have to press the red button.'' The child stood before them, her palms extended forward. Hive creatures touched her and dropped to the floor. Soon there was a large pile at her feet. Behind the open doorway large dark shapes were moving forward. Roger would remember those shapes in his nightmares. ''You go on, George,'' he said. ''I'll stay and press the button.''

George grabbed Roger's shoulder and stopped him. Then he picked up the long metal shorting pole that lay on the floor, fed it through the wire mesh of the caged-off area, and shoved its end against the red button.

There was a blinding blue-green flash, and the universe ended.

PART VII

February 3, 1987

August 15, 1992

*I doubt if there is a member of the Senate who really
understands to any degree what the SSC is all about . . .
Everything from the computer to television has come as a
result of high-energy physics undertaken in this country.
Between 20 percent and 30 percent of the gross national
product of the United States comes from high-energy physics.*
—Senator Phil Gramm (R.-Texas)

*[The SSC] will revolutionize the computer industry, the
medical community, and transform our industrial and
technological base. Economic opportunities never anticipated
will arise, scientific advancements never predicted will proceed,
and educational worlds never explored will emerge. Even if the
original scientific goals are not completely met, the knowledge
gained will completely change our lives.*
—Senator David Boren (D.-Oklahoma)

*The only thing colliding in the land under Texas will be
taxpayer dollars.*
—Congressman Dennis Eckart (D.-Ohio)

February 15, 1993

*[There is] no reason why we have to find the Higgs boson by
the turn of the century.*
—Dr. John H. Gibbons, Clinton Presidential Science Advisor,
justifying Clinton's stretchout and cost boost of the SSC project.

October 13, 1993

We're going to whip their ass.
—Congressman Sherwood Boehlert (R.-New York) commenting on
his planned floor fight in the House to kill the SSC project.

• 49

ROGER FELL INTO DARKNESS, EMBRACING HIS PLASTIC-WRAPPED backpack as he fell. As his back hit the water, there was a tremendous splash beside him. Some of the concrete floor must have come along with them, he thought. A great wave of water washed over him, thrusting him sideways, sucking him deep.

The Gulf water felt bathtub-warm and tasted salty. His head and back hit the sandy bottom hard, but he was able to right himself and push upward toward the surface. When his head broke the water's surface, he was pleased to find that his plastic-wrapped pack had enough buoyancy to support him. He coughed, then shouted hoarsely for George. There was no answer.

Roger looked around. Moonlight sparkled on the water and lights of the shoreline were visible in the distance. He attempted to stand, extended his feet downward, but the water was too deep, and his head went under. Sneezing water, he removed his water-heavy shoes and socks, shoved the socks in his jeans pockets, tied the shoelaces together, and hung his shoes around his neck. Then, embracing the pack, he began to kick in the direction of the shore. After about ten minutes of kicking, he tested the depth again. This time he could stand on the bottom. He dragged his legs through the water toward the shore. A large wave broke over him, knocking him down, but he righted himself and continued.

Finally Roger staggered out of the water and sat down on an inverted plastic bucket that someone had left on the beach. A full moon was overhead, and the moonlight gleamed across the water. He undressed, wrung the salty water from his clothes, and put them back on. He was a bit cold, but it was not too bad because the air was fairly warm. "George!" he called again. "Where are you?"

To his left he heard a call in the distance. In the moonlight he could see George walking toward him down the beach.

"Well, I see you managed to stay afloat, Roger," George said. "I'm glad the Makers didn't place their Bridgehead any higher. I hit the water pretty hard."

"As did I," said Roger, removing the plastic cover and shouldering his backpack. "Time travel, so far, has been an unpleasant soggy business."

The stilt house they had rented seventeen years in the future was not there. In its place was only a weedy lot bearing a BEACHFRONT PROPERTY FOR SALE sign. Roger found a yellowed newspaper in the tall weeds. He was able to read it fairly well in the bright moonlight. The masthead said HOUSTON CHRONICLE, FRIDAY, JANUARY 30, 1987. He laughed aloud, for a small article in the lower left-hand corner of the front page bore the headline REAGAN ANNOUNCES SUPER COLLI-DER. He could barely make out the text. It said the machine would cost $4.4 billion and be completed in 1996. He showed it to George.

"Ah yes," said George, "it all comes back. Reagan's Department of Energy got the project started with an amazingly low cost estimate that left out inflation and the cost of the detectors. The damn thing actually cost eight billion dollars and wasn't up and running until 2003. Congress was rather unpleasant about that."

They walked eastward on the beach toward the lights of Galveston and came to an impromptu picnic table made from a battered sheet of sun-bleached plywood.

"Wait a bit," said Roger. "I think we should stop here and do an inventory. I suggest we put all our possessions on this table and see what we've brought with us."

It was an interesting collection. There were two Bridge detectors, useless as detectors but fully functional as cutting lasers. George's Swiss Army knife with the toothpick missing showed dark red in the moonlight. Two key rings held keys that would not fit any existing locks, and George's had a car door lock remote control that would not be manufactured for another ten years. The eight credit cards and chip cards all had issue and expiration dates in the twenty-first century. There was $423 in U.S. currency, all signed by a Treasury Secretary who had not yet been appointed and bearing series marks of printings starting with the year 2000. There were various coins, most with dates of issue later than 1987. Roger's British passport had been issued in 2002 and his INS green card was dated 2004. George's Washington State driver's license with picture ID had an issue date of 2003 and an expiration date of 2008, sealed with a hologram. There were two personal cellphones that no longer functioned and two digital databank wristwatches that, on close inspection, were clear anachronisms. Roger's backpack contained the most glaring anachronism of all, his personal high performance lapstation containing several terabytes of stored programs and holo-ROM books and data that included the level-one download from the Makers.

"Some of this stuff is grounds for arrest on charges of counterfeiting or fraud," said George. "The money looks like high-quality counterfeiting that somehow got the dates wrong. And the credit cards are just as bad."

"The question," said Roger, "is what to keep."

George returned the knife and cutting laser to his pocket, put his watch back on, and looked at his driver's license. "I think I'll keep this," he said.

"Okay," Roger shrugged, "and I must keep my lapstation, too. It's not a crime to possess a computer that nobody is making yet, even if it's the most powerful computer presently on the planet." He used his hand to dig a hole in the beach sand. He placed the currency, key rings, postdated coins, credit cards and chip cards, passport, green card, cellphones, and a few other items into the depression. George added his SSC key card. Roger fanned the cutting laser over the objects. The blaze sparkled colorfully for a time, then quickly subsided to a pile of glowing slag. Roger kicked sand over the hole, feeling depressed. It seemed that he had systematically erased all of the important events of his life, leaving himself an empty vessel with no past and no future.

In silence they walked along the beach for a while. "We need funds," said Roger finally. "That's the key to everything else. Otherwise we're beach bums. Perhaps we could use the laser to cut open a vending machine to get some money. Or perhaps get currency from an automatic teller machine."

"We're not that desperate," said George. "At least, not yet. Besides, we'd do unnecessary damage and probably trigger an automatic alarm that would end us up in jail. With no way of identifying ourselves or explaining our existence here, we might just stay in jail permanently."

Roger nodded. "We have the ability to *Write*," he said. "Perhaps we could *Write* a plant that grows duplicates of hundred-dollar bills instead of leaves."

"That's also a crime," said George, "and when the fake money was noticed by federal agents it would attract a lot of unwanted attention. They'd probably track us down. We need to make something that isn't illegal and that has intrinsic value in itself. Perhaps we could *Write* a device that would duplicate objects of value, maybe computer chips.'' He looked at a jellyfish washed up on the beach. ''Or maybe I could modify some filter-feeding organism like a jellyfish so that it extracts gold from seawater for us.''

Roger considered this. ''I'm afraid there isn't that much gold *in* seawater. Even if the organism had a large surface area, a perfect extraction procedure, and a high flow rate, it would take months or years to accumulate a quantity of gold that had any significant value. But you've given me an idea, George.''

He walked down the sand to the remains of a beach bonfire and picked up a lump of charcoal. ''It wouldn't be difficult,'' he said, ''to *Write* a nanomachine that reorganizes these carbon atoms into a face-centered cubic crystal lattice structure with a two-atom basis.''

''Carbon crystal structure?'' George asked. ''You mean graphite?''

''No,'' said Roger, ''I mean diamonds.''

At 9:01 the following morning, Roger entered the EZ Pawn pawnshop at the corner of Rosenberg and Broadway. He and George had walked for miles along the seawall as the sun was coming up, watching the antique trolleys pass but lacking the carfare to ride them. Finally the trolley tracks turned away from the beach, and they followed them to the intersection that Roger remembered, marked by a tall monument to the Heroes of the Texas Revolution done in florid Victorian style and the long blue awning of a pawnshop.

Roger was tired, hungry, damp, needed a shave, and itched in many places from salt on his skin. ''Good morning, sir,'' he said brightly to the blue-jacketed man behind the glass display counter.

The man nodded at Roger and smiled. ''Howdy,'' he said. ''What can I do for you, friend?''

He looks like Clint Eastwood, Roger thought, noting the thin carefully trimmed sideburns. I wonder if he cultivates the resemblance. Roger placed a square of white cloth on the glass surface of the counter and opened it. On the cloth lay five round-cornered translucent octahedrons. They were uncut diamonds, one to two carats in weight, that a few hours before had grown in the moonlight from beach charcoal as George and Roger watched. Roger produce a shard of broken mirror from his pocket, showed it to the Clint person, and scratched the mirror surface with the corner of one of the stones to demonstrate its hardness. "I would like to pawn these top-quality uncut diamonds," Roger explained. "My late father was a diamond merchant in England. He had a good business in King's Lynn. When Dad died, he left me these stones. I've carried them with me for years in memory of him. But now, unfortunately, I'm in serious need of funds."

"Real sorry to hear that, friend," Clint said, grinning. "What's the problem?"

"I'm afraid I had a bit of a row with my girlfriend last night," said Roger. "When I woke up this morning, everything I had was gone. Money, wallet, watch, credit cards, car, everything. She even threw my clothes into the Gulf, but I found them washed up on the beach. Fortunately, she missed these. I suppose she didn't know what they were. I wonder if you could loan me a spot of cash for them?"

"Well, now," said Clint, removing a jeweler's loupe from a drawer behind the counter, "let's just have a look at these beauties."

Roger was pleased and surprised to learn how easy it had been to slip into the role he'd been playing. He must have a talent for acting, he decided. Roger emerged from the pawnshop with $1,200 in cash plus a brown suede jacket that fit him nicely, two Stetson hats, and two used suitcases that he had persuaded Clint, after some bargaining, to include in the deal. George had estimated that the market value of the diamonds was closer to $6,000, but the $1,200 looked very good, particularly considering that there was no documentation for the stones and that the merchandise had until recently been lumps of charcoal from a driftwood beach fire.

They walked back toward the seawall. Along the way they had a nice breakfast, and Roger began to feel optimistic. At a discount store they bought some new clothes, underwear, and toilet articles. They emerged carrying suitcases of a more substantial weight. Roger's suitcase also now contained a bag of charcoal.

They turned east at Seawall Boulevard and walked two blocks to the historic Galvez Hotel. When George couldn't produce a credit card, the desk clerk was apologetic but firm in requiring him to pay for the room for two days in advance. The bellboy took them and their suitcases to the eighth floor in an ornate elevator and showed them into a spacious room with charming period furniture, modern plumbing, and a sweeping view of the Gulf.

* * *

Roger, freshly showered, put on his starched newly purchased pajamas, pulled the curtains to darken the room, and collapsed on the bed. "I'm dead tired," he said after a few minutes, "but my body clock is disoriented from the time shift, and I don't feel sleepy. I should have bought some melatonin at a drugstore."

George, clad in a bath towel and lying on the other bed, said, "Not likely, Roger. This is 1987. As I recall, melatonin wasn't available, with or without a prescription, until about 1995."

"Really?" said Roger. "What did people do about jet lag before that?"

"They suffered," said George. "But you don't need to. Just *Write* yourself a clock adjustment protein."

Roger put his palm to his forehead. "Of course!" he said. "I must be even more tired than I feel." He put his fingertips to his arm and closed his eyes.

He slept fitfully for most of the afternoon. His dreams were populated by large flying insects that chased him as he dragged his legs through viscous water and that ate diamonds as fast as he could produce them. But when he awoke at about 6 P.M., he felt wonderfully relaxed.

George suggested a seafood dinner on the Galveston waterfront. They crossed the broad boulevard to the sidewalk along the seawall and strolled past several ancient tourist shop piers until they reached the Flagship, a hotel and restaurant built on a long pier extending from the seawall into the waters of the Gulf.

A waiter who identified himself as Bob conducted them to a table with a fine Gulf view and proceeded to recite a list of the day's specials. Roger ordered the crab-stuffed flounder. George selected the blackened redfish and a bottle of dry oaky Washington State Pinot Chardonnay with which he was well acquainted.

Roger turned the two-carat diamond on the table before them, admiring its basic octahedral shape. "The diamond business isn't bad," he said, chewing slowly, "but it won't last. I recall that at around the turn of the millennium, a new industrial vapor deposition process will become available for growing large diamonds in a variety of shapes, making all sorts of useful things with them, and selling them very cheaply."

George nodded. "But for now it's a good basic source of income to get us started. We have to be careful, though. Natural diamonds always have a few flaws and impurities. If ours are too perfect, it will give away the fact that they didn't actually come from a diamond mine.''

"I've already thought of that," said Roger. "The nanoassemblers I *Wrote* last night were programmed to include plausible impurities at the part per million level and also to put a few random flaws into the crystal structure. I'd need to do a bit of library research to get an optimum match to natural diamonds, but these should pass a cursory inspection. As I see it, our real problem will be to find a believable story for our source of diamonds. My dear late lamented old dad, the diamond merchant of King's Lynn, can only have left me so many of the things. And I might be had up for evasion of death duties by the U.K. revenue authorities or for smuggling by U.S. Customs if I'm not careful.''

"Yes, we do need a plausible source," said George. "We should buy a defunct diamond mine. Probably somewhere in Africa or South America. We can *Write* nanomachines that will seed it with a new supply of diamonds. Then we mine out the first batch and then sell the producing mine to someone in the business. That basic scheme can be used over and over. If anyone notices our string of successes, it can be attributed to our superior knowledge of diamond geology and to our ability to spot old mines with untapped veins.''

"That's tidy," said Roger. "There should be other applications of that basic strategy also. But our other immediate problem is personal documents. We can't simply get new identification. There are individuals here already who look just like us, only younger, and whose names are George Griffin and Roger Coulton. We somehow have to establish new identities. And there's also a problem with transportation. Even with our new access to cash, we can't even rent a car. We don't have the proper credit cards and driver's licenses.''

"I've been giving that problem some thought," said George. "I conclude that we will each need to establish several new identities, not just one. And in this country, fortunately, that isn't too difficult. The first step is to get a birth certificate.''

"That will be a problem," said Roger. "Could one be forged?''

"It isn't necessary," said George, "I can obtain a real one by picking an approximate birthdate, going to a big-city newspaper office, looking up the obituary notices in the microfilm archives, and finding a male baby that died when it was a few months old. Then I go to the city records office and ask for a birth certificate in the name of the deceased child.''

"But," Roger objected, "won't the records show that the child is dead?''

"No," said George. "In this country there's no effort to correlate birth and death records. People move around too much to make that practical, and there's also a deeply ingrained popular view that too much detailed government record-keeping is an attack on personal freedom. It should be easy.''

Roger stroked his chin. Suddenly he pictured Susan standing before Elvis's cage and wondered if he would see her again. Then he sighed. She's only about twelve years old now, he realized.

"Then I go to the Social Security office," said George, "and ask for a new Social Security number in the name of my new alter ego, saying that I've been living abroad for many years and had never needed one before. The Social Security people always maintain that a Social Security number is not for purposes of identification, even though it's widely used that way, so they give them out fairly freely. With my new Social Security number, I can open a bank account in my new name and put, say, forty thousand dollars into it. I can get credit cards from my bank with no problems because of my big bank balance. Then I buy a car, paying cash, and take a driver's license test, which provides me with a picture ID driver's license. Then I go to the Federal Building and get a U.S. passport, using my birth certificate and driver's license as identification.

"And *presto*! I'm a real person. If I do that several times, I can be several real people at the same time.''

"Interesting," said Roger. "I have a slightly more difficult problem. I will need to do something similar in the U.K., but I'll need some kind of valid passport even to get there. Perhaps I'll have to work on my speech patterns and learn to speak like an American, before I can get a U.S. passport and venture abroad.''

"Maybe that won't be necessary," said George. "With *Writing* we have some control of our facial characteristics. You could make yourself look like me and use one of my passports to enter the U.K. Or better yet, we could use nanomachines to produce a duplicate of my passport with your picture on it.''

"But what happens if we're caught?" said Roger. "Surely there are several illegal steps in the process you described."

George smiled at him. "Are you the same person who wanted to use a cutting laser to rob an automatic teller machine this morning? The passport operation is clearly illegal, as is getting the birth certificate and Social Security number. The story I recommend, if one of us is caught, is to claim to be a victim of amnesia. You woke up one morning with money but no identification at all, and you don't know who you are. You're only doing your best to establish a new identity by the one means open to you, so you can become a productive and functioning member of society."

"As a matter of fact," said Roger, "that's almost true."

The following day George and Roger rode a Greyhound bus to Houston. Roger was able to make diamond sales at several jewelry dealers in the downtown Houston area. The resulting stake was $13,487.

They rented two separate rooms in the downtown Marriott, each paying cash for a week in advance when they registered. The next morning they took a taxi to the archive center of the *Houston Chronicle* to do file research that would be necessary to begin their new lives.

• 50

IN LATE 1987 THE FINANCIAL PAGES OF THE *HOUSTON CHRONICLE* had noted the rise to prominence of one George Preston and his new company, Petroleum Genetics Laboratories, or PGL for short. Preston was a mysterious figure. He had appeared on the Houston oil scene out of nowhere. Even after considerable effort, the *Chronicle* financial reporter had been unable to learn anything about his background, credit history, previous experience, education, or source of financial backing. The local banks had records of substantial PGL deposits but no loans.

Petroleum Genetics Laboratories had started by using recombinant DNA techniques to "engineer" a species of rapidly multiplying but generation-limited petroleum-eating bacteria that was proving very useful in erasing the effects of oil spills. Several small Gulf Coast spills in 1987 had demonstrated the value of PGL's oil-eating bacteria and placed the company's profits on a steeply rising trajectory.

Preston had used these profits to buy up "worthless" oil leases in the long-dead oil fields of East Texas, leases for wells from which all the recoverable oil had been removed decades earlier. This had been treated as a joke at first, and in late 1987 many holders of ancient East Texas leases had rushed to sell them to this "crazy Yankee" before his money ran out, he came to his senses, or he was institutionalized.

Then in December of 1987 an unexpected thing happened. PGL's dried-up East Texas wells in the area between Gladewater and Tyler began to produce oil. Their yield curves rose, week by week, until by Christmas they equaled peak production during the golden days of Spindletop and the great Texas oil boom. In early January speculators began to buy up the dead wells nearby, but they soon found that the PGL bonanza did not extend to them. Disappointed, they sold their leases to Preston cheap to cut their losses. PGL's profits from the producing wells fueled further acquisitions. Suddenly the major oil producers came to the realization that there was a significant new player in their business.

Several of the big oil companies had already initiated well-funded research and industrial espionage programs aimed at discovering PGL's secret, when Preston revealed it to the news media at an April 1988 press conference in Houston. He announced that the privately held Petroleum Genetics Laboratories would henceforth become PetroGen, Inc., a public corporation whose stock would be listed on the New York Stock Exchange after an initial stock offering of twenty million shares at about fifty dollars per share.

PetroGen, in addition to its now-vast oil holdings in Texas, Oklahoma, Venezuela, and elsewhere and its exponentially rising revenues, had filed unique patent applications describing a genetically engineered family of bacteria that could free valuable petroleum from its bonds in porous layers of rock, sand, and shale, while at the same time trimming sluggish long-chain hydrocarbon molecules to the more marketable octane and septane sizes. As a proof-of-principle, these slimmed down, pre-refined petroleum products were already flowing freely at the PetroGen well heads. In less than a year a new blue-chip stock had been created on Wall Street.

*   *   *

August 16, 1988, was a very hot and humid Tuesday in New Orleans. The Republican Platform Committee had been meeting for a week to hammer out the new party platform. The Republican National Convention was to begin the following week in the Superdome, and thousands of reporters were converging on the Big Easy in preparation for the media feeding frenzy to come.

George Bush had campaigned hard for the Republican presidential nomination, easily outdistancing Patrick Buchanan in the primaries and gaining President Ronald Reagan's implicit support. He now had the lion's share of the convention delegates and was assured of the presidential nomination.

The real unresolved issue in New Orleans was Bush's imminent choice of a candidate for Vice President. The eleven "finalists" on Bush's short list were one by one making their way to the Marriott Hotel on Canal Street to be interviewed by Robert Kimmit, who had been an attorney with the Treasury Department before he resigned to join the Bush campaign. Bob Kimmit now had the responsibility for checking out each candidate.

PetroGen had rented an entire floor in the Canal Street Marriott just upstairs from the floors of suites that the Bush campaign organization was using as its base of operations. Roger Fulton, prominent British diamond merchant and member of the PetroGen board of directors, sat in the suite's large living room with his colleague George Preston, rising star of the resurgent Texas oil business and "Eagle-class" contributor to the Bush campaign.

"Any late-breaking news from Washington about the SSC?" Roger asked.

"Not much," said George. "There's been no mention of it during the primaries. The focus of attention in D.C. is all on the campaign, and science has no value as a campaign issue. I heard recently that the DOE added a correction to its cost estimates for inflation and now admits that the SSC might cost $5.3 billion instead of $4.4 billion. Also, certain members of Congress have decided that a very visible opposition to drugs makes a good campaign issue, and they want to be assured that the SSC laboratory and other federal laboratories will be 'drug-free workplaces,' which has become their new buzzword."

" 'Drug . . . free . . . work . . . place,' " Roger repeated slowly. "It does have a certain cadence. And I suppose it's preferable to a work-free drug place.''

George laughed. ''There's a story going around,'' he said, ''that President Reagan himself decided to set a good example for the nation by asking his Cabinet members to submit to a urine analysis test during a recent cabinet meeting. They all complied, of course, and the following day the Surgeon General came to the President with the test results. 'Mr. President,' he said, 'I'm pleased to report that you and all of your Cabinet members have passed the urine analysis test, and I can certify that the presidential cabinet meeting room is indeed a drug-free workplace. But next time, Mr. President, please don't ask everyone to pee in the same bottle.'' '

Roger chuckled. ''I suppose,'' he said, ''that we'd best get on with revising history.'' He looked uncomfortable. ''I hope that we do it right.''

George winced. ''Sometimes I wake up in the middle of the night in a cold sweat,'' he said, ''worrying about whether we're doing the right thing. What gives us the right to engage in this kind of manipulation? We think we're saving the world, but suppose we end by making things worse?''

''Worse than the Hive? I doubt that would be possible,'' said Roger. ''But in any case, history is already changing in subtle ways, even without our intervention.''

''It is? How can that be?''

''I've found evidence that events at the quantum level are having different outcomes,'' said Roger, ''even in situations where we could not possibly have had any influence. My lapstation contains an electronic almanac that, among other things, contains a twenty-year database of stock market quotations and sporting event scores. I checked the correspondence of those from my lapstation against those in newspaper files. Up to February 2, 1987, the records are a perfect match. But forward of the date of our splashy entrance at Galveston, a difference between records sets in and the discrepancies grow with time. For example, within two hours after our splashdown, a Hannover soccer team won a close match played in Munich, Germany, that should have been won by Bayern München. That isn't something we could have affected directly.''

''This is a different universe,'' said George. ''We melted it and it's recrystallizing.''

"Exactly," said Roger. "Iris described the effect of the time vortex as an unraveling of the frozen-in history of the universe, so that it has to re-evolve from the earliest point of the disruption. Apparently, during that re-evolution, every quantum event is a new game of dice with a strong chance of a new outcome. This is a new universe developing a new and different history, with or without our intervention. The general trends should be the same, of course, but detailed events from the quantum scale up are different. We should think of what we do as steering an intrinsically chaotic process rather than altering history."

George looked at his watch. "History alterations or not," he said, "we have to focus our influence on Bush's selection of a vice-presidential candidate."

"Your system of government," said Roger, "is still a deep mystery to me, I'm afraid. We're here in New Orleans to affect the nomination of the Vice President, but I fail to understand the political priorities. Why is this vice-presidential nomination so important to us? It was my impression that the U.S. Vice President is a kind of administrative spare tire, a nonfunctional ceremonial position that is of no importance unless something happens to the President."

"That's certainly been the tradition," said George, "but during the Carter and the Reagan Administrations a new tradition was established. The VP was given a leading role in the areas of science and space, in part to give him a somewhat visible activity that the President was glad to relinquish. Since the Carter-Mondale Administration, all the Science Advisors have worked closely with the VP in proposing new science initiatives and in defending the existing ones. And, of course, the VP normally has a good chance to become the next President, one way or another."

"I see," said Roger. "It's the link to science policy."

George nodded. "In our version of the future, George Bush selected Bob Dole as his Vice President. He's a rather reserved, taciturn person, but it proved to be a great choice as far as the SSC was concerned. There were some significant SSC contractors in Kansas, and Dole was interested in the project. He retained powerful connections in the U.S. Congress, which he used to protect the SSC. And of course Dole was elected in his own right in '96 and continued his SSC support. He may actually have saved the project."

"And so," said Roger, "we need to find a less effective alternative to Dole."

"The less effective, the better," said George. "Tell me about this person you and your computer picked out. What's his name? Quade?"

"Quayle," said Roger, "J. Danforth Quayle, U.S. senator from the state of Indiana. His father is a rich publisher who has pushed his son's career. Hard. Dan is good-looking. He looks rather like a vacant Robert Redford. He makes a very good first impression, has a pretty wife and an attractive family, and is an excellent and dedicated golfer. He's actually done quite well as a senator, with good press and no conspicuous screwups. Lately he's been receiving press attention as a leading supporter of the Star Wars Initiative in the Senate. He comes from the right wing of the party and is one of the few VP finalists who can pass Senator Gordon Humphrey's 'True Conservative' litmus test. And unlike Jack Kemp, he's never offended George Bush. He perhaps has only one principal failing. He's simply not very bright, even as judged by the rather undemanding standards of U.S. politics."

"Are you sure about that?" asked George. "Many politicians in this country act dumber than they are, in order to stay on the right wavelength with the home folks."

"In my one conversation with Dan," said Roger, "we discussed the space program. He's sincerely interested in it, but he seems to think that the planet Mars had canals with water in them. I'd suppose that he read Edgar Rice Burroughs as a child and never learned better, except that he never seems to have read any book for recreation except a few about golf. Perhaps his notion came from a comic book. It would be interesting to watch him in the role of leading defender of the SSC. He'd probably claim that it was being built to find a cure for cancer or something."

"He sounds like just the man for us," said George. "What did you *Write* for him when you were with him?"

"I boosted his output of an obscure human pheromone by two orders of magnitude. He would now reek of the stuff, except that no modern human is able to smell it. It comes from a feature of the human genome that was taken out of active service a million years ago when our sex and mating practices became nonseasonal. I *Wrote* a little targeted retrovirus and gave it to Danforth as we shook hands, when I was leaving after the interview."

"Was that good for him?" George asked. "I would have thought you'd be impeded by your Hippocratic wiring."

"It certainly did him no harm," said Roger, "and I combined it with a neurocoordination boost that will improve his golf game. I also *Wrote* in a temporary boost in his synaptine level, so he'll be a bit smarter for about the duration of the campaign. All very beneficial to the recipient, and therefore I could *Write* them without feeling any Hippocratic qualms. So now the rest is up to you."

George consulted a piece of paper. "Quayle's screening interview with Bob Kimmit is scheduled for tomorrow morning," he said. "I've arranged to have dinner with Bob tonight, and I'll be able to see Bush tomorrow to express my support for Quayle. If I provide a short-duration boost in sensitivity to the same pheromone for the two of them, we'll be able to create instant rapport between them and Dan Quayle. Bush is going to love his new running mate."

Roger laughed, then frowned. "But isn't there a danger for the United States in what we're doing? Suppose something happens to Bush, and Quayle has to actually function as President? We're clouding the judgments of those who should be selecting the best person to serve as a substitute President."

"We'll deal with that problem if and when it arises," said George. "We can boost Quayle's intelligence and provide him with similarly intelligence-boosted advisors, or if necessary we could get him out of the way with a debilitating disease. It's a small risk for the country and the world, compared to the danger of a probable Hive invasion. These are desperate times."

Roger nodded.

There was a knock at the door, and George answered it.

A young man with a shock of unruly white-blond hair stood outside. He was wearing PetroGen coveralls and carrying a toolbox. "Excuse me, Mr. Preston," he said. "I just thought you'd want to know that I've got all the cables and wirin' installed in the strategy suite, so you folks can watch the convention next week and use those special computers and telephones, just like you wanted. Tested ever'thang myself, and it all works just fine."

"That's great, Whitey," said George, patting him on the back. "I really appreciate your fast work."

He closed the door and returned to the conference table.

"Was that . . . ?" Roger asked.

"Yes," said George, "that was none other than Whitey Buford. When I was busy buying up East Texas oil leases last year, I decided to hire his father, Ernest Buford, to help me. He did an excellent job, and he's now a PetroGen executive. Whitey's still in high school, but we hired him for the summer. He's helping us with technical details for the convention. He's a very bright kid. He told me that he plans to go to Texas A&M when he graduates from Waxahachie High and take a dual major in petroleum geology and molecular biology. I think it's very likely that he'll get a scholarship." He smiled.

• 51

ROGER LOOKED AT HIS REFLECTION IN THE MIRRORED BACK OF THE car sun visor. He stared at the lines etched deeply into his face, the sparse gray hair, the puffy skin near the eyes. His direct control of his appearance was improving, but he'd never before used it for such extreme aging. Was he really going to look like this at age sixty-five? He looked older than his father. Perhaps it was the gray beard. He pressed his chin again, reassuring himself that it would remain in place.

Emerging from the Bentley, he retrieved his slim black leather attaché case from the backseat and locked the doors. Then he strode across the small parking lot, down one side of the cloister, and into the quad. The old Cambridge buildings brought back pleasant memories of his student days. He identified himself to the porter, pushed through the massive entry doors of the building, and climbed the worn marble stairs to the second floor.

Dr. Stanley Tern's office door was open a crack, through which Roger could hear one side of a vigorous telephone argument. "Please understand," a cultured voice said emphatically, "I do appreciate your calling me directly and relinquishing the usual anonymity, but as referee you're supposed to either approve or deny publication of my paper. You may not instruct me to rewrite my paper in order to make more generous references to your own work." Pause. "Actually, you should be glad that I did not say more about your last paper, because I'm afraid it's dead wrong." There was a long pause. "Of course it's wrong! I proved that unambiguously in section two." Pause. "May I ask if you actually *read* my paper before you wrote this referee report?" Pause. "Did you then understand what I was saying before you produced this peculiar critique of my arguments? I'm receiving the definite impression that you did not."

Roger listened quietly outside the door, recalling his own scars from past encounters with mush-headed but iron-willed journal referees.

There was another long pause before the voice continued. "Well, it appears that you leave me no alternative but to protest your misconduct in the refereeing of my paper to the journal's editorial board." Pause. "I was not aware that you were a board member." Pause. "You leave no choice, sir, but to withdraw my submission so that I may submit my work to a reputable journal that employs more rational refereeing policies. It appears that we have nothing further to discuss. Good day, sir." There was the sound of the telephone receiver being slammed into its cradle.

Roger retreated a few steps, walked forward with loud footsteps, and knocked on the slightly open door. "Dr. Tern?" he said.

A gaunt-faced man with shoulder-length dark hair looked up from the desk. "Yes?" he said.

"I am Roger Wilkins of the Iris Foundation. I'd like to speak to you if I may."

"The Iris Foundation?" Tern repeated.

"Have you heard of us?"

"Of course," said Tern, visibly brightening. "I read something in the news recently. In the past few months you're supposed to have been giving what the *Guardian* termed 'genius grants' to worthy individuals in the sciences."

"Yes, we have," said Roger.

"Well, what can I do for you?" asked Tern. "Is there something you want from me? A contribution, perhaps?"

"Not at all." Roger smiled. "Rather the reverse. But perhaps you could tell me about your new work. I've read your recent publications, but I'd like very much to know about any research directions that may not yet be in print."

Tern swiveled his chair to a file cabinet, opened a long drawer, and extracted several documents from folders. "Here are three preprints that are not in journals yet," he said, glancing furtively at the referee report on his desk, "and also two papers presented at recent conferences on quantum gravity and on relativistic cosmology, respectively.''

Roger nodded, accepted the papers, scanned their titles, then moved one to the top of the stack. '' *'Application of Clifford Algebra to Quantum Gravity . . .'* '' he read aloud. ''Interesting. Tell me about this one.''

''Very well,'' Tern began. ''What do you know about Clifford algebra?''

''Only that it's an alternative mathematical formalism for dealing with complex numbers and functions. I'm aware that some feel it provides a superior mathematical basis for some physical theories.''

''Exactly,'' said Tern. ''Last summer in France I viewed some cave paintings made by Cro-Magnons a hundred thousand years ago. Animals were painted on the cave walls, and the artist used the natural curvature and irregularity of the walls to give depth and three-dimensional character to the animals he was painting, somehow fitting the animals to the bulges and depressions of the cave wall.

''In my view, mathematics is like that. The right underlying mathematical structure enhances and enriches the physical theory that uses it, because the physical theory 'fits' the mathematical formalism. If the wrong mathematical structure is used, the physical theory does not fit. The formalism must be bent out of shape to conform to it, leading to obscurity, paradoxical implications, and other problems.

''In my view, all our present theories, but particularly quantum mechanics and general relativity at small distance scales, are cast in an inappropriate mathematical framework. The paradoxes of quantum mechanics and the lack of progress toward a valid theory of quantum gravity are both symptoms of this problem. My students, postdocs, and I have been working in this area for the past five years. I believe that we are on the verge of a real breakthrough.''

Roger nodded. ''We think so, too,'' he said. ''Let me ask how much of your time is spent writing research proposals and seeking research funds?''

Tern winced. ''Entirely too damn much,'' he said. ''Some months I do nothing else. And it gets worse with time. The science bureaucracy of the U.K. demands more and more paper justification for each shilling they pass along. Moreover, they award themselves salaries for their paper-shuffling that are far higher than the salaries of the scientists they are supposed to be serving. More and more science money is being diverted into servicing the science bureaucracy instead of funding real science. It's a national disgrace."

Roger nodded. "Fortunately, one that can be bypassed," he said. He removed an envelope from his briefcase and extended it across the desk. "The Iris Foundation likes your work and would like to encourage it. This contains a bank draft for £200,000, made out in your name. It's the first quarterly installment of your Iris Foundation award. Our legal staff will be in contact with you to advise you on how to manage the funds to minimize the taxes on the award."

Tern looked stunned as he opened the envelope. "But . . ." he said finally, "what do I have to . . . What do you expect in return?"

Roger smiled. "Not research proposals," he said. "Not budgets. Not progress reports. Just copies of your papers and the theses of your students as they are published, plus an occasional telephone or personal conversation like this one."

Tern smiled. "Your organization is quite civilized," he said. "I had no idea . . ."

"There is one more item," said Roger. He handed a single printed sheet of paper across the desk. "This is a summary of lines of inquiry in your field that we feel may prove fruitful. You have no obligation to follow them, but we believe you will find them a useful guide. We suggest that you try some of the approaches and ideas listed here, but I emphasize that this is strictly up to you."

As Tern read the sheet, his eyes widened. "Where . . . ? How?"

"I'm afraid I cannot, at this stage of our scientific relationship, divulge the source of the information on that sheet," said Roger. "I can only say that I'm sure you will find it useful information, taken as a guideline, but it must not be used as a rigid plan or program. You are under no obligation to make reference to it or even to acknowledge its existence. In fact, we would prefer that you did not."

Tern looked at Roger with suspicion. "You provide this kind of guidance to all of your awardees? How many are there?"

"We provide some limited indication of fruitful lines of inquiry to the scientists we support," said Roger. "Yours is our seventh Iris Foundation award since the initiation of the program earlier this year."

Tern now looked somewhat less agitated. "What are your restrictions on publicity and media contacts?" he asked.

"We do not intend to directly publicize your Iris Foundation award ourselves,'' Roger answered, ''but you may do so if you wish. If asked, we will acknowledge that you are an awardee. We feel that the success of your ongoing work will provide a better basis for publicity than the mere awarding of funds. But you understand your local situation better than we do. We'll leave those details up to you.''

Discussion of physics and funding continued for more than an hour. Tern was still staring at the bank draft on his desk when Roger left.

• **52**

ROGER LOOKED OUT THE WINDOW OF THE ANCIENT BUT STILL ELE-gant British Airways Concorde as it approached the Dulles Airport. In the distance he could see the Washington Monument and the Capitol Building. He could also see his face reflected in the window surface. He looked very distinguished with the touch of gray at the temples, a distinguished business figure of perhaps fifty, rather than his actual thirty-two.

With the chameleonlike body control he had learned, he could alter his weight, height, facial characteristics, even his fingerprints and retinal patterns, to match the persona he was assuming that week. Hair color was harder because of the growing time, but he had learned a few hairdresser tricks.

His present persona, one Roger Fulton, had been tied up for the past month in London attempting to streamline and shape their burgeoning financial empire. That had been fairly demanding, and he was feeling a bit out of touch with the basic work of dealing with the SSC problem.

Roger glanced at the person in the other seat. She was sleeping, but just to be sure he turned the screen of his lapstation so that it was visible only to him. Then, to refresh his memory, he decrypted the master strategy file and studied it. It summarized the plan they had hammered out two years ago in Houston, as they had struggled through the difficult initial problems of creating new identities, new appearances, new personae for themselves. The file was short and to the point. It read:

Basic Strategy

1. Generate wealth for power base; mining, oil, biotechnology, investments.

2. Create a business organization with strong investigative and lobbying capabilities.

3. Initiate Planck-scale physics research.

4. Alter Bush appointments in 1988–89: Vice President => not Dole; Energy Secretary => not Deutsch; Science Advisor => not Bromley.

5. Arrange meetings between potential SSC congressional opponents and prominent physicist SSC critics.

6. Create uncertainty over SSC magnet design and project management; conservatism => high cost.

7. Increase emphasis on foreign SSC participation; simultaneously block Japanese $1 billion contribution.

8. In 1991 extend the recession; elect Democratic President and new congressmen in 1992.

9. Kill the SSC project in Congress.

They had been doing quite well with item one. In London last week Roger had calculated that the net worth of their holdings, all carefully concealed by a network of interlocking corporations and holding companies, was, at least on paper, moving past the $4 billion mark. The multifaceted business organization was also developing well under George's guidance. He seemed to have real talents as an entrepreneur and organizer. With the creation of the Iris Foundation, money and guidance had been given to a few physicists working the right areas for item three, and this work was proceeding. They had succeeded with the first part of item four, and the tactic was working well. Unlike Dole, Vice President Quayle so far had shown little interest in scientific projects and absolutely no interest in the SSC. His attention was focused exclusively on NASA and the U.S. manned spaceflight program. Roger smiled, remembering the Martian canals.

The appointment of the Secretary of Energy was their next hurdle. All of the Cabinet slots of the Bush Administration except Energy had been filled for almost a month. The politically oriented press was awash with wild rumors about those being considered for Energy Secretary: John Deutsch, Lee Thomas, General Abrahamson, and even

Arthur Schlesinger. Roger was very curious about what George had been doing about the Energy appointment. Well, he would learn soon enough. He folded the lapstation and slid it under the seat in front of him, then pulled his own seat-back forward for the landing.

Roger knocked at the hotel room door. "How was your flight?" George asked as he ushered Roger in.

"The flight itself was quick and efficient," said Roger. "Getting here from Dulles was a problem. I wish they permitted Concorde flights from Heathrow to Washington National. One spends longer on the ground than in the air. How's it going here?"

"Well, the latest Administration budget puts the SSC cost at $5.9 billion, with completion in 1999. The DOE has finally discovered inflation and that they'll need some detectors for the machine. They're still low-balling the detector cost. I think it's intentional."

Roger nodded. "And what's the news about the appointment of the Secretary of Energy?" he asked.

"Bush is still hanging back. My contacts at the Pentagon have been working hard to dissuade him from appointing John Deutsch, who was in the lead for a while. They're pushing for someone with a military background instead. Their argument is that despite Deutsch's stint at the Pentagon, he doesn't have the background to deal with the weapons aspects of the DOE and doesn't have the command skills to shake up the department and clean up the messy leftovers from the nuclear weapons program. I think the argument is working. I'm expecting a phone call today announcing the decision."

"Who's the military person of choice? I gather General Abrahamson has been mentioned."

"I personally arranged for 'a highly placed source' to leak that to *The Wall Street Journal*," said George. "It's amazing what they will print when they hear a good rumor. But it's pure smoke. The Pentagon people are actually pushing Admiral James D. Watkins. He was a Rickover protégé from the nuclear submarine program, a specialist in shipboard nuclear reactors. He was Chief of Naval Operations until three years ago when he retired. Last year he headed a presidential commission on AIDS and did a good job in bulldozing a difficult independent-minded committee into producing the report the Reagan Administration wanted."

"Impressive," said Roger. "But what will he do for us and our SSC problem?"

"My investigators report that he's a control freak, a safety fanatic, and is always very determined to get his own way on everything he touches. During his Navy career, he would delegate the responsibilities so that everyone worked directly for him and reported to him on everyone else. He also has a reputation for being extremely conservative in the administration of his projects. He appoints only people that he's previously worked with. He takes no chances, incurs no risks. On the ships he commanded safety was the supreme watchword. He installed extra levels of procedures and documentation in the safety area. We picked up a lot of bitching from former crew members.

"One of his former subordinates told me an apocryphal joke about the admiral that had been making the Navy rounds. The story goes that when he was Chief of Naval Operations he was invited to deliver the commencement address at a high school in Virginia near his home. He accepted, but then forgot all about it. Then one Saturday morning the principal of the high school called him to say that the commencement exercises were to start in an hour, and he was coming by in his car to pick up his commencement speaker. The admiral was horrified. He hadn't prepared a speech, and he didn't have the faintest idea what to say. The trip to the high school was a nightmare, with the admiral in a blind panic, wracking his brain for any idea he might use in his speech. They arrived, parked in front of the auditorium, and rushed in. As they were approaching the front doors of the auditorium, the admiral noticed that each of the doors was labeled with a large sign that said 'Push.'

"The admiral smiled. He had found his idea and could relax. He had his theme and knew what he was going to say to the students. The principal introduced him, and he began his speech. 'Ladies and gentlemen,' he said, 'you are standing at a doorway through which you are about to pass, into a world where you must make your own way, must accomplish things that will establish the basis for your future lives. I'm going to help you in this by telling you a magic word. This word, if you use it properly, will allow you to go anywhere, do anything, accomplish whatever you want. In my career in the Navy I have used this word many times. It has allowed me to reach my present position . . . ' He went on in this vein for a long time, describing the things that he had accomplished by using the magic word that he was going to tell them.

"Finally he reached the climax of his talk. 'I know that by now you are all wondering what this magic word is,' he said. 'I will show it to you now. If you will all just turn around and look toward the back of the room, you will find that my magic word is inscribed in large letters on the rear doors of this auditorium.' The students did as the admiral suggested and turned around. Then they broke into gales of laughter. At the rear of the auditorium, written in very large letters on each door, was the word 'Pull.' "

Roger laughed. "But that Navy story isn't fair, I suspect," he said. "Surely the admiral has considerable skills at leadership and administration."

"Oh yes," said George. "And he also has very strong opinions about almost everything and is accustomed to getting his way."

"I think perhaps I'm beginning to see . . ." said Roger.

"I'm sure you can," said George. "Imagine the collision between Watkins and the scientists who are building the SSC. They're already chafing under all the new DOE project oversight paperwork that's been laid upon them. The DOE is micromanaging the SSC in a way that was never used at Fermilab or SLAC, and physicists don't suffer bureaucrats gladly. In our universe, when John Deutsch took over as Secretary of Energy one of his first acts was to streamline and simplify the DOE procedures so that Roy Schwitters, who has just been appointed as SSC director, had more freedom. There were fewer delays in making technical decisions, and the experts were able to focus more effort on the real work of building a technically difficult and demanding accelerator.

"But imagine what will happen when Watkins takes over. He'll do just the opposite. He'll want to reshuffle the SSC management completely, put his people in charge, and have them report directly to him. He'll undoubtedly institute new levels of paperwork and oversight, new chains of command. He has no conception of what's required for a successful cutting-edge science project, so he'll run the SSC construction like a Navy shipyard full of crooked contractors."

The telephone rang, and George answered it. "George Preston," he said. He listened for a time, then said, "Thank you, General," and hung up.

"That was one of our Pentagon contacts," he told Roger. "Tomorrow the Watkins appointment will be announced. We did it."

"You did it," said Roger. "Congratulations, George."

"Two down and one to go," said George and winked.

"Yes," said Roger. "There's just one more key appointment on our agenda: the Science Advisor."

"The Science Advisor appointment has been going very slowly," said George, "but we're making good progress. My contacts inside the Administration have been pushing hard for the idea that we need a Science Advisor from the industrial sector, not an academic. Our leading candidate is George Rathman, the chairman of Amgen. It's an up-and-coming biotechnology company."

Roger nodded. "He sounds like a good choice. A biotechnologist isn't likely to have much enthusiasm for high-energy physics or the SSC. Any progress on mounting congressional opposition to the SSC?"

George nodded. "I've been bringing the right people together. I recall from the SSC battles of our previous history that Senator Bumpers of Arkansas and Congressmen Boehlert of New York, Eckart of Ohio, Wolpe of Michigan, and Slattery of Kansas were among the leading opponents of the SSC in Congress. And the most vocal SSC critics in the physics community were Phil Anderson of Princeton, Rustrum Roy of Penn State, and Jim Krumhansl of Cornell. Roy is an organizer of the Science, Technology, and Society movement, Phil has a Nobel prize for theoretical work in condensed matter physics, and Jim's going to be the president of the American Physical Society this year. That gives them some social cachet, so I've been arranging social gatherings at which potential SSC-critic politicians are brought together with potential anti-SSC physicists. I can't tell how it's working yet, but I'm told that the other night Krumhansl spent an hour bending Boehlert's ear." He smiled.

"The next item on our list is the SSC magnet design," said Roger.

"Right," said George. "You're going to have to carry the ball on that one. We know that the design of the SSC dipole magnets, with their four-centimeter apertures, is marginal. They were close to the hairy edge of operability, as it turned out."

"Yes," said Roger. "Since we already know where the problems are with the design, we must find a way of bringing them to light early and making them appear to be major problems instead of minor ones. The SSC design center currently has a personnel shortage, and I've identified the temporary agency they're using to recruit extra physicist-programmers to go over the SSC reference design in more detail. I've applied for a temporary position there, using my Roger Hilton persona.''

"Great!" said George. "Give me their address, and I'll write a couple of letters of recommendation for the good Mr. Hilton, extolling his amazing programming skills and his profound knowledge of accelerator physics.''

"I did that yesterday," said Roger.

• 53

THE SSC DESIGN GROUP OCCUPIED TEMPORARY QUARTERS IN A large industrial park in De Soto, Texas, south of Dallas and north of the SSC campus site. The starkness of the building had been softened with paintings and potted plants, but it still had a temporary feel. Removable partitions divided the large open area of the hangarlike structure into small cubicles, each containing a programmer or designer.

Roger Hilton, temporary-hire physicist-programmer attached to the group, sat in his cubicle looking at magnetic field profiles that traced bright colors on the screen of his X-terminal. It was frustrating to have to use this ancient computer hardware. The small lapstation in his backpack had hundreds of times more computing capacity than the entire SSC computer complex here. But nevertheless, he was achieving his goal.

"How's it going?" asked a soft female voice behind him.

He turned and smiled at Edwina Troy, his boss, and then turned a thumb downward. "I believe we have a serious problem here, Edwina," he said. "The field of the LBL dipole design looks rather marginal to me. I think they cut a few too many corners to keep the cost down. Look at this multipole expansion of the field. See the red lines? There are big high-multipole components that simply shouldn't be there. The injected beams are not going to stack properly in the ring.''

Edwina squinted at the screen and looked worried. "We had trouble like that with Energy Doubler dipoles at Fermilab, and we had to make correction magnets to fix the problem. But with a machine of the complexity of the SSC, I'm not sure we can get away with that kind of fix."

Roger nodded. "I could try variations on the coil geometry, turn spacing and shim placement," he said. "Those are supposed to have been optimized already, but perhaps it's worth another go. But if that doesn't work, the only remedy will be to go to a larger aperture. I think we need five centimeters instead of four."

Edwina winced. "I've already looked into enlarging the aperture," she said. "You're talking about a billion-dollar design change, Roger. The magnets will get bigger, more expensive, and harder to cool. The field of each magnet will go down, so more magnets will be needed to bend the beam. But an increased number of magnets won't fit into the tunnel as designed, so we will have to come up with a new tunnel design that's miles longer, in order to accommodate the extra magnets. It's much too expensive."

"But at least the machine would work then," said Roger.

She frowned. "There is that. See what can be done with layer and spacing modifications to the coil windings. And I'll hope and pray that it works."

"I'll try," said Roger.

"Try very, very hard, Roger," said Edwina. "It will be my job to explain to the admiral that there's been a slight design problem and that the SSC is going to cost a couple of billion dollars more than we had promised him it would. He'll probably nail me to the mast as an example and make you guys walk the plank." She turned and walked away, looking depressed.

• 54

FROM THE BROAD WINDOW OF THE PETROGEN PRESIDENT'S OFFICE, George contemplated the dark brown meander of Buffalo Bayou weaving along Allen Parkway to the distant green swath of Memorial Park. He turned back to Roger. "We're running into some problems on the political front," he said. "The DOE has been clever about making SSC contracts in forty-three out of fifty states plus Puerto Rico, and that's garnered them a lot of support in Congress. Construction has started on the accelerator buildings, and the Texas contractors and Texas state lobbyists are pushing very hard in support of the project. We've been stirring up the local residents with land near Waxahachie above the ring. They've formed a fairly vocal protest group and have given a lot of publicity to the fire ant problem, but the protests are not having as much effect as we'd projected.''

Roger shook his head. "It's too bad we couldn't block Bromley's appointment to Science Advisor," he said. "What went wrong?"

"Nobody we recommended would take the damned job," said George.

Roger looked surprised. "Don't they have a sense of duty?" he asked.

"This isn't the United Kingdom," said George. "Public service is not held in such high regard here. We'd convinced President Bush that better connections between science and business were essential to long-term economic growth. The top candidates for Science and Technology Advisor were all scientists or engineers with strong ties to the business world, mostly corporate executives. Bromley, as an academic, was down on Bush's list. But then all of the corporate executive candidates declined to be considered because of the low salary and the new conflict-of-interest laws. The job only pays $72,000 per year. Any of them would have had to take a factor of three or more cut in pay and divest themselves of their stock holdings. I guess their sense of duty didn't stretch that far.

"So Allan rose to the top of the list by process of elimination, and he was appointed. His Yale connection to Bush was too much for us. He's already been very effective in presenting the case for the SSC to Congress.''

"Well," said Roger, "at least we succeeded with Quayle and Watkins. Two out of three isn't so bad in this business. It appears that the admiral's Tiger Teams are already helping to create some diversion of effort.''

"Ah yes," said George. "How did you manage that one? It was brilliant.''

"It did work surprisingly well," said Roger. "I used my BBC reporter Roger Dalton persona to get an interview with the admiral. We'd already determined that he was a stickler for safety. When we shook hands, I *Wrote* him a hormonal boost in aggressiveness and caution, both useful attributes for a Cabinet member. Then I asked him a long list of pointed questions about the rampant safety problems at U.S. national laboratories like Oak Ridge, Argonne, Los Alamos, Livermore, and so on. I implied that I was preparing a BBC exposé on the subject.

"The admiral immediately saw the potential for embarrassment, and he also saw the opportunity to bend the DOE national labs to his will. Within a week of my interview he'd recruited a few dozen of his old Navy mates, spit-and-polish retirees from his former nuclear Navy outfits. He formed them into what he called Tiger Teams. These Tigers descended on all the national laboratories like hungry carnivores on flocks of lambs. They demanded endless safety meetings, giant mountains of paperwork, a vast review and overhaul of all the lab safety procedures."

"Yes, I heard about that," said George. "Our contacts in the DOE labs report an amazing diversion of effort and loss of morale. For example, some lab technicians are boosting their status by becoming 'safety informers,' turning in scientists to the Tigers. It's like Stalin's Russia."

"Right," said Roger. "The DOE labs have essentially halted scientific research while everyone scrambles around attending safety seminars, writing detailed safety procedures for every conceivable scenario of possible disaster, and filling vast bookshelves with thousand-page documents that no one will ever read. Senior lab officials that have protested have been threatened with dismissal."

"There are definite indications that the Tigers diverted effort away from the SSC redesign," said George. "The design efforts at Fermilab, LBL, and Brookhaven are down, just when the old LBL dipole magnet design is being closely studied and reevaluated. Everyone involved is overworked, and consequently they're doing a very conservative redesign because they have no time for creative solutions."

Roger shook his head and looked downward. "Actually," he said, "I feel rather uncomfortable about what happened to Argonne. The lab was singled out by the Tigers and made an example for the rest. It was completely shut down; its science effort probably set back a year.

"And no one at any of the labs has yet figured out what hit them.

I'd feel really awful about having instigated all of that, if it wasn't in the interest of saving the universe.''

"It's interesting that all the activity surrounding Watkins's Tigers made no impression on the news media," said George. "I haven't seen a thing about it. Any idea why?"

Roger grinned. "A CBS reporter explained to me that safety is an intrinsically boring subject," he said. "According to him, safety has absolutely no news value unless there's a disaster, and even then it's only good for thirty seconds of pious moralizing."

"Well," said George, "the net effect on the SSC redesign is becoming apparent. The DOE just made an announcement about the revised project. The machine now uses eighty-eight hundred of the new five-centimeter aperture dipoles and needs an extra kilometer or so of tunnel. The new official DOE cost of the redesigned SSC has risen to $8.2 billion from U.S. federal funds, with an extra $1.6 billion expected from foreign contributions."

Roger whistled. "Total $9.8 billion . . . That's more than double the first DOE cost estimate."

"And more, in our universe, than the machine actually cost to build," said George. "The new congressional emphasis on foreign contributions is very good for us. My contacts have been promoting the idea of the need for strong international financial participation in the SSC. It isn't too easy, because there is strong feeling in Congress that all of the high-technology items, which represent most of the cost, must be built here in this country. But the most recent SSC appropriations bill contains the requirement that the SSC project must have about a billion dollars in contributions from other countries. That means Japan. Have you been able get a reading on the SSC at the Japanese end?"

"Yes, but it's rather confusing," said Roger. "The older leaders of the Japanese high-energy physics community support participation in the SSC, but the younger people are not so enthusiastic. They're afraid that projects in their own laboratories will be sacrificed, and there is a developing opposition to SSC participation. And the Japanese science funding agencies have all made it clear that they have no money for SSC support."

"No yen for the SSC?" George said. "That sounds hopeful."

"Unfortunately, it's irrelevant," said Roger. "In Japan the big decisions are always handled personally at the topmost level. If there's to be Japanese funding for the SSC, it will be decided by the Prime Minister himself. My contacts in Japan say that the Japanese Prime Minister, whoever that may be by the time Bush gets around to visiting Japan, might be willing to contribute a hundred billion yen or so to the SSC, but only if he is asked directly and personally by President Bush.''

"That's exactly what happened in our universe," said George. "There Bush would go to Japan next November, would ask Prime Minister Miyazawa directly for Japanese collaboration and support for the SSC project, and Miyazawa would agree and shake hands on it. The SSC project would get a billion dollars from that handshake.''

"We must do our best to prevent that handshake," said Roger. "Bush must now have other things on his mind, what with the Gulf War."

George smiled, then pointed to the newspapers spread on the broad rosewood conference table. "Yes, the Gulf War started last month, right on schedule," he said. "In our world, that gave a big boost to the Administration, with Bush distinguishing himself as a tough international leader. It proved to be a key element in getting him reelected in 1992, so that Dole, Deutsch, and Bromley could work on Congress during the closest SSC votes in 1993 and 1994.''

"I know," said Roger. "I recently used the holo-ROM history encyclopedia on my lapstation to analyze the history of the Gulf War. While it was in progress, there was a major internal debate over just when the Allied Forces should declare a victory and go home. In our universe, the Allies wiped out the Republican Guard in the desert, rolled into Baghdad, smoked Saddam out of his bunker, and hauled him and his top officers to Den Haag for the 1992 war crimes trials. The Den Haag trials were carefully timed to be held while the U.S. presidential race was in progress, and the Bush-Dole campaign made good use of that.

"But apparently my own U.K. government's Foreign Office at the time was advocating a more devious course, that of halting the Gulf War in the desert and leaving a weakened Saddam in place in Baghdad as a foil against Muslim-fundamentalist Iran to the east and the Kurdish communist rebels in the north. Their argument almost carried the day. If it had, President Bush would have looked much less like a conquering hero to the voters. I suspect the 'wimp' factor might have reappeared and influenced the election.''

"I see," said George. "That makes it clear, then. I must arrange a meeting with our esteemed President next week, so that I can reason with him in order to advocate a course of measured response and moderation." He grinned.

• 55

AT THE PARTY ON THE NIGHT OF THE FLORIDA PRIMARY, THE CLIN-ton campaign headquarters in Tallahassee was filled with celebrants. Across the room George recognized a familiar face. He felt a rush of anticipation. He had been thinking about this moment for six years. Now he was terrified of bungling it. He walked slowly over, drink in hand. "You're Alice Lang, I believe," he said, looking directly into her eyes.

The young woman smiled, then looked down, examining his adhesive name tag. " 'George Preston,' " she read aloud. "Oh yes, I recognize your name from our contributors list. I'm very pleased to meet you, George. You're a valued Clinton supporter. Please call me Alice."

"I must admit to you, Alice, that I'm not so much a Clinton supporter as a Bush antisupporter," he said. "I think it's time for a change. I've also given a lot of financial encouragement to Ross Perot recently."

She wrinkled her nose. "Perot? A friend of mine joined his local organization recently, but that little man scares me. Can you honestly say that you'd like to have Ross Perot as President of the United States?"

"No," said George. "Of course not. I plan for him to divert votes away from the Bush-Quayle ticket so that Bill can get elected. You've studied political science, Alice. You must know that third-party candidates always get other people elected, not themselves. Teddy Roosevelt and George Wallace are good examples of the phenomenon."

Alice frowned. "I did take a class in political science this year, but how did you know that? We've never met, have we?"

"Let's say I knew you in another life," said George. He didn't smile.

Alice laughed, then looked at him carefully. "You're not a friend of Shirley MacLaine's, are you?" She wrinkled her nose.

"No, I'm not talking about reincarnation," said George. "This was real. I met you in Waxahachie, Texas, in the year 2004, while you were there working on a story for *Search* magazine. You told me that you were born in Columbus, Ohio. You father was a lawyer, and you have two older brothers. You went to school in Columbus and always made good grades, whether you worked hard or not. In your senior year you were the editor of your high school newspaper. You liked that and decided to major in journalism in college. You came here to attend FSU because they have a good journalism school, you wanted to get some distance from relatives you didn't particularly like, and you wanted to escape the Ohio winters. You're presently seeing a law student named Steve Brown, the Perot supporter you mentioned, but you haven't decided yet whether it's serious or not."

Alice's face turned a deep red. "I feel violated, Mr. Preston," she said angrily. "You must have hired detectives to spy on me. That's despicable."

"Wait," said George, holding up his hand. "Let me continue. Your best friend in elementary school was Jane Conway, but her family moved to New York, and you missed her very much for a while. You cut your hand badly on a broken bottle when you were nine years old, but there's only a tiny scar now. You had a problem with an ingrown toenail when you were twelve, but it went away when you stopped wearing tight shoes. Your mother died of breast cancer while you were starting high school, and you've never quite gotten over that. Your cat, Boots, died the same year, and you've never had another cat."

Alice slapped him with a resounding *whack* sound, then stepped back and put her hand over her mouth, her eyes wide. Several heads turned in their direction.

George rubbed his face, winced, then smiled. "I suppose I deserved that," he said. "I understand how you must feel, Alice . . . what you must think. But you're wrong. There are no detectives, no investigations. Everything I know about you, you told me yourself. We were lovers, and we told each other everything. How could an investigator possibly find out about your friend Jane, or the toenail, or Boots, or that you wanted distance from relatives?"

"Lovers!" said Alice. "That's a filthy lie! How could you . . . ? How could we . . . ?"

"I'm a time traveler," said George. "I came from the future, or perhaps I should say one possible future. We met and fell in love in the year 2004." He handed her his Washington State driver's license and pointed to its issue date. The date of issue, sealed in plastic and protected by a hologram, was July 25, 2003.

She looked suspiciously at the picture on the license, then at him. "This could be faked," she said. "It doesn't prove anything. I admit that this man certainly looks like you, but he's older, with a graying beard and lines in his face that you don't have," she said, indicating the picture. "He looks like your older brother, and it says here that his name is Griffin, not Preston."

He nodded. "You must agree that if I was simply going to produce a fake driver's license, I would have used my present name and a better picture. I changed my name because I had to establish a new identity when I arrived here in the past," he said. "You see, there's already a previous copy of me here, and he's using my old name. Dr. George Griffin is presently living in France and doing physics at the CERN laboratory in Geneva. I'm actually six years older, not younger, than the person in the picture, but I've had the advantage of some very good biotech repair work."

Alice's eyes narrowed, and then she grinned. "A face lift? Liposuction?" she asked with a conspiratorial whisper.

"Actually, something quite a bit more basic." He laughed, then looked at the celebrating people nearby. Some of them were still watching him suspiciously in the aftermath of the slap. "Could we, um, go someplace else to talk, Alice? This is a bit public for my taste and for what I have to say. Perhaps I could buy you a late dinner, if you know a nice restaurant that's still open."

Alice studied him for a time, tapping her foot as she considered the problem he presented. "Your story is the most amazing line of bull I've ever heard, Mr. Preston. It has to be an outrageous lie. But I have good instincts about people, and somehow I trust you—up to a point. If you were a Ted Bundy clone, your line would have been a lot more believable. And I must admit that you've elevated my curiosity to the highest level it's been in a long time. Sure, I know a place that's open all night. It's shockingly expensive, too, and I mean to eat well." She gestured for him to lead the way.

*   *   *

They had been gone for half an hour when an athletic dark-haired young man arrived, a notebook and pair of law books held loosely in his arm. He scanned the room, then approached a tall girl dispensing punch. "Jane, have you seen Alice?" he asked. "The library just closed, and I thought I'd come over and help you people celebrate."

Jane smiled. "Sorry, Steve. I'm afraid you're a bit too late," she said. "Alice left some time ago with a rich Texas oilman. He's one of our big contributors."

"Oilman?" Steve said. "Who is he?"

"I believe," said Jane, "that his name is George Preston. You may have read about him in *BusinessWeek*. He's the founder and president of PetroGen. He's supposed to be almost as rich as Bill Gates. Alice has already slapped him once this evening, but they seemed to be getting along fine when they left together." She smiled after Steve as he stalked out of the room.

"I'm still not sure I understand," Alice said as the tuxedo-clad waiter was removing the gold-rimmed plates. "The universe, this future you came from, was deliberately destroyed, you said. Then how can you be here? Shouldn't you have been destroyed along with it?"

"My friend Roger and I went through a wormhole as the future was being erased," he said. "In a sense, we're an extension of the erasing process."

"But how . . . ?"

"The world has been given a second chance," said George. "Have you ever played a computer game where you can save the game status and read it back in if you don't like what happens afterward? It's rather like that, except with the real universe." He paused, watching her reaction.

Alice was frowning with concentration. "But how can there be two copies of you here?"

"Because my friend and I came through the wormhole that destroyed the future universe, and when we arrived, an earlier version of each of us was already here. It's really not much different from having an identical twin. Roger says that, in order to conserve mass and energy, as we arrived the wormhole mouth lost an equal mass, allowing us to exist and the masses to balance. He's derived some equations that explain the phenomenon, but I don't understand them. Something about back reaction and annihilation of dark matter."

Alice shook her head as if to clear her vision. "Why are you telling this to me, George?"

George looked deeply into her eyes again. "You're the only person I've ever told, Alice," he said quietly. "Perhaps that's why I did it so clumsily. For the past six years I've thought about locating you and telling you what happened. I needed to tell you. In our world, the person you would have become was very brave, and I loved her more than I ever told her. She almost succeeded in stopping the Hive invasion, and she sacrificed her life in the effort. She was killed in a horrible way, and we were able to do what we did only because of her courage. I'm sure that she would have wanted you to know what happened."

Alice nodded. "I suppose . . ." she said.

"And there is also another thing I need to tell you." He flushed and looked down at the table. "I . . . I'm still in love with that Alice, with her. At least . . . I mean . . . I feel . . . Damn this language. It isn't set up to talk about time travel. I . . . think I'm in love with you."

She stared at him, wide-eyed. "But why now? Why here? You waited all this time. You've been here for six years. Why didn't you . . . ?"

He nodded. "In 1987 you were how old? Sixteen? Your mother had just died. You needed time to get over that. You needed space to grow, to become yourself. I couldn't. Until I saw you tonight."

She looked down. "You know, after Mom died I began having strange recurring dreams. There was an older woman, but she was also me. There was a man with a beard. You?" Again she stared across the table at him.

"I don't know," he said. "But I do know that I want you to join us. There are only Roger and me now, and there's so much to do."

"But I'm only a junior in college," she said. "I need to graduate. I can't drop out of FSU. That's crazy."

"You wouldn't have to," he said. "Your summer break is almost here. You can work with us this summer and decide later if you want to continue."

She paused, looking thoughtful. "I have been writing letters and making phone calls trying to find a summer job," she said. "But I had also wanted to continue helping with the campaign. You're helping to get Bill Clinton elected? Is that part of the work you mentioned?"

"Yes, part of it," said George. "But let me be quite clear about our support of him. Bill's a very fine person, and I believe he'll be a good President. But I must tell you that our support is a means to an end. We're trying to keep the Superconducting Super Collider from being built. That's the reason we came back here. If we can't stop it, everyone on this planet will die in the year 2004."

"I still don't understand why you have to stop the SSC project," said Alice. "Does its operation do something unexpected?"

"In a way," said George. "The accelerator will work very well and will do just what it was designed for, but in the process it will make a signal that, um, will allow an enemy to find us and destroy our world. The only way to prevent the signal is by stopping the project."

"But Bill has already gone on record as supporting the SSC project," said Alice.

"He *should* support it," said George. "Except for the unpleasant side effect I mentioned, of which Bill could have no knowledge, it's an excellent science project that should be supported. But realistically, his support won't be as deep-rooted as Bush's, who is interested in anything in Texas and sees the SSC as a Republican project. Al Gore is interested in technology, but he also doesn't have a strong interest in fundamental physics or any commitment to the SSC. And Bill's new Science Advisor, whoever he will be, almost certainly won't be as effective as Allan Bromley. Besides, our projections show that a lot of first-term Democrats should be swept in with Bill, and those people, with no baggage of commitments and no particular understanding of science, should almost all vote to kill the project."

"Your projections show *that*?" asked Alice. "But no one can . . . What kind of projections are you running?"

"My colleague Roger did them. Um, Roger is—how shall I put it?—extremely smart to begin with, and on top of that he's had his intelligence boosted by the advanced biotech I mentioned. He's developed a new kind of projection technique that no one else has even heard of. And he has the advantage of knowing what happened, will happen, might happen, dammit, in our future. He has two histories against which to calibrate his technique. That turns out to be an enormous advantage."

"And what does, uh, did happen in the universe you came from?" Alice asked.

"Bush was reelected, the SSC was built, and the universe was destroyed," said George.

"And how did that involve you . . . and me?"

"That's a very long story," said George.

"I've got time," said Alice, looking at her watch. "Tell me about it."

After George had finished and was sipping his cognac, Alice remained quiet for a time.

"If I can believe you," she said finally, "you literally have the power in your own hands to cure all human ills. You can cure cancer, hemophilia, MS, AIDS—anything. And you can transfer that ability to anyone else. Yet so far you've only used that power to make money and to tinker with politics. Why haven't you done more, George? How could you *not* do more?"

"Ah," said George, "you have arrived at the place where Roger and I have been living for the last six years, the central dilemma. Of course, you're correct. We don't have to keep the techniques to ourselves. We could spread *Reading* and *Writing* through the entire population of the world in a few months. We could put the Makers' download on the Internet for anyone to access, and we could mount a multimillion-dollar advertising campaign to publicize it. And what would the consequences of that be?" He paused, looking at her.

"I don't know," Alice said finally.

"That's the correct answer, Alice. I don't know, either," said George. "And Roger doesn't know. But his attempts at predicting the outcome are frightening. Riots, revolutions, wars, terrorism, you name it . . . It would be too much of a change too fast. The human race is smart and adaptable, but probably not *that* smart and adaptable."

"But what's the alternative?" Alice asked. "You can't just do nothing."

"Oh, we *are* doing things," said George. "But we're proceeding slowly and carefully. We've prodded a few selected physicists and mathematicians in what we know are the right directions. We've encouraged them with research money. We've also done similar things on the molecular biology front. And in a few instances, we've acted more directly. No one has noticed yet, but the last flu virus to make the rounds leaves its recovered victims a bit smarter and with an improved immune system." He smiled.

"But you could cure cancer," said Alice. "Every year thousands of people die of cancer while you do nothing. My mother died of cancer, dammit."

"I know that," said George. "Look, we could save some people. In fact, we have, in a few cases. But releasing a general treatment in the correct legal way takes time because of federal government drug regulations. A biotechnology company I own is now in the middle of FDA testing of a drug that provides a fairly general cancer cure, but it won't be available outside of test groups for perhaps ten years. We're sure it works, but the FDA will only be convinced by clinical tests that take a long time. That happens to be the way our present medical system works."

"I still don't understand," said Alice.

"Look," said George, "Roger and I spent much of the first year we were here deciding how to proceed. We can't do everything. Our top priority is to stop the SSC project, in order to gain more time. We have to prevent the Hive from finding us in 2004. We've been focusing mainly on that."

"But you know how to do so much more," said Alice.

"Not really," said George. "We didn't have enough time to receive much instruction from Iris on how to use *Writing* before the Hive arrived. Consequently, we don't have enough experience to use the technique now with confidence. It has too much potential for mistakes, for doing things that are harmful and irreversible. We have to be careful, so we've only used *Writing* in very limited ways so far. We've only made viruses and nanomachines that are guaranteed to stop reproducing and die out after a fixed number of generations. To do more, we need teams of the best people working full-time on learning the subtleties of *Writing*, not just two preoccupied people with only limited time to dabble at it."

"It must be frustrating," said Alice, "having to move so slowly when you could do so much."

"If you join us, you'll learn just how frustrating it is," said George.

• 56

THERE IS AN UNDERGROUND LAYER TO THE COMPLEX OF MAJESTIC white marble buildings that are the center of the U.S. federal government. Under the busy streets and parklike lawns surrounding the Capitol Building a small subway system connects both the House office buildings and the Senate office buildings with the Capitol. Electric mini-locomotives tow chains of open passenger cars back and forth along subterranean tunnels. Senators and Congressmen are transported to their vast marble chambers in the Capitol Building to record their roll-call votes, then returned to the vast complex of congressional office buildings where most of the actual work of Congress is done and where most of the hearings and committee meetings are held. Congressional staff members, secretaries, interns, lobbyists, and visitors ride the same underground railway, playing their varying parts in the processes of the federal government.

George Preston and his new lobbyist, Alice Lang, jumped onto an open subway car just as the little train was leaving its Capitol terminus. It was raining hard outside, and at Alice's suggestion they had made the trip from House to Senate office buildings by riding the House subway, walking the length of the Capitol subbasement, and then riding the Senate subway. It was a busy route, and to George it seemed to be filled with twenty-five-year-olds in new-looking tailored business suits. These *kids* run the government, he thought.

Arriving at the Senate end of the line, George and Alice followed the signs to the Dirksen Senate Office Building. After a cursory check inside their briefcases, a security guard directed them through the arch of a metal detector. They waited for a "nonmembers" elevator and took it from the subbasement to the second floor. Finally they reached Room 229, the offices of Senator Dale Bumpers of Arkansas. Alice was greeted by the receptionist, who seemed to recognize her from previous visits, and they were shown into a conference room. "Barbara will be with you real soon," she said, her Arkansas twang proudly displayed in her speech.

"Barbara Warburton is Senator Bumpers's staff person dealing with energy-related matters, which means the SSC,'' Alice explained. "She's very nice."

"I'm not sure what we're doing here," said George. "I didn't think Dale Bumpers was on the right appropriations subcommittee to do us much good."

"I should have explained," said Alice. "Last June the House, led by our friends Eckart and Boehlert, voted 232 to 181 to kill the SSC. They zeroed out all SSC funds in the Department of Energy appropriations bill. The Senate, over Bumpers's objections, voted 62 to 32 to continue the SSC at the level of $550 million. Since the two houses of Congress passed different bills, they have to meet in a joint conference committee to iron out their differences. Bumpers wasn't appointed to that joint committee, but as an interested party he's attending as an *ex officio* member with voice but without vote. He's there pushing for adoption of the House version of the bill. He'll call Barbara immediately after the vote."

"Do you understand why he's opposing the SSC?" asked George. "It seems out of character for him as a progressive."

"I talked to Barbara about that at some length," said Alice. "Bumpers's attitude is rather like Congressman Boehlert's. He's basically in favor of supporting science, but he feels that both the SSC and the Space Station are excessive and out of scale. At a time when the focus of the government should be on balancing the budget, he thinks spending on large and conspicuous science projects sends the wrong message. He's lost some friends in the Senate over his opposition to the SSC and the Space Station, but he feels that it's a matter of principle."

George nodded. "I can respect that," he said. "It's some of those 'guns for hire' over in the House that make me feel unclean when I meet with them."

"I know the ones you mean," said Alice. "They're against the SSC because they see it as a vulnerable target of opportunity and because they want another notch on their holsters, but they're in favor of NASA's Space Station boondoggle because there's PAC money to be had from the big NASA contractors. The same day the House voted down the SSC by 232 to 181, the Space Station bill passed by one vote."

"That fifty-vote difference didn't come cheap," said George. "Those swing votes were cast by some of the best congressmen money can buy."

"While we have a moment," said Alice, "let me ask about something. The question keeps popping up of whether the Japanese will contribute to the SSC. The SSC boosters say that the Japanese will join the project any day now and will contribute a billion dollars. Will they?"

George laughed. "They're just blowing smoke," he said. "In my universe, Bush went to Japan in November 1991, right after preparatory visits from Deutsch and Bromley, directly asked Prime Minister Miyazawa for a Japanese commitment to the SSC project, and came home with a commitment of 150 billion yen. But here and now, that November visit was canceled when the U.S. economy took a turn for the worse. When Bush finally visited Japan this past January, his Chief of Staff, Sam Skinner, at our urging, dropped the SSC from the agenda of the meeting with the Japanese Prime Minister. The result was that Bush went to Japan and principally distinguished himself by vomiting on Miyazawa. He didn't bring home any SSC commitment, or much else."

Alice looked at him suspiciously. "You guys had something to do with the famous International Upchuck?"

George smiled. "Roger gave the President a benevolent retrovirus so he'd be feeling a bit below par during the meeting and wouldn't notice the absence of the SSC from the agenda. The virus may have produced Bush's problem at the state dinner, but I can't say we planned it. After Bush had returned to Washington, Miyazawa set up a joint panel to 'study Japanese participation in the SSC.' That was his inscrutable way of giving the proposal a decent burial. Don't worry. We're quite sure the Japanese won't participate. The moment for that has come and gone."

The conference room door opened and a tall woman with long dark hair entered. Alice introduced Barbara to George. "What's the news?" she asked.

"Bad," said Barbara. "We were ambushed. The House Members of the conference committee were appointed by Speaker Tom Foley. It turns out that despite the strong House vote, the House conferees were all SSC advocates, every one of them. The conference committee voted to continue the SSC at the full $550 million funding level approved by the Senate."

"At the full level?" asked Alice. "I thought that when there was a difference between House and Senate bills, the conference always splits the difference, so at best the SSC could get only half the planned funding."

"That's what we'd expected too, but there was a technical point we hadn't appreciated," said Barbara. "Since the House *deleted* the SSC appropriation altogether rather than keeping it in with zero funds, technically there was no difference to split, and so the project got its full funding. I think the SSC advocates in the House deliberately arranged to delete the appropriation, knowing full well that this would happen."

"I guess there's always next year," said George. "We should have a new Congress by then."

"Senator Bumpers certainly plans to try again next year," said Barbara, "but I'm not optimistic. The Senate vote isn't likely to change much. And if Speaker Foley always appoints only SSC supporters to the conference committee, we'll have the same scenario every year. The leadership usually gets its way in this town."

On the street outside the Dirksen Building, the rain had stopped. George and Alice found a cab that would take them to the Hilton to collect their luggage and then to National Airport. Alice looked depressed.

"After the big vote margin of the House vote, I was so sure we had succeeded," she said. "The damned project seems to have a life of its own. It can't be killed."

"It can," said George. "You must be patient. Focus on one step at a time. Your work here is done for the year, and it's time to start the next phase. For the rest of the summer you can work to get your friend Bill Clinton elected."

"Great!" said Alice, looking more cheerful. "I really need a change. Congressional politics is fascinating, but for me it has a cumulative toxic effect."

George laughed. "Some can tolerate the toxins better than others," he said. "Some years ago the various scientific societies created congressional fellowships that supported young scientists who would come to Washington and work as volunteer staff in congressional offices to help make science-related decisions. It's somewhat revealing that the chemists and mathematicians all left Washington after their year was up, like biblical refugees fleeing Sodom and Gomorrah, while most of the physicists liked it and stayed on."

"I can understand that, I guess," said Alice, "but I'm ready to leave. This town is not my favorite spot on the Earth. I wasn't cut out to be Machiavelli."

"None of us was," said George. "It makes us feel slimy, and we hate it. But we do it very well, don't we? I hope we can stop someday soon, before we start to like it."

PART VIII
July 27, 1992

October 25, 1993

Overwhelmingly, many members [of Congress] needed a symbolic act of budget-cutting. The SSC was a project that could be cut because neither the Congress nor their constituents understood it or cared about it."
> —Professor Steven Weinberg, University of Texas at Austin. Nobel Laureate

[The cost of the SSC] kept ratcheting up, and we tested the limits of Congress's endurance. The SSC showed us just how far we could go.
> —Professor Wil Happer, Princeton University, former DOE Director of Energy Research in the Bush and Clinton Administrations

It's disheartening that a large number of fairly intelligent people could do such a dumb thing . . . The government decided, in its wisdom, that high-energy physics has no future in the U.S.A.
> —Professor Leon Lederman. Illinois Institute of Technology, former Director of Fermilab, Nobel Laureate

57

"GO HOME, STEVE," SAID BERTHA. "GET A LIFE! IT WAS A NICE try, but we can't run a presidential campaign without a candidate."

Steve Brown looked up at the formidable woman who had been the Florida chairman of the Perot for President campaign. "I know, Bertha," he said. "But there are still a few things I need to finish up first. I'm not going to just drop everything and walk away. Who knows? Maybe Ross will change his mind again and decide to run for President after all."

"If he does," said Bertha, "I'll kill the little jerk. He was doing so well. He'd already pulled to within a few percentage points of Bush and Clinton in the polls, and our projections said he would have been ahead in two more weeks. It was crazy to pull out now." She patted him on the shoulder. "But *c'est la vie*, as they say in Louisiana. Take care, Steve, and thanks for everything." She walked out the front door and pulled it closed behind her just a bit too hard.

Steve looked around the deserted Tallahassee Perot for President office. Only a few days before the place had been a beehive of activity. But after Perot announced his withdrawal two days ago, the volunteers had disappeared, taking much of the loaned office furniture and equipment with them. The rent on the office, however, was paid up until the end of the month, a few desks and chairs were still here, and the WATS telephone lines were still connected.

He felt angry and betrayed. He had planned so carefully, and now it had all come apart. First there was the Alice thing. Alice was pretty, fairly intelligent, and very hardworking. He'd picked her specifically for those qualities, and she was supposed to be grateful. As he'd had it planned, they would marry when they graduated, she would get a good job, and she would support him while he finished law school.

But then that goddamned Texas bastard Preston had appeared, and somehow he'd stolen her. Alice was very secretive about what Preston had told her, but whatever it was, it had completely changed their relationship. Now she had gone off God knows where with the bastard doing God knows what. She's probably screwing him right now, he thought, the image striking him like a blow. They'd had a bitter argument the night before she left for Washington. He shouldn't have hit her, he thought, no matter what she'd said. Now she'd probably never come back to him, even if she broke it off with the damn Texan and came back to FSU.

The day after Alice left, Steve had totaled his car. He'd been angry about her betrayal, and perhaps he'd been driving too fast. He was very lucky that the driver of the car he'd hit was drunk, so he'd been able to shift the blame. The jerk's insurance company was going to pay him to replace his car, but for the moment he was a mere bike rider in a town designed around the automobile. Damn, it was frustrating.

And now there was Perot's betrayal. Before choosing a presidential campaign, Steve had carefully studied the options. Alice had pushed hard for him to join the Clinton bandwagon, but both Clinton and Bush already had large organizations full of experienced people, and both candidates were burdened with considerable negative baggage. He wasn't sure if Iran-gate or Bimbo-gate was the greater burden, but he didn't want a candidate carrying either.

It was also clear to Steve that the media underestimated Perot's chances of winning. And he soon discovered that the people running the Perot campaign in Florida were simply not that sharp and impressive. He'd seen that it would be easy to rise rapidly in the local Perot organization, possible to move upward to the national organization before the election. After he'd joined, his strategy had proved correct. He'd risen very rapidly in the Tallahassee organization until he was deputy state chairman. Perot had also risen dramatically in the polls.

But then two days ago, in the wake of the previous week's Democratic National Convention, Ross Perot had announced without warning that he was withdrawing from the presidential race. As Bertha had said, without a candidate there was no campaign. And more important, there was no organization to take over.

It was as if there was a conspiracy to keep him from succeeding, he thought. His plans were in shambles, all his careful planning destroyed. Well, he would not accept this. He'd find a way to fight back. He picked up the telephone, punched the WATS line button, consulted the media list before him, and dialed.

"*Houston Chronicle*," said a female voice.

"Hello," said Steve. "I'm calling long-distance from Florida.

Please connect me with a reporter who covers the oil industry scene in Houston.''

"That would be Tom Weatherford. The computer shows he's available. Please hold while I connect you.''

There was a ring signal, and a voice answered, "Weatherford.''

"Hello, Tom. This is Steve Brown, calling from Tallahassee. I'm working on a story for the *Tallahassee Democrat*,'' Steve lied. "I wonder if you could provide some information on a Houston oilman named George Preston. I've found several magazine articles about him, and I pulled up a credit report, but I'm looking for deeper information. I thought you might have already checked up on Preston for the *Chronicle*.''

"Ah yes, the mysterious Mr. Preston,'' said Weatherford. "Just a minute, Steve. Let me fetch my file.'' There was a pause, followed by the sound of rustling papers. "Here it is. George Raymond Preston, born in Houston, July 25, 1959, both parents now deceased, no siblings, no record of education in the Houston public school system or at any public or private university in Texas. President and principal stockholder of PertoGen, Inc., estimated net worth around one billion dollars. Corporate biography is minimal, claims Preston worked and studied molecular biology in Europe, but doesn't say where or when.''

"I noticed that his credit history only goes back to 1987,'' said Steve.

"Right,'' said Weatherford. "That's when he moved to Texas from wherever he was before that. He took a driving test to get a Texas driver's license in February 1987. He started Petroleum Genetics Laboratories in a storefront on Fannin Street in Houston in March and soon after the company began to market a whole line of petroleum-related biological products for drilling lubricants, drill tool release agents, oil spill cleanup agents, and other things.

"The whole PGL start-up was peculiar. High-technology start-up companies usually need big initial investment capital and have to invest heavily in high-tech hardware, but PGL had no financial backers I could find and no large initial hardware purchases except for office computers. Their products were so much better than anything else available that they immediately began to make lots of money. Then Preston began to buy up old garbage dumps and nonproducing oil wells.''

"Garbage dumps? I hadn't heard about that.''

"Yes, he put up factory buildings on some of the land. I guess it was cheap, but it must have been hell to stabilize it enough to construct a building on. I never understood what he was up to there."

"Interesting," said Steve, making notes. "What about Preston's private life?"

"He lives in a penthouse apartment that occupies the complete top floor of an apartment building he owns on the west side of downtown Houston. He owns two cars, a Porsche and a BMW, no chauffeur. No boats registered to him, but his company recently bought a corporate jet. He's never been mentioned on the *Chronicle*'s society page, but he's attended a number of political functions and is occasionally mentioned in connection with politics. When he's seen in public, it's usually with business associates. No indication of women friends. He was a big contributor to the Bush campaign in 1988, but recently he's switched his contributions to Clinton and Perot."

"Is Preston backing Perot, too?" Steve asked. "I wasn't aware of that."

"Guess he must have had a falling-out with the Bush people," said Weatherford. "Let's see what else there is. He has no season tickets for sports or cultural activities. The doorman of his apartment told me that he works long hours, doesn't go out much, and never brings anyone home with him late in the evening, either male or female."

Steve frowned. He'd envisioned Preston as a ladies' man, and this didn't seem to fit. Was Alice something more than a casual conquest? He needed to know more about the bastard. "How do you explain the blank credit record before 1987 and the lack of an educational history?" he asked. "Even if he moved back to Texas from out of state, shouldn't there be some paper trail of his previous credit cards and bank accounts?"

"Interesting question," said Weatherford. "*Marquis Who's Who* said that he declined to write a biography for them. Perhaps he did return to the United States from Europe, but when we see a blank like that, it usually means something else. Usually the person in question is either in the federal witness protection program or has changed his name and started over for some other reason."

"Maybe he has a prison record," said Steve, "or has drug money. Perhaps he absconded with somebody else's money and is hiding out."

"I doubt it," said Weatherford. "Preston's lifestyle has been too conspicuous for someone who's in hiding. His picture was in *BusinessWeek* a few weeks ago.''

''Hmm,'' said Steve. ''Maybe he had plastic surgery.''

''Possible,'' said Weatherford. ''He certainly looks much younger than the age forty-three his birth certificate would indicate. If I hadn't seen it myself, I'd say he was in his mid-thirties.''

''I don't suppose you've tried running a fingerprint check on him,'' Steve said.

''I don't know if you guys in Florida can get away with doing such things, but the Houston Police Department is not terribly receptive to reporters who want them to run fingerprint checks through their forensic database system in pursuit of a story. Besides, I don't have a sample of Preston's fingerprints.''

After making arrangements to keep in touch with Weatherford, Steve locked up the campaign office and pedaled to the rooming house where Alice had lived. He knew she had paid up the rent for the summer, even though she was away. He rang the doorbell, and an older woman opened the door.

''Hello, Mrs. Mitchell,'' he said. ''I'm Steve Brown, Alice's friend.''

''Oh yes,'' she said. ''How is Alice? We've missed her.''

''She's working in Washington, D.C., right now, and she's doing fine,'' Steve said. ''She just called and asked if I could find something that she left in her room and send it to her. I'd really appreciate it if you could let me in.''

The woman opened the room for him, then left. Steve put on a pair of light gloves and began to search the drawers and the bookshelf. He found nothing of interest. Finally he took a flashlight and magnifier from his pocket and walked to the bathroom.

When Steve was thirteen, he had for a time been obsessed with the techniques of finding and analyzing fingerprints. He'd read many books on the subject and assembled his own fingerprint kit with a flashlight, a magnifying glass, ruled sheets of paper, a black stamp pad, tiny paintbrushes, talcum powder, and clear plastic tape. He had taken and analyzed the fingerprints of his family and friends. He'd memorized all the fingerprint variations, the whorls, arches, overhand loops, and learned the line-counting techniques used to convert a given print pattern to a set of numbers used in computer database searches.

Now he shined the flashlight at an oblique angle to Alice's bathroom mirror and used the magnifier to look closely at the surfaces near the mirror's edges. Clear fingerprints were visible there, undoubtedly Alice's. All had a characteristic whorl pattern. He used face powder from a drawer to dust some of the glass and plastic bottles from the medicine cabinet. They bore same whorl pattern.

Returning to the main room, he walked to a corner containing a microwave and small refrigerator. Against the wall was a cabinet containing china and glassware. He was sure that Preston bastard had been here several times, particularly on the night Alice had left. He opened the cabinet and examined each glass closely.

Most of the glasses were clean. A few had clear whorl fingerprints on their surfaces. One glass, however, bore the traces of fingerprints that were distinctly different, with an overhand loop pattern unlike anything he'd found in the bathroom.

He considered this. Preston must have drunk from this glass while he was here, then washed it, and put it away. Or perhaps the prints belonged someone else altogether. What the hell, it was worth a shot.

He carefully wrapped the glass in tissue, placed it in a paper bag, clipped the bag to the back of his bicycle, and pedaled back to the Perot office.

"You're absolutely sure it was a break-in?" asked the policeman. The nameplate on his uniform read CABLE. "Couldn't this have been done by one of your volunteers? Maybe one who forgot to tell you?"

"No," said Steve. "We gave out office keys freely to our volunteers, since people worked here at all hours. And, as you can see, the door was jimmied."

Officer Cable nodded. "So you're missing some files, a cashbox containing about two hundred and fifty dollars, and a bottle of Scotch whisky. How important were the files? This sounds a bit like that Watergate thing."

"The files were confidential and sensitive," said Steve. "Contributors lists, investigative reports, privileged correspondence . . . They might have been valuable to the opposition, except that Perot has now dropped out of the race. The file cabinets, desks, computers, and almost everything else had been cleared out of the office already. We're giving up the building lease in a couple of days. I'd been saving the Scotch for a celebration, but as it turned out, we never had much to celebrate."

Cable nodded, then looked closely at the drinking glass on the desk. It had a slight brown residue in the bottom and smelled of stale liquor. "So the timing is peculiar, but this might have been a politically motivated break-in," he said. "The thief wasn't very professional. He must have helped himself to a quick drink before he left. That's good for us, because it looks like he left us a clear set of fingerprints on the glass."

Steve smiled and nodded. "I hope they help you catch the bastard," he said.

Steve waited three days, then called Officer Cable. "Any progress on our break-in?" he asked.

"Glad you called, Mr. Brown," Cable said. "I had a feeling that your break-in might be like that Watergate thing, so I pulled out all the stops. We faxed the prints to Washington and asked the FBI to check them."

"What did they find?" Steve asked.

"It's strange," said Cable. "We got a positive match to the prints from the FBI database. It pulled up the records of a guy named George A. Griffin. He's not a criminal, though, he's a scientist. FBI had his prints because while he was a student at MIT many years ago he had a high-security summer job with a Boston military contractor. We started with the contractor and tracked down his current address. It was at the CERN lab in Switzerland, so we got the Geneva office of Interpol to check on him. Griffin is now living in France near the Swiss border. It's very clear that he's not the person we want, though. He was giving a speech at a physics meeting at CERN in front of two hundred people at the exact time of your break-in. Your burglar couldn't have been him. Guess there must have been some computer screwup in the FBI's identification system."

"Strange," said Steve. "But that name sounds familiar. Out of curiosity, do you have this Griffin person's birthdate?"

"Sure do," said Cable. "He was born in Milwaukee, Wisconsin, on July 25, 1959."

58

ON ELECTION EVE THE GRAND BALLROOM OF THE LITTLE ROCK HILton was filled to capacity. Two walls were covered with large multiple television images, as the polls began closing across the continent and networks reported results and projections. Alice sat with George and Roger at a reserved GOLD AREA table in the roped-off part of the room where campaign managers and party officials could sit and chat with major contributors like George.

Roger had placed his lapstation on the table and was comparing the figures on its small screen with the wall-size screen to his left. He nodded. "Clinton-Gore is the clear winner," he announced. "The close congressional races are still in doubt, but there are definite indications of a coattail effect."

Alice smiled. Since July she had spent most of her time traveling around the country to boost the local Democratic congressional candidates with strategy and funding and to defuse the "bimbo" issue, deflating Clinton's reputation as a womanizer by spreading little jokes that had been subtly crafted by Roger to make the whole business seem ridiculous. "The miserable economy has helped Bill quite a bit," she said. "Bush took a lot of heat over the continuing recession. He really hit the wrong part of the wave."

"In our world," said George, "the recession was definitely over by October, and Bush got credit for engineering the recovery. For the past four years we've been working to stretch out the recession. PetroGen's increase in the production of domestic oil helped. Less foreign oil was bought, which kept the dollar higher and reduced manufactured exports. And we had some interactions with Federal Reserve people that persuaded them to keep the interest rates high, at a time when it would have been smart to lower them. I guess it worked."

Roger looked up from his lapstation. "It's all worked well so far," he said, "but I think it's going to be very close. Even if there's a Clinton landslide this time around, it isn't going to last very long. I'm projecting a sizable backlash in the midterm elections two years from now that will wipe out most of the Democrat coattailers and take much of the congressional establishment with them. I'm projecting that in

'94 the Republicans will take over the Senate and probably the House also. If we can't stop the SSC in the next two years, we may not be able to stop it at all.''

"What if we don't?" Alice asked.

"If we fail and the SSC goes forward," said Roger, "we would have about a decade to prepare for a Hive invasion. If we resorted to sabotage of the machine, perhaps we could extend that a bit longer. In whatever time was available, we would have to introduce *Reading* and *Writing* on a broad scale. My projections continue to show that this would be very disruptive. It might cause unimaginable wars and social upheaval. Our civilization is already strained to near the breaking point by ongoing change. We're able to absorb only so much change at a time before institutions and people begin to break down. Look what the end of the Cold War, basically a beneficial change, has done to the former Soviet states, to the former Yugoslavia, and even to the economy of Germany. We could rapidly prepare to defend ourselves against the Hive, but only with great cost in unpleasant side effects.''

George nodded. "We need more time. We have to introduce gradual changes at a rate that can be absorbed. We need several decades, not one.''

"But even if the SSC project is stopped," Alice asked, "won't some similar facility be built sooner or later?''

"That's an interesting question," said Roger. "As I think you know, the Large Hadronic Collider is now being designed at CERN and will run sometime around 2004. But its energy will be too low to make signals that would attract the Hive. We don't think another machine is likely to be started until the physics data from the LHC operation is fully analyzed and understood. I project that the decision point for constructing the next Collider will come about the year 2015, and the earliest completion of the machine would come about a decade after that, say 2025. That scenario would give us more than three decades to prepare.''

Alice frowned. "Is that enough time?" she asked.

"We think so," George said. "If not, when the decision point gets closer, there are things to do to stretch out the schedule. In any case, as soon as the Makers' download and the existence of the Hive can be revealed, the consequences of building a larger Collider will become clear to everyone and the problem will go away. Then as a society we can decide, in the long run, whether we want to hide and remain inconspicuous, or whether we want to go looking for the Hive ourselves.''

Alice nodded. "What about the immediate future? What are we going to do right now?''

"George and I have spent a lot of time predicting the effects of technological change coming too fast,'' said Roger. "What might happen if we destabilize the institutions that give our society its structure: religions, government, manufacturing, financial markets, educational and research institutions. Our conclusion is that we need to create institutions of our own that have the built-in stability against change.''

"What kind of institutions?'' asked Alice.

"In a period of a few years,'' said George, "we've managed to create a great deal of wealth from oil, mining, biotechnology, and judicious market investments. We can create more if necessary. So far much of our resources and attention have been concentrated on the SSC problem. But we've also been providing funding and guidance for scientists working in key areas that we know will lead to progress. Up to now, however, we haven't created a basic research facility of our own.

"Now, we think, it's time to move beyond the SSC problem. We must use our resources to create major privately funded scientific research facilities. My model is the old Bell Labs, as it existed before the AT&T breakup. Hire the best people, put them in a comfortable and somewhat isolated environment, give them lots of money and support, point them in the right directions, and turn them loose. We'll start by creating such institutions in both the United States and Europe. Eventually we'll undoubtedly need more than two of them. Perhaps we'll put the next one on the moon.''

"On the moon?'' Alice looked at George, wide-eyed. "I don't understand. Why focus on basic research?'' Alice asked. "We can already . . .'' She looked around as if searching for eavesdroppers, then looked down at her hands.

"Surely you realize that we're very vulnerable now,'' said Roger. "Suppose a bomb went off in this building and killed the three of us, here and now. That would be the end of our efforts—and probably of our world.''

Alice nodded.

"Right here,'' Roger continued, "I have the complete transcript of the Makers' download I carried through the time-hole. In this lapstation is information greater than the sum of all human knowledge, almost everything they sent us about their own civilization and about the seventeen other cultures they had contacted. So far, I've only scratched the surface in attempting to digest this material. Surfing about at the surface is easy. Understanding and using it will require a massive effort of many people over a period of many years.''

''At the same time,'' said George, ''there's the problem of culture shock. In our future, society was massively affected by the Snark discovery and hadn't really come to grips with it when the Hive arrived. Our civilization is accustomed to the process of slow and steady discovery, of learning at a certain rate from our own effort and sweat. If the final answers, arrived at through unknown science, using reasoning that we don't understand, are simply handed to us to absorb as revealed wisdom, how will our culture react?''

Alice frowned, thinking. ''Probably well at first. Most of us are accustomed to receiving 'revealed wisdom' from scientists. A big fraction of the public seems to think that the word 'research' means looking something up in a library or database. But in the long term, I suspect that our whole approach to scientific research and discovery might suffer. If you can learn more from communicating with aliens, why bother with the effort of doing your own experiments and research?''

''Exactly,'' said George. ''That's the dilemma. We need to create institutions that can reach some stable synthesis between the information provided by the Makers and information that comes from discoveries of our own.''

There was a roar from the crowd in the ballroom. The election results from the Midwest were coming in, and Clinton was definitely in the lead, as were Democrats in a number of congressional races.

''I've looked into the problem of new research a bit,'' said Roger. ''There are some areas where we will simply have to do our own research. Molecular biology is an obvious example. While *Reading* is a very valuable tool, it's only a tool. We need a whole new generation of molecular biologists to use the new techniques to gain more understanding of our own species and the other species on this planet. We need a whole new generation of molecular engineers to explore the implications of our new ability to *Write*. They'll need to reexplore the whole of civil, chemical, mechanical, and electrical engineering, using *Written* nano-scale biomachines. I've studied how the Makers did that, and I'm convinced that we can do better.''

"That's good news," said Alice. "I'd been assuming that the Makers knew everything.''

"The Makers and their contact civilizations are far ahead of us in most areas,'' said Roger, "but the trick is to quickly wade through the amassed knowledge until you reach the frontier.''

"What frontier?'' Alice asked.

"You need to reach a state of knowledge where you can't look up all the answers, where new basic research needs to be done. Every beginning science graduate student has to do this. It's not a new thing. The frontier has certainly been moved some distance ahead. It hasn't disappeared.

"The near future in science will be somewhat like the period following the discovery of quantum mechanics or relativity, but on a larger scale. It'll be a very difficult time for the established scientists. Their whole way of doing things is going to be overthrown. But it will be a time of great fun for the bright new students who will have an unprecedented opportunity to make the great leap forward and surpass their elders.''

"How does this apply to physics?'' asked George.

"It's a mixed bag,'' said Roger. "Astrophysics looks good in many areas. We'll have lots of new observational data from the other bubble universes, and someone will have to put it together. And there'll be new technology for new and better observational instruments, detectors for dark matter concentrations, axions, gravity waves, and neutrinos, for instance, that will need to be built, using the new engineering techniques.

"Nuclear physics looks less promising. The new research frontier exists, but it's a long way away. The same can be said of condensed matter physics. The prospects in particle physics are similar. It appears from the Makers' download that there really is a substructure to the quark, just as the preliminary experiments at Fermilab will reveal in a few years. The LHC will undoubtedly reveal more about this area. But it will require a new accelerator with special characteristics to get to the bottom of the problem, and there are some questions in this area that the Makers have not yet answered. While we could use the new engineering to construct our own private Super-SSC, to do so would certainly attract the Hive.''

"I think when we're ready, we will want to deliberately attract the Hive," said George.

Alice shuddered.

"Perhaps," said Roger, "but in the immediate future there's a better direction for particle physics than messing about with quark substructure. In particular, there's the possibility of going directly to the most fundamental structures and doing Planck-scale physics at the quantum gravity level. That's how the Makers contacted us. I don't yet understand enough to know where the frontier is for that area, or whether it would be possible for us to do meaningful research there any time soon. But the work Tern's group is doing on the problem now looks very promising."

George nodded. "Individuals can only do so much. Our funding of a few university groups is a good start, but now we need teams of people, the best minds we can recruit, working closely together on these problems." He looked around the room at the celebration. The Colorado results were being tallied, and the Clinton-Gore ticket was being projected as the sure winner. "Next week we'll announce the formation of a major new research institution. We've already been funding research using the name the Iris Foundation. I propose we call our new think tanks and basic research facilities the Iris Institutes."

• 59

STEVE BROWN TYPED PETROGEN INTO THE RECORDS COMPUTER SYStem and waited while the database program searched the file structure.

Florida State University was now closed for the Christmas holidays. Last week he'd received a tip from Tom Weatherford that PetroGen had recently been buying large blocks of property in Alabama. Steve had called yesterday about access to the Alabama Department of Records files and today had driven to Montgomery, about two hundred miles to the north. Records was located in a large low brick building not far from the Alabama state capitol building.

The pretty blonde in charge of the records computer system had shown Steve to a carrel containing a black and white X-terminal and handed him a plastic-covered page of instructions. The system was straightforward enough, and after a few minutes of practice he'd begun the real work of searching.

The computer beeped, and the screen read SEARCH HAS FOUND 7 ITEMS. This was followed by a list of reference numbers. Steve clicked on the first reference number, and the database displayed the listing. It described an eighty-acre parcel of waterfront property located on the Tombigbee River. Steve recorded the details in his notebook.

The second item was also a parcel of waterfront property on the same river. The other five items were the same. Steve tried several other search keywords, but there were no more entries. Apparently all the purchases had been recorded with PetroGen as the legal owner. He totaled the cost of all the entries. It came to over $150 million. For some reason PetroGen was investing heavily in the region along one particular stretch of river.

Steve exited the database program, gathered his papers, and strolled back to the outer office. The blonde girl was sitting at a desk behind the counter. The nameplate on the desk read KATHLEEN SCOTT.

"Through already?" she asked.

"More or less, Miss Scott," said Steve, sitting down on the chair across from her desk. "I wonder if you could tell me something. Where's the Tombigbee River and what's going on over there?"

She laughed. "Oh, that. Some people think the Tombigbee waterway project is the greatest thing that ever happened to Alabama, and other people think it's just a great big black hole for state and federal money. You see, there are some big rivers in the western part of the state—over by Mississippi?—that aren't quite navigable and that don't quite connect up. And one of our congressmen, Tom Bevill, has been up in Washington for a long time, and he runs some appropriations subcommittee . . . the one that has to do with water projects? And so he just told those Army Engineers that they should do something about connecting up those rivers and fixing them . . . so boats could go down them to Mobile and the Gulf?"

"He wants to make the Tombigbee a navigable waterway?" Steve asked.

"That's right," Kathleen answered. "So the Army started this project. And every few years the Congress gives them more money to work on it."

Steve nodded. "So how's the project been doing lately?" he asked.

"Not so well," she said. "It's supposed to be almost finished, but there's been a lot of pressure . . . for cutting budgets? And the Army Engineers don't have enough money to finish the project. Last I heard, they had stopped most of the work on it. According to the newspapers, a lot of the dredging and construction people have lost their jobs."

"What about property values on the river?" Steve asked.

"They've been way down," said Kathleen. "My Uncle Bob had some land over there, and after he died Aunt Clara had to sell it for next to nothing."

"That's too bad," Steve said. "She should have kept it. I have reason to believe the prices will go up soon."

• 60

GEORGE GRIFFIN ROSE AS THE TWO VISITORS ENTERED HIS FERMILAB office. He was apprehensive about meeting these people, even though the appointment had been arranged by the Fermilab director himself.

"Hello, George," said the taller of the men. "My name is George, too." His hair was dark blond, like Griffin's. Both men were wearing thousand-dollar suits that fitted them beautifully. They looked out of place at Fermilab. "I'm George Preston and this is my colleague Roger Fulton. We're board members of the Iris Foundation." They shook hands.

Griffin felt a surprising tingle accompanying each handshake. "I'm glad to meet you," he said. "On the phone you mentioned a job proposition. I hope you understand that I just arrived here from CERN two weeks ago, and I'm not exactly exploring job opportunities at the moment." He'd read the recent news reports about the new major research foundation with a big endowment. It seemed too good to be true.

Preston nodded. His face looked strangely familiar, but Griffin could not remember in what context. "We understand your commitment to your new position here," Preston said, "but we wanted to talk to you anyway. The Iris Foundation is now in the process of creating two major new research laboratories, the Iris Institutes. One of these will be located in Europe and the other in the United States.

The foundation has very deep pockets for supporting fundamental research. The initial foundation endowment is over $5 billion, and we expect that to grow as the companies that support it prosper. We are here to offer you the job of research director of the new Iris Institute in this country. The starting salary is around $300,000 per year, plus benefits.''

Griffin felt a rush of adrenaline. ''Research director? Surely this is a joke. You must want a prominent Nobel laureate for a position and salary like that. I'm just a mid-level high-energy experimentalist. I only make $45,000 a year, just a little more than I was getting at CERN. I don't even have a permanent job at Fermilab, just a five-year appointment.''

''I know that our offer must seem strange, George,'' said the man introduced as Roger Fulton. He had a clipped British accent. ''But we already know that you are the man we want for the job. Let me tell you a story. It begins on a warm spring day in May of the year 2004, when I was sitting alone at a table at the CERN cafeteria, minding my own business . . .''

When Roger had finished, Griffin sat quiet for a while, thinking as he looked at Preston. ''You want me to believe that you are me, but seventeen years older. If anything, you look younger than I do. You might be my younger brother.''

''I made myself younger with a bit of re-*Writing* of some basic cell biology,'' said Preston. ''I also *Wrote* a lot of other changes for my body that aren't apparent. For example, I don't have to exercise to stay in shape anymore. I'm also smarter than before, my reflexes are quicker, and I can cause my time sense to speed up or slow down by about a factor of ten. I can set my own muscle tone, and I can bench-press four times my body weight. I'm immune to cancer and other diseases. I can change my appearance and facial characteristics, too, but I haven't, except for shaving off the beard. My whiskers don't grow now unless I ask them to.''

Griffin's eyes narrowed. Was this some kind of con game?

''But . . . Okay,'' Preston continued. ''Here's some proof you might believe.'' He extracted a black stamp pad and a sheet of white paper from his briefcase and placed them on the desk. Then he held out his right index finger to Griffin. ''Look at my fingertip closely,'' he said. ''Make sure that I'm not using a rubber overlay or something.''

Griffin scratched his fingernail against the fingertip, then nodded.

Preston rolled his finger across the stamp pad and then across the paper, leaving a clear black fingerprint with a clear overhand loop pattern. "Now you do the same thing."

Griffin did so, and then looked closely at the two fingerprints. "They're the same," he said quietly.

"Okay, let's get to the point," said Preston. "What do you think of our offer, now that you understand what we have in mind?"

What if I tell you I think you're crazy? Griffin thought. "What if I tell you I'm not interested, that I like what I'm doing here?" he asked.

"I already know that you like the work," said Preston. "You'll do rather well here. Your group will clinch the discovery of the top quark in about two years, although it's going to be rather messier than you might think. You'll also turn up preliminary evidence hinting that the quark may have substructure. You and Grace will not have any children. You'll land a permanent faculty position at the University of Washington in Seattle. About the same time you and Grace will part company, and she'll go back to England. I know that you're already having problems. Following that, in my world you joined the LHC collaboration and began to work primarily at the SSC. I'm not sure what you'll do if the SSC project is canceled, probably join one of the LHC collaborations at CERN, either ATLAS or CMS. That, perhaps, won't work out so well. Roger tells me the LHC at its present design energy is unlikely to get a definitive Higgs signal. So if you're going to switch your research path, this might be a good time to do it."

How would he know that Grace and I are having problems? Griffin wondered.

"I see that you still don't believe me," said Preston. "Okay, let me tell you some things about yourself that nobody else would know . . ."

Griffin listened as Preston began to talk, listing childhood events and personal secrets. Griffin was perplexed. How could he know these things? Had he mentioned them to his coworkers, to his friends, to Grace? Did he talk in his sleep? No, there was no way this guy could know . . . he must . . . "Okay! Stop! You win!" he said, feeling embarrassed, exposed. "I give up, dammit. You must be me."

Griffin was quiet for a while. "What is the research at Iris going to be like?'' he asked finally. ''Not high-energy physics, I suspect.''

''We've told you some of it already,'' said Roger. ''As director of research, it will be partly up to you. Our plan is to select a few areas of basic and applied research and to move forward rapidly, to reach the point where we're once again doing original research instead of learning from the Makers. We want to hire a lot of bright young people, with an emphasis on quick uptake and flexibility. You'll be responsible for leading and guiding these young people. For a time it will be necessary to keep quiet about our information from the Makers, in order to minimize the culture-shock effect. We hope we can get through that period of secrecy in about ten years, perhaps sooner.''

''I've always hated secrecy,'' said Griffin.

''I know,'' said Preston, ''you were very uncomfortable with all the security during the summer job you had with that defense contractor. But in this case it's necessary, George. I also know you can deal with it when you have to.''

Griffin took a deep breath. He was quiet for a while. ''Okay,'' he said finally, ''I'll do it. But I want you to understand my reason. I'm thinking of all the people I know who might be alternate candidates for the job. And I think they'd all probably screw it up, in one way or another. So I suppose I'll have to do it myself. But let me tell you, up front, I'm not at all fond of administration, and I'm going to really hate the secrecy part. I want you to understand that.''

''I do understand, George,'' said Preston. ''I would say exactly the same thing, of course.''

Griffin frowned at him. He wondered what it was going to be like, working for a man who knows exactly how you think, who knows every thought you've ever had, up to now.

• 61

JOE RAMSEY EXAMINED HIMSELF IN THE GOLD-FRAMED OVAL MIR-ror. CONGRESSIONAL STAFF MEMBER AND SPECIAL ASSISTANT TO CON-GRESSMAN JONATHAN MATTHEWS, D.-OREGON read the gold-embossed business card wedged into the mirror frame. He'd been very clever to work on the Matthews campaign while he was finishing law school in Eugene. Otherwise, he would have been doomed to the usual indentured servitude at some big Portland law firm, spending his most productive years in some back room pounding a computer terminal, doing Lexis and Nexis research and writing briefs for the partners who interacted with the clients and pulled down the big salaries.

Here in D.C., however, he was the point man for his very own congressman. Since Jon had just been elected for his first term, Joe was in on the ground floor. It was he who interviewed most of the visitors and made the decision on who would be allowed to see the Man and who would be sent on their way after a brief discussion of why they were here, with maybe a gallery pass to the House.

Joe loved his job. He worked in this unique environment where most of the key decisions of the legislative body of the most powerful nation in the world were being made by twenty-four-year-old staff members like himself. He was living in a town where there were four women for every man. And he was making contacts that would land him a good position later—if and when.

The phone on his desk buzzed, and he looked at his schedule. The next appointment was with one A. Lang from the Tallahassee Environmental Coalition. Probably something about protecting alligators and bullfrogs. However, the appointment had been requested by the lobbyist from PetroGen, one of Jon's biggest contributors. He lifted the receiver, said that he was ready now, and walked to the reception room.

A. Lang turned out to be a woman, quite a good-looking young one, actually. The "A." stood for Alice. He noticed that his hand tingled when she shook it and wondered if that meant something special. He hoped so.

"I'm here," she explained, "to voice the opposition of my group to the SSC project in Texas."

"I'd like very much to hear about that," Joe said, radiating sincerity and concern, "and I know Congressman Matthews will be interested." He led her to his office and suggested that she join him on the sofa rather than sit on the less comfortable chair before his desk that he used for quick-turnaround interviews. "Tell me about it, Alice," he said, trying to remember what the hell this project was. A dam, perhaps?

"Our group is organizing opposition to the Superconducting Super Collider project in Congress," she began. "Congressmen Boehlert and

Eckart have been opposing it for several years, and Congressman Boehlert is supposed to be on TV tonight talking about his opposition to it. When the project was announced by President Reagan in 1987, it was supposed to cost $4.4 billion, but the price tag has risen to $11 billion and is still going up. Last year the House voted 232 to 181 to kill the project, but the congressional leadership played some tricks, and it was funded anyway. I'm here to convince you that Congressman Matthews and the other new members of the House should oppose it vigorously as an unnecessary budget-breaking boondoggle.'' She explained that high-energy physicists were digging a circular fifty-seven-mile-long tunnel into the subterranean limestone south of Dallas and filling it with a big radioactive accelerator. She gave him a copy of an as-yet-unreleased GAO report predicting that the costs would rise above $12 billion.

Joe fetched a yellow legal pad from his desk and began making notes. Jon might be interested in this one. ''This is a Department of Energy project,'' he said, phrasing it as if it were a statement instead of a question. She nodded. ''Jon is on the appropriations subcommittee that handles the DOE budget,'' he said. ''The subcommittee on energy and water.''

''I know,'' she said. ''It's very impressive that a new congressman was able to land such an important committee assignment,'' she added and smiled.

''Jon was very pleased that the leadership recognized his ability to contribute in that area,'' Joe said, thinking of the marathon bargaining session that had produced the assignment and the unsavory concessions and promises to tobacco-state legislators that had been necessary to get it.

Joe listened attentively as Alice continued her spiel. She stated that the cost of the project was out of control due to irresponsible management, that the design kept changing and getting more expensive, and that the money would be better spent in more people-oriented sectors of the government. She told Joe about the enormous consumption of electrical energy that the SSC would require, and the amount of oil, natural gas, and coal that would have to be burned to supply that power. She described the impact of the resulting CO_2 on the greenhouse effect and global warming. She described the use of fluorocarbon-based solvents by the project, and how this would damage the ozone layer. She described the drain of water from the depleted mid-Texas aquifers to supply the water needs of the machine. She described the vast quantity of limestone that would be removed to make the tunnel and the landfill problems that this would produce. She described the indigenous rabbits, deer, coyotes, raccoons, javalena pigs, armadillos, and prairie dogs that would be displaced by the SSC construction.

Joe made a few notes, but he was growing discouraged. Jon was not terribly interested in making speeches in support of displaced pigs, armadillos, and prairie dogs.

She gave him a graph showing participation by state in contracts for building the SSC. Oregon was near the bottom of the list.

That was interesting. If nothing else, he should write a letter in Jon's name to the DOE, demanding an explanation. It might generate some additional contracts in Oregon. Joe put the copy of the chart in the ACTION basket on his desk.

Finally, almost as an afterthought, she mentioned that the SSC management was spending DOE funds on works of art to put on office walls, on decorative plants for reception areas, and on parties for employees.

"DOE funds? Are you serious?" Joe asked, suddenly alert. "You can prove this?"

"Of course," said Alice. "It's a matter of public record, if you're willing to dig in the right file cabinets for it." She produced copies of spreadsheets showing SSC expenditures. "See," she said, "here are the paintings. And here's the expenditure for the 1992 Christmas party, almost $10,000, around $5 per staff member."

"Wow!" said Joe. This was good stuff. He understood very well how the federal system was supposed to work, which apparently was more than these SSC jerks did. When you were spending taxpayer money, you never, never, never spent any of it on staff parties or pizzas or office amenities or drinks in topless bars or trips to Tahiti or anything else that you wouldn't want to see in a newspaper headline. No way! Instead, you asked your *contractors* to provide the parties and drinks and trips and amenities as a no-cost contribution to the project. That way you got your parties, your ass was covered, and the contractors got a nice tax writeoff for their added expenses on the project. These SSC Mr. Science types, for all their white lab coats and slide rules, must have screwed up big-time.

"We need to show this stuff to Jon," Joe told her. "I know he'll be interested in helping." He smiled in anticipation.

LARRY WALKER SCANNED THE INDEX OF ASSOCIATED PRESS NEWS items on his terminal. This was going to be a slow day for news, even at *The Washington Post*. Perhaps today he should make a few phone calls to some of his insider sources and see if he could stir up anything.

The telephone beeped. "Walker," he answered.

"Larry," said Samantha, the front entrance receptionist, "do you have time to talk to a walk-in? There's a young lady here who says she wants to talk to a political reporter about some Department of Energy memo."

"Um, sure," said Larry, "send her up." He found an extra chair nearby and brought it back to his desk. As he was putting it down, he saw a pretty young woman in a gray business suit making her way past the rows of newsroom desks.

"Hi," he said, "I'm Larry Walker. What can I do for you?" He indicated the chair, sat down himself, and selected a new yellow legal pad from his desk drawer. He also put his small tape recorder conspicuously on the desktop and started it.

"I'm Alice Lang," she said, sitting down. "I'm with a group called the Citizens' Project for Government Oversight." She gave him a neatly printed business card.

Larry wedged the card in the top edge of the notepad. "Never heard of your group," he said. "What do you do?"

"We actively support openness in government," she said. "We're a nonprofit watchdog group that keeps an eye on the activities of the federal government. We also provide a secure conduit for 'whistle-blowers' to provide inside information to the public without endangering their government jobs. That's what I'm here about today. An internal Department of Energy memorandum has come into our possession which I think will interest you. It's a communication to Energy Secretary Hazel O'Leary from Jasper Siciliano, a DOE field office administrator in Dallas. It's about the Superconducting Super Collider project in Texas. Siciliano has the title of 'SSC Project Leader' within the DOE."

"Interesting," said Larry. "That's the big overbudget accelerator project that the House voted to kill back in June, isn't it?"

"Yes," said Alice. "The vote was 280 to 150 to kill the project. They had a similar vote last year, but this time the margin is bigger. The project was saved last year by a favorable Senate vote and some devious maneuvering by the congressional leadership."

Larry nodded. "What's going to happen this year? The same thing?"

Alice shrugged. "The Senate vote is coming very soon, and the DOE seems to be getting a little crazy. Siciliano wants to fire the SSC director and do some major revisions of the project's funding profile, effectively crippling the project but saving his own job." She handed him a letter-size manila envelope. "It's all in here."

Larry placed the envelope on his desk without opening it. "What do you know about this Siciliano person?" he asked.

"I've heard plenty about him that you couldn't print, from the scientists at the SSC. He was elevated to a position of power when Admiral Watkins became Secretary of Energy. The admiral wanted a direct line of information on the SSC, and Siciliano, who was already at the Dallas DOE office, provided it. His empire in the DOE has grown and grown. He now directs ninety-six mean-spirited paper-shuffling bureaucrats, all making life miserable for the scientists and technical people at the SSC project. Roy Schwitters, the SSC director, was recently quoted as calling Siciliano's operation 'the revenge of the C students.' "

"Ah yes," said Larry. "I read that quote in *The New York Times*. Not very politic of Schwitters to say things like that to the press."

"He's a very unhappy man running a troubled project," said Alice. "We're trying to help him by ending it."

Larry chuckled.

"I should mention," Alice continued, "that this isn't the first Siciliano memo to come to light. In 1991, with a bit of help from our people, Congress learned of the existence of the string of highly critical and sarcastic reports on the SSC from Siciliano to Admiral Watkins. An oversight subcommittee subpoenaed them. That produced a great uproar within the DOE. First they claimed the reports didn't exist. Then they admitted they did exist, but withheld them on the basis of 'executive privilege.' Finally they allowed committee staff to come to the admiral's office, read the memoranda, and make notes.

But they would not allow copies to be made. One of the staff members told me afterward that it was all a waste of time. The Siciliano memos were full of innuendos, accusations, and venom, but they contained no hard information the committee could use.''

"The admiral has sailed away, and there's a new Secretary of Energy now," said Larry. "I saw her on C-SPAN just last night. She said, as I recall, that she was 'nearly passionate' about the SSC and that she was planning to switch major contractors for the project. I take it that Mr. Siciliano has made the transition to Ms. O'Leary's DOE successfully."

"Oh yes," said Alice. "O'Leary is as leery of the SSC scientists as the admiral was, and she's added about thirty more people to Siciliano's operation in Dallas to provide even more DOE oversight." She pointed to the envelope on the desk. "Our new Siciliano memo is addressed to her."

"I see," said Larry. "This time you're taking a different route to reveal a damaging memo."

"Ah . . . yes," said Alice carefully. "Our whistle-blower is a person who was working as a temporary clerical helper in Siciliano's operation. One evening when he was working late, he happened to come across this new memorandum, which happened to have been left on the screen of Siciliano's very own PC."

"Wow!" said Larry. "Can you prove that's where it came from?"

"There's a floppy disk in the envelope," said Alice. "It contains an MS Word file for the O'Leary memorandum and files for some other interoffice memoranda and correspondence. Enough to prove its origins, if you need to. There is also a copy of an unreleased GAO report on the SSC project that we delivered to the press last June. That may also interest you as background, although perhaps it's no longer news."

Larry opened the envelope and its contents. Finally he looked up and smiled. "This is good stuff," he said. "Siciliano wants to fire the SSC director and stop the project for a year while they do a 'complete management overhaul.' That, I believe, is bureaucratese for a kangaroo court. I can imagine who he would put in charge of that."

Alice nodded. "The best thing that can be done for the SSC project now is a quick and merciful death."

Larry looked at her closely. "Why is your group so interested in 'oversight' for the SSC in particular?" he asked. "Surely there are many bigger and more appropriate targets for oversight in this town.''

"The SSC is only one of several of our projects," said Alice. "It happens to be coming up for a vote in the Senate soon, so we're focusing our attention on it just now.''

He nodded, scanning the papers again.

"Do you think you'll be running a story on this Siciliano memorandum?" she asked.

"Oh yes," said Larry. "Definitely. I'll have to call him first and ask for a clarification of the contents of the memorandum. That will serve as a confirmation of its validity, and it may also produce additional information for the story. Is your source still working at Siciliano's office? My call might compromise his job security.''

"No problem," said Alice, smiling. "He was only there for a week. He's off on another project now.''

• **63**

ROGER STOPPED THE CAR AND PEERED AGAIN AT THE CRUDELY drawn map. He had never met Sheldon Reynald or been on the Stony Brook campus before, and so far he'd found that it was dismayingly large and diffuse by Cambridge standards.

Finally, after several detours down wrong roads, he located the physics building and parked his rental car in the large lot nearby. Like most of the rest of the campus, the physics building was constructed of bare precast concrete of what must have been considered bold modern design in the late 1960s, but now looked rather dated and unfinished.

Roger found Sheldon Reynald's laboratory in the basement of the building. The lab door was open, and he walked in. A somewhat disheveled graduate student was seated before a bench in the corner, reading a paperback book. He looked up as Roger approached.

"I'm looking for Professor Reynald," said Roger. "Is he around?"

"Actually, I'm Sheldon Reynald," said the "student," pushing the book under a stack of papers. "How can I help you?"

"Roger Wilkins of the Iris Foundation," said Roger, pressing the graying beard to make sure it was secure before extending his hand.

"Dr. Wilkins," Reynald said, "this is a surprise."

"I couldn't really stay away," Roger said, "after I learned of your success with the alloy we'd suggested. I had to come and see the thing for myself. Where is it?"

"Over here," said Reynald, pointing to a cluttered lab bench. "Behold the spin battery."

Roger walked over and looked closely at the setup. An object that might have been an oversize doughnut covered with dull gray frosting occupied a central location on the table. Shiny coils of plastic-coated copper wire had been wound around and through the torus in several orientations, and leads were connected to standard laboratory measuring instruments, power supplies, and oscillators.

"It's in charge-up mode now. Would you like me to run our little demo?" Reynald asked.

"Of course," said Roger.

Reynald wheeled over a tall rack that had been against the wall. It supported a vertical slab of plywood on which were mounted row after row of lightbulbs. "This is a standard two-kilowatt load," he said. "It's made from twenty one-hundred-watt lightbulbs plus a cooling blower that uses another twenty watts. It's about equivalent to what an electric stove might use with most of its burners on. We've been pumping up the alignment of the spin battery for about an hour since the last full discharge. Now I'll disconnect the charging lines and hook it up to the load." He disconnected the doughnut-shaped object from its attached leads, picked it up from the bench, placed it in a receptacle at the top of the rack, and connected several large-diameter cables. "Ready?" he asked.

"Sure," said Roger.

Reynald flipped a switch. Immediately all the lightbulbs came on at full brightness, and the blower motor began to hum. "There you are," he said. "As you can see, there are no external connections. The electrical power is all coming from the spin battery. Its present output is about two kilowatts. It will hold that output for several days before it needs recharging. Amazing, isn't it?"

Roger looked at the gray doughnut again. "Does it get hot?"

"No," said Reynald. "Go ahead. Touch it. The copper wires heat up, but the alloy itself doesn't, except by conduction if it's in contact with the wires."

Roger put his finger on the gray surface of the doughnut. It felt cool to the touch. "The spin alignment stores the energy?" he asked.

"Actually," said Reynald, "our preliminary evidence indicates that there may be a kind of 'avalanche' of spin alignments and modified atomic structure, resulting in an unprecedentedly large internal magnetic field. Most of the energy is stored in the magnetic field. The energy density increases as the square of the magnetic field strength, you know."

"From your energy numbers, the magnetic field must be enormous," Roger said, "and the internal forces, too. How can the thing stay together against such forces?"

"We're not really sure," said Reynald. "The effect doesn't work at all if there are any cracks or structural imperfections in the alloy of the toroid. The magnetic field and degree of spin alignment are largest at the center of the alloy, while the surface field is very small. We've arranged to do some neutron scattering studies on one next week at Brookhaven to verify the size of the internal field."

"But don't you have estimates of the field?" Roger asked.

"Of course," said Reynald, looking slightly embarrassed. "On the basis of output and size, the energy density inside the thing is about half a megajoule per cubic centimeter. Therefore, if the energy is stored completely in the magnetic field, the average internal field would be around 1,100 Tesla. Of course, some of the energy is stored in the aligned spins themselves, so that's probably an overestimate."

"That's amazing," said Roger. "That's fourteen times the energy density of gasoline. Internal forces should tear the thing apart. With that amount of stored energy it should explode like a ton of TNT, yet it just sits there, not even getting warm."

"We're aware that the thing could be dangerous," said Reynald, "if the structure that holds it together were disrupted. We did some tests to determine what it takes to disrupt one of these and cause it to dump its energy. As it turns out, it's very difficult to disrupt. This one is perfectly safe, even if it was dropped on the floor. But with a suitable detonator it would make a spectacular explosive that would fly apart in a plane like a ruptured flywheel. One of the graduate students suggested that you could make a bomb that would explode in a plane five and a half feet off the ground, decapitating all the men while saving the women and children."

Roger winced. "How can it be so stable?" he asked.

"No one knows," said Reynald. "I've been playing with a theory which suggests that the same phenomenon that aligns the spins also provides increased atomic binding and structural strength."

Roger nodded. "Perhaps that's possible," he said doubtfully.

"Now I have a question," said Reynald. "Our choice of this particular copper-bismuth-holmium alloy was done at the suggestion of your foundation. I'd like to know where that suggestion came from, and if you know any more that you haven't told us. Dammit, I feel like a fraud, discovering something that is clearly of great importance, but which may actually have been someone else's idea."

"I'm afraid I can't tell you the origins of the suggestion," Roger said. "Not yet. But I can assure you that no one is going to claim that you stole their idea. When you publish your results, you're free to say anything you wish, including nothing at all, about the source of the information."

"But the spin battery is a major breakthrough," said Reynald. "It should be worth a Nobel prize. This discovery is more important than warm superconductors, because it has immediate applications. And the patent rights are going to be worth a fortune."

"Yes," said Roger. "You're about to become very wealthy. According to our contract, the patent rights will be shared equally between you, the foundation, and your university. We'll file the patent application as soon as you're ready and push it through the inspection process rapidly, to minimize any delay in publishing your results in physics journals."

Reynald nodded. "If there are no hidden problems, the chemical storage battery is obsolete. Soon everyone will be driving high-performance electric cars powered by a bank of spin batteries weighing a few pounds. It's a revolutionary technology. The availability of a cheap portable device for storing energy changes everything."

"I know," said Roger, recalling the wonders described in the Makers' download.

• 64

STEVE APPROACHED THE DESK. "ARE YOU LARRY WALKER?" HE asked.

"That's me," said the man sitting there. "What can I do for you?"

"I'm Steve Brown. I'm a law student in Tallahassee, and I just drove up from Florida. I came because I saw the piece in the *Post* you did last week about the Super Collider project and the Siciliano memorandum. It was an impressive piece of investigative journalism. It caused quite a stir, even in the Florida papers."

"I was lucky," said Larry. "I had some help on that one from a DOE insider."

"You're being modest," said Steve. "But anyhow, I came here to give you more help. There is another whole story on the politics surrounding the SSC that needs to be brought out into the open."

Larry flipped to a blank page of a yellow legal pad and selected a sharp pencil from those collected in a broken coffee cup on his desk. "Tell me about it," he said.

Steve opened his briefcase and placed a sheaf of papers on Larry's desk. "Have you ever heard of PetroGen, Inc.?" he asked.

"Hmm. Yes, I think so. A relatively new oil company that has been using bioengineered organisms to make old oil wells produce again."

"That's right," said Steve. "The founder and president of PetroGen is a man named George Preston. I've discovered that his whole identity is a fraud. He appeared out of nowhere in 1987. There are no records at all on him before that, not even a Social Security number. I've found evidence that a child with his name, birthdate, and birthplace died in 1959, the year Preston claims to have been born. He claims to have studied in Europe, but the first U.S. passport in his name was issued in 1987."

"Interesting," said Larry, "but not particularly newsworthy, I'm afraid, unless he runs for public office. Lots of people change their names for one reason or another."

Steve nodded. "It's what Preston's been doing that I think is newsworthy. Preston has a lot of political influence. He was an influential

295

Bush supporter and contributor in 1988, but more recently he's done a lot to get Clinton elected.''

Larry nodded, making notes.

"I've recently discovered that he's also been systematically causing problems for the Superconducting Super Collider project in Texas for a number of years. Here's a list of the anti-SSC organizations PetroGen has contributed to. It includes the Citizens' Project for Government Oversight that was mentioned in your article." Steve placed a sheet on the desk.

"Wait a minute," Larry said, looking sharply at Steve. "This is some kind of conspiracy theory you're pushing?"

"Oh no," said Steve, "it's an elaborate moneymaking real estate deal by a sharp operator. Preston wants to kill the SSC project to shake loose a couple of billion dollars in the federal budget this year. If the SSC is canceled, the eliminated expenditures represent funds that will still reside within the overall budget cap of the energy and water subcommittees in the House and Senate. Preston's plan is to divert that money from the SSC to an almost completed water project in Alabama. Do you know about the Tombigbee waterway?"

"Ah yes," said Larry. "I believe that Senator Moynihan once described that project as 'the cloning of the Mississippi, at taxpayer expense.' ''

"Yes," said Steve. "Well, Preston wants to snatch SSC money for the Tombigbee."

"This year that wouldn't be so easy," said Larry. "The first-term Democrats in the House want to cut budgets, not move money from one pork barrel to another."

"Ah," said Steve, "but you've been a reporter in this town long enough to know how that works. The congressional old-timers always use the enthusiasm of the freshmen for their own purposes. Tom Bevill, chairman of the House appropriations subcommittee for energy and water, is from Alabama. He's well known as a master of the pork barrel. For years he's moved federal money into the Tombigbee project from anywhere it could be found. Now the project is almost finished, and the plum of the SSC cancellation is about to drop into his lap. What do you think will happen?"

"But why is George Preston involved?" Larry asked.

Steve placed more papers on the desk. "These are the deed records of recent land purchases in Alabama. PetroGen has been buying up land along uncompleted sections of the Tombigbee waterway. The land values there are low right now because nobody believes the project will be completed any time soon. But if the SSC money is transferred to the Tombigbee, the land values will go up like a rocket. If this swindle succeeds, Preston will come away from the operation with a profit of several hundred percent, which amounts to perhaps a billion dollars.''

Walker scratched his head. "Interesting," he said, "but there's not a story here. At least, not yet."

"Why not?" Steve demanded, frowning.

"Because it's all too speculative," said Larry. "The *Post* is not the *National Enquirer*. The SSC has not been canceled, and if the congressional leadership and the powerful Texas delegation has anything to do with it, it won't be. Even if the project *is* canceled, it's very uncertain if the funds generated could be moved anywhere else. And while your information on Preston's mysterious background and land purchases seems provocative, it isn't enough to base a story on. Sorry.''

"Look," said Steve, struggling to control his rising anger, "I'm just a college student who has devoted some time to checking up on this Preston creep. With only the small amount of time I've been able to spare from my studies, I've turned up all this. I'm certain that there's a lot more there, that what I've found is just the tip of the iceberg. An investigative reporter like you, with the resources of *The Washington Post* behind you, should be able to turn up a lot more."

"Yes," Larry said, "that may be true. You've convinced me that something might be going on here. But there still may not be a story in it. I have other work to do, too, you know."

Steve shrugged. "Well, Larry, you're the reporter. Now you know what I know."

"I'd like to know one other thing," said Larry. "Why is an FSU law student so interested in an oilman with a business in Texas and land purchases in Alabama?"

Steve frowned. "It's personal," he said. "Look, I've got a long drive back to Tallahassee. I've gotta go." He stood.

Larry gathered up the sheets that Steve had placed on his desk. "I'll do some further checking," he said. "Perhaps when things develop a bit further, there may be a story here." He extended his hand

and shook Steve's. "Keep in touch, Steve," he said. "You know where to find me."

When Steve reached his car, there was a parking ticket under the wiper. He cursed and tore the yellow paper into small pieces. He'd show the bastards yet, he thought.

• 65

GEORGE AND ALICE SAT IN THE SPACIOUS INNER OFFICE OF CON-gressman Matthews. Joe had seated them here while they awaited the outcome of the House floor vote on the joint committee report that would decide the fate of the SSC.

Congressman Matthews had organized a coalition of about eighty of the first-termers and formed an alliance with the traditional budget-cutting fiscal conservatives and others to stage a House floor fight opposing the SSC project. They had garnered lots of media coverage by denouncing the SSC management for their shameful squandering of taxpayers' money on what they called "The Four P's": plants, paintings, pizzas, and parties. The House appropriations committee had voted to approve the SSC budget and proceed with construction, but on the floor of the House Matthews's mavericks had overruled the appropriations committee recommendation and succeeded in defeating the SSC appropriation by a 280 to 150 margin.

A similar initiative in the Senate, led by Senator Dale Bumpers of Arkansas, had failed by a vote of 42 to 57, and the Senate had ap-proved the SSC appropriation. Since there were differences in the House and Senate versions of the Department of Energy appropria-tions bill that centered on the SSC, it was the responsibility of the conference committee to iron out their differences and produce a com-promise. But, as it had been the year before, the conference committee had been rigged. Speaker Foley had appointed only SSC advocates to represent the House, and, like last year, the conference committee had accepted the Senate version of the DOE bill, preserving the SSC fund-ing.

Matthews's group of freshman had vowed that this time the agree-ment would not be allowed to stand. The conference committee report had to be ratified by the House, and Matthews's mavericks were staging a floor fight to reject the agreement.

George looked at his watch. The House vote on the conference committee report was scheduled for late today. It was now almost 5:00 P.M. He and Alice had been waiting here since four, and they might have to wait a lot longer.

George heard voices in the outer office. Joe Ramsey opened the door, and Congressman Matthews, followed by about a dozen other House members, the maverick ringleaders of the SSC opposition, filed into the large office.

Alice and George stood and he looked inquiringly at Matthews. "How did it go, Congressman?" he asked.

"We, won, by God!" said Matthews. "The vote was 282 to 143. We killed the fucker! We drove a stake through its heart. The SSC project, as of about ten minutes ago, is dead as a doornail." He walked across the room and shook hands with both of them, slapping George on the shoulder.

"We plan to submit a House resolution," said one of the other members, "that will require the DOE dickheads to fill in the whole goddamned tunnel!" He laughed loudly.

Joe opened a false book-front wall, behind which was a bar, consulted a list of preferences, and began dispensing drinks to the members, mostly tall glasses of straight Scotch or bourbon. Alice asked for a ginger ale. Joe looked at George and raised an eyebrow.

"I'll have a small cognac, Joe," said George. "And I'm afraid that Alice and I need to talk to Jon in private. It won't take long."

Matthews spoke briefly to Joe and then led them into a small conference room adjoining the office.

"Your group did very well this afternoon, Congressman," George said. "You saw an opportunity for political advantage, and you grasped it. You killed a big expensive project that had a relatively small constituency, just a few scientists, the Texas delegation, some miscellaneous contractors, and the usual science enthusiasts."

Matthews smiled. "And we deeply appreciate your support of our efforts, Mr. Preston."

"To you, I know, the SSC was just another pork barrel project, a particularly big one that didn't happen to be in your state. Somehow those Texas bastards had corralled a ten-billion-dollar project, and your group decided to slap their hands for being greedy. Ten or twenty million for a pork project now and then is okay, but ten billion is way out of line.''

Matthews nodded.

''Well, I need to explain two things to you, Congressman. The first is that your vote today was a very destructive thing for the *nation*. You have broken the central social contract with the scientific community of this country that has been in existence for the past five decades. For the scientists, the contract required that they work long hours, sixteen-hour days and nights and weekends, go to graduate school and live like paupers for six to ten years while they studied and worked essentially flat-out, and then move into relatively low-paying jobs, often with almost no job security, so that they can help to move forward the state of human knowledge, to gain an improved understanding of how the universe works and how we can manipulate its laws and restrictions to do new, interesting, and useful things. And they've been outrageously successful in this activity. The fruits of their basic research have become the mainspring of the U.S. economy.''

''Wait a damn minute,'' objected Matthews. ''Look at my record, George. I've consistently supported research, as long as it wasn't corporate welfare or a damned Texas pork barrel project. My vote helped to save the Space Station!''

George shook his head. ''The Space Station is *not* a scientific project, or even a good engineering project. Its construction was opposed by every major scientific professional society.

''You just don't seem to get it, Congressman,'' said George. ''For people like you, the social contract with scientists required that you support *real* scientific activity, not some aerospace contractor welfare thinly disguised as science. As a fraction of gross national product, the support of real science in the United States is quite small, considerably less than in Europe or Japan, but it has been sufficient up to now. If and when a project has been properly peer-reviewed by impartial experts and checked out for feasibility, cost effectiveness, and likelihood of success, you're supposed to support it. Once a project is started, you're supposed to see it through to completion. And you're supposed to be smart enough to distinguish between pork and valid science. In the case of the SSC, you've failed these tests miserably.

''You've blighted the plans and careers of thousands of scientists who had bet their futures on the SSC project. You've left graduate students without a thesis project, postdocs without a job or job prospects, and senior scientists without the possibility of support for their research. These people, most of whom have little understanding of politics but who have had a basic trust that good science will be supported by our government, you have betrayed.''

"*I've* betrayed?" Matthews roared. "You two have been prancing around our chambers ever since I took office, pushing us to kill the SSC. Now suddenly it's us who have done a terrible thing.''

"It is true that Alice and I have opposed the SSC. We had to, but not because it was a bad project. I can't explain to you why it was necessary for our group to oppose it. But none of our reasons apply to you. Your opposition was rooted in greed, narrow political interests, and bull-headed refusal to look objectively at the project or to consider the overall long-term good of the nation. You were wrong in your opposition, and I'm ashamed that we had to use your venality for our own purposes.''

There was another roar of outrage from Matthews, but George shouted him down. "Please let me finish, Congressman, so you can get back to your celebration," he said. "I realize that I'm destroying a carefully cultivated political relationship by telling you this, but it's necessary that at least one member of your group understands what you've done and what the consequences will be.

"You're a first-term congressman. If I have anything to do with it, you will *not* be a second-term congressman. Whether you're aware of it or not, your campaign received very large contributions from several political action committees under my control. Next year during the midterm elections you'll face stiff competition in the Democratic primary and a new and very capable Republican opponent in the final election. Your opponents' campaigns will receive very large contributions from my PACs, and you'll receive none.

"I hope you have nothing to hide, Congressman. Skillful investigators will be going over your records and background in meticulous detail. If nothing else, your opponents will hang your role in killing the SSC around your neck like an albatross.''

"Bullshit!" said Matthews. "Nobody in Oregon gives a good goddamn about the SSC. My advisors made sure of that before we mounted our opposition to it.''

"Perhaps," said George, "but my organization's polling data

shows that intrinsic public support of science runs much deeper in Oregon than you imagine. Congressman, I'm really distressed that my government is run by people like you. I want you thrown out of office, as an example to your peers that worthy but poorly defended scientific projects should not be exploited as targets of political opportunity. And I will see that all of your celebrating colleagues outside receive the same treatment as you do."

Matthews glared at George. "You're a crazy man. And you're through in this town, Preston. I know what you've been up to. I know all about your little scheme in Alabama, and it's fucking dead. All you've accomplished by your little speech is to make yourself a political pariah."

"You mean I'll never do lunch in this town again?" asked George, smiling. "I devoutly hope that you're correct. Aside from making sure that as many as possible of you are defeated for reelection next year, I no longer have a political agenda to promote. Thank you for listening to me, Congressman. I hope you'll tell the rest of your group about this conversation. And I want you to think of this conversation in November of next year as you watch the election results come in and wonder what hit you."

George held up his cognac glass, as if making a toast. "When you're defeated for reelection in 1994, Congressman, remember the 'Curse of the SSC.' "

George and Alice left quickly after that. Matthews cursed them from the doorway as they threaded their way through the revelry in the outer office and out into the hallway.

"I hadn't expected that," said Alice, looking at him. "You just dynamited our carefully constructed bridges."

George smiled. "The person you're looking at is not going to be around much longer, in any case. I've been uncomfortably visible of late, and at least two reporters, guys with the *Houston Chronicle* and *The Washington Post*, are poking into my background in far too much detail. This George Preston is going into early retirement, and a new persona with a different face and background is going replace him. Those burned bridges of yours have served their purpose and were about to collapse under their own weight." He paused and smiled. "And, by God, Alice, that little speech has made me feel amazingly good."

She smiled at him and squeezed his hand.

*   *   *

As they reached the outer building lobby, a figure in a dark coat stepped out from the wall to block their path.

"Steve!" said Alice. "What are you doing here?"

"Why, I've been waiting for you, Alice," Steve said. "I wanted to share in the fun."

"Fun?" said Alice. "What are you talking about?"

"I'm talking about the sleazy shenanigans of you and your sugar daddy here. The business of sneaking around, manipulating Congress, killing big projects, and making loads of money in the process." He turned and shook his finger in George's face. "I want you to know that I'm on to you, you bastard! I know why you've been trying to kill the SSC project. I know all about your fake identity and your get-rich-quick schemes. You're a fucking con artist."

George smiled. "I don't believe we've been properly introduced," he said. "I presume that you're Alice's friend Steve Brown. I thought that you were supposed to be at Florida State working on a law degree. Why aren't you in Tallahassee attending classes and studying for exams?"

"Because I'm learning more here, checking up on sleazeballs like you," Steve said. "I've put off my studies for a year, because I have things to do here that are more important."

"And those are . . . ?" said George.

"Exposing your cynical manipulations of our political system for your own purposes and profits," said Steve. "You see, I've found out about your land deals in Alabama. I know about the Tombigbee caper, and I know what you're up to. And I'm going to expose you, Preston. I'll make sure you don't get a damned cent of profit from all your wheelings and dealings."

"Tombigbee? Profits?" said George, frowning. Then his face brightened. "Ah, I see. Of course!" He began to laugh. "You must think . . ." He shook his head as he chuckled.

"What is it, George?" Alice asked. "What's so funny?"

"Well," said George finally, "it seems that Steve here has managed to discover Roger's wacko cover scheme. Roger thought that we would do better in our political opposition to the SSC if we had something obvious to gain from its cancellation. His theory is that politicians don't feel comfortable with you unless they can see that your motives are just as greedy as theirs. So Roger cooked up this goofy scheme. We bought some land on a river in Alabama, and then we planted stories that PetroGen wanted to kill the SSC so that money could be moved over to a water project on that river to increase the land values.''

Steve took a step back, as if he had been struck.

"I never believed it would work," George continued, looking closely at Steve, "but apparently it did. Matthews just referred to it a minute ago, and Steve here seems to have bought the story, lock, stock, and barrel. I must apologize to Roger, next time I see him.''

George and Alice were still laughing as they descended the broad staircase and caught a cab at the curb. Inside, he glanced back at Steve, who still stood at the entrance of the Rayburn House Office Building, a look of profound puzzlement on his face.

"Steve confirms the wisdom of my decision," George said. "The distinguished George Preston, founder and President of PetroGen, will soon announce that, having made his killing in the new biopetroleum industry and having been the trusted advisor to presidents, he plans to donate much of his wealth to the Iris Foundation and retire to an island in the Caribbean to live out his twilight years in the tranquil seclusion of the formerly rich and famous. The George Preston identity was my first attempt at constructing a new persona, and I made a few mistakes. For example, I stupidly used my own birthdate as his, which under the wrong circumstances could be a dead giveaway. Roger and I have become much more skillful at the construction of identities. Those reporters and your friend Steve have been getting uncomfortably close to this one.''

Alice looked out the rear window as their taxi pulled away from the curb. "I don't know what I ever saw in that jerk," she said. "In your universe, I actually married him?''

"And you put him through law school," said George.

"That's crazy," said Alice. "The world has too many lawyers as it is. I much prefer physicists.'' She turned to George and kissed him soundly.

• 66

ROGER TURNED UP THE WIPER SPEED TO HIGH AND INCREASED THE window defroster's heat setting a notch. He had flown from Frankfurt to Detroit and rented a car, expecting a pleasant drive west on Interstate 69 to East Lansing across the meadows, forests, and farmland of Michigan. Instead, he had headed into the teeth of a blizzard that seemed to grow in intensity as he approached his destination. He almost missed the East Lansing exit from the interstate and managed to slither into the exit lane at the last possible instant.

The Michigan State University campus was even larger than that of Stony Brook, and much of it seemed to be devoted to agricultural activities. He passed an impressive building with a large MSU—SWINE HUSBANDRY sign near the front entrance. He smiled, recalling that his mother had accused his father of that, once or twice. Consulting his map, he saw that the physics building must be off to the left, near the massive football stadium that loomed on the horizon. He turned the car in that direction.

The wind cut through his clothing as he walked from the semicircular driveway to the building's entrance. At least the uncomfortable beard kept his chin warm, he thought. Professor Hernando Garcia's laboratory was on the ground floor of the large limestone building. The door bore yellow signs with magenta letters warning of laser hazards and radioactivity. Roger knocked at the door, and almost immediately it opened.

"Dr. Wilkins, how good to see you," Garcia greeted him. "How was your trip?"

"Hello, Hernando," said Roger. "The trip was fine until I reached this frozen wasteland you call Michigan. The drive here from Detroit was, shall we say, memorable."

Garcia smiled. "Well," he said, "I think you'll find that the trip was worth it."

Roger took off his coat, gloves, and knitted cap and hung them on the rack by the door. "Where's this ramjet of yours?" he asked, looking around.

"It's in the little closet over here that I've instrumented with a vibration-isolated double-torsion balance," said Garcia, leading Roger to the other side of the room. He pointed to the computer screen. "The sensors read out the deflections, convert them to a force vector, and display them here. There's a feedback loop to keep the force maximized. Notice the force direction it's measuring. It's pointing at galactic latitude 48 degrees and galactic longitude 264 degrees. Does that sound familiar?"

"Hmm," said Roger. "Isn't that approximately the direction of the dipole asymmetry of the cosmic microwave background radiation?"

"Indeed it is," said Garcia. "That's the direction my axions are coming in from."

Roger stared at the display and shook his head. "An unbalanced force that points in the microwave dipole direction. That violates several of my favorite symmetry principles, Hernando. I think you'd better start at the beginning."

Garcia took a breath, then smiled. "Well, to be brief, with the help of funding from the Iris Foundation, I've suceeded in detecting axions and demonstrating that they are at least a major component of dark matter."

Roger whistled. "Axions, is it? I must confess that I never took them very seriously as the explanation for the extra hidden mass of the universe. I've always leaned toward massive neutrinos as the dark matter candidate of choice."

Garcia shrugged. "What can I say? I looked, and there they are. When I read the papers about the Reynald toroid last year, it gave me the idea for the detector. Do you remember that back in 1983 Paul Sikivie at the University of Florida suggested that if axions existed, they could be converted to photons by a big magnetic field?"

"Yes, I remember looking into that," said Roger, "but I thought there was an experiment by groups at Rochester and Brookhaven, and they didn't see anything."

"Sure," said Garcia. "They were only using a field of about a Tesla, and they were looking in the wrong place."

"I see," said Roger. "With a Reynald toroid, you can get a field that's a thousand times larger."

"Yes," said Garcia, "and the axion conversion probability scales with energy density, not field, so my detector is a million times more sensitive than theirs. Even at that, I tried their technique first, and it didn't work."

"Why not?" Roger asked.

"The Rochester-Brookhaven experiment attempted to convert axions to microwave photons and detect the photons by varying the tuning of a microwave cavity, hoping to hit the right photon wavelength. I tried the same thing, but it didn't work. It's now clear it failed because the conversion isn't going into photons."

"No photons?" said Roger.

"No," said Garcia. "The axions are converted to something else that moves at the speed of light. I don't know what that might be. Neutrinos? Gravitons? Supersymmetric particles?"

"Wait a moment," said Roger. "If you're not detecting photons, what are you detecting?"

Garcia smiled. "I decided to try tuning the axion wavelength instead. I mounted two Reynald toroids with opposite fields on an optical bench pointed along the direction of the dipole asymmetry and varied their separation. When I hit a center-to-center separation of about five centimeters, strange things began to happen in my instruments. After a lot of testing, I discovered that, among other things, on resonance there is a net force pushing on my apparatus."

"How do you explain that?" Roger asked, pushing on his beard.

"As I told you on the telephone yesterday, it's a ramjet. The axions, which are more or less at rest in the cosmic background reference frame, are moving through my apparatus at about $\frac{1}{800}$ of the speed of light. If and when they're converted to massless particles like photons, they move away at the speed of light. The speed increases by a factor of 800 and brings with it a change in momentum. So although we can't directly detect either the axions or the particles they're converted into, whatever those are, we can detect the momentum change of the conversion process. The momentum is absorbed by the Reynald toroids. We see a maximum force vector that points toward the incoming axions."

"I see," said Roger. "But how can you be sure the momentum kick is coming from axions?"

"Well," said Garcia, "the old Sikivie paper can be used to predict the response of the detector under various conditions of field strength and orientation. Pseudo-scalar particles have certain unique symmetry properties. All of the predictions agree very well with our measurements."

"How big is the force?"

"I can get up to a few hundred dynes of thrust from my small prototype, and there are ways of getting more. It's not enough for levitation, but it should be sufficient to drive a small fuelless space probe anywhere you want."

"But it only produces thrust in only in the direction of the dipole asymmetry," said Roger. "That doesn't sound too useful."

"No," said Garcia. "The maximum is in the direction of the incoming axions, but the thrust is perpendicular to the plane of the magnetic field lines. You can point that anywhere in a hemisphere, and as the velocity builds, the incoming direction becomes the direction you're moving in. With a curved trajectory, you could launch a probe in any direction you wanted."

"A few hundred dynes isn't much thrust, though," said Roger.

"But the faster it goes through the axion medium," said Garcia, "the more axions per second enter the field and the more thrust you get. That's why I call it an axion ramjet."

"Wait a minute," said Roger. "The thing accelerates forever? With more and more thrust? That's not possible, Hernando. It would soak up all the mass in the universe."

"Remember," said Garcia, "ramjets are always limited by the difference between inlet and exhaust velocity. In this case, the exhaust velocity is lightspeed, but the input velocity depends on how fast the object is moving through the axion medium. As the device approaches lightspeed, you lose the momentum kick because velocity change between in and out goes to zero. The device has its limits. It doesn't work well near the speed of light. But it's going to be useful, I think."

"Useful . . ." Roger repeated. "You're being far too modest, Hernando. You've invented a space drive that produces thrust without using any fuel. We can send probes to the stars. And maybe go there ourselves."

Garcia smiled.

As he walked back to his car through the swirling snow, Roger's mind was racing. This effect of Garcia's was definitely not mentioned in the Makers' download. Could the Makers be concealing it, for some reason? Or had they never discovered it?

Roger weighed the alternatives, thinking of Iris. It was simply not the Makers' style to conceal information. They didn't know about the effect. Perhaps in the Makers' Universe in the vicinity of their solar system the axion density was too low to show Garcia's effect. He had discovered a new phenomenon that the Makers did not know about.

Roger smiled. Mankind had reached the frontier.

• 67

THE NEW CAMPUS OF THE IRIS INSTITUTE U.S.A. STOOD ON A ROCKY bluff along the broad southern edge of Lopez Island, one of the San Juan group that clustered in North Puget Sound just south of the jagged international border separating Washington State and British Columbia. The several buildings recently constructed on the site formed a crescent facing southward toward the spectacular view of the blue waters of Puget Sound and the Olympic Mountains behind them.

George Griffin met his three visitors at the rooftop helicopter pad and walked immediately to the young man who was about his height. "Hello, Charles," he said. "I like your new face."

Charles Lewis, the new president of PetroGen, Inc., who had once been George Preston, who had once been George Griffin, smiled. "Roger's right," he said. "Everyone should change his name and face once in a while. It's like cleaning house. It gets rid of a lot of excess baggage and keeps you on your toes. At PetroGen, though, I have to be careful not to be too much like the old president. I wouldn't want to confuse our staff."

Griffin conducted them downstairs and into the new conference room atop the central building. "I haven't yet had the opportunity to kiss the bride," he said. He kissed Alice on the cheek.

"We had a private ceremony, with Roger as best man," Charles said. "We would certainly have invited you and Grace if we'd decided on a larger wedding."

"No problem," said Griffin. "I've been away from here too much as it is."

"How does Grace like the San Juans?" Alice inquired.

"This change has been very good for her," said Griffin. "She's a lot more relaxed and happy now. And also, she's pregnant . . .'' He looked at his hand, then at Charles. "I don't know what that is going to make you. An uncle? A godfather?"

"Uncle Charles will do fine," said Lewis. "I haven't seen you since the November elections, George. What do you think of the big turnover in Congress?"

Griffin stroked his beard. "Your friends the SSC-killers certainly lost their seats in droves. Here in Washington State, every member of the House who voted to terminate the SSC was thrown out of office. Was all of that your doing?"

Charles smiled and shrugged. "One only does what one can. The problem is that these flinty-eyed Republicans who replaced the Clinton-wave Democrats may not be a change for the better. I don't think they understand in complete detail how they got elected. It will be interesting to see how Newt and his Newtonian Congress carry the ball for the next two years. I'm glad that we have no large political agenda to deal with in the immediate future."

"How is the recruiting for the institute going, George?" Roger asked.

"Very well, actually," said Griffin. "We've persuaded some of our university groups to relocate here. They form the nucleus of the effort. With the cancellation of the SSC, we've also been very successful in our recruiting in computing, accelerator design, and particle physics, both theory and experiment. Biotechnology has been a bit harder, but there's been a minor shakeout in the industry lately, which has helped us." He looked out the window. "Also, the site helps. There are lots of scientists and technicians with a deep-seated desire to escape the East Coast or the L.A. area or Silicon Valley for a more tranquil environment with lower housing prices and plenty of waterfront property." He looked at Roger. "How's the recruiting going at Iris Institute Europe?"

"Very well," Roger said. "With the depressed state of science in the U.K., the recruiting has been fairly easy. The Cornwall coast is an appealing location, with many of the attractions of this one. Tern's group and others came from Cambridge, and we were able to pinch a number of Brits from CERN who were glad to return to the U.K. at a decent salary. Also, the meltdown of the U.S.S.R. allowed us to recruit many scientists from the former East Bloc countries. They're much more understanding of the Iris secrecy restrictions than are many of my own countrymen.'' He sighed.

''Have you considered recruiting your younger self?'' Griffin asked, winking at Charles.

''Young Roger is only twenty-one now and has another year at Oxford,'' said Roger. ''I remember that year very well. He needs it to grow and mature and learn. After that, I plan to recruit him. I'd hate to have him waste several years getting a Ph.D. at Cambridge learning obsolete physics and mathematics, when I could teach him so much more.''

Charles nodded. ''I'm having an easier time with that in our new commercial enterprises. Applications of the Reynald spin battery are already making us lots of money and also generating considerable interest among scientists in our new industrial laboratories in Galveston. Industrial scientists understand trade secrets, and they don't feel such a compulsion to publish their results immediately. But I'll still be very glad when this phase of our operation is over.'' He looked across the table at his alter ego. ''How is the medical end of the project shaping up?''

''That's going to take some time,'' said Griffin. ''Actually, it's quite frustrating. We have in our hands a broad spectrum of cures for all human ills: AIDS, cancer, flu and the common cold, all genetic diseases, excess fertility, even acne, hair loss, and dandruff. But we can't release them yet. We must first discover how to produce the appropriate proteins and retroviruses without *Writing* them. After that, we must get the approval of the Food and Drug Administration or its equivalent in other countries. That will take years or even decades. And we will need to give the existing biotech industry a piece of the action, so we don't destroy it. It's going to be very tricky for a while. We've been using Roger's new projection techniques to evaluate the impact of various scenarios for releasing new drugs. Sometimes the second-order social effects are amazing.''

Roger grimaced. ''That's too bad,'' he said. ''It seems to be easier to invent a space drive than a cure for athlete's foot.''

''That reminds me,'' said Charles. ''We have a new industrial component. PetroGen has just spawned an offshoot company, SpaceGen. We bought out one of the ailing California aerospace outfits that had been sliding toward bankruptcy since the Cold War ended. We renamed it and moved the corporate headquarters to New Mexico.

We're setting up an organically grown laser launch facility there, near the old White Sands proving ground. Soon we'll start boosting small payloads into low Earth orbit. We have some nanodesigns that will eat the space junk that's been accumulating in LEO and make it into useful stuff. Then we start intensive probing of the moon and the asteroid belt, where more raw material is available. We've assembled a team that's doing a preliminary design for a permanent manned moonbase. And with the Garcia drive showing promise, we may be launching a series of unmanned interstellar probes before long. It's amazing how everything opens up when the launch cost goes down and the drive efficiency goes up. It's the dawn of a new space age."

Roger nodded. "We're going to need that technology. Tern's team at Iris Institute Europe has been making real progress in understanding the Makers' maths. It's now clear that the mathematics used by the Makers is a variant of Clifford algebra. It's like finding the Rosetta stone. We have the code key to their formalism. There's a realistic possibility of doing Planck-scale physics, once we master the formalism and gain more insight into the techniques.

"But the catch seems to be that Planck-scale experimental work will have to be done in space. Preferably well-removed from the sun's gravity well, which means outside the solar system. Otherwise, the gravitational curvature is too disruptive. We're going to need infrastructure to support a base out in the Oort cloud."

"Iris Institute Oort," said Alice. "That has a nice ring to it. I'm pleased there's a legitimate need for physics research in space. I spent too many hours in Washington listening to comparisons of research at the SSC and on the Space Station. Most of the NASA science presentations were embarrassing."

"NASA is a problem," said Charles, "but one, I think, that can be dealt with." He smiled in anticipation.

• 68

THE SKY-FILLING DISK OF THE DIM YELLOW-ORANGE SUN WAS JUST rising on the east coast of the northern continent when the new universe was discovered. The Hive Mind's latest breed of extradimensional Lookers signaled the find, triggering rapid transmissions that rose to a screaming pitch on all frequency bands as communications from separated components stitched across the planet. The Hive Mind gave orders. Resources must be refined, machines must be constructed, energy banks must be recharged, a new strategy of conquest must be put into place. Workers all over the planet scurried to fulfill their tasks, refining materials, producing parts, assembling machines, simulating alternate courses of action, making ready for the next great attempt at Hive colonization.

• AFTERWORD

October 28, 1994

We have had to focus a lot of our time on helping [the physicists] let go of the idea that they can stay in high-energy physics and getting them to focus on transferable skills . . . It's really a shock to the system.
　　　　　—Marie Snidow, SSC outplacement councilor

The loss of a job is a traumatic experience for anybody. The loss of a career is devastating. I spent fifteen years doing physics . . . my investment and my career went out the window.
　　　　　—Kate Morgan, former SSC physicist now employed by Citicorp, Dallas

February 1, 1995

Once upon a time, science did have a voice in determining [national science] policy, but that was long ago . . . What science needs more than anything else are vibrant spokespersons who can communicate with the public and with the policymakers. Otherwise, I dread the coming debacle that seems to be brewing in our nation's capital.
　　　　　—Professor Leon Lederman, Illinois Institute of Technology, former Director of Fermilab, Nobel laureate

• Introduction

THIS NOVEL IS A WORK OF "HARD" SCIENCE FICTION, THAT SUBSPE-cies of the science fiction genre in which the protagonists are often working scientists, careful attention is paid to the scientific accuracy of technical details, and scientific problem-solving is an important plot element. Hard SF inherently has special problems because the reader may be easily misled into believing that fictional "rubber" science needed as extrapolation for the plot structure is real and factual, or that real scientific facts used to give the work verisimilitude are fictional.

The present novel also has another problem, because it uses a fictional plot woven with as much plausibility as possible through the recent real but unlikely history of the initiation and cancellation of the Superconducting Super Collider project by the United States Congress. In this Afterword, I want to try to sort out the factual from the fictional science and politics of the work, because I think this may be of considerable interest to the readers of this book. However, the novel stands as a work of fiction without any follow-up explanations, and for some, reading this afterword may actually spoil the ending. Therefore, read this *only* if you are interested in the nuts-and-bolts of the science and politics.

I would also like to state here that I had no personal stake in the SSC, aside from being in the midst of writing a novel about it when the project was definitively canceled in October 1993. The kind of physics research I do at the CERN laboratory in Geneva using relativistic heavy ions was never planned for the SSC and might have been added to the physics research program there only at considerable additional expense and delay. Therefore, I consider myself an informed but unbiased observer of the history of the doomed project.

For those interested in the "Alternate View" columns referred to below, these can be found via my Web site at:

http://weber.u.washington.edu/~jcramer

"Bubble Universes" and Inflationary Cosmology

The idea of isolated bubble universes, as used in this novel, comes from a variant of the current standard model of cosmology, the Big Bang model with inflation (or rapid exponential expansion) at the early stages. Bubble universes are not required by inflationary cosmology, but they are a logical consequence of the scenario that describes the initial universe as a volume of space that is supersaturated with energy. A localized phase transition is spontaneously initiated in this space and the bubble of altered space begins to expand. This process is perhaps nucleated by a magnetic monopole, rather like a bubble of steam forming around a grain of dust in liquid water heated above its boiling point. The result is that an expanding bubble universe forms, inside which is normal space while outside is the energy-saturated space of the initial universe. The walls of the bubble are expanding with an exponential growth rate, driven by the energy liberated in the space phase transition at the interface. This is what we call the Big Bang.

In this scenario, there is no reason why this should have happened only once, at a single nucleation point. Therefore, a multiplicity of bubble universes has been postulated, all forming independently within the same overall cosmos. Each is a closed universe, essentially a black hole that is expanding because of an excess of kinetic energy, and each such bubble universe is completely isolated from all the others.

Connections and communication between one such bubble universe and another would only be possible if there was a wormhole connection, the scenario used in this novel, or if two universes made contact by a collision. There are theoretical papers in the physics literature that discuss what happens when one bubble universe collides with another. You wouldn't want to live in such a universe, and fortunately we don't. We know this from the COBE-measured uniformity in all directions of the 2.7°K microwave background radiation from the Big Bang.

EINSTEIN-ROSEN BRIDGES AND WORMHOLE PHYSICS

In 1916 Einstein first introduced his general theory of relativity, a theory which to this day remains the standard model for gravitation. Twenty years later, he and his longtime collaborator Nathan Rosen published a paper in *Physical Review* 48:73 (1935) showing that implicit in the general relativity formalism is a curved-space structure that can join two distant regions of space-time through a tunnellike curved spatial shortcut. The purpose of the paper of Einstein and Rosen was not to promote faster-than-light or interuniverse travel, but to attempt to explain fundamental particles like electrons as space tunnels threaded by electric lines of force. Their electron model subsequently proved invalid when it was realized that the smallest possible mass-energy of such a curved-space topology is that of a Planck mass, far larger than the mass-energy of an electron.

The Einstein-Rosen work was disturbing to many physicists of the time because such a "tunnel" through space-time, which came to be known in the late 1930s and '40s as an "Einstein-Rosen bridge," could in principle allow the transmission of information faster than the speed of light—in violation of one of the key postulates of special relativity known as "Einsteinian causality."

In 1962 John Wheeler and a collaborator discovered that the Einstein-Rosen bridge space-time structure, which Wheeler rechristened as a "wormhole," was dynamically unstable in field-free space. They showed that if such a wormhole somehow opened, it would close up again before even a single photon could be transmitted through it, thereby preserving Einsteinian causality.

In 1989 Kip Thorne and his graduate student Mike Morris showed that an Einstein-Rosen bridge, by now called a wormhole in the literature, could be stabilized by a region of space containing a negative mass-energy. They suggested that an "advanced civilization" capable of manipulating planet-scale quantities of mass-energy might use the Casimir effect to produce such a region of negative mass energy and, starting with vacuum fluctuations, might create stable wormholes. Later work by Matt Visser suggested the use of cosmic strings of negative string tension, also solutions of Einstein's equations, as an alternative mechanism for stabilizing wormholes.

In the present novel, the techniques used by the Makers and other alien races to produce stable wormholes are never completely described, but they clearly involve vast quantities of energy and the use of Planck-scale physics that is presently unknown to us.

High-Energy Physics

The high-energy physics portrayed in the first half of this novel is a fictionalized account of a very real activity. This branch of experimental physics research is carried out by very large experimental groups, often a thousand or more physicists working together on a single very large and expensive experiment that, as it is being built, pushes the cutting edge of technology. About 12 percent of physicists involved in basic physics research in the U.S.A. work in this field, which is supported by about 50 percent of the non-NASA and non-DOD basic research funding, a fact that generates some resentment in other subfields of physics. The large experiment collaborations are typically led by one "spokesperson," a physicist possessing unusual leadership skills that are sometimes accompanied by idiosyncratic personality quirks.

The leading high-energy physics experiments of the 1990s are being performed at the LEP electron-positron collider at CERN near Geneva and at the Fermilab proton-antiproton collider near Chicago. LEP has four large experiments, ALEPH, DELPHI, L3 and OPAL, which have mainly focused on precise determination of the masses and widths of the Z^0 and $W^\pm$ bosons, the mediating particles of the weak interaction. Fermilab has mounted two large collider experiments, CDF and D0, both of which recently reported the discovery of the top quark with the unexpectedly large mass of about 180 GeV. CDF has also recently reported preliminary evidence suggesting that quarks may have substructure, may be composites made of even smaller and more fundamental particles.

The next generation of accelerators for high-energy physics was supposed to have been the LHC at CERN and the SSC at Waxahachie. The detectors for the LHC will be ATLAS and CMS, used to study proton-proton collisions, and ALICE, used to study heavy ion collisions. The two SSC detectors were to have been SDC, a detector using a large solenoidal magnet, and GEM, a detector designed for gamma rays, electrons, and muons. The fictional LEM detector in this novel bears some resemblance to GEM, but its leadership does not. The cancellation of the SSC project has, of course, ended all work on SDC and GEM.

A handful of the physicists formerly working on the SSC and its detectors have successfully made the transition to CERN and are working on the LHC facility or the ATLAS or CMS detectors, but many others, particularly the younger physicists who had staked their careers on the future of the SSC, have been forced out of physics research altogether. Many are now working in the computer industry or on Wall Street. The cancellation of the SSC project has dealt a devastating blow to the future of high-energy physics in the U.S.A. Regrettably, in this real world there is no Iris Foundation to provide an alternative.

The LHC (and the SSC, if it had been built) will produce small regions of space that contain the concentrations of energy comparable to the first nanosecond of the Big Bang. However, there is no reason to think that the regions of ultra-high-energy density created in the collisions will generate "signals" or will provide a medium for the creation of wormholes or alien contact. These ideas were added to further the plot of the present novel.

TIME VORTICES AND TIMELIKE LOOPS

One of the issues raised by the Thorne-Morris work on wormholes centers on the possibility of producing a "time-hole," a wormhole that connects two regions of space-time across a timelike interval. Here the word "interval" means $x^2 + y^2 + z^2 - (ct)^2$, where x, y, and z are the distances in space (in meters), t is the time interval (in seconds) and c is the velocity of light (in meters per second). A positive interval is dominated by the space contribution and is said to be "spacelike," a zero interval balances space and time along a speed-of-light trajectory and is said to be "lightlike," and a negative interval is dominated by the time contribution and is said to be "timelike." The sign of an interval is not changed by relativistic transformations from one inertial reference frame to another, so a timelike interval in one frame is timelike in all frames.

A transversable wormhole spanning a timelike interval is, in effect, a time machine. The Thorne-Morris work demonstrated how any wormhole might be converted into a time-hole. This, for the first time, has led to serious consideration of the physics of time machines and time travel in mainstream physics literature. One consequence of this consideration, first pointed out by Stephen Hawking, is that a vacuum fluctuation instability occurs when the ends of a developing time-hole first begin to span a timelike interval. Practitioners of quantum field theory have severe problems in dealing with paths through space-time for which the net path interval is zero (time equals space). Hawking has speculated that if a wormhole entered this domain, the vacuum fluctuations at such a "Cauchy horizon" would build up and destroy the wormhole. He has suggested that "nature abhors a time machine" and will frustrate all attempts to create one.

In the present novel, I have used a variant of the idea that nature abhors a time machine to destroy, not the time machine, but the entire section of space-time history spanned by the time machine or "time vortex" in the universe in which it is created. The universe is destroyed and must re-evolve along a different path of history that does not contain a time vortex or a timelike loop. This approach, as far as I know, is new in science fiction as a solution to the paradoxes created by time travel.

THE INTERPRETATIONS OF QUANTUM MECHANICS

In this novel, the interpretation of quantum mechanics advocated by Iris is actually the transactional interpretation, which I originated about a decade ago and published in the July 1986 issue of the physics journal *Reviews of Modern Physics*. The transactional interpretation is a nonfictional alternative to the better-known Copenhagen interpretation of Bohr and Heisenberg and the "many worlds" interpretation of Everett and Wheeler. In 1995 the transactional interpretation was featured in John Gribbin's widely read popular science book *Schrödinger's Kittens*.

Briefly, the transactional interpretation associates the psi star complex conjugates of quantum wave functions that appear everywhere in the quantum formalism with "advanced waves" that travel backward in time to "confirm" each incipient quantum transaction with a quantum handshake spanning space-time. This idea is based on the Wheeler-Feynman absorber theory published in 1945. The transactional approach resolves the interpretational problems of nonlocality and wave function collapse implicit in the quantum formalism, explains some of the arbitrary-seeming features of quantum mechanics, and offers a number of other advantages over its rivals. It resolves all of the quantum mechanics paradoxes that have been troubling the field of quantum physics for six decades.

In the present novel, the transactional interpretation is used as a way of justifying and providing a mechanism for the universe-destroying actions of the timelike loop created by the Makers. It also serves another more philosophical purpose, demonstrating by example that the transactional interpretation is not rigorously deterministic and that the evolution of the universe from future possibility to present reality need not advance along a flat spacelike surface as the future crystallizes into the present.

Readers who are interested in learning more about the transactional interpretation and have access to WorldWideWeb can find a hypertext version of my *Reviews of Modern Physics* paper on the transactional interpretation at:

http://www.npl.washington.edu/tiqm/TI_toc.html

THE FERMI PARADOX AND THE KIRKWOOD ZONES

The ''Fermi paradox'' is the name given to the conflict between our expectation that life, even intelligent life, should be very common in the universe and the manifest absence of any evidence of intelligent life except on this planet. Supposedly, during the Manhattan Project in the 1940s, there was a lunchtime discussion at Los Alamos on the high probability that intelligent life must have independently evolved elsewhere in the universe, after which Enrico Fermi looked around the table, spread his hands, and asked, ''But where are they?''

There is a broad literature attempting to answer Fermi's question, but it remains unresolved. The ''Drake equation,'' a probability product of all the individual probabilities for conditions needed to produce intelligent life, usually leads to the conclusion that there should be many other intelligent species even within our own galactic neighborhood, yet radio astronomers have yet to detect either radio emissions that might be a deliberate attempt at communication from another species or accidental radio emissions of a high-technology civilization. With the exception of Earth, our universe seems strangely empty of intelligent life.

The solution to the Fermi paradox used in this novel was first presented in one of my "Alternate View" columns in *Analog* magazine, which was published in the January 1986 issue. It is based on two seemingly unrelated ideas, the notion of punctuated equilibrium in evolution as derived from the analysis of the fossil records by paleontologists, and the existence of the Kirkwood zones in the asteroid belt of the solar system.

Charles Darwin had envisioned evolution as a smooth continuous process in which species progress through natural selection. The fossil record, however, seems to tell a somewhat different story. It shows that species sometimes rapidly evolve to fill available ecological niches, then show little evolutionary progress for tens of millions of years, until there is a break in the fossil record in which everything is changed. Some species disappear while others again rapidly evolve to fill newly vacated niches, and the process repeats. The cause of these "punctuation marks" in the erratic course of evolution is not well established, but it is suspected that they are the result of large-scale natural disasters that disrupt the environment, cause massive die-off of some species, and give others the opportunity to evolve to occupy the vacated niches in the newly emerging ecology.

A dramatic example of this punctuated equilibrium process is the Cretaceous catastrophe that occurred some sixty-five million years ago. It is now fairly well established through the pioneering work of physicist Luis Alvarez and his coworkers that a large iridium-rich carbonaceous chondrite meteorite, probably an asteroid, struck the Earth in the vicinity of what is now the Yucatán peninsula, depositing a great quantity of dust in the upper atmosphere and killing off the dinosaurs and many other plant and animal species. The Cretaceous catastrophe provided mammals with the opportunity to evolve, to occupy ecological niches formerly occupied by reptiles, and to achieve their present dominance in life on Earth.

The second idea comes from the existence of the Kirkwood zones in the asteroid belt of our solar system. Among the band of orbits that comprise the asteroid belt that lies between the orbits of Mars and Jupiter, there are empty bands of orbits at certain distances from the sun in which no asteroids are found, even though many asteroids populate nearby orbits. When the science of chaos came to prominence about a decade ago, it was realized that the Kirkwood zones are regions in which asteroid orbits become chaotic due the cumulative perturbations of the planet Jupiter. The effects of Jupiter's gravitation build up because its orbital period is in an integer ratio to that of a Kirkwood asteroid so that, for example, Jupiter is in the same place on every third asteroid orbit.

If an asteroid should wander into a Kirkwood zone due to some random interaction with its neighbors, this perturbation would soon propel the asteroid out of its Kirkwood zone orbit, with a fairly high probability that it will be deflected into a new orbit that transits the inner solar system. Thus, the solar system has a built-in launch mechanism for providing a supply of large rocks that can collide with Earth. It has been estimated that from this mechanism alone a large asteroid might collide with the Earth with an average interval of twenty million years, a rate that is consistent with the fossil record of "punctuations."

We can combine these two ideas to obtain the variant view of an evolution process that is "pumped" by intermittent asteroid collisions, alternating between times of catastrophic species die-off and rapid change and periods of stable environmental conditions during which species equilibrium is reestablished. Clearly in this scenario there is some optimum rate for the pumping. If the pump runs too fast, the process is too wasteful of life and there is not enough time for equilibrium to be reestablished before the next catastrophe. If the pump runs too slowly, the species may become too deeply embedded in their ecologies to respond well to change, and in any case the rate of evolution will be slowed.

My hypothesis in the present novel, based a bit on the anthropic principle, is that the evolution pump rate in our solar system by a fortunate and improbable accident is near the optimum, and that this has caused intelligence to evolve on Earth more rapidly than it has elsewhere in our galaxy and our universe. We are therefore early arrivals on the scene. We do not receive the radio signals or emissions of other intelligent species because there are none.

This lonely solution to the Fermi paradox, I should add, is not well known or widely accepted in the SETI community, nor to my knowledge has it even been discussed in reviews of the subject (perhaps because so far it has been published only in my column in *Analog* magazine).

TELEPRESENCE AND VIRTUAL REALITY

My column in the November 1990 issue of *Analog* on virtual reality (VR) was one of the first popular accounts of this emerging technology, but since that time VR has been the subject of so much media hype that it should not require any explanation here. On the other hand, the related technology of telepresence, as used in the present novel, has not received much media attention. Telepresence was the subject of my July 1990 *Analog* column. I believe that, in the long run, telepresence will have a much greater impact on our lives than VR.

While no high-energy physics laboratory has yet invested in telepresence in the way described in this novel, I am confident that this development is inevitable. A precursor, video-conferencing over the Internet, is already widely used in the field. The basic point here is that machine-pattern recognition is intrinsically very difficult but human-pattern recognition is easy; robotic manipulation of arms and bodies is difficult but human control of "robot" arms and bodies is easy; computer generation of a VR environment is difficult but "real" reality is already here to be used, locally or remotely. It's just a matter of getting the cost of suitable remote units down to a reasonable level and paying for the bandwidth needed to use them.

I teach physics at the University of Washington in Seattle, and I do physics research at the CERN laboratory in Geneva, Switzerland. I look forward to the time when I can use telepresence to do both things on the same day.

INTELLIGENCE ENHANCEMENT

The development of the drug synaptine in the novel is pure make-believe. The objections of Francis Crick to the name used for neural networks is real, but I somewhat distorted his arguments for my own purposes.

There has been a group within the megavitamin and life-extension movement that has been experimenting with various over-the-counter and prescription drugs as a way of boosting intelligence. There is already an emerging folklore centering on which drugs, vitamins, and dietary supplements do and don't work in achieving the goals of boosted intelligence and memory improvement.

I am confident that in the next decade or so developments in molecular biology and protein synthesis will produce real and effective intelligence-enhancing drugs, with or without the unpleasant side effects described in the novel. When this happens, the impact on theoretical physics will be somewhat like the impact of metabolic steroids on athletic records. It is quite true, as Roger observed, that even a small gain in human intelligence will go a very long way when one is working at the cutting edge of a field which uses intelligence as its principal tool. And the impact on society in general will also be very profound. The present world desperately needs more intelligence and needs to have the available intelligence used more effectively.

READING AND WRITING DNA

In studying the history of technology, one finds that the first use of an emerging technology is to make tools to use that technology better. Lathes and milling machines are used to make better lathes and milling machines. Electronic circuits are used to make oscilloscopes and voltmeters for making better electronic circuits. This should be no different with genetic engineering and nanotechnology.

In this novel, the fully mature biotechnology of the Makers has given individuals the fully realized capabilities for decoding, simulating, and interpreting DNA, RNA, and nanomachines and for synthesizing DNA, RNA, and nanomachines for their own purposes. This seems to me to be an inevitable long-term product of this technology.

The "Fountain of Youth" enzyme that restores the end segments of DNA strands and allows them to continue to participate in cell division processes is real. The DNA end segments that may be acting as countdown timers to limit cell division are called "telomeres" and the enzyme that restores them is called "telomerase." Intensive research now in progress focuses on this enzyme and its real biological effects. I hope they get it sorted out soon. I could use some.

REYNALD TOROIDS, AXIONS, AND SPACE DRIVES

The Reynald toroid is a strictly fictional solution to the frustrating problem of energy storage. In principle, magnetic fields are an excellent way of storing energy since the energy storage increases as the square of the field strength. A 290 Tesla magnetic field has the same energy density as gasoline (and converts to electrical energy much more cleanly and efficiently). However, we are presently limited to relatively small magnetic fields ($\sim$10 Tesla) by the limited mechanical strengths and low electrical conductivity of presently available materials.

The Reynald toroid is supposed to be made of a ''magic'' alloy that supports a closed loop of magnetic flux in its interior and simultaneously grows in mechanical strength to sustain it. I wish I knew how to make one.

The axion is a could-be particle that is a side effect of a theory that explains the CP violation in the decays of K^0 mesons. If axions exist at all, they would have been produced in large numbers in the early Big Bang. Therefore, invisible axions might be the source of ''cold dark matter'' that seems to form most of the mass present in our universe. It was shown theoretically in 1983 by Sikivie from symmetry arguments that axions could be converted to photons in a strong magnetic or electric field. However, experiments attempting to convert axions to detectable microwave photons using this effect have so far failed.

The hypothesis in the present novel is that (a) axions exist and are the principal source of dark matter, (b) that they can be converted to unspecified speed-of-light particles (not photons) using the intense fields present in Reynald toroids, and (c) that the momentum kick from the conversion permits their detection and also has potential use as a ''space drive.'' All of these hypotheses are physically possible, but none is supported by any presently available evidence.

• The Political Background of *Einstein's Bridge*

PRESIDENTIAL APPOINTMENTS

Dan Quayle's selection as George Bush's running mate at the 1988 Republican Convention was a great surprise at the time and has never been adequately explained. The choice appears to have been an impulsive act on Bush's part, which in the long run seriously damaged his presidency.

Professor John Deutsch of the MIT Department of Chemistry, former director of the Office of Energy Research at the U.S. Department of Energy (DOE) and present director of the Central Intelligence Agency, was mentioned as a top candidate for Bush's Secretary of Energy in early 1989 before Admiral James D. Watkins was selected. Had Deutsch been appointed Energy Secretary, the SSC project would have been handled very differently by the DOE and might never have been brought to the point of cancellation.

Professor D. Allan Bromley of Yale University was named Science Advisor and director of the Office of Science and Technology Policy by Bush in mid-1989, but not until a number of industrial scientists had turned down the job because of its relatively low salary. Bromley proved to be perhaps the most effective Science Advisor in the history of that office. In early 1992 he came very close to succeeding in arranging a Japanese contribution of $1 billion to the SSC, but, according to his own memoirs, was frustrated in this attempt by Sam Skinner, at the time when Skinner was briefly Bush's Chief of Staff. Skinner deleted discussion of the SSC contribution from the agenda of Bush's meeting with Japanese Prime Minister Miyazawa in January 1992. If there had been a second Bush Administration, Bromley would undoubtedly have been more effective than his successor, Dr. John H. Gibbons, in justifying the SSC to the 1993 Congress.

DOE OVERSIGHT OF THE SSC PROJECT

The U.S. Department of Energy and its predecessors, the Energy Research and Development Agency (ERDA) and the Atomic Energy Commission (AEC), have had a long history of successful management and oversight of large and expensive construction projects designed and built by physicists: nuclear research reactors, plasma physics machines, and nuclear and high-energy particle accelerators. The DOE had developed excellent oversight procedures for physics construction project management that had struck a careful balance between responsible oversight, good physics, and good technical decisions.

However, when the SSC came along during the Reagan Administration, it was such a large and politically visible project that the upper DOE management panicked and abandoned the lessons of its own history. The DOE was still reeling from the cancellation of its previous big accelerator project, the Isabelle Collider at Brookhaven, which had been halted before completion because a poor superconducting magnet design had delayed the project and because physicists at CERN had already discovered the Z and W weak-force bosons, the principal physics goal that Isabelle had been designed to accomplish.

The DOE management under Reagan decided that the SSC project needed to be watched much more carefully than previous DOE physics construction projects and insisted on much more direct DOE control. The freedom and prerogatives of the SSC laboratory director were therefore severely restricted, with much more direct DOE oversight and participation inserted in the chain of decision-making processes. From the start of the SSC project, a morass of new bureaucracy, paperwork, and micromanagement was created. The SSC designers and builders, most with years of experience from other DOE construction projects, found the new procedures obstructive and offensive.

Then with the Bush Administration Admiral James D. Watkins became Secretary of Energy. This appointment had very unfortunate consequences for the SSC project. Watkins's desire for personal control caused him to increase the bureaucracy and paperwork associated with SSC oversight by another order of magnitude. He also extensively revised the SSC management structure, installing people that he trusted in key positions while displacing physicists and experienced accelerator builders from the decision chains.

This reorganization was very detrimental to the SSC project. According to an article in *Physics Today*, Congress developed ''a sense that the project was not being handled well. In fact, the physicists at the SSC had been cut out of the administrative loop by a management group brought in by Watkins. This created a perplexing paradox: SSC and Universities Research Association [URA, the contracting organization responsible for management of Brookhaven and Fermilab, as well as the SSC] leaders criticized the DOE for too much oversight and authority, but [Clinton's Energy Secretary Hazel] O'Leary told Congress that the department had exercised too little oversight and authority.'' Roy Schwitters, SSC director, characterized the DOE's massive oversight efforts in an interview with *The New York Times* as ''the revenge of the C students.''

The safety Tiger Teams described in the novel were one of Watkins's most controversial and morale-destroying innovations. The "Siciliano memo" scenario of the novel bears some resemblance to events involving one Joseph Cipriano, the head of the SSC program office in Dallas, who was ordered by Watkins to report directly to him. Cipriano's office grew to sixty permanent staffers, with forty more staff on temporary assignment from elsewhere in the DOE. O'Leary, when she took over from Watkins, did indeed assign yet another thirty DOE staff to Cipriano's office for SSC oversight in the year before the project was terminated.

The existence of Cipriano's secret memos to Watkins, apparently highly critical of many aspects of the SSC project, became known to Congress in 1991, and they became a bone of contention between the DOE and Congressman Howard Wolpe, an SSC opponent and chairman of the House Science, Space, and Technology Subcommittee on Investigations. The DOE at first denied that the memoranda existed and then attempted to claim "executive privilege" to avoid producing them. Finally, in response to great pressure, the DOE permitted Wolpe's subcommittee staff members to come to Watkins's office to read the Cipriano memos, but would not allow copies of them to be made.

In 1993, in the aftermath of the 280 to 150 House vote to kill the SSC, another Cipriano memo surfaced, this time the draft of a letter to Energy Secretary Hazel O'Leary. A group called Project on Government Oversight somehow obtained the document directly from the word processor in Cipriano's own office and delivered it to *The Washington Post*. According to *Physics Today,* the letter suggested that the immediate removal of SSC Director Roy Schwitters "may be the only way to keep the lab from falling apart before the Senate vote." It claimed that morale at the SSC lab was low and that "confidence in the existing management is practically nonexistent and costs and schedule trends are worsening at an alarming rate." Cipriano reportedly suggested putting the project on hold for a year to resolve the management problems and to provide time for the preparation of "reduced scope or phased implementation alternatives" for the SSC's construction. Cipriano proposed that the SSC's 1994 budget be cut from $640 million to $400 million to honor existing contracts but not to start new ones. The memo appears to have been a last-ditch attempt to preserve the DOE bureaucracy associated with the SSC by sacrificing the physics goals of the project.

THE SSC COST ESCALATION

When Reagan announced the approval of the SSC project in 1987, the cost widely quoted in the news media was $4.4 billion. This was a cost quoted in 1988 dollars that did not include inflation and did not include the cost of the detectors needed to actually do physics experiments with the machine. Later in 1987, the DOE provided a revised cost estimate including a modest allowance for inflation and an added $0.5 billion for detectors, bringing the total to about $5.3 billion. Even at the time, it was admitted that the inflation rate and detector cost used were rather low. In early 1989 under the new Bush Administration, the SSC cost estimate rose to $5.9 billion when a more realistic inflation rate was used. This disingenuous cost concealment by the DOE, which had been a successful tactic for smaller DOE construction projects in the past, proved disastrous for a project with the visibility of the SSC. It gave the impression, even in its beginning stages, that the cost of the SSC project was out of control.

After intense design work on the SSC project was begun, the previous preliminary design of the superconducting magnets with four-centimeter apertures, done by the Central Design Group at Lawrence Berkeley Laboratory, was carefully reexamined. This process was carried out in the highly conservative justify-every-step-with-a-paper-trail bureaucratic environment that had been created by Admiral Watkins. After some agonizing the SSC design team led by Dr. Helen Edwards, previously of Fermilab, decided that to be sure the design would work it would be necessary to increase the dipole magnet aperture from four to five centimeters. This decision was reviewed by a group of outside accelerator experts. Although there was a minority within the review group that argued for holding to the four-centimeter apertures, the majority consensus of the review confirmed the decision to change to five-centimeter apertures as a conservative choice that would assure successful operation of the machine.

The Drell Panel, a separate group composed mainly of theoretical physicists, considered the option of reducing the operating energy and scaling back the physics goals of the project, in order to hold to the old budget. They rejected this option as unacceptable. The five-centimeter magnet design change raised the price of the SSC from $5.9 billion to a hotly debated new cost that stabilized at about $8.6 billion.

When the Clinton Administration replaced the Bush Administration, an early budget-tightening decision was made to stretch out the SSC construction schedule, moving the date of completion from 1999 to 2003. This decision had the effect of increasing the overall cost of the project while reducing its yearly cost. The result was that the total SSC cost rose by about $2 billion, from $8.6 billion to over $10 billion. Later in 1993, a month before the SSC was terminated, the DOE's *Baseline Validation Report* advocated another increase in the safety and contingency margins, moving the completion date to 2004 and increasing the cost to $11.5 billion.

The media coverage of the SSC project dealt only superficially with these increasing cost figures. It created the impression of another out-of-control government project with a cost that had almost tripled since its start and might double again before the project was finished.

I can see four separate reasons for the rising SSC cost: (1) the initial deliberate "lowball" attempt by the DOE under the Reagan Administration to conceal the true cost of the SSC project by ignoring or minimizing inflation and leaving out the approximately $1 billion cost of the detector systems that the accelerator would need; (2) the 1989 redesign of the accelerator, motivated in part by the more conservative SSC management attitude that had its seeds in the escalation of DOE oversight under Admiral Watkins; (3) the decision by the Clinton Administration to delay completion of the project by four years; and (4) loss of confidence in the SSC project by several budget review groups as a result of the previous increases and the evidence of management problems, which caused them to repeatedly add more and more contingencies and safety factors to the estimated cost of the project.

FOREIGN CONTRIBUTIONS TO THE SSC

Arranging foreign contributions to a large physics project like the SSC is reminiscent of the fairy tale of the Little Red Hen: No one wants to do the work of growing the wheat, milling the flour, and baking the bread, but everyone is eager to eat it. Physicists from every country will want to use the forefront facility once it is completed, but no national government wants to help pay for constructing a big facility in another country. In the case of the SSC, this problem was further complicated by the schizophrenic view asserted in Congress and elsewhere that (a) there had to be major foreign contributions but (b) the cutting-edge technological spin-offs from the SSC should only benefit U.S. industrial firms, not foreign ones. Many members of Congress nevertheless viewed foreign participation in the SSC as a key issue. They took the failure of such contributions to appear as a deal-breaking breach of the agreement between Congress and the DOE.

The memoirs of former Science Advisor D. Allan Bromley, as mentioned above, describe his failed attempt to arrange a meeting in late 1991 or early 1992 between President Bush and Japanese Prime Minister Miyazawa, during which Bush was to directly ask Miyazawa for a billion-dollar Japanese contribution to the SSC. The request was deleted from Bush's agenda, never made, and as a result the SSC project suffered an ultimately fatal blow.

SSC RHETORIC IN CONGRESS

The rising SSC costs and increasing opposition to the SSC produced a tendency toward hyperbole among the supporters of the project, as can be seen from some of the quotations used in the section breaks of this novel. This rhetoric, modeled on similar tactics used by NASA but executed here less effectively, produced a backlash that damaged the credibility of the project and focused congressional attention on its potential technological spin-offs (or lack thereof), rather than on the intrinsic scientific and intellectual merit of the project.

The sad thing is that many of the outrageous assertions made by the desperate SSC supporters contain a kernel of truth, and phrased more carefully would, in many cases, become accurate statements of the technological benefits that our culture has derived from past support of basic research in science. It is acknowledged in the physics community that active researchers do not spend enough time communicating the excitement and accomplishments of their field to the public in general and the U.S. Congress in particular. Here, however, we see an example of the downside of such communication when it is provided under pressure.

The exaggerated and counterproductive claims made on the floor of Congress were the carefully phrased statements of scientist SSC advocates, after they had been modified, dumbed-down, filtered, and hyped by receptive and well-meaning congressional staff and members of Congress. Descriptions of the accomplishments of basic research in science in general became the accomplishments of high-energy physics. Statements of how high-energy physics had aided in the development of the computer industry, for example, were transmuted into claims that the field had single-handedly invented and developed the computer. And so on. The lesson here is that one-shot communication under the time pressure and the information vacuum that are characteristic of a hot congressional debate can be ineffective and even dangerous.

CONGRESSIONAL OPPOSITION AND THE SSC VOTES

The opposition to the SSC in Congress was surprisingly slow to develop. Even in 1991, after the official DOE cost of the project had moved from the initially announced $4.4 billion to $8.6 billion, an attempt to kill the project in the House was voted down by a margin of 251 to 165. However, the worsening U.S. economy, the freshman congressmen swept in with Clinton, and the rising emphasis in Congress on balanced budgets and cost-cutting, particularly after the 1992 election, resulted in House votes to kill the project of 232 to 181 in 1992 and 280 to 150 in 1993.

The lukewarm support of the SSC by the Clinton Administration in 1993 and the decision to stretch out and escalate the cost of the project also became large factors in its demise. Science Advisor John Gibbons failed to provide the support for the project that his predecessor, Allan Bromley, had. Energy Secretary Hazel O'Leary proclaimed during her confirmation hearings that she was "not passionate" about the SSC. By September 1993, when her passions finally became somewhat aroused, she only took ineffective steps to reshuffle the major SSC contractors and increase the already bloated DOE oversight of the project. Neither President Clinton nor Vice President Gore was willing to make broad personal appeals, as George Bush had, on behalf of the SSC to House members before the two critical votes in June and October.

Despite unfavorable votes in the House, the SSC was saved by a maneuver of the House leadership in 1992 and was almost saved again in 1993 by the same maneuver. When the House and Senate differ in their legislation, a joint conference committee composed of members

of both bodies is appointed to resolve the differences. In both 1992
and 1993, House Speaker Tom Foley appointed as House representatives on the conference committee only members who were SSC
supporters. Consequently, in both 1992 and 1993, the conference committee agreed to the Senate version of the legislation which included
continuation of the SSC project. However, any conference committee
action must be ratified by the House as a whole. In 1993 a floor fight
led by Congressman Sherwood Boehlert (R.-NY) rejected the conference committee report by a vote of 282 to 143. At this point, the SSC
supporters conceded defeat, and the project officially died.

   Opposition in Congress came from several sources: (1) fiscal conservatives like Boehlert and Senator Dale Bumpers (D.-Arkansas),
who appeared to understand the scientific value of the project but felt
that on balance the nation could not afford the expense at this time;
(2) "sore losers" of the competition for choosing the SSC site, who
felt that the decision to place the project in Texas was politically
motivated and were resentful of the power in Congress of the Texas
delegation; and (3) scalp-hunters who would soon face tough reelection campaigns and who wanted a large and conspicuous government
project which they could say they had killed. The latter group included
many of the 114 freshman members of the House who had been swept
in with Clinton, about 70 percent of whom voted to kill the SSC.

   Freshman Congressman Jon Matthews (D.-Oregon) and his staff
assistant, Joe Ramsey, are fictional. Senator Bumpers and Congressmen Boehlert, Slattery, Eckart, and Wolpe are real.

WHO KILLED THE SSC?

   There is plenty of blame to go around. Here is my list of the seven
top contributors to the demise of the project, in roughly chronological
order:

1.   The Central Design Group led by Professor Maury Tigner of Cor-
     nell and based at LBL in the 1980s, for producing an initial SSC
     design in 1986 that turned out to be marginal, leading to the
     eventual redesign that increased the project cost by $2.7 billion.
2.   President Ronald Reagan and members of his Administration, for
     allowing the DOE to misrepresent the cost of the project

in 1987 by minimizing the effects of inflation and by omitting the $1 billion cost of the detectors needed for the project.

3. President George Bush and members of his Administration, for appointing Admiral Watkins as Energy Secretary and for failing to formally request Japanese participation in the project when he had the opportunity.

4. Admiral James D. Watkins, for crippling the SSC project with a human wave of DOE bureaucrats and Navy-oriented managers that slowed and hampered every aspect of the project, increased its estimated cost, and destroyed congressional confidence in the project's management.

5. Dr. Roy Schwitters, SSC director, for permitting the expenditure of DOE funds on office amenities (paintings and decorative plants) and morale-boosting gatherings like Christmas parties. The fraction of SSC funds involved was very small and amounted to only a few dollars per employee, but its impact in Congress was quite large and helped to create the impression of poor management that led to the project's termination.

6. President Bill Clinton and members of his Administration, for appointing Hazel O'Leary as Energy Secretary, for deciding to stretch out the time scale of the project by four years and thereby adding $2–4 billion to its estimated cost, and for "benign neglect" instead of support for the project in Congress.

7. The United States Congress, for its failure of will in seeing the project through to completion after initial approval, for failing to understand the scientific purpose and value of the SSC project, for debating entirely the wrong issues in deciding its fate, and for consistently failing to develop any long-term science policy for the nation that can be depended on from one year to the next.

WHERE DID THE SSC MONEY GO?

The cancellation of the SSC project produced a billion-dollar windfall in 1993 that could be diverted to other projects in the general category of energy and water. There is some evidence that at least some of the SSC funds went to such pork barrel projects rather than to an actual reduction in the federal budget, but it is very difficult to track the windfall or to establish a correspondence with other projects in the slippery interior of the pork barrel.

The Tombigbee Waterway mentioned in the novel is a real ongoing federal pork barrel project being carried out by the U.S. Army Corps of Engineers in Alabama and Mississippi, but its connection with the SSC cancellation is purely fictional (if rather plausible).

THE AFTERMATH OF THE SSC KILLING

It is perhaps worth noting that the described scalp-hunting strategy of certain congressmen did not, in most cases, facilitate their reelection. For example, in my own Washington State none of the five members of the House who voted to kill the SSC in 1993 (Cantwell, Inslee, Kreidler, Swift, and Unsoeld) was reelected in 1994, and Speaker Tom Foley, a key SSC supporter, was also defeated. The "Curse of the SSC" in the novel, for whatever reasons, seems to have been a real phenomenon. Of the four cosponsors of the 1992 SSC cancellation amendment in the House who were at the center of SSC opposition, only Sherwood Boehlert was reelected, while Dennis Eckart (D.-Ohio), Jim Slattery (D.-Kansas), and Howard Wolpe (D.-Michigan) were all defeated in 1994. Overall, of those members of the House who voted to kill the SSC on June 15, 1993, about a quarter of them either lost or did not run in the 1994 election. On the other hand, of those who voted to continue the SSC, six-sevenths were reelected and returned to office. No comparable pattern is apparent in votes on the Space Station during the same period.

The some two thousand people, physicists, engineers, and support staff that were directly or indirectly employed at the SSC laboratory all lost their jobs. The carefully assembled pool of accelerator construction expertise brought to a focus in Waxahachie has been dissipated and lost. The high-energy physics community in the U.S.A. remains in a state of disarray. The field has been badly wounded by the SSC decision. There is an ongoing effort within the DOE and the U.S. high-energy physics community to join the physics effort at the CERN LHC project. However, any large-scale participation in the CERN accelerator must be negotiated at the federal level by the DOE and must include substantial contributions to CERN.

At this writing (December 1995), the DOE itself has been under attack by the new Republican-dominated 104th Congress, and for a time its continued existence was in doubt. Moreover, a congressional committee recently deleted from the DOE budget the $6 million intended as a first step in joining the LHC project at CERN. This will make such negotiations difficult.

The U.S. accelerator designers have not been completely discouraged by the cancellation of the SSC project. Recently a new international effort has begun that would leapfrog over the old synchrotron technology of the SSC and LHC to initiate a new project, a Linear Collider, which would be able to reach effective collision energies even higher than those that would have been accessible with the SSC.

We live in interesting times.

—John Cramer,
Munich, Germany, and
Seattle, Washington,
Summer and Fall, 1995

• Acronyms and Definitions

AEC

Atomic Energy Commission, the U.S. government agency that first funded major projects in high-energy physics and that was the predecessor to ERDA and the Department of Energy.

ALEPH

A large solenoid magnet and time projection chamber for the LEP collider at CERN, used since about 1988 with electron-positron collisions to study Z and W bosons.

ALICE

A detector planned for the LHC collider at CERN and planned for operation about 2005, to be used for the study of ultra-relativistic heavy ion collisions, usually between lead nuclei.

Argonne

Argonne National Laboratory, one of the large DOE national laboratories, located south of Chicago and east of Fermilab.

ATLAS

A detector planned for the LHC collider at CERN and planned for operation about 2005, to be used for the study of proton-proton collisions.

axion

A hypothetical pseudo-scalar particle that is considered a possible source of dark matter (*see entry*) in the universe. The axion, if it existed, would have a very small mass, would interact only very weakly with normal matter, and might be converted to a photon in the presence of a very strong non-uniform magnetic field.

BBC   British Broadcasting Corporation.

Bevalac   An early high-energy synchrotron accelerator constructed in the 1950s at Lawrence Berkeley Laboratory and used to discover the antiproton. Closed in 1992.

Bridge   A three-dimensional wormhole, usually connecting separated Bubble Universes, in the terminology of the Makers.

Bridgehead   One end of a wormhole, i.e., a wormhole mouth, in the terminology of the Makers. Note that a Bridgehead may be meters across, or it may be so small as to resemble a fundamental particle.

Brookhaven   Brookhaven National Laboratory (or BNL), one of the large DOE national laboratories, located on Long Island, east of New York City, at the site of WWI Camp Yappahank, an Army training base.

Bubble   Maker terminology for Bubble Universe (*see next entry*).

Bubble Universe   One of a number of completely isolated subuniverses, evolved during the Big Bang in separate nucleation events leading to exponential expansion, as implied by the inflation scenario of "the standard model" of cosmology.

CDF   Collider Detector at Fermilab, one of the two large detectors constructed at Fermilab in the 1990s to use the colliding proton-antiproton beams produced by the machine. The top quark was discovered with this detector in 1993–94.

center of mass system   The inertial reference frame in which the overall momentum of a system of particles is zero. Used in relativistic kinematics. Sometimes called the CM system.

CERN   *Centre Europénne pour la Recherche Nucléaire,* European Organization for Nuclear Research, the major European center for research in high-energy physics, funded by nineteen member nations and located just west of Geneva, Switzerland, spanning the Swiss-French border and sprawling over the French countryside. Operates the large SPS and LEP accelerators and is presently constructing the LHC accelerator in the LEP tunnel.

CIA   U.S. Central Intelligence Agency.

Clifford algebra   An unorthodox approach to the algebra of complex numbers and matrices that is currently viewed as a "growth area" in theoretical physics. There are some theorists who feel that the formalisms of relativity and relativistic quantum mechanics become simpler and more transparent when reformulated using Clifford algebra.

CMS   Compact Muon Solenoid, a detector planned for the LHC collider at CERN and expected to operate about 2005, to be used for the study of proton-proton collisions.

collider   A relatively new type of high-energy physics accelerator that produces two accelerated particle beams that are brought into head-on collision. This allows all of the available energy to be used in the collision, rather than losing a large fraction of it to motion of the center of mass of the system, as is the case when a relativistic particle beam strikes a target at rest.

Cornell

Cornell University, located in Ithaca, N.Y., operates a high-energy electron accelerator facility funded by the U.S. National Science Foundation.

cosmic background

Radiation produced one hundred thousand years after the initial Big Bang when the universe cooled enough for free protons and electrons to combine to form neutral hydrogen atoms. At this point the universe became optically transparent and radiation with a broad "black body" frequency spectrum was liberated. Due to the progressive red-shift as the universe expands, this radiation now has a characteristic temperature of 2.7°K.

Cosmotron

An early high-energy synchrotron accelerator constructed in the 1950s at Brookhaven National Laboratory and used in early high-energy physics experiments. Closed in the late 1960s.

D.C.

District of Columbia.

D-FW

Abbreviation for the Dallas–Fort Worth International Airport.

D0

D-Zero is one of the two large detectors constructed at Fermilab in the 1990s to use the colliding proton-antiproton beams produced by the machine. The D0 experiment provided supporting evidence for the discovery of the top quark.

dark matter   Evidence from a number of sources indi-
                         cates that the universe has considerable
                         mass that cannot be accounted for as vis-
                         ible stars or even using the best estimates
                         of the total amount of normal matter. This
                         excess mass is attributed to "dark matter,"
                         and the identification of dark matter is a
                         major unsolved problem of contemporary
                         astrophysics.

DELPHI   One of the four large collider detectors of
                         the CERN LEP facility.

dewar   A vessel for holding cryogenic liquids,
                         constructed like a large thermos bottle.

DNA   Deoxyribonucleic Acid. The basic read-
                         only library containing a sequence of in-
                         structions for the construction of proteins
                         residing in all cells.

DOE   Department of Energy.

EA-3   East-Area Experiment 3. A fictitious des-
                         ignation for one of the smaller experiments
                         of the Superconducting Super Collider lab-
                         oratory, according to this novel.

EA-4   East-Area Experiment 4. A fictitious des-
                         ignation for one of the smaller experiments
                         of the Superconducting Super Collider lab-
                         oratory, according to this novel.

Einstein-Rosen bridge A three-dimensional "wormhole" in four-
                         dimensional space-time; a topological de-
                         fect in space-time that provides a shortcut
                         between one region of space-time and an-
                         other; a little-understood solution to Ein-
                         stein's equations of general relativity.

element numbers

The alien Tunnel Maker refers to the chemical elements by their atomic number. Those mentioned are: 1 = hydrogen, 4 = beryllium, 6 = carbon, 8 = oxygen, 10 = neon, 14 = silicon, 26 = iron, 29 = copper, 82 = lead, and 92 = uranium. All of these are elements that might be found in a high-energy physics detector.

Energy Doubler

Short for the Energy Doubler-Saver, the name given to the Fermilab conversion of their synchrotron from "warm" to superconducting magnets in the late 1980s.

EPA

Environmental Protection Agency.

ERDA

Energy Research and Development Agency, a predecessor of the present Department of Energy.

FBI

Federal Bureau of Investigation, domestic investigative office of the U.S. Department of Justice.

Fermilab

One of two major high-energy accelerator facilities in the United States operated by the U.S. Department of Energy. It is located near Batavia, Illinois, south of Chicago.

FET

Field-Effect Transistor, a voltage-controlled solid-state electronic device that regulates the flow of electrical current and is a principal component of integrated-circuit electronics.

FSU

Florida State University, located in Tallahassee, Florida.

GEM

One of the two major collider detectors planned for the SSC laboratory. The acronym stands for Gamma rays, Electrons, and Muons, the three particles the detector was designed to detect. Canceled along with the SSC accelerator project in late 1993.

general relativity

"The standard model" theory of gravitation developed by Albert Einstein about 1916. It describes the actions of gravity in terms of the curvature and geometry of space-time.

GeV

Giga-electron Volts or 10^9 electron volts. This is the standard unit of energy used in particle physics. The mass-energy of a proton at rest is about 0.94 GeV.

GPS

Global Positioning System, a portable electronic device that uses signals from a system of navigation satellites to determine the three-dimensional location and changes in location of the device.

graduate student

A university student who has completed a bachelor's degree and is working on an advanced degree, usually a Ph.D. degree.

ISABELLE

A DOE-funded proton-proton collider that was under construction at Brookhaven National Laboratory when the project was canceled in 1983 due to problems in superconducting magnet construction.

jets	Clusters of energetic particles observed to emerge from collisions of high-energy particles. Attributed to the emission of a high-energy quark or gluon that, due to color-string breaking, gives rise to a group of correlated particles.
KIRO-TV	A television station in the Seattle area, broadcasting on Channel 4 and affiliated with the ABC Network.
LANL	*See Los Alamos.*
LBL	Lawrence Berkeley Laboratory, a large DOE-funded national laboratory founded by E. O. Lawrence and located in Berkeley, California, adjacent to the University of California campus. In 1995 the name of the laboratory was changed to Lawrence Berkeley National Laboratory and the acronym changed to LBNL.
LBNL	*See LBL.*
LEM	Leptons and Electro-Magnetic interactions detector, the fictitious designation for one of the large collider experiments of the Superconducting Super Collider laboratory, according to this novel. LEM bears some resemblance to the planned GEM detector of the SSC.
LEP	Large Electron-Positron collider, an accelerator facility that has been in operation at CERN since about 1988.
Lexis	A database service used by the legal profession.

LHC	Large Hadronic Collider, an accelerator facility to be constructed in the LEP tunnel at CERN and that will collide protons at an energy of 8 TeV. The completion of the LHC was postponed when the pressure from the SSC project was removed, and the facility is now scheduled for initial operation about 2005.
Livermore	Short for the Lawrence Livermore National Laboratory or LLNL, one of the two DOE-funded weapons laboratories located at Livermore, California, about fifty miles east of San Francisco.
Los Alamos	Short for the Los Alamos National Laboratory or LANL, one of the two DOE-funded weapons laboratories. LANL is located atop a mesa at Los Alamos, New Mexico, about fifty miles northwest of Santa Fe.
LLNL	*See Livermore.*
L3	One of the four large collider detectors of the CERN LEP facility.
Makers	A race of intelligent aliens evolved from amphibians that has a high-technology civilization approximately a thousand years in advance of ours.
mass-energy	Physicists tend to consider mass and energy to be equivalent, using Einstein's relation $E = mc^2$, and the masses of fundamental particles are often quoted in energy units. The mass-energy of a stationary particle is its rest mass, expressed in energy units. The mass-energy of a moving particle is the sum of this and its kinetic energy.

Mathematica   A symbolic algebra and mathematics program widely used by theoretical physicists and produced by Wolfram Research, Inc., Urbana, IL.

MIT   Massachusetts Institute of Technology, located in Cambridge, Massachusetts, a suburb of Boston.

mr/h   Abbreviation for Milli-Rem per Hour, a measure of ionizing radiation dosage. Natural background radiation in our environment exposes the average person to about 300 mr per year of radiation.

MRI   Magnetic Resonance Imaging; originally called "nuclear magnetic resonance imaging" until the term "nuclear" was dropped by the medical profession to avoid alarming patients.

nanometer   A length of 10^{-9} meters, approximately the size of a molecule.

NASA   National Aeronautics and Space Administration, the federal space bureaucracy.

Nexis   A database service used by the legal profession.

NSA   National Security Agency, the federal intelligence agency charged with the responsibility of intercepting messages and breaking codes. A very secret organization whose acronym is sometimes interpreted to mean "No Such Agency."

NSF   National Science Foundation, the second most important funding agency (after the DOE) for the funding of particle physics research.

Oak Ridge   Oak Ridge National Laboratory (or ORNL), a large DOE-funded national laboratory constructed during WWII for separation of uranium-235 for the Manhattan Project and located in the hills of Tennessee, about seventy miles from Knoxville.

OPAL   One of the four large collider detectors of the CERN LEP facility.

ORNL   *See Oak Ridge National Laboratory.*

Planck mass   The mass, set by the gravitational constant, of the smallest possible black hole. It is the heaviest possible mass for a fundamental particle. The value of a Planck mass is about 10^{23} eV or about 0.6 micrograms.

postdoc   A postdoctoral fellow. This is the usual job title of a physicist who has received his Ph.D. and wishes to go on in physics research. It is a "journeyman physicist" position characterized by relatively low pay and long working hours.

QCD   Quantum ChromoDynamics, the theory of quarks, gluons, and the color force. A key element of the standard model of particle physics.

quantum gravity   A unified theory, not yet formulated but widely sought after by theoretical physicists, that combines gravitation and quantum mechanics in a single mathematical framework. As one prominent physicist has observed, "The only thing we presently know about quantum gravity is its name."

rest mass   The mass that a particle has at rest, as opposed to the larger mass it would have when in motion due to relativistic mass increase.

Reynald toroid   A fictional device described in the novel that employs spin alignment and high magnetic fields in a torus-shaped alloy for compact energy storage.

RF   Radio Frequency, usually referring to radio waves or electrical oscillations at frequencies between 100 kHz and 500 MHz.

RNA   RiboNucleic Acid, the string of nucleic acids transcribed from DNA and containing a sequence of instructions for the construction of proteins residing in all cells.

SDC   One of the two major collider detectors planned for the SSC laboratory. The acronym stands for Solenoidal Detector Collaboration. Canceled along with the accelerator project in 1993.

SETI   The Search for Extraterrestrial Intelligence, a series of searches carried out mainly by radio astronomers seeking directed signals or by-product radio waves produced by a civilization of intelligent life forms inhabiting another star system. No evidence of such signals has ever been detected.

SLAC

Stanford Linear Accelerator Center, one of two major high-energy accelerator facilities in the United States operated by the U.S. Department of Energy. It is located near Palo Alto, California, just south of San Francisco.

SLC

SLAC Linear Collider, an experiment designed to use one-pass colliding beams from the SLAC linear accelerator in an attempt (which failed) to do definitive measurements of the Z and W bosons before the LEP machine at CERN and its detectors came into operation.

spin battery

See Reynald toroid.

SSC

Superconducting Super Collider, a double synchrotron designed to produce a head-on collision between two protons, each accelerated to an energy of 20 TeV. The SSC project was canceled in 1993 by the U.S. Congress.

Tesla

A standard international unit used to measure magnetic fields. One Tesla is about as large a magnetic field as can be obtained from normal "warm" magnets, but superconducting magnets can do more. The SSC was designed to use superconducting 6 Tesla magnets, and the LHC magnets are designed to produce fields of up to 9 Tesla.

TeV

Tera-electron Volts or 10^{12} electron volts. This is another standard unit of energy used in particle physics. The mass-energy of a top quark is about 0.18 TeV.

3-D

Three-Dimensional, as in 3-D graphics presenting a separate stereoscopic view for each eye of the user.

Tiger Teams

Groups of safety specialists and military retirees dispatched by Energy Secretary Admiral James Watkins to review the safety procedures and problems of the DOE-funded national laboratories in the early 1990s. Commonly referred to at the national laboratories as the "Safety SS."

Tombigbee Waterway

A water project of the U.S. Army Corps of Engineers in Alabama and Mississippi aimed at dredging and linking the Tombigbee and Tennessee rivers so as to produce a navigable waterway leading to the Gulf of Mexico.

torsion balance

A delicate but precise scientific instrument that measures minute forces and torques by observing small deflections of torsion springs or fibers.

URA

Universities Research Association, a nonprofit management bureaucracy representing the group of universities. The URA operates Fermilab, Brookhaven, and also operated the SSC laboratory until its closure in 1993. The URA was blamed by some DOE officials for loose oversight contributing to the SSC project's cancellation.

vertex

A point from which many particles emerge, for example the point at which a proton-proton collision occurs in a collider.

VLSI   Very Large Scale Integration, the technology that permits placing complete computers or other elaborate electronic circuits on a single chip of silicon.

VR   Virtual Reality, the technique of sensing head position and feeding an appropriate simulation of reality to each eye and ear separately, to create the very realistic illusion of a reality that, in fact, exists only within a computer.

W$^{\pm}$ The charged mediating particles of the weak interaction, with mass energies of 80.6 GeV. Predicted by "the standard model" of particle physics and discovered at CERN in the early 1980s.

Z^0   The neutral mediating particle of the weak interaction, with a mass energy of 91.161 GeV. Predicted by "the standard model" of particle physics and discovered at CERN in the early 1980s.